Cookie

The Fluffy Cupcake Book 3

Katie Mettner

Cookie

"It is easy to fall in love, but it is not easy to tell them how you feel about them, especially when that person is your best friend."
Unknown

Cookie

One

The Fluffy Cupcake. Let's face it. The name is delightful. It conjures the image of golden sponge cake swirled with buttercream icing and covered in a smattering of sprinkles. Prefer chocolate? We have those too! The mere idea of it has you saying, *yes, please!* That's precisely what the townspeople of Lake Pendle have been saying about our cupcakes for over fifty-seven years. To give credit where credit is due, my mother is the reason The Fluffy Cupcake has enjoyed years of success. Haylee Pearson has been the head cupcake of this bakery for almost forty years. Fitting since my dad, Brady, has called her Cupcake for going on thirty-six of those years.

About thirty-one years ago, I was born. Cookie Marie Pearson. Seriously, that's the name Mom and Dad bequeathed me with and is legally registered on my birth certificate. In hindsight, Marie would have been an appropriate nickname when I hated my not-so-common name, but there was no choice by the time I was old enough to make that choice. Everyone in my life was firmly entrenched in calling me Cookie, Cooks, Cooky-Coo, or any other hundred nicknames my dad gave me. I've learned to embrace the name and use it to my advantage over the years.

As a second-generation Fluffy Cupcaker, I made cookies my schtick. While my mom was The Queen of Cupcakes, I prefer the magic of cookies. As the new master baker at The Fluffy Cupcake, I had to set myself apart from my mother. Setting myself apart as a baker in this town was imperative, but it wasn't easy. Since I took over the baking six months ago, I'm happy to report that I've hooked the town on my cookies as quickly as Mom did with her cupcakes. A smile tipped my lips as I got busy stacking cookies in rows to load the cookie wagon. Initially, I worried people were buying the cookies to be kind, but that worry quickly disappeared when dozens of cookie orders started pouring in for parties and graduations.

It's not easy following in the footsteps of Haylee and Brady Pearson, let there be no doubt, but I've trained alongside my mother since I was born. First, I banged on measuring cups and rolling pins in a playpen by the baker's bench. The real fun began when I was old enough to stand on a stool and reach the bench. With a propensity for sweets, I gravitated toward the fancy cupcakes and tarts my mom would display daily. I became her baker's helper, fetching ingredients and taste-testing every new recipe. My dad loved standing at the other end of the baker's bench, watching us while he made beautiful artisan bread loaves. Thankfully, he already had an assistant, so I didn't have to feel guilty for sticking by Mom's side.

Athena Halla was Dad's righthand woman at the bread station since before I was born. She worked her way up through an apprenticeship and became a master baker like her bosses when she was twenty-four. Her step-mom, Amber, is my mom's best friend and business partner here at The Fluffy Cupcake. Amber does the books, and Mom does the cupcakes. It's been that way for years, but this year, it's changing. Soon, The Fluffy Cupcake will become The Fluffy Cupcake 2.0 when we take ownership in a few short days. That *we* includes Athena and her brother, Ares.

Ares Halla is Amber and Bishop's son. When he was seventeen, he decided Lake Pendle wasn't big enough to hold his dreams and headed for the big city after high school. When he drove out of Lake Pendle thirteen years ago, I made sure not to see him off. Why? Well, we used to be best friends until he abandoned me for the lure of the city, but that's a story for another day. From what Athena tells me, he's now some hotshot businessman in Minneapolis. He may be part owner of The Fluffy Cupcake on paper, but I was happy he wouldn't be sticking his nose in a business he had no interest in running. I hadn't seen him in thirteen years and I was happy to keep that record going. If I found myself in the same room with Ares Halla, there's no telling what I might do. It would probably end with me popping him in the nose, so it's better if we don't see each other.

As the clock counts down to the final days before my parents hand me the keys and head for Florida, we have one last thing to do. That one thing is finding someone to do our books. Amber has run the financials for the bakery since the beginning, and while I had business skills, they weren't at *running an entire business* level. My mom promised they would have someone in place before they signed the business over, but she hasn't hired anyone yet. While panning cookies this morning, I decided if Mom couldn't tell me the new hire's name, I'd start looking for someone myself. I'd make it my first official act as the new owner of The Fluffy Cupcake.

"I'm heading out, Athena!" I called from the back door.

"Be careful," she said, walking toward me as she wiped off her hands. "If you run low, let me know. I'll send Taylor out to your location with more."

"Thanks," I said with a wave as I closed the back door.

Taylor was Athena's wife of twenty years, but they've been together longer than I've been alive. I was ten when they married at The Fluffy Cupcake, and I got to make their wedding cake—with a bit of help from my mom. Over the years, Taylor has done everything from front of the house to baking, but she has settled in as the front-end manager and special occasions director. That means she works with brides to find the perfect wedding cake and other companies who need cakes, cookies, bread, and buns for their events. Since today is a busy Saturday, she's on delivery duty. To say The Fluffy Cupcake was a family affair was spot on, except for the one member who thought he was better than all the rest of us.

Ares Halla.

We grew up together, scrapped together, baked together, and got in trouble together. We generally did everything together until he turned seventeen and went from a gregarious jokester everyone loved to hang out with to a serious, almost militant, jackass. Sorry for the language, but it's the only word fitting of the man. Not only did he decide Lake Pendle wasn't enough for him, he included his family and friends in that declaration.

I rolled my eyes and started down the street, pushing my cookie wagon toward the farmer's market. Actually, his exact words were, "the world is a big place, Cookie Pie," —yes, he called me Cookie

Pie, don't judge— "and I want to experience it. I'm leaving Lake Pendle and never looking back. There's nothing left for me here."

And that was the day I went from a fun-loving teen to a jaded young woman whose world had crumbled with one sentence.

There's nothing left for me here.

That sentence has simultaneously wrecked me and motivated me every day since. To say I was relieved that I hadn't let on about my crush on Ares Halla was an understatement. Dating him would have been a terrible idea considering our families were so intertwined, but I still dreamed about going to prom with him or turning our regular Sunday ice cream trips into an actual date. Thankfully, my seventeen-year-old self was smart enough to recognize that if there was nothing left for him in Lake Pendle, that included me.

My parents say I changed that year. They say I turned serious and forgot how to have fun. They weren't wrong, but my heart was shattered into ten thousand tiny pieces when my best friend of seventeen years said I wasn't enough for him. It seems to me that would change anyone. Ares has returned to Lake Pendle over the years, but I've made it a point to be busy or out of town. Despite the short drive, his visits were infrequent enough that Aunt Amber always planned weeks in advance for his arrival. It wasn't hard to find something going on somewhere else on those weekends. It was better that way.

No, it was easier that way.

I shushed my sassy inner self. It was always right, but I wanted to be right for once.

If you stopped thinking about Ares Halla, that might help.

I let loose another eye roll as I pushed the cookie cart to my spot on the sidewalk and locked the wheels. As soon as the business transfer was done, I'd return to pretending Ares Halla didn't even exist. I'd done it for a decade and could do it for at least six more until I died a sad, lonely woman.

Kidding.

Hell would freeze over before I let *thou who shall not be named* ruin my life. It was time to stop pining for someone I couldn't have and didn't want—mostly—kind of, maybe—and start dating again.

With that resolution made, I pushed the umbrella up, popped the button to lock it, and prepared for business.

WELCOME TO LAKE PENDLE

"Home of The Fluffy Cupcake and not much else," I muttered as I passed the sign announcing my arrival in my hometown. Okay, so that's not true. Lake Pendle is a lovely small town on the edge of the lake with the same name that keeps tourists here year-round for swimming, boating, fishing, cross-country skiing, and sledding. The tourists keep the town businesses alive, and the businesses helped turn the town into a green space—meaning they made improvements to the infrastructure that encouraged walking and biking as the simplest way to get around town.

I glanced around me at the BMW I was driving and sighed. Moving home meant it would be in the garage more than it was driven, but I didn't care. This car reminded me of my time in the city, and I'd love to forget that time. It was time to sell it and buy something that fits more with who I am now—maybe a Chevy or a Ford, but nothing sporty or red.

Returning to Lake Pendle was all about reinventing Ares Halla. I couldn't do that if I held onto the albatrosses from the past. Sitting at a stop sign, I glanced in the rearview mirror. Speaking of albatrosses. My ridiculously expensive designer luggage with all the bells and whistles lined the backseat. Just the sight of them made me cringe. That Ares Halla was insufferable and I couldn't figure out what anyone liked about him. Even I didn't like him.

A thought struck me as I put my foot on the gas again. It wasn't time to reinvent Ares Halla. It was time to *find* him again. Find the boy I used to be and figure out what that boy would have done with his life if he hadn't run from the life he'd always wanted. It was

Cookie

time to do some honest work and get back in touch with my roots
before I made any decisions about my future.

Then there was that fence that needed mending. From what I've
been told, a careless hand split it down the middle thirteen years
ago. I couldn't let it continue. I had no idea how I was going to
mend it, especially if I couldn't get near it without getting splinters,
but I'd figure it out. Then again, maybe I deserved those splinters
and should take them like a grown-up. I tipped my head back and
forth a few times. There was no maybe about it. I deserved the
splinters, but the pain would be worth it if it gave me a chance to fix
things.

I drove past the farmers' market and smiled. That was one thing
I had missed about my hometown. Our farmers' market was always
the place to be for everything from fresh produce to fancy cupcakes.

Cupcakes.

Wait. Did I just see what I thought I saw? I steered the car to
the right and parked behind a cube van marked with The Modern
Goat's logo. Instantly, my mouth watered for one of their smoked
fish sandwiches. Okay, so that was another thing I had missed about
Lake Pendle. I added it to my immediate to-do list, but first, I had to
see if my eyes deceived me.

I climbed from the car, glad I'd dressed down in jeans and a
sweater. It was bad enough that I was driving a BMW. A three-
piece suit and tie would make me stick out like a sore thumb in this
town. I aimed to be welcomed back into the fold. I couldn't alienate
myself the first day home. I strolled down the brick pathway that
made up the outside edge of the farmers' market. Most of the
market was covered by a giant wood and steel pavilion. The
pavilion was used for music events and festivals when the market
wasn't open. But every Saturday from spring through fall, the place
was filled with products I only dreamed about getting in the city.
Oh, sure, you could get organic veggies if you wanted to pay twice
as much for carrots, but they still wouldn't taste like Mr. Mandel's
fresh ones.

Ahead of me was a quaint, white food cart with old-fashioned
spindle wheels, a pink and white Fluffy Cupcake logo on the front,
and a pink and white umbrella offering a bit of shade from the
noonday sun. Under it stood the fence I needed to mend.

Cookie Pearson.

My Cookie Pie.

I snorted at the thought. She would likely not appreciate it if I called her my Cookie Pie. It had been nearly thirteen years since I'd seen her, and I couldn't help but stare. She had always been a pretty girl, but the last thirteen years had turned her into a knockout that made my mouth water. Seeing her again reminded me just how badly I'd screwed up my life. Her long brown hair was pulled back at her nape with a band that matched the starched white of her baker's uniform. She had inherited her mother's body shape, and had hips and an ass that any girl would pay an excellent plastic surgeon to recreate. A little piece of my sad, schoolboy heart thudded inside my chest. I wanted to pull that band out of her hair and let her locks kiss her shoulders the way they used to in high school. Back when I was the one she ran to instead of the one she ran from.

A long deep breath steadied my nerves, and when her customers departed, I stepped up to the cart. "Well, look at you, Cookie Pie. You built the cookie wagon you designed in the tenth grade."

The woman I had missed so much for too long lifted her head, and the look in her beautiful blue eyes told me more than she wanted me to know. She had missed me, but she was angry deep to her soul. I deserved the anger and would take it all if it meant she could heal.

"Ares?" Oh, boy. The stunned tone of voice told me no one had clued her in about my return to Lake Pendle.

"It's me, Cookie Pie. I just got to town."

"Do.Not.Call.Me.That," she hissed, leaning over the cookie cart after she closed the sliding door on the top. "What are you doing here? Aunt Amber didn't mention you were coming for a visit."

Hmm. My assumption was correct. The most important person in this scenario was in the dark about my return. Probably so she couldn't run away.

"Really?" I asked with my head cocked. "I'm surprised no one mentioned that I was moving home."

"Moving ha—home?" she stuttered, and I nodded, this time letting an easy smile come to my lips. "Why are you moving home?"

"I can't do my new job from Minneapolis." My gaze ate her up from top to bottom, and I licked my lips, even if my mouth had gone bone dry. "It will be hands-on while I get my feet under me again."

She lifted one perfectly sculpted brow and folded her arms across her more than ample chest. "What poor sucker hired Ares Halla?"

"You," I answered, but thought better of it. "Actually, that's not true. I guess you could say we'll be co-workers. I'm here to claim my rights to The Fluffy Cupcake." Her mouth opened, but I held up my hand. "Don't worry. I won't be messing around in your kitchen." *Unless you want to*, my inappropriate brain added. "I'm more a behind the scenes kind of guy. I'll be there to ensure The Fluffy Cupcake stays in the black."

Two

I gripped the edges of my cookie wagon and held on for dear life. My head spun as I tried to process what was happening. I was afraid if I let go, I might zip off into the great unknown. How did I not see this coming? I should have, without a doubt. Ares has a degree in finance, but the idea he would return to tiny, measly Lake Pendle, which by his own declaration held nothing for him, never crossed my mind. Why hadn't anyone told me? I refused to let him see me sweat, but it took every last bit of energy to summon enough sass to speak.

"What? You're going to stoop so low as to work in Lake Pendle? Are we supposed to feel blessed by your return to save us? You didn't care about The Fluffy Cupcake thirteen years ago, so forgive me if I find it hard to believe that you care about it now."

His forehead wrinkled a bit before he spoke. That always meant he was confused but didn't want to show it. "I don't know where you got that impression, but you're wrong. I've always cared about The Fluffy Cupcake. The difference is, no one needed me there for the last decade. Now, they do, so here I am."

Where did I get that impression? From the jerk standing in front of me! I needed you here for the last decade, but I guess I just wasn't enough for you.

That inner voice sometimes made me smile. I plastered one on my face and pointed it directly at Ares. "I see, so the prodigal son returns. Should I curtsy, or would you rather I gush with platitudes of thankfulness for saving our cupcake?"

He whistled and bounced up on his toes, which I noticed were clad in high-end tennis shoes rather than dress shoes. His cashmere sweater hugged his chest, telling me he spent a fair amount of time in a gym, and his jeans hugged his asset like a glove. "Well, well. It looks like Cookie Pearson hasn't changed a bit."

How wrong you are, Ares, and little do you know that you're the reason for it all.

"You think you know me, but you don't. You gave that right away when you left town and never looked back."

My barb hit home, and he held up his hands in resignation. "If you say so. I need to head over to my parent's house for lunch. I'll see you tomorrow?"

"Tomorrow?" I asked, nausea roiling through my gut.

"For dinner and the contract signing."

"You're coming to the contract signing."

"Of course, Cookie Pie. I'm sharing Mom's fifty percent of the business with Athena."

The way he stared at me as he said that made sweat trickle down my spine. It sucked that he was ridiculously gorgeous, making it impossible to tear my gaze from him. My body was desperate to have him while my mind reminded me how much I hated him. Okay, hate was a strong word. How much I hated what he did to me. There. That's better.

"Looking forward to it," I said between gritted teeth.

As he walked away, I couldn't help but notice he was no longer the scrawny string bean boy I grew up with. He was a tall, muscular, polished man that probably looked incredible in a suit and tie, or lounging in my bed wearing nothing, if the way he wore those Levi's was any indication.

Cookie! Stop thinking about Ares in your bed naked! Tight buns and cocky swaggers lead to trouble, I scolded myself. *Keep your eye on the prize.*

My eye was on what I thought was the prize until the prize decided I was the booby prize. Since then, the bakery has been my prize, but at the end of a long day, or the start of an early one, it was harder and harder to face the day alone. As Ares climbed into his obnoxious BMW and drove away, I couldn't help but wonder how his return would change The Fluffy Cupcake, and me. When I gazed into his eyes, I could see that boy I used to share all my secrets with, and a tiny part of me wanted to pull him toward me. I wanted to be the one to remind him of all the beautiful things Lake Pendle had to offer him if he opened his heart to it. The bulk of me, though, wouldn't let that happen. I wouldn't let Ares Halla hurt me again. His first betrayal nearly killed me, and I wouldn't survive a second round, especially now that we'd be working together.

Slowly, I packed up the cookie wagon and lowered the umbrella, confident of one thing. If Ares thought he had any say in how we run the bakery, he had another think coming. He couldn't waltz into a business he deserted for bigger and better things and pretend like he owned the place. Laughter bubbled from my lips. Okay, that was a poor choice of words, but the same concept. He would earn his stripes, or he wouldn't have a say in anything other than the price we paid for flour.

I pushed the wagon back to The Fluffy Cupcake with haughty indignation. He wasn't going to walk back into my town and my bakery and expect it to be all about him. Ares would learn the hard way that ego and self-centeredness had no place in Lake Pendle *or* The Fluffy Cupcake.

Cookie Pearson was the same sassy girl she'd always been, except she wasn't a girl anymore. She was all woman, and I had a hard time convincing my libido that she was off limits. Cookie was my best friend—okay, ex-best friend—and my inappropriate thoughts better move to the backseat and stay there. Chances were high they wouldn't, though. It had been too long since a woman of Cookie's caliber had challenged me, and I had to admit, it turned me on. I was excited to know there were more sparring matches to come and more chances for her to show me who she's become since I left. She wants people to think she's all sugar and spice and everything nice, but I know the truth. There was way more spice than sugar, and we'd gotten into plenty of trouble as kids because of

15

it. The time-outs, groundings, and extra chores had always been worth it, though. We had been inseparable and unstoppable back then. Back before everything changed in my life. Unfortunately, in hindsight and with maturity, I see how much the changes in my life affected hers, and that wasn't fair.

I drove through Lake Pendle toward home and could picture us on the street corner by The Fluffy Cupcake, playing with sidewalk chalk and jump rope. Almost twenty years later, that sidewalk hosts a beautiful patio with tables the bakery uses for book clubs and early morning breakfast meetings. It was a business improvement that my Aunt Haylee made happen and one Cookie continued to foster. Cookie lived to see people enjoying her creations with friends and family and made it a point to spend time on the patio talking with people about their lives as well as her creations.

I pulled the car to the side of the road and took in the bakery. My gaze was drawn to the quirky but cute hand painted cupcake on the door. It beckoned you inside as though it was an old friend. Cookie's love for her business was displayed in the left window that was layered with bread, pastries, cupcakes, and a prominent display of specialty cookies, as well as the bright spring flowers growing from the pots near the door. While Athena and Taylor were deeply entrenched in the bakery, too, there was no question that Cookie was the reason the bakery thrived like a living, breathing entity.

My insider information told me that she had implemented many successful marketing campaigns and had several more in the works. I could see it would fall to me to keep her from expanding the bakery too quickly. It was a formidable task, but I looked forward to the challenge of working as a team with the same goals in mind. It had been too many years since I'd been challenged, so I was ready to go head-to-head with Cookie Pie. I knew I'd enjoy every minute of it. The Fluffy Cupcake and Cookie Pearson had to go on the backburner for now, though. It was time to go home.

Home.

How long had it been since I'd genuinely felt at home? Not even in the physical sense as much as having a place where I could be myself. In all honesty, not since the day I pulled out of Lake Pendle as a teen.

I slipped the BMW into the driveway next to my dad's car and climbed out. With that one action, I was home. There was a settling in my soul this time when I spied the suitcases in the backseat. They were the silent sentries of my new life in a place that had always let me be me, even if I hadn't realized it at the time. I grabbed my overnight bag and briefcase then turned to take in my childhood home. Emotion welled within me to know this wasn't just a weekend trip. I could find a life here that had meaning and that was honest and true to who I am now.

As it turned out, I wasn't a big-city kind of guy. I was a small-town boy who bit off more than he could chew but had too much pride to admit it when it came down to brass tacks. Wasn't there some old saying about adversity building character? I may have taken it to the extreme over the last decade of my life. Adversity may build character, but I learned that sometimes the character you see in the morning isn't someone you're proud to be.

In fact, I'd hated that guy with a severe jawline, caffeine-crazed eyes, and a sharp tongue. With every passing year, I knew he would have to go if I was going to make it to thirty-five without suffering a stroke or a heart attack. A few months ago, my dad mentioned he was about my age when he moved to Lake Pendle. He was looking for a quieter life and a place to heal his soul. My half-sister, Athena, was grown and at college, but dad had barely cracked the lid on his thirties. He didn't want to be alone anymore and hoped making a change would bring him someone special to share his life. Then he met Mom and the rest was history. He reminded me that change is scary, but look what he'd have missed if he hadn't taken a chance on a little town in the middle of Minnesota.

I followed the scent of charcoal around the path to the backyard, where the man himself stood. "Hey, Dad."

"Ares!" he exclaimed, setting his pop can down to hug me. "I'm so glad you're here."

"Thanks." I smiled as I stepped out of his hug and took in the yard behind him. "The place looks great. Where's Mom?"

"In the house. She's working on lunch."

"Sounds great. I'll go say hello, be right back."

The ramp that led into the house from the deck bounced under my feet when I walked up. I had spent years of my life running up and down it, unconsciously memorizing the feel and sound of the wood over the years. It didn't sound or feel the same anymore. I made a note to look at it and make any needed repairs.

"I'm home, Mom," I called, stepping into the kitchen and setting my bags by the wall.

"Ares!" she exclaimed, rolling over to hug me. "I've missed you, sweetheart."

After kissing her cheek, I stood up and smiled. "I missed you too. It's a little surreal to know I'm here to stay."

"I'm so happy you agreed to return and claim your rightful place at The Fluffy Cupcake!"

Mom was grinning from ear to ear, but I couldn't help but think about those exact words coming from Cookie's lips. She hadn't been grinning when she'd said them. As I replayed it, I saw the absolute devastation radiating from her eyes. I was missing a massive piece of the picture when it came to Cookie Pearson, and right then and there, I vowed to find it, even if it took me years.

"I needed a change," I said with a shrug, as though I wasn't a shell of a man standing in my childhood home. "I'm looking forward to the chance to keep the bakery in the family. I know Athena and Taylor are too. Where are they?"

"They're still working, but they should be home any minute. Can you run the meat out to Dad? We'll eat on the deck since it's so nice out."

"Sure," I said, waiting as she rolled to the refrigerator and stopped her chair. She pushed a button that lifted her into the air to reach into the fridge and grab a plate of beef kabobs.

Mom had been critically injured when she was a teenager. A tornado swept through town, and she went with it. After years of rehab, she had a left leg that was damaged beyond repair. That was the very reason she married Dad. She needed a new brace that was ridiculously expensive and outside the realm of a self-employed bakery owner to pay for out of pocket. My dad was a teacher and had insurance through the school district, so by marrying her, he could get her the brace she needed. They both admit it was in a moral gray area, but Mom was the only one who struggled with it. My dad knew he was doing the right thing. In his opinion, his only choice was to help a woman who was in terrible pain. The brace would lessen her pain, allow her to keep working and care for herself, which in the end benefited society. The marriage was supposed to last thirty days, but here we are, thirty years later and they're just as in love today as they were the day they said their vows. All these years later, I would say the end justified the means.

Mom used that brace to lead a semi-mobile life until I was in high school. She couldn't walk long distances but could work and stay upright around the house. Then she got an infection in the leg that they couldn't cure. The choice was to amputate the leg or die. Even if the choice was obvious, it was hard. In the end, she had a hip disarticulation, meaning her entire leg was removed at her hip. Since then, she has thrived without the pain that limb had given her for years, but due to the injuries to her arms from the tornado, and her age, she opted for a custom wheelchair rather than a prosthesis that would be difficult or impossible for her to use. The chair allowed her to do everything she wanted in a way she hadn't been able to do since she was a young girl.

"Your chair still blows my mind," I said, accepting the plate of kabobs from her.

She patted the armrest and smiled. "There's a lot packed into this baby. But you know Dad—"

"Nothing but the best for my little tart," we said in unison before we dissolved into a fit of giggles.

"He loves you so much, though," I said with a wink.

She got that dreamy look in her eye whenever Dad was mentioned. My dad wore the same look every time he caught sight of Mom, even after thirty years. I could only hope to find something half that extraordinary in my life. I had incredible role models on how to love wholly and completely, but I hadn't found the woman to put that kind of look in my eye.

That's a lie, and you know it.

I ignored that inner voice and focused on my mom. "He does, and I'm looking forward to our retirement. I'm so glad you'll be here and part of our lives again."

"Except you won't be," I said, a frown marring my face. "Here, I mean. You'll be thousands of miles away in sunny Florida."

The words were barely out of my mouth, when her eyes filled with tears. I noticed her hand tremble as she tried to activate the joystick on her chair. I grabbed the back of it so she couldn't turn away.

"Mom? What's the matter?"

"Nothing, dear," she said, but I also heard her voice tremble. "Better get the meat to Dad before he comes looking for it. I'll be right out."

I let go of the chair, and she zipped down the hallway toward their bedroom. All I wanted to do was run down there and comfort her or tell Dad so he could, but I didn't. Something told me not to. A little voice said she didn't want my dad to know something was wrong, even if I didn't know what or why.

Dad took the plate, chatting about how great it was for me to be home, but my mind was still on the woman in the house. I'd seen that reaction hundreds of times in my life. Every time a thunderstorm rolled in or a watch was issued, that same look would cross her face. Her PTSD was still that strong all these years later. I glanced upward, but there wasn't a cloud in sight, and they weren't predicting rain for days.

I didn't know what was going on, but in time, I would sit down and have a little chat with Amber Halla.

Three

The walk back to the bakery gave me time to get good and worked up about Ares' surprise return. To say I was not amused was an understatement. I was livid! Why on earth had no one told me? Instead, I had to hear about it from his lips! I parked the cookie wagon outside the door and stomped into the bakery.

"Why was I the last to know that Ares Damn Halla is joining the team?" I yelled the question from the storeroom, but my anger pulsed ahead of me. Athena stood like a deer in headlights when I made it to the baker's bench. "I thought we were sisters!" I slapped my hand down on the bench to get her attention. "It's always sisters before misters! Even if that mister is your brother!"

"I was sworn to secrecy by threat of my job, Cookie. I tried to warn you. Remember when I said to relax about finding a numbers guy?"

"Your exact quote was, give it time, and everything will work out. That's not a warning, Athena. That's an inspirational sticker!"

"What is going on in here?" My mom came out of the small office by the walk-in cooler and stopped short when she saw me.

"Mom, what are *you* doing here?" I asked, putting extra emphasis on you. "Plotting to ruin my life with more fun surprises?"

"Office. Now." She pointed to the open door, and I stomped past her without saying another word to Athena. Mom closed the door behind her as I flopped into a chair, rightly put out. "To answer your question, I was preparing the final paperwork for the transfer dinner tomorrow night."

I leaned forward and pounded my fist on the desk. "I want to know why no one told me Ares Halla was claiming his shares to the bakery!"

Cookie

My mother was silent. All she did was stare at me with a brow raised. I'd lived with the woman for twenty-one years and knew she wouldn't answer me until I chilled. Fine, she wanted chill, I'd give her chill! I flopped back into the chair and crossed my arms over my chest. For added emphasis as to my state of mind, I jutted my chin out in a righteous teenage pout.

"This," she said, motioning around my body, "is why we didn't tell you."

I touched my temple with disbelief. "Did it occur to anyone that I was going to find out? Athena thought of it, but you threatened her job if she told me. Her job, Mom?" I whipped my arm out toward the door in frustration.

"We were going to tell you tonight, so you had time to cool down before dinner tomorrow."

"That doesn't explain why no one told me the minute Ares agreed to take the position."

She motioned around me again and then gave me the palms up. "Better to keep you in the dark as long as possible. Aunt Amber was worried you'd sabotage his return if you knew about it."

"This is…" I paused and shook my head, my teeth grasping my lower lip for a moment as I searched for the words that wouldn't come. "Unbelievable."

"You have to admit that you get a little worked up regarding Ares."

"My personal relationship with Ares has nothing to do with the business that we're running. If a change is made to how this business runs, I need to be informed immediately. I can't believe you went against your own daughter. Worse, you thought so little of me to believe I would try to sabotage his return. I may not be happy, but I would never do that. He has a right to this business just as much as I do. Had you told me about it, like a mature adult, at least I would have had time to prepare myself for the inevitable. Instead, I'm blindsided by him in the middle of the farmers' market!" I tossed my arm out at the door again in a dramatic overture.

Mom held up her hands to calm me. "I'll admit that I didn't think that one through. I should have considered that you might see him before we could talk to you about it. I apologize that you were put on the spot. But he's here to stay now. You'll have to accept that. I know you have a crush on him—"

I jumped up from the chair before she could finish. "Had! That ended the day he drove out of Lake Pendle without a backward glance."

"Ares has visited many times over the years, Cookie. You're the one who's never here when he's home."

"I have a business to run. I can't work my life around Ares' return visits like he's some small-town celebrity or something. Besides, this has nothing to do with Ares and everything to do with the fact that my inner circle didn't have my back. My inner circle, the people who were supposed to be my ride or die, kept this from me because apparently, that's how little they think of me. More than anything, that's what hurts. You'll never understand the embarrassment and hurt I just went through at his hands. I don't know how I'll ever forgive or trust any of you again."

"You're blowing this out of proportion, Cookie," Mom said, her exasperation loud and clear. Too bad. She should be in my shoes right now.

"No, I'm not, and the fact that you can't see how badly this hurt me tells me you never even considered my feelings when you and Amber made this decision. You should have stood up for me and told your best friend that I'm not an eighteen-year-old teenage girl anymore and I can handle my own business, but you didn't do that. You didn't believe in me," I said, pointing to my chest as tears gathered in my eyes. "Never, in all my years of life, did I ever think you'd be the one to break my heart and shatter any self-confidence I'd built since Ares left the first time." Mom tried to speak, but I cut her off with my hand. "You know what? Take my name off the reservation for tomorrow's dinner. I won't be attending. Now that I know how little everyone thinks of me, I certainly won't be missed." I walked to the door and grasped the doorknob, tears falling down my cheeks. "I can't believe Dad went along with this, too." My earlier anger turned to sadness, and my heart crumbled. "With one careless decision, you blew up my entire world and what's worse, I never saw it coming. That's on me." I wanted to say more, but all that came out was a choked sob.

Cookie

"Cookie, wait—" Mom called, but I was already dashing from the bakery and up the stairs to my apartment.

Once inside the door, I sank onto my couch and let the tears fall. I was a joke to my own family. How would I ever show my face anywhere in Lake Pendle again?

My plan was made and I'd already implemented it. I'd stay curled up in the corner of the couch with the blanket over my head and a book in my hand until the day I died. It was the only solution for this situation. Knowing how little they thought of me, there was no way I could face my family again. What had been pure anger turned to sadness when I learned that both of my parents went along with a plan to leave me standing with egg on my face.

"I'm coming in, Cooks," a voice called from the front door. I'd heard her coming up the stairs, but I didn't get up. Refer to the above plan with questions.

The door opened and closed, and I grunted from under the blanket. "I don't want company, Rye." My voice was nasally due to the gallon of tears I'd shed over the last four hours.

The couch cushion depressed, and the blanket fell away when she put her arm around me. "I heard what happened."

"Did you know too?" I asked in a barely-there whisper. I couldn't sit with the idea that Rye was also in on it. If my best friend knew that Ares was coming home and didn't run to me the moment she heard, then I was truly alone in this world.

"No. I swear to you on my life, Cookie. Had I known, I would have told you. I suspected it might be the case since he's a numbers guy, but when I asked Haylee and Brady, they said no."

"So, they lied to you too."

"It appears so. They knew I would tell you if they were honest with me."

"At first, I was angry that he was back. Then I was angry no one told me, but when I found out they did it on purpose, my heart broke," I whispered, my voice bearing all of my sadness. "Just leave me here to die."

"I'm sorry, Cookie. If it matters, Haylee told everyone at lunch what happened. She feels terrible."

"I almost believe that, Rye."

My best friend sat quietly next to me and rubbed my shoulder, allowing me to feel what I needed to feel without judgment. Rye moved to Lake Pendle in the middle of our junior year. As a foster child, moving to a new school in the middle of the year was old hat as was the incessant bullying she put up with every day. She hadn't even flinched when kids started in on her about her name or her face. 'Rye,' they'd say, 'as in bread?' and then bust into giggles. Living with a name like Cookie, I could commiserate with her, but when they started mocking her because she had facial scars, cochlear implants, and a slightly garbled voice, I got good and mad. One day, while a kid was up in her face imitating her, I popped him in the nose. That earned me an in-school suspension for three days, but it was worth it.

We've been fast friends ever since. Rye is the sweetest person you've ever met and would do anything for anyone. She's also hardworking and determined to make a life for herself. A life she never thought she'd have when she was a child. Rye claims her 'disaster of a face,' not to mention being deaf, was why she never got adopted after her mom died when she was two. I think, in some odd way, that makes her feel better. While I could acknowledge her pain and grief from feeling unwanted, I couldn't accept her lack of self-esteem. I loved her face and told her she should take pride in it. It was her face, and loving it for all the trials and tribulations she'd been through was the only answer. I taught her how to use makeup to cover the scars from her multiple surgeries to build her a nose when she was born without one and to close the deformity of her lip and palate. Not so she could *hide*, but so she could *live*. She gained confidence when something as simple as makeup slowed the bullying at school. I also kept her at my hip since I had earned a reputation as someone not to cross.

Apparently, it didn't take much in Lake Pendle to scare kids straight. A bloody nose and a whispered promise to hurt him worse if I ever saw him talking to Rye, and Ben never made eye contact with either of us again. Now, he works at the bank in town. Thankfully, he's no longer a jackass. I'm glad that was just a phase. Ben talks to me now but usually does it from a few feet back.

After I got in trouble at school, my dad wanted to meet the girl I'd resorted to violence to protect. When I introduced Rye, they could see she needed love and guidance more than anything. We offered to take her until she turned eighteen, and her foster family couldn't get her out the door fast enough. Rye wanted a job, so my parents hired her to work the front of the bakery on the weekends. In the end, we both needed a friend, so the universe made it happen.

Rye had only worked at the bakery about a month when early one Sunday morning, she came in to find no donuts in the case and an empty fryer in the back. That was the day she took over the donut frying position. She would work every morning from two a.m. to six a.m. before school. When she graduated, she studied everything she could get her hands on about the art of making and frying donuts. My dad hooked her up with a short apprenticeship in the city so she could learn more advanced techniques and recipes. When she returned to The Fluffy Cupcake, she implemented everything she'd learned. Since then, she's expanded our donut and pastry business tenfold.

Rye has her apartment in my parent's basement but hasn't been ready to leave the nest. That was part of the reason I moved to the small apartment above the bakery when I turned twenty-one. I wanted to give her time to be an only child, even if she was no longer a child. My parents call her their bonus daughter and love having her there. While they're in Florida, she'll take care of the house, but I'm a little worried about how she will do emotionally. She's depended on them to help her heal from her childhood, and while she knows it's time for more independence, it will still be an adjustment. If I leave the bakery, it will be even worse for her.

I blinked twice.

Did I just think that?

I had because it might be my only option to deal with the utter embarrassment they'd put me through today. How was I going to show my face there ever again? My cheeks heated at the mere thought of it. Rye got up and went to the kitchen, returning with two glasses of wine and some tissues.

"Want to tell me what happened?" she asked, handing me a glass.

"Ares showed up at the farmers' market and accosted me at the cookie wagon!"

"Accosted you?" she asked with her brows in the air.

"Fine, he talked to me, but that's basically accosting me! He acted like he hadn't been gone for thirteen years, and we were going to pick up our friendship where we left off in eleventh grade. He even called me Cookie Pie!"

Rye bit her lip, and I could tell she was trying not to laugh. "Not Cookie Pie!" She put her hands to her face in *Home Alone* style. I did nothing but glower at her. She sighed and shook her head. "What else did he say?"

"That he's moving home and taking Amber's position at the bakery. He gloated over the fact that I didn't know he was taking the job."

"I was hoping he wouldn't figure that out immediately."

"Keep hoping. It was a little hard to hide my surprise when face-to-face with Ares. The thing is, he doesn't want to be in Lake Pendle, Rye. He said that to my face!" I dug my finger into my chest to make a point. Better to feel the pain inflicted by my hand than my family's.

"You don't know that," she said, taking my hand from my chest. "Ares has been in the city a long time. He could be ready for a change. Hell, for all you know, he's a completely different person. Maybe you should give him a chance to prove himself one way or the other."

"It doesn't matter now. I won't be working at the bakery, so I'll never see him. Problem solved."

Rye reared back and grasped my chin. "What? No, no, no, no. You can't quit the bakery, Cookie. No. I need you there!"

Her voice transformed into a garbled throaty growl I couldn't understand, something that happened whenever she got emotional, so I signed 'stop' and waited for her to quiet. "My family thought I would sabotage Ares' return, Rye. How can I face all of them, much less him?"

"I know you're hurt, confused, and sad," she signed, her hands jabbing the air to emphasize her fear and unhappiness. "But don't make any decisions you can't take back until you've had time to consider it. Okay?"

Her eyes told me she needed me to say okay more than I wanted to say it, but she had my back, unlike all the others, so I did. "Okay. Maybe I'll feel differently about things tomorrow."

"I know you will," she said, her voice clear again now that she was calmer. "Take tonight to decide how to approach things and talk to your family tomorrow. They deserve your anger, but you deserve to take over the bakery. You've worked too hard all these years to give it up now."

"I know," I agreed but at the same time shrugged. "But I can't work with people who will lie to me."

"Understandable," she soothed, rubbing my shoulder as I drank my wine. "I happen to know the bakery is empty tonight until one a.m. I know you like to bake when you have something to think over."

"I would, but my mom would likely stop in, and I'm not ready to face her yet."

"That's true. How about a girls' night at home? Popcorn, a horror flick, and a bottle of wine."

I rested my head on her shoulder and sighed. "Thanks, Rye, for always knowing when I want to talk and when I don't."

"That's what sisters are for," she promised, giving me a tight squeeze.

After handing me the remote control, she stood and went to the kitchen for the popcorn. Growing up, I had three sisters; Athena, Taylor, and Rye. In the blink of an eye, I learned there was only one true sister after all.

Four

The moonbeam on the water led me to Cookie's location better than a beacon. One benefit of growing up with someone is that you always know their secret spot. Though, this particular one hadn't just been hers. It had been our spot whenever school or family overwhelmed us. While I lived on the lake, it wasn't the same as having a special place to go with your best friend. It was a little piece of land that Brady bought from his friend near the public beach access to Lake Pendle. The story he tells is that it's the place where Haylee started to see him as more than an employee or friend. When it came up for sale, he couldn't let it slip through his fingers. In fairness, it was one of the most romantic spots in town, but it was also a secluded spot to stare at the stars and let go of the day's frustrations. Something told me Cookie's world was spinning out of control, and this would be where she'd go when looking for a few moments of escape from her problems.

From what Rye told us, she wasn't in a good place—not that I would expect her to be. When I approached her this morning, I thought she knew I was joining The Fluffy Cupcake team. I could only imagine how she felt when she had to find out from me rather than her family. Her body language had said anger, but she always used anger to hide hurt. I'd spent enough years with her that I should have thought of that immediately. I'll admit I'm a bit rusty on the life and times of Cookie Pearson, but maybe I can change that tonight.

I momentarily stood at the top of the hill, my gaze taking in the woman below. An empty wine glass rested in the sand near where she had stretched out to gaze at the night sky. Whenever she needed answers, she would flop down in the sand and spread her arms like a cross. She once told me she wished the stars could give her honest answers. I told her they could if she listened to what her heart was saying while she gazed at them. Tonight, I hoped she'd forgotten that advice. The last thing I wanted was for her to quit her job at the bakery, but according to Rye, that was a genuine possibility. My job was to convince her that quitting wasn't the answer and there were other ways to resolve this situation.

I balked when my mom and Aunt Haylee asked me to check on her. There was no question in my mind that I was the last person she wanted to see, but they insisted. Haylee said I was always the one to calm her down and help her sort out her head when she was in a tough spot. That was true. Then. Now, not so much. I would need a little bit of luck and a whole lot of patience. We all knew if Cookie didn't want to do something, she wasn't going to do it, and that included forgiving her parents for being absolute idiots. Privately, I'd told my dad that I would step aside if no other solution could be found to this problem. The Fluffy Cupcake needed Cookie more than it needed me. Anyone can do paperwork and payroll, but not just anyone can breathe life into a business the way Cookie did.

"Great minds think alike," I said when I was partway down the hill. I didn't want to scare her, so I thought it best not to sneak up on her.

"I want to be alone, Ares." I could hear the tears in her voice, which hit me right in the gut. I was the reason she was sad, and I was not too fond of that for so many reasons.

"Maybe it's better if you aren't," I said, lowering myself to the sand beside her.

She sat up and turned to face the lake. "Maybe, but sitting with the crux of the problem isn't going to help me clear my head."

"That's fair." I poured a glass of wine from the bottle I'd brought and motioned at her glass. With a heavy sigh, she held it out for me to fill. I let the silence linger as we drank the wine. The sound of silence was occasionally broken by waves lapping on the shore and the hoot of an owl. She sniffed a few times and discreetly wiped her face with her shoulder when she thought I wasn't looking. I'd give her that dignity without commenting. She'd had a rough day, and while I felt responsible for it, I also knew it was only indirectly my fault.

Katie Mettner

"Our families could have handled things much better than they did," I finally said, breaking the silence as I filled our glasses again. "But you know what they say about hindsight."

She refused to look at me, and I wouldn't force her to do anything she wasn't comfortable doing. I was here to get a feel for her mental state and nothing else. I wasn't here to judge her or offer advice she didn't ask for or need.

"I know all about hindsight," she whispered, and I couldn't help but think her comment had nothing to do with what happened today. "It's one of the least helpful phrases in the English language. It never fixes the problem."

"True. I feel terrible that my return has caused so much upheaval."

"Don't." She said the word quickly and with precision. "What they've done is on them, not you. If they had acted like adults and treated me like one, we wouldn't be sitting here right now."

We'd still be at each other's throats.

That inner voice was correct. Mom and Aunt Haylee had offered an opportunity to mend a little piece of the fence, and I grabbed the hammer and nails on the way out the door.

I ran my hand through the sand under my legs, and the warmth it held was soothing on my skin. "If it matters, my mom feels terrible about this. She was the one who convinced your parents not to say anything to you."

"I don't understand why, Ares. Am I that much of a bitch?"

"No," I said, facing her even if she refused to make eye contact. "You're not a bitch, Cookie. My guess is my mom wanted me back in Lake Pendle so badly that she couldn't risk anyone talking me out of it."

Cookie groaned and dropped her head into her hands. Her long fingers buried themselves in the long chestnut locks, and I couldn't tear my gaze away. She got her daddy's eyes, but everything else was her momma. She was drop-dead gorgeous and not in a small-town girl kind of way. More in that she didn't know she was drop-dead gorgeous and that every boy in school wanted to date her. She had dated none of them. At first, I was worried it was a self-esteem issue regarding how she was built. Some would call it an hourglass figure, but I called it delicious.

31

Cookie

Back then, I was a seventeen-year-old boy with a crush on his best friend. It took everything I had not to plant my hands on her sweet hips and my lips on hers. That desire hit me straight away as I gazed at her tonight. Dammit. I thought I'd gotten Cookie Pearson out of my system, but it appeared pieces of her had stuck around. There was zero chance Cookie would look twice at me after this fiasco, which made my anger at my mother rear its ugly head. I sucked in a deep breath and let it back out. It was easier to be angry with her than to remember it stemmed from something we didn't understand. My mother was a different woman than the one I saw two months ago when they came to the city. My dad noticed the changes, too, but avoided my questions when I asked them.

Without consent or approval, my hands grasped Cookie's elbows, and I gently caressed her arms with my thumbs. She lifted her head to reveal so much pain in her sky-blue eyes. My heart paused when I realized this was more than a hurt ego. They had crushed her soul in a way I wasn't sure was repairable.

"I would never do that, Ares," she whispered, shaking her head. "That's what hurts the most. The people who raised me believe I would." She stuck her finger in her chest and tried to say more, but her chin started to tremble.

"I know you wouldn't, Cookie. I'm sure my return to Lake Pendle was unwelcome news today, but I remember the girl I grew up with well. That girl was quick to anger but just as quick to forgive. Despite obstacles, she knew what she wanted and was driven to make it happen. My return to The Fluffy Cupcake might feel like an obstacle, but I assure you, it's not. Is it a change? Yes. Does it have to be a bad change? I don't think so."

Her chin trembled for a moment before she spoke. "I'm already over the news that you'll be working at The Fluffy Cupcake. I do the baking, and you do the books. As long as you aren't in my kitchen, I can deal. It only took me an hour to come to that realization, but none of that matters now that my world has imploded. My job is gone because they couldn't give me the courtesy of an hour."

"Wait," I said, my head cocked. "Your job is gone? Haylee fired you?"

Cookie's shoulders slumped forward when she shook her head. "No, but I'm going to quit."

"I don't see how quitting your job correlates when you're the one who was wronged. Besides, you're about to own The Fluffy Cupcake. You can't quit."

"Well, I also can't work there knowing that everyone thinks I'm some immature bitch who would go behind their backs and sabotage the business that was about to be mine! Do you think I want to work with Athena every day when I know she put her job above doing the right and decent thing? Do you think I could ever be comfortable in that bakery again, knowing what they think of me? Could you do it?"

She had a point. I'd left the city for the same reason, but that was the right choice for me at the time. I had no skin in the game when it came to that business. The same could not be said for Cookie.

"Listen, Cookie Pie—"

"Don't.Call.Me.That," she hissed. "You don't get to pretend like we're still best friends. We aren't."

I lifted my hands off her elbows and held them up in my defense. Talking was getting us nowhere. I would have to pull out the big guns if I wanted to get it through her stubborn head that she couldn't leave the bakery. "What do you say we get out of here? I know a place that will turn that frown upside down and might even help you find some clarity."

"That would make you a miracle worker, Ares Halla, and I know you're not that."

"Maybe I am. You can't be sure. I've changed a lot in thirteen years, Cookie."

She lifted her gaze to mine and held it longer than I was comfortable, but I didn't break the connection. I needed her to see how much I had changed since we were kids. I'm no longer the boy she remembers. When she didn't say anything, I held my hand out. "What do you say?"

A shiver ran through me when she slipped her soft, warm hand into mine. Touching her again loosened the tension in my chest. I sucked in a deep breath, and for the first time in years, fresh air filled my fully expanded lungs. When I let it out, some splintered pieces of my soul had found their place again.

"I'll go, but I'm taking the wine." Cookie's words were slightly slurred as she grabbed the wine bottle. She would have toppled over if I hadn't grabbed her waist and held on tightly. The warmth and sensation of her sweet hip against mine were electrifying and comforting. It was like meeting someone for the first time and coming home again. When I headed out to find her tonight, I knew my task would be arduous. I never expected my emotions would come into play, though. As we walked up the hill to the sidewalk, I couldn't help but think that the things left unsaid between us all those years ago were bubbling to the surface. One way or the other, we had to learn to coexist at the bakery, but truthfully, I hoped we could do more than coexist. I needed a friend, and being back in Cookie's presence reminded me that we used to be good together. We used to understand each other to the extent we could finish each other's sentences. If given enough time and attention, I wondered if we could return to that place again. As the stars twinkled above, I resolved to do everything I could to close the gaping gulf of pain and anger between us. That was the first step. That was the most critical step and my focus for the foreseeable future.

Joy. Laughter. Trust. Love.

They were four small words that held my entire world within them now. As a kid, I believed Cookie would be mine forever. That boy was gone, but the man I'd become had far more determination and grit. He also had all his skin in the game. If I played my cards right, I might have my cookie and eat it too.

Five

Why was I walking down the sidewalk with Ares without protest? I
didn't need Ares Halla, his surprises, or anyone in this town, for that
matter, except for Rye. I needed Rye. Thank God she didn't have
any part in this. I probably would have driven straight out of town if
she had known and not told me. That wasn't how Rye flew, though.
She flew straight and always to me. At least someone understood
loyalty in this town. I glanced to my left at the man who had shown
up unexpectedly and without expectations. It made me wonder if, at
some level, our friendship never died. Maybe it was hibernating all
these years, waiting for us to come together again.

Ares tells me he's not the same person he was when he left
Lake Pendle. Logically, I knew that was true. He had matured, got
an education, and lived in the real world. A world I would never
understand, nor did I want to. I was happy to grow where I was
planted.

"It wasn't because I was lazy, either," I slurred. I'd had too
much wine, but then again, was there such a thing as too much
wine?

"Lazy about what, Cookie?" he asked, his gaze meeting mine
when he glanced down at me.

"About growing where I was planted. I did that, but I didn't do
it because I was lazy."

"On the contrary, Cookie. I've looked at the books, and you
must be doing something right with the income you're bringing into
the bakery now. Laziness has nothing to do with it."

"I'm glad you see things my way." I nodded, wishing I could
shut up, but the wine was talking now. "The Fluffy Cupcake was all
I ever needed to be happy." A thought struck me that forced a laugh
from my lips. That wasn't true, I needed him more than anything,

but I wasn't about to say that. "I know you didn't feel that way, and that's fine, but I was just sayin'. If you're going to grow where you're planted, it's not always because you're too lazy to find a new pot."

I expected him to laugh, but he only squeezed my waist again.

"I don't think this is a good idea." What can I say? I'm a weak woman when wine is involved. I should have told him no sooner, but the wine slowed my reflexes. Speaking of, I brought the bottle to my lips and drank. The grapes were sweet and heady, and I moaned a little as I swallowed. "I love wine."

"I can tell," Ares said with laughter. It reminded me of when we were in high school and lying under the stars on the beach. Ares was always the more serious one in our friendship, but he laughed easily and often when we were alone with the stars.

"Don't you think I earned it today?" I asked, taking another swig. Lord, have mercy. No one better look out their window right about now. Imagine if someone told my mother I was walking down the street with Ares Halla and drinking wine from a bottle. She'd have a cow! Wait. It no longer mattered what she thought about me. She already thought the worst. Time for another swig! Ares grabbed the bottle from me and pulled it away.

"Maybe we should save the wine until we get where we're going. I'd hate for you to fall and hurt yourself."

"Joykill," I huffed. "Where are we going? I'm tired. I've been up for like…," I begged my brain to do the math, but its answer was nothing more than wine o'clock. "A babillion hours."

His burst of laughter made me smile against my will. "A babillion? How long is that, exactly? I'm a numbers guy, and no one can tell me."

"Like, a lot of hours. So many. A babillion."

He squeezed my waist as he laughed, and I languished in the sensation of his touch. It had been too long since any man had touched me, but an eternity since I'd been in the safety of my best friend's arms.

Ex-best friend! Don't let the wine cloud your memory of his transgressions.

I nodded my head along to that inner voice. Right. I had to work with him, but I didn't have to be friends with him! Hell, I didn't even have to work with him. I could go home, pack my things, and drive out of town. With my certifications, I could get a job anywhere. I didn't need this little town to survive. While all that might be true, my heart didn't want to hear it. I didn't know who I was without Lake Pendle and The Fluffy Cupcake. I was the face of The Fluffy Cupcake now. The idea of walking away from my legacy was almost too much to bear.

"You didn't answer my question. Where are we going?"

"We're here," he answered.

I glanced up and came face-to-face with…my bakery? "You brought me home? How is that a surprise?"

He dug in his pocket and produced a key. "I didn't bring you home. I brought you to one of our favorite places as a kid."

"Ares, I don't want to—"

He turned and put his finger to my lips. "Don't talk. Just follow me."

He unlocked the door and helped me through it before he closed and locked it behind us. Great. Now I was locked in the bakery with Ares. Just when I thought life couldn't get worse. I stood by the baker's bench and waited while he flipped on the lights. He dug up a pan and then disappeared into the cooler. Now was my chance! I could run to my apartment while he was otherwise occupied. I ordered my feet to move, but they wouldn't. They held me in place, awaiting his return. As he walked toward me, I was struck by what a handsome man he'd become. He was tall at nearly six three and had muscles from stem to stern. With each step, his thighs rippled under his jeans, and I could almost picture the six-pack he carried under his tight, ridiculously soft cashmere sweater.

Stop gobbling him up, Cookie! Have some self-respect!

I tried, but the wine must have broken my self-respect bone because I couldn't stop. I gobbled up everything from his barely-there goatee to his coffee-brown eyes to his hair that he still wore tossed to the side with a bit of Dippity-do. Those eyes held secrets, though. They held an endless abyss of pain and, while I couldn't be sure, what looked like fear. What did Ares Halla have to fear? He had everything going for him, both personally and professionally.

Cookie

On the other hand, I was a hotter mess than the cookies he was about to put in my industrial-sized oven. Wait. Why was he putting cookies in my oven? "Ares, those are already baked."

"I know," he said with a smile, closing the door and returning to the bench. That's when I noticed the rest of what he'd brought with him from the cooler.

"Buttercream icing," I said with a sigh. "Are we making Cookie Pies?"

He smiled and winked before checking on the cookies. Ares once dared me to make whoopie pies for the class Halloween party. I see it for what it was now, but I would do anything to make Ares happy back then. So, I stayed up and made whoopie pies for class the next day. They were the hit of the Halloween party, and our classmates started calling them Cookie Pies. They were the number one requested treat at every school party. The name, while ridiculous, stuck, and we'd called them that ever since. They were the one thing Ares could make without help, so whenever we were alone in the bakery, he always made them for us.

"I don't think you've made me a Cookie Pie since the eleventh grade." I sighed with girlie delight as he pulled the cookies from the oven and loaded two with icing before capping them with the second cookie. "Double dark chocolate chip. How did you know?"

"I still remember everything about you, Cookie." He handed me one and held his cookie up like we always did when we were kids. "Long live the cookie queen." We clinked our cookies together and took a bite at the same time.

Our moans of delight bounced around the empty bakery. They sounded far dirtier than they should to my ears, but maybe it was just my sex-starved body who thought so. I could have convinced myself of that until I made eye contact with Ares. His brown ones had melted into pools of chocolate as he gobbled me up the way I had him. It made me a bit self-conscious since I wasn't the thinnest woman on the planet. Fluffy would be a better word. I own a bakery, for heaven's sake.

If someone asked me to describe myself, I could do it in four words: tits, hips, and ass. If a guy wasn't staring at my tits, he was staring at my ass. It was a mighty fine ass in its own right, but it was broader than most. When you add the hips, you get a look that reminds a person of an hourglass…if the bottom bowl is more bulbous than the top. I was lucky to have inherited this glorious body style from my mother. I rolled my eyes, but the wine made it nearly impossible to get them to face forward again. When they did, I couldn't help but notice that Ares' gaze wasn't pinned on my tits, hips, or ass. He gazed into my eyes as though he could see the words written on my soul. Being that open and vulnerable with the man I'd hated with every fiber of my being for the last thirteen years was unnerving. I worried that the reason for my anger was written there for him to read as well, so I looked away.

Remember, he's the reason your world was turned upside down.

Was he, though? I wasn't so sure anymore. It could be argued that he was also an innocent victim of this event. He had no way of knowing I was still in the dark about the bakery changes when he approached me this morning. They let him hang out to dry just as much as me.

"It's not fair, you know."

"What's not fair?" He set his cookie down on the table and brushed off his hands.

"This. You. Me. Everything."

"I don't understand, Cookie."

I motioned my hands around in the air while fighting back the tears. "What they did," I finally managed to whisper. "You got caught up in it too, and that's unfair."

He slowly walked toward me. "True, but they didn't lie to my face. They just let me assume things that weren't true. I wish I had the forethought to ask them, but it never crossed my mind that you wouldn't know. To that end, I've made a decision."

"About?" I asked, staring at my feet rather than into those brown eyes I still liked to get lost in.

"The bakery. I'm going to bow out. I'll hold my shares, but you can hire someone to do the books. Someone you feel comfortable having in the bakery."

My heart sank, and tears flooded my eyes. "That's even more unfairer!" I exclaimed. "Is that a word?"

Ares laughed, but it was tight and uncomfortable as he wiped a tear from my cheek with his thumb. "I think so, but words aside, I don't care as much about what's fair as I do about what's right. The right thing for me to do is walk away."

"But then they'll think I made you do it! Then I'm the bitch they believe me to be! There is no good answer here, Ares."

"No, Cookie Pi—Cookie, I'll make sure they understand it was my decision."

"Then you'll leave town again, and everyone will be sad *and* mad at me. It also doesn't solve my problem of how I work here again when everyone hates me."

I tossed my arms to the side and motioned around the empty bakery before bursting into tears that featured loud, racking sobs. All the hurt I'd been holding in for years came pouring out, and I couldn't stop the flood. "What am I going to do, Ares?" I asked, the words nearly incoherent through the tears.

Ares put his arms around me and held me to him, his fancy cashmere absorbing my tears as they fell. He rubbed my back and rocked me, whispering it was okay to feel my feelings. I glanced up and tried a shaky smile.

"You always used to tell me that when we were kids."

"I did," he said, a smile coming to his lips. "You kept such tight control of your emotions, but sometimes, you needed to let that anger or sadness out so you could move forward."

"Wise advice," I agreed with a shaky breath.

"I have more," he said, walking me toward the back door. "It's late, and you've had too much wine on too little sleep." Ares pulled the door open, helped me out, and walked me up the stairs to my apartment. "It's time to get a good night's sleep and worry about everything else once the sun is up."

My apartment was cool and inviting when we walked through the door. Ares helped me to the couch, sat me down, pulled my shoes off, and set them aside. I pulled my phone from my pocket and grimaced at the ten missed calls and five texts from my mother. Ares grasped the phone gently and set it aside.

"Tomorrow is soon enough, Cookie. I'll let her know you're okay on my way home."

I nodded, but the tears started again and stole my words. Ares swung himself onto the couch and pulled me over onto his shoulder.

He rubbed my arm with one hand and used his thumb to brush away tears from my cheek.

"Cookie, would you like me to call Rye and have her come over? I don't want to leave you alone when you feel like this."

I nodded against his chest, but what I wanted was for him to stay. That tiny voice of self-preservation was smart enough to stop me. My heart was already shattered. It could not withstand the pain of spending a night with Ares Halla only to watch him walk away again.

Six

It was late by the time Rye arrived at Cookie's apartment. Thankfully, Cookie had fallen asleep on my shoulder, so I carried her to her room and let Rye settle her into bed. It was hard to walk away from the girl who used to run to me when her life was in turmoil. Then I remembered how she clung to me at the bakery and wondered if she, in an unconscious way, still ran to me during those times. I had to admit that it felt good to be needed. Holding her as she wept with pain and disappointment broke something inside me, though. She was never so emotionally overcome, even at the height of her angsty teenage years. Cookie burns hot but cools off fast and forgives easily. Once she took a moment to think things over, she could always find an answer to any problem. I feared that wasn't the case this time. She was stuck between a rock and a hard place.

I paused and gazed up at the sky. The stars twinkling over Lake Pendle were brighter than you could ever hope to see in the city. They danced all night without pollution to dull their light. Considering my tumultuous return to town thus far, some of me wanted to pretend the real world didn't exist and the stars were all that mattered. Unfortunately, that wasn't how the world worked once you were an adult. The real world was often tumultuous, and the only way past it was through it. I'd learned that one often as a child. The feelings taking root inside me, though, were the ones I hated. They were the reason I left this town all those years ago. It felt like karma that my first day back was so contentious. I had run from this town for all the wrong reasons, and the universe was making it clear that now was my chance to fix it.

As I started walking again, I had to admit that I didn't hate the feelings associated with holding Cookie in my arms. I wouldn't say I liked that she was in so much pain, but having my arms around her

42

comforted me as much as her. She had turned to me when she was sad, which was the most unexpected outcome of this fiasco.

She didn't hate me.

At least tonight, it felt like she didn't hate me. Maybe tomorrow, she'd revert to the usual cold shoulder routine when I was in the room. Tonight, I didn't care about tomorrow. I would revel in being the one to make her feel slightly better. Cookie is the very definition of extraordinary in how she runs the bakery and sees life. I yearned to connect with her again, hoping that I might see life the way she does. Cookie believes that simple trumps complicated, both in baking and life. She believes if you can help someone, you do, regardless of the time or difficulty it adds to your life. Most of all, Cookie believes family is everything, and you always have their back. Hers didn't this time, so tomorrow, I hope she remembers the first half of that belief.

I walked past Haylee and Brady's house, and all the lights were out but one near the front window. A lone figure was sitting on the couch, and as I walked by, Aunt Haylee waved once. Rye had assured me she had told them Cookie was okay, so I didn't stop. I was too tired to deal with anything more tonight, and nothing Cookie had shared with me would be any comfort to her mother. I'd rather not be the one to tell the woman I had always considered my aunt what her daughter was considering. I'd rather Cookie had time to cool off and think things through. Telling Haylee her daughter didn't want the bakery could cause an unnecessary blowback on everyone.

My parents would long be in bed at this late hour, but they'd left a light on for me. It beckoned me as I walked down the street, reminding me I always had a home. I was never happier to see it. The day had left me exhausted and, oddly enough, exhilarated. I had anticipated some ups and downs, but I wasn't expecting the entire rollercoaster ride it had become.

I jogged up the ramp to the front door and slipped inside, leaving my shoes by the door. My belly grumbled, and it hit me that I hadn't eaten anything but half a Cookie Pie since lunch. The fridge would have something to hold me over until morning. I padded into the kitchen and pulled open the appliance door. In the center, right under the light, sat a covered plate with a ham and cheese sandwich, and fruit. I pulled it out with a smile. Once a mom, always a mom, I thought as I plowed through the food. When I worked at The Fluffy Cupcake in high school, I could always count on her to have a plate of food ready for me whether I went in early or came home late.

A box of Cookie's classic white chocolate macadamia nut and craisin cookies sat on the counter, and I couldn't help but reach for one. They were my guilty pleasure, and Mom always had a box here whenever I visited. After the day I had, it was bittersweet to bite into the cookie. I wanted to enjoy its sweetness evenly balanced with the tartness of the craisins, but I couldn't stop worrying about Cookie and the future of The Fluffy Cupcake. Athena was an incredibly talented artisan bread baker but wanted nothing to do with the pastries. Sure, she could pinch-hit, but she didn't have the eye that Cookie did for that side of the business. The Fluffy Cupcake sells an inordinate amount of bread, but it sells four times that of cakes, cupcakes, and cookies. That's not even factoring in the wedding cakes. If we lose Cookie, we may as well close up shop.

I tossed the rest of the cookie in the trash and turned toward my room. That's when I caught a glimpse of a figure on the deck. After I slid open the patio door and stepped out, I spoke. "Mom?"

"Be careful, Ares. The ramp broke at the end."

The spot she spoke of was unmistakable, and I sighed internally. I knew it was soft, so I should have mentioned that to Dad today. I hopped over the broken spot and knelt to inspect it.

"The whole ramp needs to be replaced," she said, her quiet, sad voice floating through the darkness.

"I'm surprised Dad hasn't done it."

"I haven't told him it's a problem. I thought it could wait until school was out. He's tired, and I already create enough work for him daily."

I grabbed a chair and spun it around to sit by her. "Dad doesn't look at it that way, and you know it. What if you had gotten hurt when it broke?"

"Karma, I guess," she said flippantly.

"How were you going to get back inside?"

She shrugged again. "Your dad would wake up eventually and notice I wasn't there."

Something was seriously wrong with my mother. She had been through so much but never let it get her down. Then again, maybe she was tired of acting okay even when she wasn't. She deserved that right after all these years.

"How was Cookie?"

"Upset. Hurt. Broken," I answered truthfully. "She doesn't understand why all the people who raised her think she was the kind of person who would sabotage her own business. She told me it took her less than an hour to come to terms with me being back in town, but she doesn't know if she will ever come to terms with her family thinking so poorly of her. She's seriously considering leaving the bakery."

"What? No," she gasped, her hand to her heart. "Cookie *is* The Fluffy Cupcake now! If she leaves, everything crumbles."

I held my hands out in self-defense. "I know, but you have to look at it from Cookie's point of view. How can she continue to work with people she can't trust."

Mom grimaced and bit her lip to keep it from trembling. She focused her gaze out over the lake rather than make eye contact. "I'm not proud of what I've done, Ares. I want you to know that. Honestly, not telling Cookie about you coming back had nothing to do with her and everything to do with me."

"I know," I agreed. "You wanted me home and wouldn't risk even the slightest chance that someone might talk me out of it."

She nodded and wiped her cheek on her shoulder. "We had to tell Athena for obvious reasons, but no one else knew. I—I screwed everything up, and I don't know how to fix it."

"Give it time," I said, squeezing her shoulder. "Cookie will never leave the bakery. She is that bakery. With enough time and clarity, she will see that."

"Maybe you could remind her that we won't be there, so the only person she will have to work with is Athena."

"Who wanted to tell her but feared losing her job." My words were more pointed than I intended, but I couldn't take them back.

"She feels awful about not telling Cookie, too. She told us the other night it was time to tell her since your return was imminent. I didn't listen."

"We all make mistakes, Mom. All we can do is own up to them, ask for forgiveness, and move forward."

"I will," she agreed quietly, "But I told Hay-Hay that it's best if I don't have anything more to do with this beyond signing my part over to you and Athena. I won't be at the dinner when it's held."

"Listen, Mom. We can worry about all that later, okay?" I asked, hugging her around her shoulders. "Let's give Cookie some time, and then we'll move forward as a family the way we always have."

She didn't answer me with anything other than a nod. Somehow, I would have to convince her to let me help her into the house so she could sleep.

"Ares?"

I jumped and turned to the door where my dad stood. "Be careful! The ramp is broken."

Dad flipped on the light and frowned when he saw the wheel-sized hole at the bottom. "Dammit, I should have fixed that when I noticed it was soft."

I squeezed his shoulder when he made it down the ramp to us. "You've been busy at work wrapping up a long career. I'll fix it tomorrow. In the meantime, would you carry Mom to bed? I can get her chair over the hole if she's not in it."

Dad knelt beside Mom's chair and brushed a stray lock off her face. "Tart, why didn't you call for help?"

"She said it was karma."

"Oh, sweetheart," he whispered before he scooped her into his arms. "It's all going to work out, but I can't have you getting sick or hurt this close to my epic retirement party, right?" Mom didn't answer. She just clung to him, her shoulders shaking with tears of regret and fatigue. He carried her inside while whispering words of comfort into her ear.

As they disappeared, I momentarily leaned against the deck railing and stared at the stars. All I could think was love hurts, but it also heals. I had to pray Cookie could see that too.

Seven

"Hey, little brother," a voice said, and I turned from the lake to see
Athena making her way down the lawn. Taylor likes to say her wife
is tall, dark, and gorgeous, and she is. My dad says the first time he
held Athena, he saw all her wisdom within her eyes. She was an old
soul, but she would change lives, including his. That was the reason
he'd named her Athena. When I came along, it only made sense to
name me Ares. Like us, Athena and Ares were half-siblings and the
goddess and god of war. Their relationship was a constant tug of
war for power, but that was never in the cards for Athena and me.

Our relationship was unlike most sibling relationships. Athena
was nineteen when I was born, so if I wasn't in Mom or Dad's
arms, I was in hers. She was less my sister and more a second mom
in my early years. Since I graduated from college, we've tried to
morph it into a typical brother-sister relationship, but I don't think it
will ever be typical. I still look to her for advice when I need help
sorting out my head.

"What's up, sis?" I asked, scooting over so she could sit next to
me on the bench that looked out over Lake Pendle. My Dad bought
the house sight unseen when he got the job in Lake Pendle thirty-
some years ago. He then spent four months in a cabin on the lake
while it was renovated just in time to move in and meet Amber the
next day. After years of hard work and devotion, the property was
beautiful. My dad vowed to love Mom in sickness and health, and
he says that promise included making their life accessible, including
the lake. With a system in place to get Mom down the hill, they love

Cookie

to spend a summer afternoon floating on the lake as though they're newlyweds instead of retirees.

Athena and Taylor live next door in the house that was Amber's childhood home. When her parents passed away about twenty years ago in an accident in Florida, the house went up for sale. Since Athena and Taylor lived in the tiny apartment above the bakery that is now Cookie's, they jumped at the chance to buy a home on the lake. Amber and her sisters were incredibly generous and sold it to them below market value, so my sister has returned the favor by renovating and restoring the rundown property to its former beauty.

"I saw your fix on the ramp," she said, putting *fix* in air quotes. "You took a hell of a burden off Dad's mind with that."

"The metal plate is a temporary fix that will support Mom's chair, even if it's ugly. I've ordered a modular ramp, and once it arrives, I'll pull the old one out completely. He'll never need to replace this new one."

"I'm sure they'll appreciate that when they return to visit. Sadness fills me whenever I think about them leaving, so I'm glad you're home for good, little brother." She shoulder-bumped me with a smile and then put her arm around me in a half hug. "It is for good, right?"

"I hope so, at least for a long time to come. In all honesty, it's taken me by surprise how happy I am to be home."

She raised a brow. "Has it really, though?"

I turned my gaze back to the lake. "You've noticed."

"It would be hard not to. The last few times you've been home, we had to practically push you out the door to get you back to the city on time for the work week. You were coming home unannounced and sleeping half the hours you were here. After everything that happened a year ago, we were worried about you. I'm glad their retirement convinced you to make a change."

I spun on the bench to face her. "Wait. They didn't retire to get me to come home, did they?"

Why hadn't I considered that a possibility? Probably because I couldn't see a way out of the hell I was living in then. I desperately needed a straw to grasp, and they offered me one.

"No, but the timing worked out well," she said with a shrug. "Dad is almost sixty-five and is more than ready to leave the district and spend all his time with Mom. Besides, it took me almost a year to convince them to retire. Someone had to, or they'd still be running that bakery from the nursing home."

I chuckled and nodded in agreement. "True. They could have easily put it in yours and Cookie's capable hands long ago."

"To be fair, they have as far as the day-to-day stuff goes. Mom does the books from here, and Haylee rarely works unless Cookie needs extra help during the wedding season. Brady comes in to bake occasionally, but it's because he misses it, not because we need him."

"You can take the man out of the bakery, but you can't take the bakery out of the man."

She chuckled and hit me with a finger gun. "Exactly. Speaking of Cookie, how is she?"

"Last night, when I left her apartment, she wasn't doing too hot. It wasn't about my new position at the bakery, either."

Athena sighed, and her lips thinned. "She's upset that everyone kept the information from her. I get that." Her gaze darted to the lake. "I didn't agree with the decision not to tell her if that counts for anything."

"I'm surprised they told you." I turned toward her again. "That was unfair to you."

"We're splitting Mom's share in the bakery, so they had to tell me you were coming back to claim your percentage. They low-key threatened me with my job if I told Cookie. I still should have done it, but I thought they would tell her before you arrived. Hindsight says I should have taken better care of my friend."

I groaned, and the sound echoed across the lake. "I'm sorry, sis. You were put in a bad position by no fault of your own. I don't believe it's my fault, but I feel like it is. I suppose Cookie read you the riot act?"

"If looks could kill, I wouldn't be talking to you. Cookie threw around the sisters before misters theory just as Aunt Haylee dragged her into the office. After that, well, you know what happened."

Lunch had been a somber event when Haylee showed up in tears. Rye had gone over to be with Cookie, and the rest of us sat picking at our food. Mom disappeared into the house and never returned, and Brady walked Haylee home with an apology for ruining my first day back. It was a real mess that wasn't my fault. I was the reason for it, but I wasn't the one who had botched it with Cookie.

"I wish I could figure out why Cookie was so hostile. Yesterday, she was sarcastic and catty even before she knew I was moving back for good. She acts like I insulted her and her entire family."

Athena shook her head, but I noticed a smile tip her lips. "Kid, for being a numbers whiz, you sure can't add two plus two."

"What does that even mean?" I asked as she stood.

"What's important is that you do the math yourself, Ares. All I'm going to say is, tread lightly with Cookie. She will need some time to accept your return."

"Cookie told me last night that she was over the idea of me working at The Fluffy Cupcake after an hour. What she can't get past is what everyone did to her. She's considering leaving the bakery."

Athena's gasp was loud as she sat back down. "No! You can't let that happen, Ares! She lives and breathes the bakery; without her, there is no bakery. She wasn't working this morning, but I expected she wouldn't be. When Rye came in to start the donuts, she said Cookie was sleeping. I should have gone to see her this morning before leaving work, but Rye insisted she needed more time."

I held my hand out to calm her. "I'm sure Haylee is over there now, but I told Cookie last night that I would walk away before I'd let her. I can keep my shares and pay someone else to do the books."

Athena's frown lines deepened. "Then you'd leave town again. None of us want that, Ares."

"I'm sure I can find work here. If I can't, I can always open a firm."

"I'll go over and make it right with her. Or at least apologize for not doing what I should have done when this started. You know I have to keep that job, though." Her gaze darted to her house before it landed back on me. "I'll make it clear to Cookie that it will never happen again, and we're a team."

"Maybe it's time you tell her why, too," I suggested. "Especially after this debacle."

Athena grimaced at the suggestion, and I could see that would be a hard no. She held out her hand where an SD card rested in her palm. "I suggest you get familiar with the information on this disk. If you start working at The Fluffy Cupcake, Cookie won't cut you any slack regarding your lack of knowledge about the business. If you want to thaw the ice queen, the information on this card is your magic hair dryer."

I thought I'd done a decent job of thawing Cookie out last night, but I couldn't tell my sister that, or she would demand a blow-by-blow. After lifting the SD card off her palm, I flipped it over several times. "Mom gave me copies of the books, Athena. I don't need a second set."

"Trust me, Ares, what's on that card has nothing to do with numbers and everything to do with dreams."

I tipped my head and stared at her in silence for a moment. "Why won't anyone give me straight answers? Why all the puzzles and cryptic messages?"

Athena walked backward a few steps before she answered. "You need to earn your stripes, but more than that, you must earn your place here again."

"The way you figure it, letting me flounder around will humble me?"

"No, but wisdom is gained through experience, Ares. Your experience with The Fluffy Cupcake and Cookie Pearson is outdated and disconnected. I just gave you the information you need in a way that keeps your slate clean so you can write your future."

"Athena?" She stopped and turned back to me. "I need wisdom about Cookie now. It can't wait."

She pointed at the SD card in my hand. "That has all the wisdom you need."

When she disappeared behind the fence, I stood and gazed at the SD card. Could this tiny piece of plastic hold the secret to finding my way back into Cookie Pearson's good graces? Last night was a start, but I would need more in my arsenal than Cookie Pies and a shoulder to cry on.

I jogged up the hill toward the house and prayed my footfalls brought me closer to the wisdom I'd need to pick up where I left off in mending that fence.

Who used my head as a punching bag? That was the only question running through my mind when I reached the bathroom sink. The woman reflected in the mirror was frightening. Her hair stuck up in all different directions, and the dark bags under her eyes carried a heavy load. The incessant pounding at her temples told her the wine had fists.

"How are you going to face the day, girl?"

The woman in the mirror didn't answer, so I tossed my pajamas on the floor and stepped under a stream of warm water. Too much wine mixed with exhaustion had won out last night. That was my only explanation for falling asleep on Ares' shoulder while we waited for Rye. The next thing I remembered was Rye waking me to say she was going to work and that I should sleep in. Sleep in? Fine. I was never returning to the bakery, so I may as well get used to sleeping in. The thought alone made my heart spasm painfully in my chest. All the sleepless nights I'd put into improving and building the business would be wasted if I walked away now. While my head knew that, my heart was too broken to listen.

Once I was out of the shower and dressed, the pounding in my head ceased, and the woman in the mirror came back to life. A little coffee, and she might be able to form a sentence without crying. The low hum of my business running below me brought tears to my eyes, and one fell over my lashes—so much for not crying. I used to find the sound of the mixer thwapping dough and the happy voices of customers floating through the air comforting, but not today. Today, it was heartbreaking.

While I waited for the coffee to brew, I took a bite of a dark chocolate cookie. The flavors exploded in my mouth the same way they always do, but this time, they came with an image of Ares holding his Cookie Pie in the air and toasting the cookie queen. I couldn't help but notice that Ares had become a different person since he'd left town so many years ago. His gregarious personality was muted by experience and maturity. I occasionally caught glimpses of the boy I used to know, like when he knew exactly where to find me last night because it was our special place, or how he knew that even at my lowest moment, a Cookie Pie would make me smile.

I tipped my head when I realized I wouldn't have a problem working with Ares at the bakery. I wouldn't have a problem separating our failed friendship from our professional relationship. My mind replayed the night before when I sobbed uncontrollably into his cashmere sweater. I should probably offer to pay the dry-cleaning bill for that. I snorted as I poured a cup of coffee and took a sip. In fairness, I wasn't in my right mind last night. All my good sense had left the building between the emotional trauma and the wine. Now sober, albeit with a bit of a headache, my good sense had returned and told me leaving the bakery wasn't the answer. I already knew that, but—

A sharp knock landed on my door, and I sighed. It could be Rye. Then again, it could also be Ares. Worse yet, it could be my mother. To answer or not to answer? Another sharp knock, and I knew who it was. Rye and Ares would have announced themselves, but my mother would not.

Eight

I opened the door, and my mother stood there with a box of cinnamon rolls in one hand and a tissue in the other.

"Hi," she said, and I heard so much regret, pain, fear, and fatigue in that one word. "I was hoping we could talk. I brought your favorite." She held up the box and gave me a shaky smile, so I stepped back and motioned her in.

As I closed the door, I took a deep breath and begged my foggy brain to remain neutral and listen to what she had to say. I had to walk through this and to do that, I had to hear her side of the story. When I turned back, she'd set the rolls on the coffee table and sat on the couch, clutching her tissue.

"How's Dad?" I asked, sitting in the chair across from her rather than on the couch.

"He wanted to come, but I asked him not to until we'd had a chance to talk. He had nothing to do with the decision not to tell you about Ares returning. While it's true that he didn't tell you, he was in a tough spot."

"Seems like Aunt Amber put a lot of people in tough spots."

"Without argument," she agreed as her fingers twisted the tissue. "Something is going on with her, and I haven't figured out what it is yet, but Ares returning was a light she could see in the darkness. I think that's why she begged me not to tell you about his decision to return. The idea of being this close to having him home," she said, holding her fingers nearly together, "was all she could see at the end of a long tunnel. Nothing else filtered when we tried to talk to her. It didn't matter if it was me, Bishop, Dad, or Athena."

"Ares tells me he was kept in the dark too."

"He was, which I also didn't agree with but was afraid to push too hard considering her mental state lately."

"None of that explains why you didn't tell me once you knew it was a sure thing, like when Ares had given his two weeks' notice or let his lease go on his apartment. At that point, nothing I could say would stop him. Oh, and also, I didn't have any contact information for him!" I took a breath and forced the anger down. Devolving into yelling at each other wasn't going to solve this problem, and I wanted nothing more than to solve this problem. I love my parents wholeheartedly and don't like being angry with them. I never have. That's why I've always tried to keep the lines of communication open. I had to do the same now, even when they left me feeling hurt and betrayed.

"There's always a way to find someone, Cookie. We both know that. Did I think you would try to find him and cause a problem? No. Did Aunt Amber? I can't answer that question. Six months ago, she wouldn't believe you'd sabotage the business, but she's changed since then."

I nodded my agreement. "Aunt Amber has, but again, you could have come to me and explained everything happening with the bakery merger. We could have had a conversation like the grown adults that we are, rather than you treating me like I'm still a teenager. I can see that Aunt Amber has changed, but none of this needed to happen."

"Hindsight," she said, nodding as she wiped her tears. "In hindsight, you're absolutely correct. That's what we should have done. I'm just scared I'm losing my best friend, and because I let that control me, I'm going to lose my daughter instead."

Mom broke down into tears and tucked her chin to her chest to stem the sobs as she dabbed at her eyes. My chest was heavy, and my heart was constricted with more emotions than I could name. All I could do was run to her and gather her in my arms. I rocked her gently, ironically much like Ares had done for me last night, and waited for her tears to subside.

Once she was quiet, I handed her a clean tissue and leaned forward on my thighs. "You're not going to lose me," I whispered. "Did I feel hurt and betrayed yesterday? Yes, but I think I deserved to feel that way."

Cookie

"Of course," she whispered, swiping at her nose again. "You had every right to feel betrayed. We did betray you. Our alliance should have been with our daughter without question."

"That said," I continued, sitting up to face her. "I now understand all the other things you couldn't control in this situation. That doesn't make it right, but it puts it in the perspective that you had just as much of a rock and a hard place as I do now."

Her nod was quick, and she let out a shaky breath. "I was going to tell you before Ares got back. I just didn't realize he was going to get here so early. Ares said you're thinking about leaving the bakery. Please, don't do that, Cookie. I promise that you won't have to work with any of us anymore. Rye had no idea this was going on. We purposely didn't tell her either. Also, don't hold this against Athena. She wanted to tell you. She told Amber daily that she had to let you in on it, but Amber refused to listen. That said, you can let Athena go if you feel more comfortable working with a completely new team."

The gasp that escaped my lips was loud in the quiet room. "I would never fire Athena! I would leave the bakery first. She has worked so hard to build on Dad's success with the artisan bread side of the business! I'm not cruel. Besides, she will own twenty-five percent of the business now."

Mom held out her hands to quiet me. "I want you to see all of your options, Cookie. I know you and Athena are like sisters, and she wants to talk to you, but I asked her to wait until a little later. I don't want you to feel ganged up on when you did nothing wrong."

"I'll talk to her. I'm starting to see it's not Athena's fault, either. There seems to be a lot of rock and hard places going on around Aunt Amber."

Mom took my hand and squeezed it. "So, you aren't leaving The Fluffy Cupcake?"

"For a hot minute, I considered it my only option. But with time and talking to you and Ares, I can see that's not going to fix anything. This fiasco has more to do with Aunt Amber than me, and I'm going to look at it that way. My mental health is far more stable than hers right now, so in the end, maybe you all made the right choice. I don't know, but I do know I can't walk away from a business that I've poured my soul into for my entire life."

"I'm so relieved," she whispered, squeezing my hand. "Once we sign the papers and make the bakery yours, I'm going to get to the bottom of Amber's problem. I hope she'll be more open with me when for the first time in three decades, we can be friends without worrying about business getting in the way."

The irony hit me. "It's just the opposite for Ares and me. We've been friends for three decades and will now be business partners."

"But you haven't been friends with him for three decades," Mom said with a raised brow. "That's the reason we're sitting here this morning. Something happened between you and Ares in high school, and your dad and I are worried that he hurt you somehow."

I stood and walked to the window that overlooked the side of the bakery. I had made it a point never to tell anyone what Ares had said. Rye had overheard him, so she was sworn to secrecy to avoid hurting my parents. At first, I thought he was just blowing off steam, but when he doubled down and stopped wanting to hang out, I got the message that he meant what he said. By the time we graduated, I was too angry to speak of him without a fit of rage or tears.

Now, here we were, both adults and right back where we started.

"He didn't hurt me, at least not physically," I said without turning.

"But emotionally?" Mom asked next to my ear, making me jump. I was so lost in thought I didn't hear her coming.

"It wasn't like that, Mom."

Okay, so I lied to my mother, but after everything that's happened, it was an innocent white one.

"He was your best friend, but you had no emotional connection to him? Is that what you're trying to sell me?"

"No, that's not what I meant," I said, rolling my eyes since she couldn't see me. "Okay, full disclosure, yes, Ares hurt me emotionally, but not how you think."

"I think you were in love with Ares, and he broke your heart when he left town."

I hunched my shoulders at her words. It was an automatic response to the memories of that time when I had carried so much pain around inside, knowing I wasn't good enough for the person I loved more than life itself. "I wasn't in love with him," I vehemently denied. Whether she believed me or not didn't matter, I had to keep the façade from crumbling. "I don't want to talk about this."

When I turned away, she grabbed my elbow to hold me in place. "You don't get a choice anymore, Cookie. It's time we talk about this. We must clear the air so everyone can start new when we turn the bakery over to you."

I shook my head, my eyes filling with tears again while I bit my lip to keep it from trembling. Finally, I managed to tell her the real reason I didn't want to talk. "I've kept this a secret to protect you."

"No one knows?" she asked, her head cocked in confusion.

"Well, Rye knows because she overheard him say it once, but I made her swear never to utter a word to anyone. I'll tell you, but you can never tell Aunt Amber or Bishop, and you may *never* say a word to Ares." I stressed the word *never* so heavily that my voice sounded like a demon had possessed my soul.

"Protect us from what?" Mom asked, her gaze holding mine. She had done that my entire life whenever the stakes were high. She knew I couldn't lie straight to her face.

"From feeling like I felt when he said it to me," I said, jamming my finger into my chest. "Feeling sad, angry, broken, and not good enough. Like the runner-up in the biggest event of your life."

"Cookie, sweetheart, what on earth did he say?"

I took a deep breath, shaky as it was with a painful chest, and said the words I'd never uttered to anyone. "When Ares told me he was leaving Lake Pendle and never looking back, there was more. He said this town had nothing to offer him, and it was time to get out before he was trapped here at the bakery in a dead-end job for the uneducated and unmotivated. He couldn't imagine being stuck here for the rest of his life. I'd asked him, what about us? We'd been best friends our entire life—" I paused and bit back the tears that threatened to fall. I had to finish, but I was afraid my voice wouldn't hold out for the rest of it.

"It's okay, Cookie," Mom whispered, rubbing my upper arms as I shivered. "Something tells me even Rye doesn't know this part?"

"No," I whispered before I cleared my throat. "No one knows this part but me, and I'd planned to keep it that way forever, but now he's back. You deserve to understand, but I still don't want Aunt Amber or Bishop to know."

"I won't tell them," she promised, wiping away a stray tear with her knuckle. "This stays between you and me."

"When I asked him about our friendship, he told me he wanted to experience the world outside Lake Pendle. It was time for a new life, new adventures, and new friends. He said I might be happy to stay and work at a tiny bakery for the rest of my life, but it wasn't for him. Upset, I whispered what about our dreams for the bakery, and he said he had bigger and better dreams to chase that didn't include me. He said our friendship had only lasted as long as it had because you and Aunt Amber were friends, but it was time to grow up and realize that childhood friendships have no place in the adult world."

"Oh, sweetheart," Mom whispered, pulling me into her arms. "I'm so sorry. I wish you had said something sooner."

"I couldn't," I said in a choked whisper. "I couldn't do that to you and Aunt Amber."

Mom rubbed my back and held me tightly, rocking me back and forth. "I wish you had, but I understand why you didn't. It's hard to hear someone you love say something like that when you've worked your whole life to make something out of nothing. Did you guys have an argument that may have led him to say that?"

I shook my head against her shoulder. "There was nothing, and trust me, I've had thirteen years to replay what happened. Everything was normal other than we were focused on career planning and college applications at the time. He planned to go to business school and work at the bakery on the weekends, remember?" She nodded and wiped away another tear from my cheek. "Then one day, it was like a switch flipped, and he became someone I didn't know."

"It's hard when people we love change like that," she agreed, kissing the top of my head.

"Love as a friend," I clarified because I wasn't going down that road today.

Cookie

She chuckled, and I could hear that she didn't believe me. After squeezing me one last time, she smiled and held me by my shoulders. "If that makes you feel better, we'll roll with it." I opened my mouth to object, and she put her finger over my lips. "I'm not arguing with you, Cookie. Thank you for helping me understand what happened. I don't know why Ares changed, but you're right. One day he was his usual self, and the next day he couldn't wait to go to college and get out of town. We all saw it, but we thought the school had convinced him to attend a four-year college. We all assumed he'd be back. None of us foresaw what has happened since. Knowing all this, I think hiring someone else to do the books would be smart. You shouldn't have to work with him."

"I can work with him, Mom, but I can never trust him again."

"Understandable," she whispered with a sad smile as she handed me a tissue. "However, you're the one who has put the time and talent into the bakery to make it what it is today, so if you don't feel comfortable working with Ares, you say the word. Dad and I always thought it was a simple teenage crush gone wrong, but knowing what he said, I'm not sure he deserves to be part of the dream you've chased to make the bakery what it is today."

"Maybe not," I agreed, "but he does own part of the business now. One way or the other, he will benefit from my hard work. So, if he's willing to put in the time, I will give him a second chance to prove himself worthy of The Fluffy Cupcake."

Because he will never be worthy of me, I thought. *That ship sailed, and it wasn't returning to the harbor.*

Mom took my hand and squeezed it. "Baby, you have always been the sweetest, most forgiving person I've ever known. When you offer someone a second chance, they make something of it. Dad and I have seen it happen over and over in your life. I truly believe Ares will step up and put that second chance you're offering to good use." She kissed my cheek and then led me to the couch to sit. "Now, how about having a cinnamon roll with your old mom while we figure out the rest of this situation?"

I sat and took a bite of the fresh roll, the icing melty and warm, just how I liked it. I couldn't help but think that maybe Ares had bigger and better dreams to follow, but mine had always been this building and the people inside it. That was the kind of dream that mattered, in my opinion, and the only one I'd continue to chase. Ares Halla, be damned.

Nine

It had already been a long day, but it wasn't over. Yesterday, after talking to my mom, Athena, and Aunt Amber, I felt like the air had been cleared as much as possible. Aunt Amber had made herself sick worrying about what she had done to me, so I did my best to assure her that while I was hurt and sad to learn the truth, I also understood there were extenuating circumstances to the situation. Yes, I lied, but it was the kind of lie that only I had to live with, and it was one I was alright with holding. In truth, I could see that Aunt Amber was struggling, and I couldn't add to her burden in good conscience. We had to start with a clean slate come Tuesday morning when we opened the bakery under new management. It took me longer than it should have to convince her that we all wanted her at the dinner, but eventually, she agreed to come. After talking, we also agreed to postpone it a day so she could get some rest and feel better. Part of me thinks she only plans to come and deal with the legal side of things, but I would take it as a win for now.

With dinner postponed, I decided baking would help me smooth out the rough edges of how I felt about the whole thing. Baking always helped me sort out my feelings and compartmentalize them. Shortly after midnight, Athena came in, and we had a chat. It was relaxed and easy, and I assured her that the predicaments we found ourselves in were not fair, nor did they have a playbook on the right way to approach them.

None of the above helped me figure out how to work with Ares, though. I searched online, but there was no playbook on how to own a business with your childhood crush who did you wrong, either. Shocker, I know.

Ultimately, telling my mom what happened all those years ago felt good. Not having to carry that burden myself was freeing. While it probably hurt her to hear it, we both agreed that something had happened to make him say it. Ares had been as invested in moving up the ranks of The Fluffy Cupcake as I was, so his sudden about-face had confused everyone. I made her promise at least ten times that she wouldn't tell anyone but Dad before I let her leave. It would break my heart if it got back to Amber and Bishop. They had worked hard to give Ares the opportunities he had, and it would crush Amber to hear what he'd said all those years ago. Did he feel the same now? I doubted it, but I'd find out soon enough.

Since Amber wasn't feeling the best, we decided to have the transfer dinner at Athena's and Taylor's house rather than a restaurant. I insisted on ordering food from The Modern Goat, though. Athena was a gem in hosting the dinner, but she wouldn't spend the entire day cooking when this was as much about her as it was about me.

There was a light on in the bakery when I got to the bottom of my stairs, and I cocked my head when I heard the mixer running. No one should be working tonight. We were closed until Tuesday morning.

"Mom, is that you?" I called out after I unlocked the door and walked in. "Why aren't you getting ready for dinner? We have to be there in thirty—" I stopped speaking when I saw the woman standing by the bench. It wasn't my mom. "Rye? What are you doing here? We're supposed to be at Athena's in thirty."

"You go ahead," she said, grabbing a pan from the proofer box. "I'll get an early start on the baking."

After I took the pan from her and put it back in the box, I turned her to face me. "Rye, you're invited to dinner. We want you there."

"I know," she said as she shrugged. "But this is a big event in your family. It's changing the dynamics in a passing of the torch kind of way. I'm not family and shouldn't horn in on such an important night."

My blood pounded through my veins, fueled by frustration, fear, and anger from the last few days, but I pushed it back and tried

Cookie

to see the situation from her eyes. "Rye, you are family. Don't you see that? In our parent's eyes, we are their daughters."

"That's nice of you to say, Cookie, but it's different. They gave birth to you. I just kind of walked into their lives one day."

"Maybe, but as Dad would say, you were one of us in that one second. Who do you go to when you need a hug?"

"You, Haylee, or Brady."

"Who do you go to when you need advice?"

"You, Haylee, or Brady."

"Who do you trust to keep a roof over your head and a place for you to work?"

Her sigh was heavy this time before she answered. "Haylee and Brady, but Cookie, I know they're being charitable. You can't compare their love for me and their love for you."

"Aha!" I said, sticking my finger up in the air. "You just proved my point. Their love for you. Their love has nothing to do with charity, Rye. It has everything to do with their hearts and nothing else."

"She's right," a voice said from the bakery's doorway. I turned to see my mom standing there. She walked into the bakery with a dress in one hand and shoes in the other.

"Haylee, what are you doing here?" Rye asked without making eye contact. "You should go so you aren't late for dinner."

"We have plenty of time before dinner," Dad said, walking in behind Mom. "It's time for you to get dressed."

Rye bit her lip, and her gaze drifted between us. I could tell she was close to tears and didn't know what to do. Dad walked over and pulled her over onto his shoulder for a hug.

"We love you, Rye. You never have to question that—"

"That's not what I'm questioning," she said, pulling away and swiping at her eyes. "I'm not even questioning. I'm just saying that tonight is super important and—"

"We want you there," Mom assured her. She nodded at Dad, who pulled out an envelope from his pocket.

"We were going to do this later tonight, but now feels like the right time." Dad tapped the envelope on the bench. "Rye, we've loved you for thirteen years and will for eternity."

"The same way we love Cookie," Mom added, and Dad smiled.

64

"She's right, and that's why we want you there tonight, but if you need proof of that in writing, you'll want to read this." He handed her the envelope, and Rye took it, her hands shaking as she pulled out the papers and started to read. Soon, the papers were shaking, too, and I had to put my arm around her and hold them still.

"You—you want to adopt me?" The question was quick and quiet, but it held a multitude of emotions within it: shock, joy, fear, love, and a tinge of disbelief.

"We do," Dad said with a smile on his face. "We didn't know there was such a thing as adult adoptions until I saw something about it online. I looked into it, and as it turns out, if you're willing, we can go to the courthouse together, and you can become Rye Pearson in heart *and* name."

"Do you want to be our daughter in name too?" Mom's voice was choked when she asked the question. My dad put his arm around her and kissed her temple. His love for her shone in his eyes every time he gazed at her. Mom was a foster child who grew up with Amber's family. They never adopted her but always wished they had. Mom was going to make sure she never had those same regrets.

Rye started nodding, tears streaming down her face as I took the papers from her. She ran to Mom and Dad, throwing her arms around them and sobbing into Dad's chest. "You always make me feel so loved," she said between sobs and hiccups.

"Because you are," Mom assured her, rubbing her back. "You have been part of the family since our daughter wrapped her arms of protection around you. We will always do the same. Now you no longer have to question it."

"Rye, I give you my last name, but the greatest honor is mine to know you have chosen to carry it. If you get married, and your name changes again, all the love of the Pearson name transfers. It will remain yours."

"Forever," Mom said, kissing the top of her head.

I tossed the papers on the bench and ran to them, throwing my arms around them in what could be considered the first official family hug. There is no greater feeling in the world than knowing you are loved, so tonight, I would choose to celebrate the joy of found love and not the pain of love lost.

The past two hours had been the very definition of torture. It began when Cookie walked in looking good enough to eat. Literally. She wore a red sundress with spaghetti straps and a slit to the knee. The way the material fell across her hips drew my eye and fueled my imagination. I could picture the dress flowing over her curves to cover them, but I could also picture my hands sliding up those same curves to relieve her of the dress. The moment she walked into the room, I had to fight my attraction to her. Not only was that torture, but it was confusing. Cookie had grown into a beautiful woman, but she was my childhood friend, and it tipped my world on its axis to think of her as anything more. I tried to focus on memories of our childhood years together at The Fluffy Cupcake, but the only thing my brain showed me was us standing in the bakery two nights ago with her head on my chest. It was almost like the calendar had reset, and nothing before that moment mattered.

Something mattered, though, and I had yet to figure out what it was. Cookie was amicable and wore a gigantic smile, but she had also spent the last two hours pretending I wasn't sitting here with my gaze pinned on her every movement. Good on her for being able to do that because I sure as hell couldn't. I noticed that Aunt Haylee had given me the cold shoulder, which wasn't normal. I wondered if Cookie had told her something about the other night. To say I was frustrated with the whole evening was an understatement. I couldn't wait to sign the papers and escape this awkward situation. We'd start fresh with our first bakery meeting as the new owners tomorrow. We'd go over our goals and then open on Tuesday morning again, ready to move forward. I hoped, anyway.

The information Athena had shared with me on that SD card also flashed through my mind. Cookie had a lot of plans, and those plans told me one thing—she was one hell of a businesswoman. According to my parents, she's self-taught in business and marketing. She didn't go to college, instead stepping right into her role at the bakery upon graduation. Cookie wasn't content to simply work at the bakery. She had to follow in her parent's footsteps. She became a master baker at the ripe old age of twenty-three and is also a certified master pastry chef. Those distinctions are evident in her baked delights but also in the plans she has for the business. Everything I read said she is a second-generation baker and is proud to hold that distinction.

I had to give her credit for her steadfastness regarding her place in the world. Cookie knew what she wanted and went after it without a second thought about what she might miss out on. If I had to guess, I'd say she didn't look at staying in her hometown as missing out on anything. Lake Pendle held everything she needed to be happy in this world. I wasn't that focused or strong.

That's not true. You went after what you thought you wanted.

I tipped my head in agreement with my inner self while I finished my second glass of champagne. I went after what I wanted—at the time, but I wasn't strong enough to walk it back when I realized I was missing out on a life with Cookie and nothing else. Now, I sat around a table with my family as an outsider with a glass of liquid courage. Only it didn't feel like liquid courage. It felt like liquid stupidity. Too much more of it, and the chances were high that I was going to say something to that stunning woman that I shouldn't. Like demand to know what the simmering underlayer of anger was every time she looked at me.

"It sure has been wonderful being with you all here tonight," Brady said as he stood from his place at the table. "The Fluffy Cupcake has been part of our family," he paused, and when his gaze found Haylee's, their connection was palpable in the room. He took her hand and held it between his. "Truthfully, The Fluffy Cupcake has built our family and we couldn't be happier that it will now be in the hands of the people who maybe love it even more than we did. It seems with each generation, the bakery changes and grows, creating more memories for our family and the families of Lake

67

Pendle. I can't wait to watch the business thrive under the capable hands of our daughters and son. The sky is the limit with the talent you all bring to the baker's bench."

Haylee stood and made eye contact with everyone around the table. When she got to me, I was nervous that she'd see everything I'd been thinking about her daughter since we walked in the door. I met her gaze, and her eyes narrowed, assuring me that something had changed between us over the last few days, and it wasn't good.

"Now, to the reason we're here tonight," Haylee said, motioning at Mom and Dad, who nodded, as Mom leaned her head on Dad's shoulder. "I speak for all of us when I say we love you, and we're so very proud of you. We have seen you take the baton and run with it over the last few years as we've lessened our presence at The Fluffy Cupcake. As of Monday, when these papers are filed," she said, tapping a stack of folders on the table. "The Fluffy Cupcake will officially change hands. As you know, fifty percent of the business is mine, and fifty percent is Amber's. We are splitting the stock evenly between our children, with the caveat that if anyone wants to leave the business, they must sell their stocks back to the remaining owners, and it must be split evenly. As of tomorrow, you will each hold twenty-five percent ownership in the bakery. As the shares will be split evenly, no one will hold the majority of the stock, so full agreement on all changes to the business will be required."

Athena cocked her head in confusion. "Haylee, only Ares and I will split stock. Cookie will hold the majority with your fifty percent."

"While Cookie is our only biological child," Haylee answered, "our soon-to-be adopted daughter, Rye, has contributed to building this business for the last thirteen years. She has put as much blood, sweat, and tears into it as Cookie has, so it is with Cookie's full agreement and encouragement that Rye will receive twenty-five percent of the shares to the bakery."

Rye popped up from her chair like a Jack in the box. "No, no. You can't give me Cookie's shares of the business. She earned those when she was born. I've only worked for you for the last dozen years. That's not the same."

"A baker's dozen, actually," Brady said, making a joke that didn't hit home with Rye.

Her eyes were wild and frantic when she pinned them on Haylee. "Seriously, guys, you can't do this. I don't want you to do this. It's not fair to Cookie."

Cookie stood and put her arm around Rye. They were friends in high school, but I could see they had become sisters while I was away. The Pearsons loved Rye deeply. She had come into their lives unexpectedly but was welcomed with joy and understanding. I remember when Cookie popped Ben Harding right in the nose for bullying Rye. It made Cookie a legend in Lake Pendle as someone who stood up for the underdog, no matter the consequences. One might think that was what was happening here tonight, but that wasn't the case at all. I'd been gone for many years, but even I understood this was about family and nothing else.

"Rye, being born into something means nothing," Cookie said, sparing a withering glance at me before she continued. "Being present, doing the work, implementing ideas, and being a team player makes a business successful, not birthright." Another scorching glance of disrespect was sent my way. "You've done all of those things and then some. So even though you're about to be my sister legally, you've been my heart sister for the last thirteen years. We've worked side by side, and just like Athena, without you, the bakery wouldn't be where it is today."

You made your point, Cookie, I thought, biting back a huff and an eye roll.

"It's your choice whether you accept the shares or not, Rye," Haylee said. "We can't force you to sign the papers, but we can encourage you to consider them. I understand it's hard for you to see that you deserve this, and I understand why. I experienced those same feelings when The Fluffy Cupcake was handed to me. Kids like us grow up with a preconceived notion that we don't deserve good things to happen to us, but nothing could be further from the truth. We deserve all the good things that happen to us. Look around you. Look at what you built from love when no blood was involved."

Cookie squeezed Rye's shoulder and wiped a tear off her face. "We've thrown a lot at you tonight, sis. Emotions are high for all of

69

us, but we had to bring this up to everyone tonight for obvious reasons. I hope you'll consider signing the papers and making the bakery a permanent part of your life."

"It already is," she whispered, shaking her head as she tried to keep from crying. "Growing up in foster care, I never thought I'd find anyone who would love me like my mom did before she died. Then I came to Lake Pendle, and what was supposed to be my last stop to nowhere turned out to be my first step to a new life. I owe that to you guys, which means you owe me nothing. Cookie should have all the shares, so she has the majority of the say in the business. That's only fair, right?"

"Wrong," Cookie said, turning and taking Rye's hands. That put her right in my line of sight, so I busied myself with my glass to avoid eye contact. I couldn't take many more of her caustic looks without melting through the floor. "Some of us got to this table by default, and some got here by dedication and determination. We all have a place around the table, and I don't want the majority rule in the business. That doesn't benefit anyone, Rye. Cooperation and teamwork will move The Fluffy Cupcake into the next century. I want you and Athena around the baker's bench to do that. That's the only way, in my eyes."

I couldn't help but notice she'd left me out of the girl gang. To be fair, I wouldn't be at the baker's bench as the finance guy, but I could read between the lines. She didn't think I would stick around long. Even if I did, they wouldn't welcome me with open arms. That wasn't new to me. I'd lived that life for the last nine years, but I was here for a change. That change would start with Cookie's attitude toward me if I had anything to say.

Rye turned to my mom and dad, who sat at the end of the table. "Did you both agree to this too?"

"With a resounding yes," Mom said with a smile. "Sweetheart, you've been part of this family for years, and I know Haylee wouldn't have it any other way. It's no different than me splitting my shares between Athena and Ares. Athena isn't my daughter by blood, but she is by love. She's devoted her life to the business and deserves a piece of the pie she's worked so hard to bake."

"Nice bakery analogy, Mom," I said while laughing. "It always comes down to baked goods in this family."

"Because that's what built us," Amber said, smiling at Haylee. "When we were young kids with no clue what we were doing, we would never have dreamed that we'd be here tonight. To be clear, Rye, yes, I agree to you being a partner with every part of my soul. You are my niece and always will be."

Rye nodded, but her lips momentarily quivered before she signed 'I love you' to my mom, who signed it right back. Then she turned to Athena and me. "Do either of you have a problem with me being part of the business?"

"I would have a problem if they hadn't offered you shares, Rye," Athena said with a wink. "You will hear zero arguments from me."

"If I had any doubts after witnessing this exchange," I said, keeping my gaze on Rye and not letting it drift to the woman next to her, "they would be squashed by my deep dive into the books. I'm a numbers guy who looks at business in black and red. You have contributed significantly to keeping the bakery in the black, and that's all I need to know when making a business decision. Along with being loved by everyone here, you're a valuable asset to the bakery that we can't afford to lose. Offering you shares to the business ensures that you'll be here for years to come. You'll hear no argument from me."

"That's seven yeas," Haylee said. "What's your vote, Rye? Should I hand out these folders to the new owners of The Fluffy Cupcake?"

Rye started signing, and Cookie immediately translated. We all learned to sign when Rye first came to town, but I was rusty enough now that I appreciated the help.

"I'm signing because I'm hard to understand when I'm emotional. I had to be sure you weren't offering me the business out of pity or obligation. The truth is, I know better than that, but Haylee is right. It's hard for someone like me to trust in the good things that come along in life. Then I look around this room and remember that you're all the best things to happen to me, so my vote is..." She stopped and folded her hands under her chin. "Yea."

Three letters. One word. A lifetime of acceptance for a woman who never thought anyone would accept her. I watched as hugs were shared between Rye and my family, and all I could think was that maybe there was hope for me yet.

Ten

My caramel pecan rolls, baked to golden perfection, sat on the table in the warm sunshine. The pecans sprinkled each roll just so and the caramel dripped slowly down the sides, coating each roll in sticky goodness. I was looking forward to sinking my teeth into one, but first, I had to get the coffee ready. I told Taylor to come in with Athena, so I would take care of coffee duty as well as baking duty. I didn't mind, though. After all, this is my place now, and the time and effort I put in will only return to me in spades. That was why I showed up at three a.m. to start baking and preparing for tomorrow's reopening.

After our meeting, Athena would start working on bread for our regular orders on Tuesday, then Rye and I would arrive at midnight for business as usual. Tomorrow's baking wasn't my concern, though, as I stood filling the carafe of coffee. I had to focus on this meeting and ensuring Ares knew precisely where he sat in the pecking order. He would be heard, but he wouldn't be in control. If I accomplished nothing else at this meeting, I'd be happy.

More than likely, that was going to be easier said than done. Ares had sat through last night's dinner rather smugly but left as soon as the papers were signed. Not a surprise considering he wasn't great at sticking around. I snorted as I carried the coffee pot to the table with mugs, cream, and sugar. If Taylor were here, she'd whip up coffee drinks to fancy any tastebud, but I wasn't Taylor. They were getting regular coffee. They could like it or lump it.

Another snort escaped my lips. Ares would probably lump it. He had lived in the city for so long that he likely couldn't drink regular coffee. When we were in high school, he drank coffee by the thermos load on the mornings he'd open the bakery. He took it black with two sugar cubes, and it had to be cubes. God forbid you gave him a packet of sugar and expected him to use it. I chuckled evilly as I picked up the container of sugar cubes and hid it behind the counter, then dumped a pile of sugar packets on the tray instead. Childish? Sure. Hilarious? Absolutely.

I checked my watch and gave a satisfied nod. My goal was to be ready and waiting by nine a.m. and I had ten minutes to spare. I sat, poured a cup of coffee, and officially began my wait. I leaned back and sipped the brew, staring out the window at the town of Lake Pendle as the sun turned it a golden orange of the new day. People stopped every so often to read the sign on the door, before they'd smile and jog up the street to the bank. I'd dropped off an excellent selection of goodies with Janice this morning for her to share with anyone looking for a fix. I couldn't leave the people of Lake Pendle donut-less for an entire day! Was it a profit loss? Yes, but it was worth it if it kept my customers happy.

"Cookie?" Rye called from the back room.

I grabbed my phone and hit a button, sending a preloaded text that said, 'front.' When we were in high school, we had started using texts to tell each other where we were. It was better than yelling, especially when my parents banned it in the house. I don't know what we'd do without technology now.

Rye came around the corner with a smile. "Thanks for the assist," she said, joining me at the table. "Oh, those look amazing as always."

I poured her a cup of coffee and handed her a plate for her roll. "I thought we'd need a little fuel for this meeting of the minds. I'm glad you made it before Ares. I want to be sure we're on the same page."

Rye nodded as she stirred cream into her coffee. "We are. I know what to do. We tag team him if we have to, but we don't let him take over the meeting."

I gave her a finger gun. "I know we're supposed to be a team, but we can't let Ares think he's the team leader."

"No, because you are."

"Did you see how smug he was last night at dinner? I wanted to pop him in the nose."

Rye tipped her head as she cut into her roll. "Smug? That wasn't what I saw. He appeared awkward to me."

I raised a brow the same way my mother always raised hers. I guess I had inherited a few convenient things from her besides my inconvenient body shape. "Ares Halla is never awkward."

She motioned around in the air while she chewed. "Maybe not awkward as unsure? I don't know. I turned my processors off for part of dinner because so many voices overwhelmed me. Since he was right next to me, I observed him while we ate. I couldn't hear what he was saying, but I could read his body language. He was unsure of his place at the table. I guess I can understand why. While Ares was away, we tightened the family bond without him. My unprofessional people reading skills told me he was watching the events unfold like an outsider instead of someone inside the circle."

Thinking back over the evening, I could see what she was saying. "You could be right, but if that's the case, it's on him. We've always been here."

"Maybe that's why he's back now," she said with a shrug. "It's possible he's decided the city wasn't all it was cracked up to be."

"I hope so. If that's the case, then Ares is more likely to stay and put in the time and energy the bakery needs. The sky is the limit on this place now."

"It is. I think that's why I'm still in shock this morning."

"About being adopted or owning a bakery?" I asked, leaning back in my chair. Due to my baking schedule, I hadn't talked to her since the meeting.

"Both," she said on a breath.

"But you're here this morning," I pointed out. "That's a good start."

"Little secret?" she asked, and I nodded for her to continue. "I want this. I mean, there was no question that I'd work here for the rest of my life. I was happy and content knowing I had a secure job for as long as I wanted it. If I had lost this job, it would be hard to find another bakery that would give me a chance, so to know that I own part of it now—" She made the mind-blown motion with her hands. "I don't know if it's right to want it as much as I do, though. I'm still torn about it this morning."

"Why wouldn't it be right to want it?" I asked, the confusion evident in my voice. "It was given with pure intentions and with no stipulations other than to sell it back if you leave, which is the same stipulation we all have to follow."

Rye waved her hand in the air while she swallowed her coffee. "I mean, it never crossed my mind that I'd own part of it one day. It would always be yours, and I was happy you wanted to keep me on. But owning part of it means…"

"Making decisions that affect everyone?"

"It's a lot of responsibility."

"It is, but you aren't doing it alone. There are four of us, well, technically five. Athena and Taylor share Athena's shares since they're married."

"But she doesn't get voting rights? I didn't understand that part."

"The shares are in Athena's name, so she is the only one who gets technical voting rights. However, the state of Minnesota is a community property state, so since they're married, they share the shares."

"Just like Brady and Haylee."

"Right. Technicalities aside, Taylor is such an important member of the team that we'll always take her thoughts and ideas into consideration. That's why I insisted she come to the meeting today. Taylor is the one who ends up implementing most of the ideas when it comes to the front of the store," I said, motioning at the windows. "It's only fair that she's in on the ideas from conception."

"I'm glad you see it that way. I do too. Everyone's ideas should be heard."

"They will be, including yours," I promised. "Setting the shares up to require majority rules means any idea brought to the table can be discussed and refined before voted on, and you'll have help implementing those ideas. Do you have ideas you want to bring to the table?" I sensed she did but she was afraid to say anything and make waves.

She nodded quickly. "A couple of things, but I don't want to bring them up today. We'll have a lot to review, which could get overwhelming. From now on, I thought we could do a short meeting each week, maybe ten or fifteen minutes max, to talk about one aspect of the bakery. We'd have designated weeks for bread, pastries and cakes, special orders, and finances. That would be the time to bring up ideas for that specific department. Does that make sense?"

"It makes sense to me," a voice said.

We both turned to see Ares, Athena, and Taylor standing in the doorway. I motioned them in and scooted over for Athena to sit, but she and Taylor took the chairs next to Rye, leaving me with Ares. I had failed to teach these women the concept of sisters over misters. I rolled my eyes with a heavy sigh and scooted my chair further away as he dug into the caramel rolls with gusto. When he poured a cup of coffee, I bit my lip in glee, waiting for him to demand sugar cubes. Instead, he drank it black without a word. My shoulders slumped in defeat. Okay, he's changed, but that doesn't mean I have to like him. Unfortunately, I still did. With that depressing thought, I moved on with the day.

"Good morning, Athena and Taylor. How are you both today?" I asked the question with a clear purpose. To put Ares in his place as the person I was least concerned with this morning.

"Great," they answered in unison.

Taylor grabbed a roll and then rubbed her hands together. "I was looking forward to what you'd have ready to snack on. You didn't disappoint."

Her giant bite of the pecan roll ended the discussion, so I left them to eat in peace before we started the meeting.

"What about me?" Ares asked thirty seconds later.

"What about you?" I asked in return.

"Aren't you going to ask how I am this morning?"

My internal evil smiled at the question. He couldn't stand being left out. At least that much hadn't changed since we were kids.

I took a short tour of his long form dressed in a chamois shirt and jeans that were tight in all the right places. He looked good enough to eat, but there was no way I'd ever let that show on my face. I shrugged. "You look the same as you did last night. Who's ready to start the meeting?"

While I moved the tray of goodies out of the way and prepared my computer presentation, I couldn't help but smile.

Cookie – one.

Ares – zero.

I glanced at the clock to see two hours had passed in the blink of an eye. We had a lot to discuss, but thankfully, we all seemed to be on the same page regarding expectations for the bakery. I was concerned Cookie would try to take over the meeting, and I'd been correct, but she had done it in a way that made everyone feel like an equal team member. That included me. Color me surprised after the greeting I received upon arrival. But I knew her game, so I played it exactly how she wanted me to. I let her dominate me straight out of the gate. I could respect that she was the big cheese as long as she didn't disrespect my role in the bakery when she did it. Thus far, she listened to everything I had to say about the finances, and we adjusted ideas and shelved others that weren't ready for development yet.

"Have we touched on everything now?" Cookie asked as she walked back to the table from her computer. "I know there's a lot to digest here. I want to give you time to think things over and make notes so you can ask any questions you have."

"Almost," I said, shuffling through my portfolio to find the needed document.

"You have something else to bring to the table?" Cookie suspiciously asked as she sat next to me again.

"I do," I said when I found the paper and laid it before her. "This." I motioned at it and waited for her to read through the application. I could tell she was not impressed when she glanced up at me.

"A cookie competition? You seriously brought a cookie competition to the table?"

"Not just any cookie competition," I said, pointing at the logo at the top. "A Cookie Heaven Small-Town Cookie Competition."

Katie Mettner

"I don't care if Gordon Ramsey is sponsoring it, I'm not doing a baking competition. You remember what happened the last time The Fluffy Cupcake was involved in a baking competition?"

"That was completely different, Cookie," I reminded her. "Darla attacked your mom because she was jealous of her and Brady, not because she baked good cupcakes. Besides, that was thirty years ago. You need to let it go."

"Did you tell me to let go of my mother's near-fatal attack on this very property? I don't think that's something you should let go of," she said, using air quotes. "As a woman, I should always have that in the forefront of my mind as I go about life."

I held up my hands in defense, but I noticed Rye, Taylor, and Athena were trying not to snicker. "That's not what I meant, Cookie. I meant that you have to stop using it as a reason not to participate in some of these events. An event like this could change this bakery forever. The prize money alone is worth it. Not to mention the bragging rights, trophy, and features in papers, magazines, and cookbooks that come with a win. Cookie Heaven is the top traveling competition in the world, and you could do much worse than to win one of their competitions."

"While that may all be true," Cookie said, pointing at a spot on the application form, "it clearly states that the cookie must be an original recipe and never been sold before. Where would I find the time to create an original cookie recipe and perfect it with only three weeks until the competition?"

"I mean, it's not like you have a raging social life. You don't date or have a steady boyfriend, not to mention you practically live in the bakery. If you need extra help with the other baking while perfecting the cookie, I'm sure your mom would come in and help."

"Absolutely not," Cookie growled. "My mother is no longer an owner or employee at The Fluffy Cupcake. My first tenured act as the owner will not be to ask my parents for help to win a cookie competition!"

Rye held up her finger to her best friend. "I hear what you're saying, Cookie, but I also hear what Ares is saying, and he's not wrong. Winning a competition like this could rocket the bakery into a whole new stratosphere. What if I help you with some of the regular cookie baking so that you can devote time to creating an original recipe? I can handle working a few extra hours for three weeks. We've done more with less time in the past. Not to mention, twenty grand is nothing to sneeze at for a prize-winning cookie recipe."

The time had come to play my trump card. "That twenty grand would go a long way in starting the Cuckoo for Cookies catering truck."

Cookie's head swung toward me in slow motion. "You know about the catering truck?"

"I know about everything. I'm the financial guy, which means I have to know our current plans and your plans and dreams for the future. Your dreams are my dreams now."

Cookie rolled her eyes so hard I feared she would never return them to centerline. "Oh, right, my dreams are your dreams. Well, my dream is not to participate in a cookie-baking competition."

"Neither is mine," I said patiently, "but I'd appreciate it if you'd at least think about it. Think about what it could do for the business. If you're worried about being attacked, I'll follow you everywhere. I'll be your shadow. You could call me your cookie bodyguard."

Cookie immediately broke out into a fit of giggles. Soon, she was laughing so hard she couldn't speak. Tears were running down her face, and even the other women started to giggle. "Sorry," she said, waving her hand in the air to get control of herself. "I was picturing it in my mind. You trailing behind me everywhere I went like a vampire hiding from the sun. Considering I have at least fifty pounds on you with hips wide enough to knock anyone off me and an ass to finish the job, I don't think I'll need a bodyguard. But thanks for your concern."

My gaze traveled the length of her before it met hers again. If only she knew what I was thinking about those hips and ass. If only I could stop thinking about those hips and ass. It would be much more convenient if I could see her as my childhood friend and not the voluptuous woman she is today.

I cleared my throat before I spoke so I didn't sound like a prepubescent boy. "If that's the case, then I don't see any reason why you can't join the competition. You'll have help with the other baking, and I'm always here to taste test. As far as I can see, nothing is standing in our way but you."

"Except that you're forgetting one small thing," Cookie said. "If I win, it will look a little fishy, considering I'm a master baker and own a bakery. Adversely, if I don't win, what will the community think? They'll lose confidence in the bakery if I can't produce a winning cookie."

"There's a defeatist attitude if I've ever heard one," Athena said, shaking her head.

All I could think was, *thank you, sis.*

"The community already knows you can bake," Athena said. "They don't need a contest to tell them that your cookies are the best in the state. Professionals enter these contests and win them all the time. That's kind of the point. It's like a professional writing contest. Of course, a publisher will enter their best writers in the contest. That just makes sense. They can't all win, but that doesn't mean they're bad writers."

I held my hand out at my sister as though to say *exactly.* "What are you afraid of here, Cookie?"

"I'm not afraid of anything!" She huffed and snatched the paper off the table. "Fine! We'll do the cookie competition! It won't be laughable that a woman named Cookie is entering a cookie competition for Cookie Heaven or anything! Imagine the guffaws at my expense when I explain that Cookie is my real name!"

I bit my lip to keep from laughing. Cookie really could get herself riled up over the littlest things. But I wasn't about to push her, considering she was willing to do the competition. "It won't be laughable once they taste your cookies."

She lowered the paper, and her gaze caught mine again. I worried she could read the innuendo I had tossed into that sentence. "You have such confidence in me, Ares Halla. Considering you haven't been around for years, what do you know about my cookies?"

"I know they're perfectly sweet, expertly crafted, and crumble at just the right time. They're excellent with a pile of buttercream icing or all alone. I may have been gone for years, but your cookies have only improved. Little secret? My mom always had Cookie

81

Pearson cookies on the counter when I came home for a visit. I did notice you were always missing, though."

She gasped and held her hands to her face like Home Alone. "What? You cheated on your city life by eating cookies from The Fluffy Cupcake?"

"Cookie Pie, I promise you no one in the city makes cookies the way you do. That's why I have no worries about you entering this competition. You're the best in the region."

"You're promising me here today that if I win, we'll seriously consider the Cuckoo for Cookies catering truck?"

"Absolutely," I agreed. "While I don't understand everything you have planned or why anyone would want a food truck at their wedding, I'm sure you've done extensive research. I hope you'll sit down with me and discuss it so I can understand it better. If it will benefit the business, then it's definitely on the table. I put it to a vote that if you come up with a winning cookie recipe and pull this off, then, to the winner goes the spoils." I glanced at the other three women, who all nodded their agreement.

"For once, I agree with Ares," Rye said. "This could put us in excellent shape come wedding season next year. I know it's daunting for you, but you'll step up and make a cookie that will knock everybody's socks off."

For the first time in twenty minutes, Cookie had a smile on her face. "All right, I'm throwing my hat in the ring in the name of the Cuckoo for Cookies catering truck! I'll start researching and baking cookie options for everyone to try. Once we decide on a winner, I'll perfect it and prepare it for the competition. There's no time to waste!"

The grin I wore was ridiculously cheesy, but I didn't even care. The cookie competition was my way back into Cookie's good graces, and I would use every last second of her cookie research to my advantage.

Eleven

"He thinks he can tell me what to do," I muttered as I slammed another pan on the baker's bench. "I'll show him!" I spun around to grab the mixing bowl and ran into a body. "Rye! I didn't know you were still here."

"Even I couldn't miss the sound of the pans slamming around back here. Something you want to talk about?"

It wasn't like I didn't notice the smartass grin she wore. She was talking about the meeting with Ares. "Did you hear him? Did you hear how obnoxious he was about the cookie competition?"

Her shrug was easy when she threw it at me. "Ares was very reasonable. He laid out his reasons for wanting to do it and gave you a choice. I'm not sure what you're upset about right now. You should have a smile on your face and a happy heart that the bakery is now yours. You've worked so hard for this, Cookie. Don't let Ares take that away from you. He may own part of it on paper, but you own it in heart, and that's what matters. We'll continue to run the bakery as a big happy family with one black sheep," she teased until I finally smiled. "Don't let him get you so worked up this early in the game."

"He's infuriating, though! He walks in here in those *previously made famous by Ares Halla* chamois shirt and blue jeans looking like a Greek Adonis as though he's never been gone!" Rye opened her mouth to speak, and I rolled my eyes. "You know what I mean. I'm just saying he didn't have to show up looking good enough to eat."

"Was he supposed to grow horns in the city?" Rye asked, rolling the mixer bowl over.

"It would have been nice!" I exclaimed. "Did you hear him in there?" I asked, jabbing my hand toward the front of the bakery.

"It's not like you're dating or have a boyfriend or a life, for that matter," I repeated in my best imitation of him. "So smug and self-assured, as though he knows everything there is to know about me! For all he knows, I do have a boyfriend! He's new to town. How would he know?"

Rye held her hands out to me in the sign for calm. "I was hoping that part had gotten lost in the cookie competition debate, but my hopes have been dashed."

"Oh, no," I said, spinning to dump sugar into the mixer bowl. "It took me thirty minutes after Ares left to remember it and about thirty seconds after that to become enraged that he had the audacity to say it. There's a word for guys like him."

"Correct?"

"Jackass!" I huffed, dumping in the shortening. I froze with the spatula halfway back to the bowl. "Did you say correct?"

"I did," Rye said, taking the baking utensils from my hands and leading me away from the dangerous tools. "Because he is. Should he have said it that way? No, but he's not wrong. You don't date, and you don't have a boyfriend."

"I date!" I exclaimed. "I date all the time."

"That's..." She bit back laughter and had to take a deep breath before she continued. "Hilariously untrue, but it gives me an idea." Rye slowly rubbed her hands together, and a sly smile lifted her lips.

"I'm scared," I answered tongue in cheek, but I was only half kidding. When she got that look, it usually meant she was hatching an evil plan.

"Hear me out," she said, grasping my shoulders. "It's time to start dating."

I groaned, the sound filling the kitchen in a way that said I wasn't just annoyed but also frustrated and sad. "Thanks, but no thanks."

"I said, hear me out," she repeated pointedly, so I motioned for her to continue. "Serial dating any and every eligible guy we can find."

"Whatever for?" The confusion was loud and clear in my voice.

"To torque off Ares Halla, of course!" Her laughter was indeed evil when she let the cackle rip, and while the idea was terrible, her laughter made me smile.

I held up my finger. "One problem with your plan, Rye. Ares doesn't care who, when, or if I date."

"I'm not saying you're wrong, but you're wrong. I think he cares more than you or he knows yet. Besides, could it hurt to try? I've known you for thirteen years, and in that time, you've gone on three dates."

I rolled my eyes. "I've been on more than three dates. Besides, it's not like you're dating either." That was a total cop-out. She was correct; I hadn't dated much since high school. The one guy I'd wanted to date left town, and while I had a few relationships, I hadn't found anyone interesting enough to fill his shoes.

"I'm not dating because no one likes my face. You're not dating because you're still hung up on a guy who doesn't deserve you. It's time to get out and meet other people before your entire life is wasted on a man who is too obtuse to see what he's missing."

She crossed her arms over her chest and waited for an answer. Was she right? Was I losing out on life because I couldn't get over him? I stared at the ceiling, momentarily slack-jawed before stiffening my spine.

"Okay, say I wanted to date someone to torque off Ares. How would I do it?"

She answered with a glint in her eye and a wicked smile. "Leave it to me and prepare to reenter the dating world, Cookie Pearson."

The last three days since the bakery reopened, I had spent getting a handle on all the computer programs for ordering at The

Cookie

Fluffy Cupcake and reviewing the financial records. I had been in my parent's basement since Tuesday at noon when I left The Fluffy Cupcake, and it was now Friday night at eight p.m. I wanted to see Cookie and was itching to hear about her quest for the perfect cookie recipe. The bonus was I'd get to be in the same room with her while she told me about it. My sister had mentioned that Cookie would be at the bakery at nine to make a few test batches before starting her regular baking.

My mouth watered at the thought of hot, sweet cookies on my tongue. I groaned aloud as I walked down the street, fighting against the image of being in Cookie Pearson's bedroom. She'd kill me before that happened; if she didn't, Uncle Brady would. A shiver ran down my spine at the thought. There was an uncomfortable situation I wanted to avoid at all costs. Brady didn't like it when a guy so much as looked at Cookie, much less touched her. On the upside, they were headed to Florida in a few short months, so once they're gone, Cookie might find some much earned freedom.

The thought led me from Cookie to my mom. She'd cried for two days after the dinner Sunday night, and when she stopped, she also stopped talking. Dad assured me she was fine and that the bakery transition had made her emotional. I wasn't convinced. I knew few people better than my mother, so I had no doubt there was more to her emotional lability. I could hope that constantly reassuring her that I was home to stay would be enough to turn her around, but thus far, that wasn't the case.

I set aside the situation at home and contemplated the best way to approach Cookie tonight. I wanted to hear about her cookie recipe, but I also wanted to hear about the catering truck. While I had some information from the SD card, I wanted her candid explanation, hopes, and dreams for it. It's easy for someone to put their plans on paper, but describing the emotions attached to those plans is much more challenging. I hoped that while she was making cookies, we could talk about where she wanted to go with this new aspect of the business. If I had any say in it—

Movement ahead caught my eye, and I paused. The sun was starting to set, and I couldn't be sure, but it appeared Cookie was standing with a guy near the bakery door. I immediately noticed her defensive stance with her hands on her hips and her feet braced wide. Whether she was angry or in danger, I didn't know, so I moved into the shadows and edged closer to listen to what they were saying.

"Let's go back to your place for a nightcap," the guy said while he loomed over Cookie.

"Sorry," she said in a not-so-conciliatory tone. "As I've said twice, it's time to start baking. Thanks again for dinner. I had a lovely time."

That would sound like a sincere thank you to anyone else, but I knew Cookie to a T. She was aggravated, and knowing her as well as I did, I could also hear a ribbon of fear in her voice.

"You own the place," he said, taking another step toward her. "You can make time for a drink with me, considering I paid for dinner."

"While I appreciate that you paid for dinner," Cookie said between gritted teeth, "That doesn't change the fact that I'm on a tight deadline. I can't wait any longer to get started. I'm happy to pay you for my entrée if that will make us even."

The man roughly grasped her elbow and shook it. "I don't want you to pay for the entree! I want you to have a drink with me," he growled.

"You need to let go of her," I demanded, stepping out from behind the patio set.

"Who the hell are you?" the dude asked, but I noticed he didn't drop her arm.

"Ares," Cookie said with a quiver in her voice. "Thanks for working an extra baking shift tonight. We are so behind." She tried to shake the guy's hand off, but he didn't let go.

"Well, we do have to get those cookies done." I made eye contact with the asshole, who was still manhandling my best friend. "I asked you nicely to take your hands off of her."

"Who the hell do you think you are? This is between Cookie and me."

"Cookie wants you to get your hands off of her, too," Cookie added.

The guy dropped her elbow and took a step back. "You bitches are all alike," he muttered as he started to walk away.

Cookie

"Better a bitch than a jackass like you," Cookie replied. The guy spun around, but I stepped between them.

"I would suggest you keep walking," I growled, "or you'll be in the hospital wishing you had."

He looked me up and down for ten seconds before he chuckled and shook his head. "Like you're going to take me. I'd say bring it, but I have better things to do than squash your tiny bug ass."

The Jackass, as he would now be called, took off down the street. I watched to be sure he wouldn't return, and by the time I turned, Cookie was already unlocking the door. I walked in behind her and locked it. When I turned to her, I noticed a shiver go through her. "Come here," I whispered, pulling her against my chest. "What were you thinking letting him walk you back here?"

"Everyone knows where I live, Ares. It's not a secret."

"I know, but you still have to be careful. You can't leave yourself open to an attack."

"Weren't you the one who told me to let it go regarding my mother's attack?" She glanced up at me, her eyes filled with obstinate fire.

"I was speaking of that only professionally. Who was that asshole?"

"Some guy that Rye knew, and she set us up. It was our first and last date."

"Agreed. If you ever see him again, steer clear."

"I'll try, but he was handsy the entire night. When I tried to part ways at the restaurant, he followed behind me. I probably should have walked to my parent's house, right?"

"Probably," I agreed, tightening my arms around her shoulders. "But that's a hard call when you're a thirty-year-old woman and haven't lived at home for a decade. Try to avoid him, but if he gets handsy again, I give you permission to reprise your role as Lake Pendle's nose breaker."

Her laughter filled the bakery, and the sound slowed my pounding heart. She'd had a scare, but I was here for her, and I hoped this was another step closer to patching the gaping wound in our friendship. "I do have that to fall back on," she said, still chuckling.

88

"He must be new to town and didn't get the memo," I whispered, giving her a tight hug before releasing her. "But, Cookie, seriously, you must be careful with guys like that."

"Understood," she said before turning and walking to the back of the bakery, flipping on lights as she went. "Thanks for the assist, but you don't have to stay."

"Maybe I want to stay." I braced my hands on the baker's bench and stared her down where she stood by the office door.

"You don't even know how to bake."

"I've learned many skills over the last thirteen years. Maybe baking is one of them." I raised a brow as a challenge and waited for her to make her move.

After a long pause, she tossed her arm up at me. "Suit yourself. I'll be out in a minute." She disappeared into the office with a click of the door.

She probably hoped I wouldn't be here when she returned, but her hopes would be dashed. I grabbed an apron off a hanger, threw it around my neck, walked to the oven, and flipped the switch. After checking to ensure the racks were rotating, I prepared her workstation the way I used to in high school.

It appeared Cookie had started dating again, so I would have to fast-track my plan to prove to her that I was in it to win it. Maybe, in the process, I'd prove that if she was in the market for a new boyfriend, I was submitting my application.

Twelve

I banged my head against the office door and let out a breath of frustration. My first attempt to make Ares Halla jealous had backfired on me big time. The Jackass, as I was now calling him since I couldn't remember his name, not only bored me to death, but he wouldn't stop touching me. No matter what we were doing, he had to be touching me. By the time the appetizer arrived, it was clear that Rye and I would need to discuss what kind of guys she set me up with in the future. I was all for meeting new people in my conquest to make Ares jealous, but I wasn't all for meeting every jackass in a tri-county area. Truthfully, tonight's date cured me of any desire to continue this dating façade, but I had no doubts that Rye wouldn't let me give up that easily. Whenever I thought about what I was doing, my stomach got all squashy. Initially, I thought it was a great idea to make Ares angry or jealous by serial dating, but my gut told me otherwise. My gut told me it was wrong to lead the other guys on, knowing I'd never commit to a relationship with them. I wasn't interested in a relationship with anyone, much less with a knuckle dragger like…Blake! That was his name. Blake. Jackass was better.

You're interested in a relationship with Ares Halla, my inner voice reminded me.

I shed my sweater and grabbed my bakery coat from the locker to quiet that voice. After buttoning the coat, I smoothed it over my chest, which was still warm from Ares' hug. An involuntary shiver racked me. Hugs from Ares had always made me feel better as a kid, but now his hugs made me feel things for him that I shouldn't. Our history was black and white, and he had made it clear years ago that our friendship only existed because of our parents. Granted, now that we're adults, we could change that, but I didn't see how I could be friends with him again. We could be friendly at work, but I couldn't let it go any further than that. Not if I wanted to protect my heart.

Did I wish things were different? Yes. I could remember when Ares and I had fun together, and I longed for that kind of relationship again. It didn't help that the dating pool in Lake Pendle was stunningly shallow, and the hope of finding anyone half as great as Ares was slim. It only took one date to remind me why I hadn't been on one in years. All it did was fill me with an ache to have a relationship with Ares like we used to have. An easy camaraderie that made you feel loved and cared for whenever you were together. That had been missing from my life for a dozen years. Now that he was back, my soul called to him all while my heart ached. It ached from the knowledge that we can never be more than friends.

"You can do this, Cookie," I said to psych myself up. "You can talk business and keep anything personal out of it." A snort escaped as I reached for the door handle. "Sure, but can he?"

With the question unanswered, I took a deep breath and returned to the bakery. In seconds, I noticed that Ares had set up my workstation. "Wow," I said, taking stock of the supplies. "You still remember how to set up my station after all this time."

"I did it every weekend for four years, so it's muscle memory. I'm sure you've changed things, but you've got your staples ready and waiting."

"Thanks, Ares. Now the only thing I'm missing is a cup of coffee," I said with a smile.

"I can fix that." He tossed me a grin and then dashed to the front of the bakery. I couldn't help but smile as I listened to him fill a pot and set the machine to brew. Maybe a little bit of that boy I used to know was still in there. I hoped it was the part of him that used to like spending time with me, made me laugh, and always stood up for me. That was the Ares I wouldn't mind reconnecting with and the Ares that would make working together as partners easy.

While I rolled the mixing bowl over to the bench, I realized that since he'd been back, at least two of those three things were true. He'd made me laugh several times and stood up for me tonight. Part of me wanted to think he enjoyed spending time with me, but that was up for debate. Ares could have an agenda. Rye keeps telling me it's time to bury the hatchet, and I will, professionally. He'll never apologize on a personal level, so the personal hatchet will remain unburied. I'd be a fool to open my heart to that kind of pain again.

Determination not to let Ares sweet talk me guided my hands as I filled the mixer with base cookie ingredients. The smartest thing to do was put the man in the other room out of my mind. It wouldn't be easy, but if I hoped to survive working with him, I had to find a way to compartmentalize what happened when we were kids with where we were now. As the mixer worked its magic, my mind's eye showed me all those years we spent talking, laughing, and sharing every moment of our lives together. Maybe Rye was correct, and the universe was trying to tell me something, but I couldn't listen. At thirty, I was way too old for a childhood crush, no matter how good it felt to be in his arms again.

Mesmerizing. That word ran through my mind as I watched Cookie bake. The motions transported her somewhere as she created, poured, stirred, and tested. She added ingredients to the mixing bowl without even measuring. Somehow, she knew precisely how much to use for the perfect cookie every time.

"Are you going to tell me what you're making?" I asked, standing near the oven. "I'm dying to know if you've come up with a recipe for the contest."

"Would you grab me the muffin-top-only pans from the shelf? I need two."

The muffin top only pans, I thought as I grabbed them from the shelf and carried them back to the bench. She was making cookies, so why the muffin pans?

I waited while she expertly ladled the dough onto the pan and slid them into the oven. After setting the timer, she closed the door and clapped her hands like she had just invented cookies for the first time.

"We're about to find out," she said, pointing at the oven. "You inspired me the other night, so the original recipe I'll submit for the cookie competition will be The Fluffy Cupcake Amazing Cookie Pie." She waved her hand in the air. "Or something like that."

"Seriously?" I asked. "You're just messing with me, right?"

I noticed her shoulders deflate a bit, and she sighed. "You don't like the idea?"

"Are you kidding? I love the idea! I'm surprised, though. You think they'll stand up in a competition like Cookie Heaven?"

"Well," she said with a glint in her eye, "these aren't just any Cookie Pies. We're taking them to the next level, so I will need your help to decide on the best one. Tonight, I'm making Dark Cherry Chocolate Cookie Pies."

"Oh!" I exclaimed with a clap of my hands. "The muffin top pans will bake the cookies to look like a moon pie!"

"For the perfectly symmetrical look to every cookie," she said, pointing at me with her finger. "But it won't be just any buttercream icing. We're using cherry buttercream with a center ribbon of fudge."

"I already know I'm going to love them. They're a winner."

"But wait, there's more," she said with laughter. "Tomorrow night, I'm making Monster Cookie Pies."

"Like in the shape of Cookie Monster?"

She threw her head back and laughed the way she used to when she was a kid. There was nothing I wanted more than to walk over to her, bury my hands in her long brown hair, and kiss her senseless. I couldn't. I wouldn't. I didn't want to risk the bond we were building by asking for more than she could give. I had to bide my time and strengthen this bridge I'd built if I was going to find my way back into her heart.

"While that's a cute idea, and I may find a pan so I can sell those in the store, that's not what I meant. A monster cookie pie is a white cookie base with M&Ms, chocolate chips, butterscotch chips, nuts, and toffee. The icing will be chocolate buttercream, and we'll roll the edges in sprinkles."

I tipped my head side to side when she finished. "Don't get me wrong, they sound delicious and fun, but I'm not sure they're right for a competition like Cookie Heaven."

She leaned her hip against the bench and stared me down. "Tell me why you feel that way."

"They sound a bit too," I searched for the right word for a moment. "Childish? I'm sure they'd sell out in minutes to every kid in town, but I don't know if the judges on Cookie Heaven would feel the same way."

"You're right, it would be a risk, but I'm doing it in the name of research. You see, I'm going to taste-test each cookie with the community. Tomorrow morning, Taylor will sample the Dark Cherry Decadence Cookie Pie. The next day, she'll sample the Abominable Cookie Pie, which will be what we call the monster ones; the third day, she'll sample The Raspberry Chocolate Truffle Cookie Pies. We'll then use that data when deciding which cookie will go to the competition."

"Raspberry chocolate truffle? Please tell me I get to taste that one?"

"Well," she said with a shrug, "if you're here two nights from now, you'll get to taste one. It's a chocolate cookie base with tiny raspberry truffles and a raspberry preserves center surrounded by vanilla buttercream icing."

"That's a winner!" I exclaimed, licking my lips. "Oh, I want to taste one right now."

She was laughing when she pointed at me. "Something tells me, no matter what Cookie Pie I make, it'll be your favorite."

A grin split my lips. "You could be right about that. But, seriously, Cookie, they all sound delicious. I think you've found a unique recipe that the judges won't see coming but will find fun and fancy. Do you think it will be legal to use this recipe since we've made them before?"

She walked closer to me and leaned against the bench. "I've made them before, but never for the store, and I've never sold them. It doesn't say that it can't be a family cookie recipe. It just says you can't have profited off the recipe you're using. Since I can prove I've never sold them in the bakery, I think we'll be fine."

"I'll reread the rules just to be sure, but I hope you're right. Regardless of how the competition turns out, we need to start selling all these Cookie Pies in the store."

She tapped my chest with her pointer finger. "For once, we finally agree on something, Mr. Halla. I plan to work them into the cookie rotation after the competition ends. Regardless of the outcome of the contest, we still win. So do the people of Lake Pendle, who will enjoy these mouthwatering delights year-round. I have ideas for the holidays and special occasions, as well."

"I can't love this more than I do right now. It's a great idea, and I'm surprised you didn't start selling them sooner. They were always such a hit with the kids in school."

She took a step back and focused somewhere over my shoulder. "It didn't feel right."

"What didn't feel right? Selling Cookie Pies in the bakery?"

"Making them without you here," she clarified. "As a kid, I only made them to make you happy. They brought me no joy once you were gone."

I took a step closer and grasped her hand in mine. It was warm, soft, and trembled as I ran my thumb across her knuckles. "I'm happy to be back too, Cookie. Things haven't been great between us since I left for college, but I want to change that. I want to be friends again."

When she glanced up at me, her eyes filled with fire. She shook off my hand and walked over to the oven. "Oh, you want to be friends again? You mean you're ready to continue our forced friendship now that you're back in Lake Pendle? I don't think so, Ares. We can work together, but we will never be best friends again. I can't say I know for sure if we ever were to begin with."

She grabbed the hot pad, swung the oven door open, and pulled the cookie pans out, all while I stood in dumbfounded silence. What was she talking about? I had no idea, but her tone told me she believed every word. Was my plan to get back into her good graces dead on arrival?

I stood there in silence and watched her move back and forth between the bench and the mixing bowl as she prepared the icing

Cookie

for the cookies. Her determination to pretend I didn't exist was admirable, but in her determination, I found my own. I would not give up on this woman just because the going got tough. Something had happened to make her believe I didn't want to be friends, but that was not the case. I had missed her with a painful yearning since I left home at eighteen. Every time I returned home to Lake Pendle to visit, she wasn't around, and now I saw it for what it was. She was avoiding me, probably to save face with our parents. I desperately wanted to know why, but her posture told me asking her tonight would be futile. She'd had enough of a struggle with that jackass earlier, she didn't need me to add to it.

When she swiped at her face with her shoulder, I noticed the silent tears that ran down her cheeks. Something deep inside me broke wide open, and all of the pain and bad experiences I'd carried since moving to the city fell into that pit before it closed tightly forever. None of that mattered anymore. Cookie was all that mattered now. If it took me thirteen more years, I'd prove to her that I wanted to be her best friend…and so much more.

Thirteen

After a long week of baking and taste testing, I was finally ready to hash out the numbers for the Cookie Pies. I refused to let Taylor tell me anything about the customers' reactions. I had to keep my head in the game when it came to baking, and I didn't want opinions to skew a recipe one way or the other. Now that the cookies had been made, consumed, and voted on by the community, it was time for The Fluffy Cupcake team to decide which one we would use in the competition. I was confident that we had three solid contenders, which meant regardless of Cookie Heaven, we had endless new cookies to rotate through the case and for special orders. That alone was worth the extra hours I put in this week.

Ares had shown up all three nights to help me bake, even after my unexpected tirade the first night. I expected him to tuck tail and run, but he'd surprised me by showing up each night with a cup of coffee, a smile, and an eagerness to bake. He didn't ask more of me than I was willing to give, but he did taste each cookie, and his moans of satisfaction told me the cookies were a success. The sound also turned my gut into gooey goodness, but I never let it show. I also didn't let the praise he'd heaped on me go to my head. Just because he liked them didn't mean everyone would. He was already biased, considering he'd been eating Cookie Pies for years, even if these were his first official ones in a long time.

Every morning when we parted ways, I trudged up the stairs filled with hate at how easy it was to be with him, talk with him, and work with him. His personality had softened since high school, and he no longer felt the need to strut around like a cock ready to crow. Ares was content to watch, listen, and learn, which I was not expecting. Don't get me wrong. It was refreshing but also unsettling. The more effort he put into learning how we did things at the bakery, and the more time he spent making the products, showed me that maybe he was here to stay. Everyone assured me that was the case, but I had to wonder if the going got tough, if he would go too. Maybe that was just the skeptic in me, but I was willing to teach him the ropes while I continued to protect my heart.

I'd talked with Rye about the whole dating situation, but as expected, she refused to let me give up so easily. She apologized profusely for how badly the night went with Blake and was glad Ares was there to step in and send the guy packing. I admitted to her ears only that I was glad he'd shown up when he had. I probably could have taken the guy on, but I was glad I didn't have to, and Ares was able to diffuse the situation. In light of my jitters, she agreed that we should start small for the next first date and work our way up.

From here forward, I'd meet the guy for drinks at The Modern Goat, which was classy but comfortable. Since the bar was always busy, there would be plenty of people around for safety. We'd meet there, and I would ride my bike rather than walk, so there was no way he could follow me home. I could drive, but I don't want them to know my car right off the bat either. If I got a bad vibe from the guy, I planned to send a preloaded message to her, and she'd call me with an *emergency* I needed to tend to. It was sad that women had to devise such intricate plans to keep themselves safe in the dating world, but I wouldn't leave myself open to danger like the last time. I didn't want to kiss too many more frogs in my pursuit of the prince, either. Unless the next couple of dates held my interest, I'd probably give up on the dating scene. While a girl has needs, some can be met with a rechargeable silicone Johnson. Those come with no expectations. They do their job and go back into the drawer until they're called upon again.

Especially when the one person you want to date and who has the only Johnson you're interested in, is off limits, my inner voice reminded me.

A huff escaped my lips. "Thanks for the reminder I didn't need." My cheeks flushed with heat at the thought of Ares and his Johnson, which I tried to avoid thinking about for various reasons. There were so many reasons, but I'd throw them all to the wind if I thought for one second that we stood a chance together. I know better, and that's why those reasons are always at the forefront of my mind when I deal with him.

Tonight, I'd be dealing with him. The four of us were meeting up here before we started baking for the night. I needed to know which Cookie Pie we would promote on Cookie Heaven, so I could order the best ingredients to make multiple batches this week. I would have to perfect it and practice making it in the allotted time for the show. After tasting each one, I was confident they could stand independently at any competition without further tweaking. Still, I'm not cocky enough to ignore constructive criticism if it improves them.

I'd saved a Cookie Pie from each batch in the cooler in case we needed a tiebreaker tonight, so I set them and four plates out on the baker's bench. If the numbers were close, we could try the cookies again. It was also a great way to taste the cookies a few days out to see how they hold in the cooler.

"Cookie?" a voice called from the front.

"In the back, Athena," I answered.

When she walked through the door, her brother was tailing her. He had his briefcase in one hand and a bottle in the other. Ares set the bottle on the baker's bench and lowered his briefcase to the floor.

"It's like you read my mind," he said, eyeing the cookies. "I was hoping we'd get to sample them again."

Athena swatted him on the arm and laughed. "You don't need to taste-test them again. You already know which one you like the best."

"All of them!" he exclaimed, his laughter filling the bakery. My heart rate ticked up, and I cursed it. Ares' spontaneous laughter had always done that to me. The sensation used to make me glow from the inside out, but now it brought tears to my eyes. It appeared I would suffer forever from this crush that could never be anything more. The mere idea was torture.

I cleared my throat. "What's with the bottle?" I asked since I was too far away to see the label.

"To celebrate. Once we pick a cookie, we'll toast its success with one of Lake Pendle Liquor's finest champagnes."

"So, you know, mediocre," Athena clarified.

Cookie

We all chuckled since it was true. Lake Pendle Liquor's clientele was not high-end by any means. They were happy with the latest Minnesota craft beer or a bottle of wine with a screw-off cap. "Don't you think popping a cork might be premature?" I asked. "We still have a long way to go in this competition."

He disappeared into the front of the bakery and returned with four coffee mugs. "No, I don't think it's premature. We're not celebrating you winning the competition. We're celebrating our first success as a new team at The Fluffy Cupcake. A new product for the case even if the competition doesn't work out."

Athena smiled, and I shrugged. "Well, who am I to argue with the finance man? Once Rye gets here, we'll review the numbers from Taylor. I'm hoping we have a winner by a landslide, but I'm also worried the split will be even. If that happens, we'll test the cookies again and use their hold rate as the deciding factor."

"Hold rate?" Ares asked.

"How the cookie tastes, looks, and stays together several days after baking," Athena answered.

"Oh, that would be important. Not so much for the competition, but when we implement them into the bakery."

"Exactly," Athena agreed. I could tell she was proud of her brother for digging in to learn what he didn't know and not being afraid to ask questions of the women who knew the answers.

"Not that they're going to stick around long," he said with a head shake. "They're too damn good. They'll sell out immediately every time you make them."

"I can't worry about that right now, though," I said. "First, I have to perfect the cookie for competition. We have so much to do, but I've got a few more long nights in me if it means we secure the funding for the bakery truck."

"That's what I like to hear," Ares said with a smile. "I suspected your competitive streak would emerge once you got your teeth into a recipe. Besides, no one stands a chance against Cookie Pearson's Cookie Pies." He winked at me, and it felt oddly intimate, even with his sister in the room.

I cleared my throat again while I checked my watch. "Where is Rye? She should be here by now." I pulled my phone out to check for a text just as the front door opened and closed.

When she joined us, she was disheveled, sweating, and panting. Her hands were flying almost faster than I could read them. "I'm sorry I'm late! I didn't feel well and fell asleep. Sorry for signing, but I don't have my processors on because my head hurts."

I put my hand to her forehead, only to pull it away immediately. I signed as I spoke. "Rye, you have a fever. You need to go home."

She signed back, "No, I have too much work to do tonight. If you sign for the meeting, I'll put my processors on for work."

I glanced at Athena and Ares. Athena was shaking her head no, and Ares gave me the no-go sign at his throat. "I don't think that's smart, Rye. You shouldn't be working if you're not feeling right. It's too dangerous," I signed.

"You need my help," she responded. "You can't do all the baking and donut frying alone."

Ares walked around and stood in front of Rye. "I'll help," he signed, leaving us without words. Not just because he offered to work but because he could sign.

"You still remember how to sign," Rye signed, and Ares shook his fist at her in the sign for yes.

"Some," he signed. He turned to me. "Tell her to go home. We'll make sure the baking gets done. I'll help you with cookies, and when Athena comes in for bread, we can transfer to pastries."

"Taylor will be happy to come in early and help finish the donuts," Athena offered.

I signed the message to Rye, and she frowned. "What about the meeting? This is the first important meeting of the business. I can't miss it. Stupid ears." She paused in her signing to hold her head.

She was in agony, and I suspected Dad would need to drive her to the ER tonight rather than wait until morning. While she was distracted, I flicked my gaze at Ares and mouthed, *text my dad to pick her up.* He nodded and pulled out his phone, tapping out a message.

Athena walked over and signed. "You're miserable, Rye. We appreciate your dedication, but you don't have to suffer to be a member of the team. You need to take a night off to get better rather than push yourself until you get sicker." She held up her finger and then grabbed a notepad and pen. She handed them to Rye and signed, "Write down your vote and leave it under the sample dome in the case. If we need a tiebreaker, your vote will be it. Fair?"

Rye shook her fist in the yes and signed, "Thanks for understanding." She tipped to the left, and Ares grabbed her elbow and righted her again.

"Cookie?" Dad called from the front of the bakery, and I sighed with relief.

"Dad's here to get you," I signed to Rye.

"How did you call Dad?" Her hands slapped together as she formed the signs, a surefire bet she was mad.

While I loved that she started calling them Mom and Dad, I also had to smooth things over. "Ares texted him," I signed. "You're in no shape to walk or drive. You can hardly stand up straight."

Dad walked into the bakery, and I explained the situation. "I think you should take her right to the ER. I'd do it, but I need to bake."

"I got her," he promised me. He put the back of his hand to her forehead before he signed, "Points for trying, sweetheart, but you need meds and a bed before you even think about operating machinery."

Her face said it all, and he wrapped his arm around her, assuring us he'd keep us updated on her condition as they left the bakery.

"I wish she hadn't felt like she had to come in feeling so poorly," Athena said.

"I guess you have to look at it from her point of view," I said. "She didn't want us to think she couldn't hack owning part of the bakery."

"Which is silly since we can't control when we get sick. It could be one of us tomorrow," Ares said.

"True, but I don't imagine she was thinking that way. Rye is always worried that her disability will keep her from being successful in life."

"Are you serious right now? That woman is more successful than half of the people in Lake Pendle, and she's done it with such determination, honesty, and desire to serve the people," Athena said, an edge of anger to her tone.

I held my hands up in front of me. "You're preaching to the choir, sister. But we can all relate to letting our fears and worries sneak in during significant life changes. I'm sure that's what Rye is going through right now. We sprang the bakery ownership on her, so she hasn't had as long to come to terms with it as we have. She'll be fine in a few days once she realizes we consider her an important part of the team. I would put off the vote if I could, but we need to make a decision. Every day we wait is a day less that I have to get ready for the competition." I glanced at Ares, and the look on his face said I was correct.

"She got to vote, so I think she'll be fine with any cookie we pick. I agree that we need to decide tonight, though. The sooner we know, the sooner we can hype up your appearance on Cookie Heaven."

"Maybe we should wait on the hype?" I asked. "What if I don't do well? I'd rather not have egg on my face, or in this case, cookie, when I have to slink back into the bakery the day after the competition."

"No, we can't wait on the hype," Ares argued. "While this competition isn't your dream, there is a dream behind it. We need to get the people of Lake Pendle behind us to gain momentum for the day of the competition. You know Cookie Heaven wants people talking up their favored competitor on social media. As for slinking, you won't be doing that anywhere the day after the competition. Win or lose, you've created a viable product for the case. I don't know how Athena feels, and I know we'll have to run it past Rye, but it's my opinion that once we start selling the Cookie Pies in the shop, the profit goes into the bakery truck fund until we have enough to take it from a dream to a plan."

"That idea has my vote," Athena chimed in. "We must run it past Rye, but we all know she won't object."

A smile tipped my lips at the idea that we were one step closer to the bakery truck. It had been a dream for so long that it felt weird to think it was almost within reach. "It gets my vote, too," I agreed, clapping my hands near my chin. "If I can win the competition, we'll be much closer to having the funding we need to make it sustainable. Let's decide on the winning cookie!"

Cookie

Ares set his briefcase on the bench and opened it, pulling out a sealed manilla envelope that said TOP SECRET in red ink. "Taylor was trusting no one," he said with a wink as he handed it to me.

I chuckled, but my insides were vibrating with nervous excitement. If we wanted to sell these cookies, people first had to like them. "Why is this so heavy?" I asked, hefting it up in the air a couple of times.

"From what Taylor tells me, people had a lot to say," Athena explained, motioning at the envelope. "Those are the comments."

After I tore the envelope open and dumped the pile of comment slips on the bench, I grabbed the first one. "These should be illegal," I read, chuckling at the comment. It only took a few more comment sheets to see that people loved them. "I'm so relieved," I admitted, leaving the pile in front of me. "It's going to take some time to get through all of these, but it seems the majority thought they were delicious."

"I'll go through them tonight while you're baking and pick out any that have actual suggestions that would be helpful," Ares said, motioning for me to put them back in the envelope. "Now for the consensus."

I picked up the white envelope I'd set to the side and greedily tore it open. After scanning the sheet of paper inside, my smile only grew.

"Well, what's the verdict?" Athena impatiently asked.

"As expected, the Abominable Cookie Pie was a hit with the ten and under crowd as well as surprisingly, males over the age of thirty."

"I'm not surprised," Ares said as he eyed the one in the middle of the table. I hated to see the poor guy suffering, so I pushed it over to him.

"Help yourself, it did well, but it's not our winner."

He grabbed it and took a bite, moaning as he chewed. "It would win if all the judges were men over thirty."

Athena and I both laughed while I pointed at the paper. "The Chocolate Cherry Decadence and Chocolate Raspberry Truffle were neck and neck, but it looks like, for the community, the raspberry truffle edged out the cherries. And I quote, "Everyone loved the mini truffles!"

104

"Who are we to argue with everyone?" Athena asked, wearing a grin. "That one gets my vote too."

"Mine too," Ares agreed. "I also think the truffles elevate the cookie to competition level. Anyone can do anything with cherries, but the mini truffles and preserves is genius level baking."

I held up my finger and jogged to the front of the bakery to grab Rye's vote. When I returned to the baker's bench, I held it up. "Let's see which one Rye voted for." I made a show of opening it and flipping it around for them to see.

"Truffles!" Athena said with a clap.

"That's three votes for the truffles. What say you?" Ares asked.

"Truffles," I agreed with a nod. "They're challenging to make, but you're right about them elevating the cookie to competition level. Want to know the secret that all three of these cookies have in common?" I motioned at the plate in the center of the bench.

"Do tell," Ares said, licking his fingers of the buttercream icing.

"They're all gluten-free."

I dropped that bomb and waited for one of them to say something. It was Athena who spoke first. "If you aren't pulling my leg, you are the cookie master. I would never have guessed. Did Taylor know?"

"Yes, but only so she knew everyone could try them."

"Don't most gluten-free cookies crumble apart almost immediately?" Ares asked, his head tipped to the side.

"Usually, but not the ones made by Cookie Pearson," Athena said, crossing her arms over her chest. "She makes gluten-free cookies that we ship to people, which arrive in one piece."

"Are you going to make them gluten-free for the competition?" he asked me and I nodded.

"I am. I want to bring something to the table that everyone can eat and show people with dietary restrictions that businesses are willing to cater to them."

"Brilliant," Ares said, a giant grin on his lips. "Just brilliant. I'm so proud of you, Cookie. Tell me they won't all be gluten-free when we start selling them, though."

Cookie

"No. When we sell them, I'll make both options for the case. Let me guess. The finance man is worried about the cost per cookie."

"Can you blame him?" he asked. "The cost difference between regular and gluten-free flour is like a Ford and a Maserati."

"Wow," Athena whistled, "little brother knows his stuff."

He shot her a deadly look, and I bit my lip to keep from laughing. "Finance man doesn't need to worry. So, Chocolate Raspberry Truffle it is?"

"Unanimously," they both agreed.

"Great," Athena said, grabbing her coat and purse. "I'm heading home for a nap and will return at two a.m. You two behave now, you hear?"

With that, she swept from the bakery and we heard the door open, close, and lock.

Ares grabbed the bottle from the table. "I think we'll stash this in the cooler for now. Our celebration will have to wait because the donuts can't."

While he disappeared into the cooler, I jogged to the office, grabbed something from the locker, and met up with him back at the bench.

"What's this?" He took the shirt I was holding out and inspected it. "Whoa, a bakery uniform with my name on it."

"You're part of the team, and team members get uniforms. I wasn't sure of your pants size, so we can order those in the morning. That is if you'd like some uniforms. I really wasn't sure how much time you planned to spend back here, and I'm in no way saying you have to, but I just wanted—"

He laid a finger against my lips. "You said it yourself. I'm part of the team now, and that means stepping up and stepping in whenever another team member needs help. This shirt makes me feel like you've accepted me, at least tentatively, as part of the team."

"More than tentatively," I assured him. "You've proven that you're dedicated and ready to contribute to the business over the last week, and you've done it on the fly. Your actions tell me, at least for now, that you're in it to win it."

106

"More than just the time being," he whispered, his gaze holding mine. I worried my eyes would tell him everything I didn't want him to know about how much I loved having his hands on me. "I'm here to stay, Cookie. It's going to take you some time to believe that, I know, but I didn't come home on a whim."

"Okay," I whispered, still holding his gaze. "You have my tentative work trust."

"Tentative work trust? That feels weird to say, much less try to understand."

"It means that I trust you're here at the bakery for all the right reasons."

"But I don't have your tentative personal trust?"

I didn't answer other than to tip my head.

"I will change that," he promised. "But I'll only take what you're willing to give."

While the sentence was innocent, the look in his eyes told me what his words didn't. He wanted more than a work relationship and he was determined to make it happen. I watched him peel his sweater off and button up the white shirt with a blue name patch that said 'Ares' on the right breast. It transported me back to a time when we had personal trust. I used the next moment to remind myself what happened to my heart the last time he broke my trust.

I spun on my heel and headed to the cooler for supplies. Maybe I could trust him to help me get the donuts done, but I couldn't, and I wouldn't, trust him with my heart ever again, even if he did still own it.

Fourteen

I had taken over frying the yeast donuts an hour ago so Cookie could work on cupcakes. Cake donuts were my nemesis, but yeast donuts I could fry like a pro, flipping the drum sticks as effectively as Rye. Okay, that's a stretch, but I wasn't a total loser at it. Once fried and cooled, I'd start decorating them until Taylor arrived to help. One way or the other, we'd have a full case in the morning.

"Tell me about the Cuckoo for Cookies idea," I said while I flipped the perfectly golden-brown crullers over.

"I thought you read the information already," Cookie answered from where she was piping icing on a cake with precision.

"I did, and while it was a helpful overview, I'd like you to tell me about your ideas. It will help me get a better handle on what you have planned."

She rested the pastry bag on the bench and shrugged. "I guess that's not breaking the rules as long as no decisions are made, right?"

I pointed at her with the drum stick in my left hand. It still fascinated me that fancy drum sticks were used to flip donuts in bakeries across the country. "No decisions, just information."

"Once I got the mini cookie wagon up and running for the farmers' market, I was surprised by how quickly I sold out of cookies every time. People started asking me if I was going to be at the local fairs and events. One woman asked if I would bring the wagon to her outdoor wedding and serve cookies and cupcakes. I realized I needed a cookie wagon on steroids to do those things. I was thinking that couples or venues could hire us to be there for the rehearsal dinner, in the morning with pastries as the wedding party got ready, and then in the evening for cake or alternatively, any dessert they want at the wedding or event."

"I could see where that might be useful, but I'm not sure there's enough draw yet for that kind of service in this area, is there?"

"No," she admitted, which lifted my brows as I pulled the crullers and moved on to long johns. "That's where the other events come into play. Cuckoo for Cookies could be used for the farmers' market, the fair, birthday parties, and work events. The little cookie wagon just doesn't hold enough and someone from here always has to bring me more stock halfway through the farmers' market, which isn't a good use of labor hours. We're talking about a small-town local market bringing that much business to the wagon, Ares. Imagine what I could sell with a truck at some of these bigger events."

"I can picture the Cuckoo for Cookies wagon pulling up to a birthday party and the kids going wild. Or a family reunion!" I exclaimed, shaking off a drum stick.

"Right!" she enthusiastically agreed while she pulled pans of Danish from the oven, expertly stowing them on cooling racks and refilling the oven with cookies ready to be baked. She looked like an orchestra conductor the way she moved the pans with such symmetry and precision. "What will really make it stand out will be the options for dietary restrictions like gluten-free, vegan, and nut free. Most kids with food allergies are left out at parties because the host doesn't have the ability to cater to them. I could change that with the cookie wagon. Eventually, I'd like to build it to the point that I can apply for a booth at the Minnesota State Fair."

I paused in my donut flipping and turned to her. "The Great Minnesota Get-Together? That's a lofty goal, Cookie."

"Go big or go home, right?" she asked with a shrug as she went back to decorating her cakes while the cookies baked. We only had a few more minutes alone before Athena and Taylor would come in to start the rest of the baking.

"Would you bake on the truck or is it strictly to transport and serve."

She tossed her head back and forth before she lifted it to make eye contact. "If I could get something that had space for convection ovens and a small mixer besides the refrigerated cases, then yes. But that could get pricey, so I may have to start small and work my way up."

109

Cookie

"It sounds like you've put a lot of thought into this." I pulled out all the long johns and lowered in the rack of twists.

"It's the cookie wagon I already run but multiplied in space and convenience. My thought is, once we have the money in hand, I'll buy any food truck I can get my hands on, store it for the winter and work on gutting it and restaging it to fit our needs. It'll take a year, but buying new is out of the question."

"What about buying a concessions trailer instead?" I asked, an idea forming as we talked. "One that could be pulled with the bakery van?"

She paused in her decorating, and I could tell it was something she hadn't thought of before. "That would work. It might even work better than a truck."

"Plus, you don't have the expense of maintaining another motor," I said, pushing the rack of finished donuts to the side and grabbing an empty one. "Not to mention, when you can't use it in the winter, it's easy to store."

"I'll research that," she said as the timer went off on the oven. "I'm glad we talked it out. I can already see where a concessions trailer would solve many of the tripping points I've been hitting regarding a truck."

"Always happy to talk things out with you, Cookie."

I hoped she would read between the lines there. She didn't trust me, and I wanted to know why. If she'd talk with me about it, I could work to make it right.

Rather than respond, she picked up her cake and carried it to the cooler. Then again, maybe that was her response to the idea of talking things out with me. A sigh escaped as I pulled out the last of the donuts and pushed both racks toward the decorating station behind the fryers. I may as well get started with the icing and decorating while I waited for Taylor. With any luck, Rye had prepared all the supplies for tonight and put them in the cooler. I pulled the door open and startled Cookie who juggled her cake for a second before getting it up on the shelf safely.

"Sorry," I said, stepping into the small cooler. "I didn't mean to scare you. Just here for the icing supplies." The shelves were closer together than they were when I worked here the last time. It was clear that the bakery had outgrown the cooler space. That was something I'd been trying to remedy with the budget. "I think we should look into getting some refrigerated cases for the back room," I said, glancing around. "We're full up in here."

"It's a huge problem," she agreed as I took a step closer to her, now nearly chest to chest. "It's the main reason we have to bake so much every day. There's no space to bake ahead and hold anything. If I had space to make cakes and cookies ahead of time, it would really change the flow of the bakery and make us more productive."

"Then I think we need to hold a meeting to discuss options," I suggested, pressing her against a rack as I tried to sneak past her. "There's money in the operating budget for it, so I'm confused why it hasn't been done."

"I didn't want to bother Aunt Amber with it." Her shoulder shrug told me that my mother had become a problem long before my return. "I thought it would just be easier to wait until we owned the place."

"Understandable at the time. Now, we need to fix this and fix it fast. When can we meet?"

"No need to have a meeting," she said, her voice breathy as I closed in on her. "We're all in agreement that we need more cooler space. It's up to the finance guy to figure out how much we can spend. Once we know that, we can sit down and find viable options."

"I'll get the information to you by tomorrow," I whispered, my heart barely beating as we stood in the cooler, chest to chest, with our gazes locked.

"Tha—thank you," she stuttered.

I took another step forward and she pressed her hands to my chest to steady herself. Heat bloomed through me from her touch and brought me to life again for the first time in too many years. "I've missed you, Cookie Pearson," I whispered as I lowered my forehead to hers. "In ways I can't describe with words other than to say your touch makes my heart beat again. Being with you makes me feel like everything will be okay. I haven't felt that way in thirteen years."

"I didn't want to miss you." Her neck bobbed as she swallowed hard. "Even though I did. The thing is, we're not kids anymore."

Cookie

"No, we're not," I agreed, my lips dangerously close to hers. Less than an inch and I could lay my lips on hers and drink from her the way I'd dreamed about since I was fifteen. My gaze flicked to her lips which were plump, parted, and pink.

Don't be a coward, just kiss her.

It took everything I had to fight that voice. Kissing her too soon was a surefire way of sinking the mission. I wanted to prove to her that I'd changed and moving too fast wasn't going to accomplish that. That said, I wondered if kissing her would prove that I'd changed in a faster, more distinct way. She'd said it herself. We were adults, and maybe it was time to take things by the horns.

I lowered my lips toward hers as a buzzing filled the cooler. She jumped away from me and hurried toward the door. "The cookies!" she exclaimed, her face flushed and voice breathy. "They're going to burn!"

She punched open the door and took off, leaving me standing there with my body on fire and filled with a desire that only she could quench. My heart, on the other hand, was on fire with only one thing.

Hope.

Fifteen

This date was as inconvenient as a root canal. I had a baking competition in two days, and I'd rather be downstairs putting the finishing touches on the new cookie, but it was too late in the game to back out now. At least it was only a drink, and if the guy was a total no-go, I'd be back home in less than an hour to start baking. Who knows, maybe he'll be a witty conversationalist and we'll talk the night away. My internal eye roll said that was unlikely. I stared at the woman in the mirror and wondered what she was doing. None of these guys were Ares, so dating felt partly like cheating and ultimately futile. My fingers hovered near my lips and I sighed at the memory of those minutes in the cooler when Ares was just inches from them. Would I have let him kiss me if the timer hadn't gone off?

The truth was reflected brightly from my eyes. Yes. I would have let Ares kiss me and I would have liked it. I had known that much since I was fifteen, but that didn't make it right. Then again, maybe it would make everything right. That, in a nutshell, was the struggle. While trusting him could get my heart broken all over again, it might also heal it. Do I play it safe and keep him at arm's length or do I throw caution to the wind and let things play out? One would protect my heart from getting broken again, but I would never know if Ares was my soulmate. The other could give me that answer, but could also pulverize my heart.

I shook my head and walked away from the mirror. "You don't have time for an existential crisis, woman. You've got a date."

Grumbling, I grabbed my keys off the table by the door and shook out my shoulders. This dating thing felt like karma had come calling. I embarked on the activity with the glee of making Ares jealous, but I was the one suffering. Last week, when he rescued me from Blake, he didn't look jealous. He just looked concerned for my safety.

Pausing at the bottom of the stairs, I wondered if I was reading Ares all wrong. Maybe the fact that I was dating didn't make him jealous because he didn't care. I grabbed my bike from the back of the bakery and hopped on it. "Last night in the cooler, he looked like he cared," I muttered, my own thoughts confusing me.

I put Ares out of my mind and focused on the evening ahead. It was ridiculous to ride my bike the half a block to The Modern Goat, but it did give me the option to ride to my parent's house if the guy tried to follow me home. After last week, there was no way I was risking that again. Sure, most people know where to find me, but I could protect myself by having my dad get me to the bakery safely if something went horribly wrong.

"Jonas," I said aloud as I biked down the street. "His name is Jonas." I leaned my bike against the rack and walked into the bar, determined to make this date better than the last one. Rye had described him as tall, dark, and handsome. He also wore glasses, and he had on a blue shirt. I started to roll my eyes but stopped just in case he happened to be in the bar already. A glance around the nearly empty space said he wasn't. Since I was early, I sidled up to the bar for a little liquid courage.

"Hey, Cookie! What's happening, girl?"

The bartender, and co-owner of The Modern Goat, was an old friend from high school. "Hi, Emily, if you can believe it, I'm here on a blind date."

She stood stock still for a moment before she burst out laughing. When she calmed down, she waved a hand in the air and tried to speak. "Great joke. You don't date."

"I decided it was time to get back on the old elephant."

She tipped her head. "I think the saying is horse."

"Oh, I know it is, but this feels more like an elephant."

She snorted while trying to hold in her laughter. "Sorry, but this entire conversation is hilarious since the dating scene in Lake Pendle leaves a lot to be desired."

"How would you know? You're married to the class clown a.k.a. class president a.k.a. the winning quarterback."

"I work in a bar," she answered as though that should be enough of an answer.

"You make a valid point."

She grinned and handed me a glass of wine, my go-to whenever I was in her establishment.

"Does this have anything to do with Ares Halla returning to town?"

I made a sound that I hoped was indignant rather than denial. "No." I aimed for flippant, but it sounded desperate to my ears. "But I'm not getting any younger. Now that I own the bakery, I have a little time to start going out again."

"I see, I see," she said, biting her lip to keep from smiling, which told me I had not succeeded with indignant versus denial. "Maybe you should just date Ares. The entire class knew you two were made for each other."

The sound I made was somewhere between a pfftt, snort, laugh, and gag. "Wrong." That was all I could think to say. Especially since, for many years, I had thought the same thing.

She held her hands up to calm me. "I think one doth protest too much, but you know I've got your back, so if you need saving, order a whiskey sour. I'll come to your rescue."

I raised my glass to her and smiled. "I appreciate that. Here's to Jonas, may he not be a total dunder."

I moved to a table where I could see both doors to the bar while I awaited a tall, dark, and handsome man wearing glasses and a blue shirt. The Modern Goat had a separate dining room from the bar, as well as a large patio they used in the summer when tourists flocked to town to hang out at the lake. Ironically, the restaurant had opened around the same time my mom and dad had started dating, so they were celebrating their third decade in business.

After a stroll through my Facebook feed, and two games of Bakery Story, Jonas was still MIA. The bar was busy as we approached the eight o'clock hour and I was ready to leave. The date was set for seven-thirty, so I'd clearly been stood up by Mr. Tall, Dark and Handsome in a blue shirt. It didn't bother me one bit. It made deciding on a second date super easy. Standing, I pushed in my chair and slipped into my coat. "Sorry, Jonas, your loss," I muttered as a loud, rowdy group of guys walked in. I diverted for

Cookie

the back door to avoid them. Were customers supposed to use the back door? No, but I had been delivering baked goods here for years, so I was exempt from customer rules.

If I hurried, I could be home, changed, and have the ovens fired up in under fifteen minutes. Tonight, Rye would be back and I could focus all my attention on the Cookie Pies between my other batches. With any luck, after tonight, I'd have everything dialed in to make the cookies competition worthy.

The sun was setting when I stepped out the back door and I noticed a cool breeze had picked up. I paused to zip my jacket, when someone stepped out of the shadows near the bike rack. "We meet again," Blake said, pinning me up against the building. "My buddy Jonas did me a solid getting you here tonight. I owe him a beer," he said, tracing a finger down my cheek in a way that sent a skitter of fear down my spine. "You owe me a kiss, darling."

Instinctively, my hands went to his chest to push him away. "I don't owe you anything. Get away from me!" I yelled.

He slapped his hand over my mouth. "All you bitches are the same. You think you can lead a guy on and then just walk away, but you can't lead me on. I get what's owed me and I'm not afraid to take it if I have to."

"She owes you nothing," a voice from my left said. "I would suggest you let her go before the cops get here. They tend to frown upon men threatening women."

"You again," he snarled, when he turned toward Ares.

It gave me the opening I needed. I brought my knee up between his legs and sent his little boys into orbit. He grunted as he curled over on himself, so I gave him an upper hook to the nose just for the hell of it. I hoped it left a lasting impression that he'd remember the rest of his life. He started howling like a rabid animal, but I didn't wait around to see what he'd do. I ran to Ares and fell into his arms as a squad car came to a squealing halt at the curb.

"Thank you," I cried, grabbing hold of his shirt as my spine shuddered from fear and adrenaline.

"All I did was give you an opportunity," he said, kissing my forehead. "You're the one who took him out."

"I was so scared," I admitted as the cops came running toward us.

"It's okay," he whispered. "I got you."

He turned me away from the guy writhing on the ground to address the officers. I was happy and grateful to be in the safety of his arms again after all these years. When he cupped my face and encouraged me to rest my head on his shoulder, I vowed to stop this dating nonsense. He'd rescued me from karma twice now and I wasn't going to risk a third time.

"Here, drink this," he said, handing me a cup of steaming hot liquid. "It's tea with honey and whiskey."

I didn't argue, just brought it to my lips and sipped the sweet but spicy liquid. "Thanks," I said, not making eye contact with him as he sat beside me on the couch. "I'm so glad you were there tonight."

"I think you would have gotten out of it on your own, but I'm glad I was there to give you an opening."

"Something tells me you weren't just happening by," I said, taking another sip. It was strong, but with any luck, it would chase the final shivers away. The cops had arrested Blake and charged him with attempted sexual assault. I gave them my statement but it was likely a good lawyer could get him out of the charge and back on the streets. Either way, I got my licks in on Blake and that was enough for me.

"Rye told me what you were doing tonight."

"Of course, she did." My sigh was heavy but his laughter was light.

"Don't be mad at her. I told her I was worried after what happened the other night, and she agreed that she had screwed up with Blake. Just so you know, I had no intentions of getting between you and your date. I waited outside to make sure you got home safely and for no other reason. I saw you get up and leave, but when you didn't show up at the end of the alley to get your bike, I knew something was wrong."

"I can't even be mad about it," I said, gulping down the rest of the tea. Maybe it would calm my nerves. "I didn't want to be there, but Rye told me I couldn't give up on dating so quickly."

"Why did you start dating? My dad told me you haven't dated anyone in years."

"He's right," I said with a nod. After your comment at the first meeting for The Fluffy Cupcake, I decided to start again."

"If that's the case, I'm terribly sorry and it wasn't intentional," he said, taking the cup from my hands and setting it on the coffee table. When he turned back, he took my hand and didn't let it go. "What did I say?"

"That I wasn't dating, and I didn't have a boyfriend or a social life, so there was no reason I couldn't enter the competition."

He tipped his head and his eyes told me the moment he remembered the conversation. "I did say that, but I meant nothing by it other than you could make time if you wanted to do it."

"I know," I agreed with a shrug. "But you know how I get sometimes."

"I do," he said, but he was smiling when he said it. "I'm still sorry that I'm the reason for all of this. That wasn't my intention. I'm not sure what your end game was with it, though."

"Me either." I shook my head as I stared at our hands clasped together. "That's a lie. My end game was to make you jealous, which in hindsight was ridiculous, but Rye convinced me you'd silently seethe if you knew I was dating all these other guys."

"Rye was correct."

My next words froze on my tongue. "Wait, what?"

He shrugged, but I could tell he was forcing the nonchalance behind it. "The idea of another man's hands or lips on you infuriates me. I don't have a right to feel that way, but I do."

"Another man's hands?" I asked, my thoughts spinning in my head. "That implies that—"

"I want to be the only man to touch you," he finished, giving me a slight lip tilt. "I've tried to hide how I truly feel about you, Cookie, but it's becoming harder and harder to be the good guy when I see guys like Blake treating you like garbage. You're just so–" He made the mind blown motion with one hand before letting it drop, then fell silent while he stared at our hands clasped together.

"I'm so what, Ares?"

He lifted his gaze to mine and pinned me with those chocolate eyes I wanted to dive into. "Beautiful. Brilliant. The whole package. Trust me, I didn't expect to return to Lake Pendle and still carry this crush on my best friend, but the moment I saw you passing out cookies from your long-awaited cookie wagon, I knew it was going to be an uphill battle."

"You think I'm beautiful?" The question carried such an air of incredulousness that I almost laughed. "Do you need glasses?"

"Stop," he said, putting his finger to my lips. "Do not start about your hips and your ass. Some might argue they're your best physical attributes."

"Some?"

"Okay, me. I would argue that, but my point is, you always undercut any compliment given to you when you deserve every single one of them whether those compliments are about your baking skills or your body."

Was this happening? Was Ares Halla admitting that he liked me or, at the very least, found me...sexy? Between the scare earlier and the whiskey, I was afraid my head or heart was going to explode before I could make sense of this.

"Wait. Still carry a crush on your best friend?" I asked, the conversation reaching me in bits and pieces.

"I know, we aren't best friends—"

I cut him off with the wave of my hand. "I meant the still part. That word indicates it's been there for a while."

"Only about fifteen years."

"You had a crush on me when we were kids? Why didn't you say anything?"

"Two words. Uncle Brady."

I grimaced and nodded my understanding. "Good point. But we haven't been kids for a long time, Ares."

"You haven't been talking to me for a long time, Cookie. When I did come home, you'd be gone, so I didn't know what to think. I still don't."

Cookie

"I can't talk about this tonight, Ares," I said, nearly tripping over my tongue to get it out. "It's already been a long night and I still have to bake."

"I know," he whispered, brushing a lock off my forehead. "There's a lot of history between us that we have to address. It doesn't have to be tonight as long as I know you're willing to talk to me. I want to figure this out."

"Figure what out?" I asked, wanting to move away from him but unable to fight against the pull of his orbit. It had always been that way for me and it scared me to think he felt the same way about me.

"This magnetic draw between us. The one that's been here since we were kids. Like we were born of the same spirit in two separate bodies." I snorted with sarcasm but he grasped my chin and brought my gaze back to his. "I've screwed up a lot over the years, and I'll admit that I wasn't always the best at talking about my feelings. I want to change that now if you'll give me a chance."

"A chance is all I can promise tonight, Ares," I said, that familiar burn in my eyes. I wanted to cry with happiness that he still liked me and from the painful memories that tried to edge that happiness out.

"A chance is more than I deserve, Cookie," he said, his thumb caressing my cheek. "I promise not to screw it up."

"I hope not." I rested my hand against his cheek and his beard tickled my palm, but his heat was the only thing I could focus on. "My life has been black and white since I lost you, but since you've been back, color started creeping in around the edges again. I can feel the warmth of the sun on my back and appreciate the birds' songs in the morning. I don't want to lose that."

"You won't," he promised, putting his finger to my lips. I kissed it without conscious thought. "I'll be here until you see everything in technicolor."

"Then you'll leave again?" I asked, the tremble in my voice giving away how much I didn't want that to happen.

"No, then I'll hold your hand and walk beside you. I'm not leaving again, Cookie. This is my home now."

Those five words came out with so much emphasis it was hard to deny them. His actions the last few weeks made it hard to deny

120

them. Ares was all in, it appeared, and for the first time in thirteen years, I wanted to believe him too.

"I hope that's true, Ares," I whispered, looking anywhere but at him. "When you approached me at the farmers' market, it took me by surprise, but that flame I always carried for you sparked in my soul. I hated every second of the sensation, but it told me that we had unfinished business and nothing would improve until we finished it."

"I know how to finish it."

"I'm glad someone does because I don't even know where to start."

He lowered his forehead to mine, and I inhaled the scent of him: sunshine and almonds. My heart reacted to the boy I remembered from childhood, but my body reacted to the brush of his skin against mine.

"That's because where we start and where we finish are the same place," he whispered. His gaze dropped to my lips and before I could take a breath, his lips were on mine.

Oh, God, was this happening? Was I finally kissing my best friend? I lifted my chin, letting him know I wanted this. I wanted so much more, but if this kiss was it, then I would be forever grateful for the little bit of Ares Halla I carried with me. Hating him be damned. That had gotten me nowhere the last thirteen years, so maybe, just maybe, this wasn't the end but rather the beginning—a clean slate to write a different story than the one we could wipe away.

It was almost too much to hope for. Instead, I threw myself into the kiss I'd wanted for many years. His gentle hands directed my head to the side so he could take the kiss deeper while keeping it close-lipped. I trailed my hand up to bury it in the hair at the nape of his neck. He'd always had the softest hair, and I teased him that he must use baby shampoo to keep it so soft. I moaned, the sensation of touching him again nearly overwhelming. I kissed him, knowing he wanted it as much as I did. When he trailed his tongue between the crack of my lips, I wondered if he wanted it even more than me.

I parted my lips and waited. Would he take a taste or back away from the fire consuming us? A long moan escaped his lips when he felt the opening, but he held back. He broke the kiss, and his gaze drifted to mine. "Is this happening?" he whisper-asked.

My nod was short before his lips were back on mine. He dipped his tongue in this time, no longer hesitant to explore all of me in one kiss. We stayed locked together with our hearts pounding for each other until we were desperate for air. Correction— desperate for air *and* solid ground. The moment his lips touched mine, the floor fell away and left me floating on a cloud.

"Thank you for sharing yourself with me," he whispered with his forehead on mine again. "Just so you know, you blew my daydreams about kissing you out of the water."

"Same, but it wasn't the physical act," I whispered, tracing his jawline.

"No, it was everything else. That kiss took all the broken pieces of my heart and reassembled them," Ares said, his hand holding mine to his face. "Your kiss has that kind of power over me. I wanted you to know that."

"Same, Ares, same," I promised as I closed my eyes and inhaled deeply. It wasn't a lie or mouth music to make him feel better. Little pieces of my heart had found their way back together during that kiss.

"We better get going," he finally said, his words laced with disappointment.

"You don't have to bake tonight, Ares. Rye will be back in as normal."

"I know she will be," he agreed with a smile. Something about his tenderness made me ache to be in his arms. "But when I bake with you, I feel alive. Please, don't take that away from me yet. I promise to stay out of your way as long as I can be there watching and learning."

"Okay," I whispered, the desperation in his eyes more than my heart could take. Those eyes said every word he spoke was true and I couldn't break his heart by shutting him out. "You can help me with cookies and when we're done, I'm sure Rye or Athena will have a job or two for you."

"That's good enough for me. Thank you, Cookie, for understanding even without understanding."

His barely-there beard was soft and smooth against my skin when I rested my hand on his cheek. Touching him again was captivating. Emotional. Calming. "There's a lot that I don't understand, but if I can make our future better than our past, then I'm willing to try."

"Me too," he said with a smile as he brushed his thumb against my temple. "Tell me what I can do to help you get through tonight, and I'll do it, no questions asked. We still have to tell your parents about the incident, too."

Telling my parents about Blake dragged an involuntary groan from my lips. "I don't want to think about that right now. I want to be in your arms again where I feel safe."

"Now that's a request I have no trouble filling," he whispered as he wrapped me up in his arms and put his lips back on mine.

Wrapped up in him, I had to consider the possibility that we could be more than business partners. He had a lot of questions to answer, but tonight I sensed that he never shared the real reason he left Lake Pendle. I could spend time trying to puzzle that out, or I could spend time soaking up the warmth of his arms and the feeling in my chest when he kissed me. I decided that, just for now, I'd let my heart be open to the possibility of change.

Sixteen

What was happening right now? That question kept running through my head as Ares drove me toward my parents' house. He insisted on driving, saying walking in the dark tonight wasn't safe. He was probably right, but I didn't want to hear that Blake could already be out of the clinker. Even though he was driving, he hadn't let go of my hand since we climbed into the car. The biggest question I kept asking myself was if that time on the couch, when our lips were as connected as our souls, had really happened.

"I'd rather be baking," I said as we approached the neighborhood.

"I know, because that's who you are, but it's important that your folks know what's going on."

"I'd like to think I'm more than just a baker."

"Cookie, baking has been part of you since your creation in a way it never was for me. At three, you didn't care about Sesame Street. You cared about sesame seeds. At ten, you created new cookie recipes on the back of your notebook during social studies. As a teenager, you didn't care about Friday night dances. You cared about Saturday morning weddings. Baking is about knowledge, skill, and a heavy dose of intuition. It's also about learning while being a teacher and endless cups of patience. More than that, it's about love, devotion, and selflessness. It's about caring for people during the happiest and saddest parts of their lives. It's about being humble when you should be proud. You're happy to hide in the back so the cookies and cakes you bake with love can take the stage. All of that is who you are, Cookie. You have that innate ability to create in a way that doesn't make sense to those of us who can't. So, when I say baking is who you are, I mean it as the highest possible compliment. I hope that makes sense."

I let what he said replay in my mind, but focused on how he'd said it. What he said made sense, but how he said it was why it would stay with me for the rest of my life. The words were said like a reverent prayer, as though he had a newfound ability to be honest about his feelings for the first time.

"It made more sense than anything anyone has ever said to me before, Ares. It made me feel seen. Not just for what I accomplished at the bakery, but also for what I accomplished in the community."

"I know that's the reason you had such a visceral reaction to our parents lying to you about me coming home. The idea that you might lose that connection with the community was more than you could bear."

"It would be like you no longer being able to add," I agreed. "I have so many dreams to pursue and without the bakery, those dreams would die."

He brought my knuckles to his lips and brushed a kiss across them. "We're going to pursue those together now because—"

"My dreams are your dreams," I finished, far less sarcastically than I intended.

"They are," he agreed, pulling to the curb and putting my car into park. "After what happened in the city, I yearn for dreams that I can believe in, even if they didn't originate in my mind. Your dreams are the kind of dreams that help people, not hurt them. That's what I'm looking for in my life now."

I raised a brow at his mention of the city. That was the first time he'd said anything about his life there since he'd returned. I wanted to know everything, but I was sure pushing him too far or fast would not accomplish that goal. If I wanted absolute honesty from him, I'd have to be patient, so I bit back the question on my tongue.

"It makes me happy to know you think my dreams are worthy of chasing. Not everyone wants to build a cookie wagon."

"I want to," he said with a smile. "I'm also working hard on your online marketplace plan. It's doable if we have our ducks in a row."

"When your mom wasn't excited about it, I put it on the back burner. The amount of work required of the finance person is intense, so they'd have to be excited about it to do it right. I'm glad you see the value in it."

"Are you kidding? Shipping The Fluffy Cupcake cookies and treats across the country is a sound business in this day and age. I'm working on it in my spare time."

"Which you haven't had much of," I said, eyeing my parent's house. "That's on me."

"Wrong," he said, cupping my chin and turning it to face him. "We're in this together. I brought the cookie competition to you, so I had to be ready to step up and help where needed. I love every single second of what we're doing together, Cookie. Don't ever think I'm not happy with my decision to return. Over the last two weeks, my life has done a one-eighty, and it was just in the nick of time." He let out a sigh and rolled his shoulders, dropping eye contact. "Are you ready to do this?"

I wasn't. I wanted to learn what happened in the city and why it changed him. That would have to wait, though, so I nodded once. "It's no big deal. We'll give them the facts and leave everything else out, right?"

"Right," he said, tapping my nose before climbing from the car and coming around to help me. "Just don't expect your parents to follow that plan."

Sarcastic laughter escaped my lips as we walked up the pathway. He knew my parents as well as I did, and he was absolutely right. They would not be happy if I tried to gloss over any part of this story. We were climbing the steps to the front door when my dad opened it.

"Cookie? Ares? What are you doing here? Is everything okay?" He looked at his watch, the late hour likely throwing him for a loop. "Did something happen to Amber?"

Ares waved his hands as we stopped in front of him. "No, Mom is fine, I promise."

"Is Mom home?" I asked. "I'd rather only explain this once."

"Of course, honey." Dad held the door open while Ares and I walked into my childhood home the same way we had thousands of times over the years…together. It was the first time in thirteen years, but to me, for that one brief second, it felt like nothing had changed.

126

"Who is it, hon—" Mom paused in the kitchen doorway when she saw us. "Cookie? What's going on? Ares? Did something happen to Amber?" Her voice shook at the end of the question as Dad slipped his arm around her for comfort.

"Amber is fine. Apparently, this has to do with Cookie."

Mom's gaze flicked between Ares and me, and the look in her eye told me she was already jumping to conclusions, so it was time to derail them. "There was an incident tonight," I said, walking to the couch to sit. Ares joined me and put his arm around my shoulders, which raised both parents' eyebrows. "Is Rye home?"

"Yes, but she's sleeping," Dad answered as he and Mom sat. "Should I wake her?"

"No, I will fill her in later tonight. Ares thought it was wise that I tell you what happened before you hear it in town tomorrow."

Dad leaned forward and clasped his hands together. "This sounds serious."

"It is," Ares said, and I noticed his jaw ticking as he clenched his teeth together.

I glanced at him for a moment before I answered. "Last week, Rye set me up on a blind date that didn't end well. In fact, if Ares hadn't come along when he did, I don't know what would have happened."

"Did he try to get physical?" Dad asked, making a fist. "What's his name? We'll have a chat."

Mom rolled her eyes and reached out, taking my hand. "Are you okay, honey?"

"I'm fine. I thought it was over and behind me until tonight."

"When she had another blind date," Ares said, a bit too disapprovingly for my taste, but I bit my tongue to keep from jumping down his throat in front of my parents.

"Did Rye set you up again?" Mom asked.

"She did, but this wasn't her fault. She didn't know the guy had been put up to it by Blake."

"The dude from the first date?" Dad asked, and I nodded.

"When tonight's date didn't show up, I snuck out the back door of The Modern Goat, thrilled I could head home and bake. The problem? Blake was waiting for me in the alley."

127

Cookie

"I walked up as he had her pinned against the wall with his hand over her mouth," Ares said, his body vibrating with anger where he sat next to me.

"We didn't let him get away with it this time," I jumped in, knowing they were going to freak out. "We called the police and Blake was taken to jail on assault charges. I know someone is going to tell you this in the morning, so I wanted you to understand what happened."

"You just happened to be there both times, Ares?" Dad asked with a high degree of suspicion.

"The first time was luck. I was walking to the bakery to see if Cookie needed help, and they were in front of the building. Tonight, well, I made Rye tell me where her date was so that I could keep an eye on her. I wanted to make sure she got home safely."

Dad stuck his hand out. "I appreciate you watching out for my girl, son."

Ares shook his hand and then shrugged. "I didn't have a good feeling about that guy from last week, so I'm glad I threatened to steal Rye's favorite donut frying sticks if she didn't tell me."

Mom and Dad laughed in unison, which was a relief. My biggest fear was they'd overreact and we'd end up fighting about my rights as an adult woman.

"That's dirty," Dad said, a smile still on his face. "What did the police say would happen now?"

"They would try to keep him in jail overnight and have him arraigned in the morning. He will get out but will not be allowed any contact with me."

"But that doesn't mean he won't try," Dad jumped in. "Don't let your guard down."

"Don't worry, Uncle Brady, I've got her back. He won't get near her again." His declaration was accompanied by his arm tightening on my shoulder.

"I'll be careful," I promised. "Is my old room open if Blake shows up around the bakery? That would be my biggest concern."

"Of course, of course," Mom promised. "You're always welcome here, baby."

"There isn't much more to say. I'll keep you posted on what happens, but I'm one hundred percent certain it will be all over town by morning."

"Especially when people find out she sent his gonads to the moon and finished him off with a hook to his nose," Ares said, trying to bite back a smile.

"That's my girl," Dad said with a satisfied nod. He glanced at Mom for a moment. "Ares, I was going to call you tomorrow. I have a question about an investment. I was wondering if you could take a look at it and tell me the best thing to do?"

Ares turned to me. "Are you okay to stay for a few minutes? I know we need to start baking."

I noticed Mom and Dad raise a brow at each other, but I ignored them and nodded. "Sure, we have a few minutes."

Ares squeezed my shoulders once and then stood, leaving the room with Dad. Mom stared me down until I asked an uncomfortable 'What?'

"I'm just trying to figure out how Ares is involved in all of this."

"He just told you, Mom," I said, immediately on the defense.

"I'm also trying to figure out why you decided to start dating again, now of all times."

I shrugged and avoided eye contact. "It was time to get back out there."

"Now that Ares is home."

"It has nothing to do with Ares, Mom, but I can't wait around for the right guy to come to me. I've wasted enough of my life on the wrong guy."

"Is he the wrong guy, though? Maybe you decided, consciously or subconsciously, that dating would make him jealous."

"Did you talk to Rye?" I asked, frustration clear in my voice. "She promised not to tell you about our plan!"

"Rye never said a word," she replied, that one brow up in the air again. "But thanks for confirming it."

"Ugh!" I groaned, stomping my foot. "I hate it when you do that!"

Mom just laughed and leaned forward. "All I'm going to say about the matter is this; from what I just saw, dating to make Ares

Cookie

jealous worked. That said, I would like you to stop going on blind dates until this thing with Blake is cleared up. It's not safe."

I held my hands up in front of me. "Trust me, when Rye comes in tonight, I'll let her know our experiment in serial dating was a disaster, and it's over."

"Rye was in on it, too?"

"It was her idea," I said with another shrug. "She knew how frustrated I was with Ares when he made mention of my lack of dating life at our meeting a few weeks ago. We couldn't let it stand."

"That's the pot and the kettle if I've ever seen it."

I bit back a smile, so she didn't think she was funny. "Rye said she doesn't date because no one likes her face, but I don't date because I can't get over my childhood crush."

Mom tipped her head back and forth a couple of times. "She's wrong about herself, but right about you. This," she waved her hand around between us and behind her where the men went, "proves it."

"Mom," I said on a sigh.

"Don't Mom me. I might be old, but I remember being thirty and watching my life slip away due to a crush on a guy I was too afraid to take a chance on."

"It's been thirteen years, Mom."

"That's true, but your dad worked with me every day for seven years while he waited for me to be ready. He already knew we were made for each other. He just had to wait for me to know it too."

I stared at the floor with my hands clasped together and thought about the kiss on the couch just an hour ago. "Maybe we were made for each other, but too much time has passed and there's too much history between us now to overcome."

"No," she said, shaking her head. "Those are the excuses you're using to protect your heart from being broken again. You have to open your heart and take a chance, Cookie."

"I'm trying," I said, finally looking up and right into her loving gaze. "I'm taking it slow and getting to know him again."

That kiss didn't feel like you were taking it slow, that little voice whispered.

"By helping you bake?"

130

"Right now, yes," I said, leaning back on the couch and crossing my legs. I had to play it cool with her or she would know that my crush on Ares was stronger than ever. "We're getting to know each other again over the baker's bench. I'm working on the cookie for the competition, so he's baking off some of the simple cookies and helping Rye with donuts and pastries."

"I didn't know he knew that much about bakery work."

"He used to work there when we were kids, Mom," I reminded her.

"Yes, but his skills didn't go past putting donuts in boxes for people, remember?"

"Well, that was then, and now, he's quite capable if you give him direction. He's been a lifesaver since I started this cookie project. Once that's done, then he can go back to the books."

"I haven't heard much about this cookie competition other than what Rye has told me." Her tone was loud and clear. She was annoyed I hadn't talked to her about it.

"That's my fault. I should have run it all past you, but I've either been sleeping or working."

"Do you think you'll have a quality product by Friday?"

"Absolutely," I assured her, then gave her a quick rundown on what I was baking for the competition.

"Cookie Pies. Now there's a throwback. Great idea, though. It's outside the box a bit but they still fit the rules. I can't wait to see how you do with them, but be careful, Cookie. Competitions can be ruthless."

A shiver went through her and I leaned forward, taking her hand. "I know you're still scarred from the Darla incident, but I'll be fine. Darla didn't stab you because you made good cupcakes, and you know it. Besides, she got her comeuppance when she was shivved in the shower for being a bully. She's gone and we don't have to worry about her anymore."

"I know," she said, letting out a breath. "I still worry about you, though. I'm your mom."

"When it comes to both the competition and Blake, I'll be careful, and I'll never be alone."

"I can see that," she said, looking over her shoulder. "Ares was the last person I expected you to be with tonight."

"We've made some strides toward being friends again. It's early days, but I decided if we have to work together, then we have to get along. I'm willing to bury the hatchet for the good of the bakery."

"For the bakery…"

"Mom," I said in a warning tone.

"What? I'm just saying the way he had his arm around you didn't look like it had anything to do with the bakery."

"Right now, for me, it's about the bakery. I can't speak for Ares."

Mom nodded along as though she agreed with me, but I could see that she didn't. Hell, I didn't even agree with that statement. I was burying the hatchet for the bakery, but more, I was burying it for myself. I had spent too many years hating him, hating myself, and hating the way our relationship ended not to grab the chance to leave all that behind when it came my way. In the end, we may end up nothing more than friends, but I'd rather be friends than enemies any day.

Uncle Brady led me out to the patio after stopping by the kitchen for a couple of beers. I loved that over the years, he hadn't changed. He worked hard, played hard, and loved hard.

He handed me a beer and sat in one of the lawn chairs, waiting for me to do the same. "Thanks for looking out for my girl."

We tapped bottles and took a sip as the stars twinkled above us. "I still care about Cookie, sir," I said, lowering the beer to my lap. "I don't want to see her get hurt."

"Neither do we," he said, looking down his nose at me as he brought the bottle to his lips.

"It's not like that, sir. We're only learning to be friends again." It was embarrassing how hard I was lying to this man and wishing we both believed it. I could still feel Cookie's lips on mine and craved the taste of her now more than ever.

"Which is a good place to start."

"Something tells me you don't need help with an investment."

"Not the kind you're thinking of, no," he said with a tip of his head. "I was hoping we could form an alliance of sorts."

"An alliance?"

"To take care of Cookie. I'd like you to be with her as much as possible to protect her. Can you do that for me?"

"No, sir, I can't," I said immediately, setting the beer on the table in front of us.

"You just said you care about Cookie," Brady said, frustration filling the air between us.

"I do, and that's why I won't form an alliance with her father. Sir, I have loved your daughter probably since the day I was born." His brows went up and I nodded, giving him the palms up. "It took me a long time to come to that conclusion and I know I hurt Cookie in the process."

He opened his mouth to say something, but snapped his jaw shut and took another drink of beer. I waited him out rather than try to fill the silence. "While I'm not surprised by this information, it only makes all the more sense for you to form an alliance with me to protect her."

"I'm going to protect her, sir, but it's going to take a lot of time and effort to prove to her that she can trust me. If she ever found out I was working behind her back with her father, she'd never forgive me."

Uncle Brady smiled and tipped his bottle at me. "Good boy."

"That was a test?"

"In a way, but it was also to learn your intentions toward my daughter. I've known you since the day you were born, Ares, which is why I was so surprised when you left Lake Pendle the way you did after graduation. You didn't just hurt Cookie. You broke her. Every part of her heart and soul crumbled like a cookie and fell into a pit that she's locked away for thirteen years. Only you can find that pit and fix those broken parts of her."

Cookie

I pressed my fist to my chest and coughed. "Thanks for the brutal imagery, Uncle Brady."

He shrugged as he set his beer on the table next to mine and stared out over the backyard. "It was brutal to watch your own child go through something like that, Ares. There was nothing we could do to help her once you were gone. In the blink of an eye, she lost the half of herself she'd always depended on. All of us together couldn't be that for her despite how hard we tried. Then things got desperate and we had to take drastic measures just to keep her here with us. A year later, when she came back to us, she wasn't the same girl. She was pieces of that girl held together by hatred, love, and inexplicable pain."

"Wait, are you saying what I think you're saying?" The beer curdled in my stomach and I wanted to vomit all the pain and anguish from my soul.

"Yes, and you know firsthand how difficult it is for parents to watch their children go through something so horrible. I should be beyond angry with you for what you did to her."

"But you're not?" I asked, meekness filling the words.

"I'm not. I don't believe in letting someone else control my life, and that's what I'd be doing. But, and this is a heavy but, I also can't pretend it didn't happen."

"Understood, sir," I agreed. "I just wish I knew what happened. Can you tell me?"

"Absolutely not," he said with a chuckle. "Cookie will tell you that when she trusts you. When she really trusts that you aren't going to hurt her again."

"Great," I muttered.

"Hey, look at it this way, bud. You have two things going for you."

"Two things?"

"Yep, the first is you've been gone thirteen years. We're a family of bakers and thirteen is our number."

I couldn't hold in my laughter. "True, I hadn't thought of that. What's the second thing?"

"You've been home for almost three weeks and you're sitting on my deck talking to me after driving here in Cookie's car." He lifted a brow and I nodded once. "Whatever you're doing, it's working, so keep going and don't be afraid to bleed a little for her. She's worth it."

I nodded, and folded my hands together in prayer. "I learned that the hard way, Uncle Brady, both then and now. I do have a question for you."

"Hit me."

"If I can get Cookie back to where she trusts me again, do I have your permission to date her? I don't know if it will all work out, but if it does, I have to be sure she's not going against her family's wishes."

"She's a grown woman who can make her own decisions, Ares. Our wishes don't matter when it comes to her heart. My dad bones want to tell you to keep your hands off my daughter, but I won't for one simple reason. I remember being a thirty-year-old guy aching for the chance to be with the only woman he'd ever truly loved. That said, you'd better respect her and don't fu—muck it up."

I beat back the smile and simply nodded my head instead. "Heard and understood. Thanks, Uncle Brady."

"For what?"

"For the grace of understanding when you could hate me for what happened to Cookie."

"I don't hate anyone, Ares. I also know back then you were a kid who saw things just a little differently than my daughter. I may not have liked how you went about it, but you had every right to go. Maturity is gained, though, not promised."

I nodded along, wishing I knew what to say, so I said the only thing I could think of in the moment. "I tell Cookie now that her dreams are my dreams. She thinks I'm being sarcastic when I say it."

"But you aren't?"

"No. Not in the slightest. I chased what I thought was my dream, and it turned out to be a nightmare. But Cookie," I said, shaking my head as I tried to get across to the most important man in Cookie's life what I saw for my future. "Her dreams are pure and honest. She understands integrity and hard work. She isn't afraid to give her all to the dream, whether it benefits her alone or everyone. Her dreams don't come attached with a dollar sign. And those, I've learned, are the only kind of dreams that matter."

Cookie

"Ares," Brady said, squeezing my shoulder. "You know my daughter better than you think you do, and that's going to be the reason you can teach her to trust again. Cookie is great at giving second chances, but I assure you, there is never a third."

"I won't need a third, sir," I promised.

He leaned back on his chair with a smile and tipped his head before he finished his beer. I had won Uncle Brady's trust. Now I just had to win Cookie's.

Seventeen

"Hey, Mom," I said as I walked into the kitchen early Thursday afternoon. "How are you doing today?" I stopped on my way to the fridge to kiss her cheek and she patted mine.

"I'm good, sweetheart," she said while she pointed at the fridge. "I saved you some lunch. I know you've been working long hours at the bakery. I noticed the BMW is gone, though."

"Yep," I confirmed as I pulled the plate out of the fridge. "It was the last piece of my old life and it was time for it to go. There is zero purpose to driving a car like that here. I traded it in for a Chevy. I'm going to pick it up later today."

"I'm happy to see you making a home here, Ares. I just wish we were going to be here to spend it with you."

I leaned against the edge of the counter and took a bite of the sandwich. When I finished chewing, I tipped my head to the side. "It's not like you're going to be gone forever, Mom. You're only going for the winter."

She looked down at her lap rather than answer and it was two more bites of my sandwich before I realized she was crying. I set the plate on the counter and knelt in front of her chair, tipping her chin up. "Mom, you've got to tell me what's wrong. We can all see that you have a problem and we want to help, but we can't if we don't know what the problem is."

"I want to tell you." she said through her tears, "but I'm scared of your father."

"Why on earth are you afraid of Dad?" I asked, confusion filling me.

"I should say I'm afraid of his reaction. I guess I'm afraid of all of your reactions."

"Whatever it is, Mom, you just have to tell us. I promise we'll react with love because that's what this family runs on."

"He's right." My dad's voice filled the room, and I glanced up to see him standing in the hallway. I hadn't heard him come in and was surprised to see him so early in the day.

"Dad? What are you doing home already? It's only two."

"I finished my meeting, so I thought I'd swing by home and pick up something to eat before returning to the office. Now I'm glad I did."

He loosened his tie and walked into the kitchen, pulling a chair over to sit next to Mom. "Tart, if you think we can't see something is going on, you don't put much faith in us. I was hoping it was just the bakery turnover and my retirement, so I haven't pushed you on it, but I can see it's something more. I'm not going to let it go on any longer. It's time to tell us what upset you so we can help you fix it."

"You can't fix it. That's the problem," she cried. "No one can fix it. It's just too much."

"Too much what?" Dad demanded.

"Too much change," I said slowly, the truth dawning on me. "Losing the bakery, you retiring, me coming home, and then going to Florida all in the matter of a few months."

"Is Ares correct?" my dad asked, taking her hand and kissing her knuckles even as they shook in his hand. She didn't answer him with words. She just nodded as tears fell from her eyes and down her cheeks. "I thought you were excited to turn the bakery over to the kids so we could have more time together. It feels like that's changed since we decided to retire."

I noticed how her pupils had dilated when I said Florida and the fear that filled them. The picture snapped into focus, and I gasped. "Mom, you're not upset about retiring. You're upset about going to Florida."

Dad gently wiped her face with a towel before he spoke. "Is that true?"

"I don't think I can do it." Her words were staccato as she forced them from her lips. "As the day draws closer, it's harder and harder to think about anything else."

"You're safe here with us, Tart. Tell us why you don't think you can go to Florida," Dad said, encouraging her to speak openly. "No judgments from us. We're here to listen."

More tears fell as she shook her head while her lips trembled. Finally, she managed to speak. "This is my problem, not yours, and you shouldn't have to suffer anymore because of it."

"Tart, you know in this family that if one of us has a problem, we all have one. Right, Ares?"

I answered immediately because I could hear the desperation in his voice, which was mirrored in my gut. "He's right, Mom, and if Athena were here, she'd say the same thing. When I was going through hell in the city, we all went through it. That's how we get through it, together."

"How about if I make an educated guess, and you tell me if I'm right," Dad said. When she didn't respond, he just went ahead with his thought. "I think you're afraid to go to Florida because of storms, but you're also afraid to tell me that and let the PTSD ruin something else for me."

Her soft sob into her hand was enough of a confirmation for us. I went to the fridge and got her a bottle of water, encouraging her to take a sip so she didn't work herself up until she passed out. "I thought I could do it," she said after she lowered the bottle to her lap. "I thought I could do it for you, Bishop, but the closer we get to leaving, the more terrified I become. I know you want to go somewhere warmer in the winter, but I don't think I can physically force myself to do it. I'm afraid my heart will give out from the fear, Bishop," she cried, nearly crumbling to the floor. Dad grabbed her and brought her onto his lap while I took the water bottle from her hand.

He held her to him and flicked his gaze to the counter where her pills sat. I grabbed her anti-anxiety medication and carried it back to Dad, who tucked one under her tongue while he worked to calm her.

Once she could breathe normally again, Dad rested her head on his shoulder and kissed her forehead. "Baby, I only wanted to go somewhere warm for you. The doctor said it would help your pain not to suffer through the long Minnesota winters. I thought you wanted to go to Florida because your sister and her family are there."

"They are, but Mom and Dad also died there in a horrible accident, Bishop. I'm paralyzed with fear about being there, and while I wish that weren't true, I also don't know how to change it."

"You can't change it, Mom," I reminded her. "That's not your fault, though. You have to remember it's not your fault."

"PTSD doesn't take vacations, honey," Dad said. "The last thing I want is for you to be unhappy for a second of our time together now that we can spend it how we want. We will not be going to Florida this winter."

"Bu—but, Brady and Hay-Hay are expecting us to go with them."

"I'm not so sure about that," Dad said. "Haylee knows there's a problem, and she told me she would quote, pester you until you told her what the problem was so we could address it."

Mom's lips lifted in a small smile. "That sounds like Hay-Hay."

"Since I suspected this might be the problem," Dad continued. "I did a little research and learned that Arizona has very few storms between October and June. Would you consider researching with me to find places in Arizona that might be safe to spend part of the winter? Maybe leave after New Year's and come back on Memorial Day? With Ares home now, it might be the best of both worlds to be here for the holidays and then escape the cold Minnesota January and enjoy a little time in the sun. I've known Haylee and Brady long enough to know that they'll change their plans on a dime to be with us."

"I would like that better," Mom said, her voice still shaking. "I want to find a place where we can go and enjoy our time together, but I don't want to be terrified the entire time we do it. I also don't know how I'd even be able to live in a motorhome, much less try to navigate through the sand in Florida. I'm afraid in the end, all of it would put me in an early grave."

Dad tightened his arms around her as though the idea of her being gone was too much. "Florida is officially off the table," he said firmly. "We'll talk with Brady and Haylee, but I know they'll be on board with changing our plans."

"I just wish this didn't creep in on every plan we make. After all these years, you must be tired of dealing with my irrational fears about storms."

The shame in her voice was loud and clear, even though she should have no shame having survived a tornado.

"Sweetheart, your fears aren't irrational. If anything, you are one of the few people still on this earth who understand a storm's power over us. When we said our vows, I said I would love you in the good times and the bad, in sickness and health, until death do us part. That may have been thirty-some years ago, but I still mean them today. I don't care where we go or where we live. As long as I'm with you, I'm happy."

"You're too good to me, Bishop," she whispered, her hand to his face. "You should be mad as hell, but you're not."

"I could never be mad at you, Tart. Am I sad that you thought you couldn't tell me this? A little bit, but I also understand that your brain doesn't work the same way mine does. I can offer you grace in how you told me because I'm relieved you finally told me."

"I'll stay here with Mom for the afternoon," I told Dad. "I know you need to get back to the office."

"I'm not going anywhere," he said firmly. "They can get along without me just fine over there, and they'll have to start in another few weeks anyway. I'll stay here, run my sweet wife a bubble bath, and plan a little winter vacation once she feels better."

"If you're sure," I said, wanting to give him a second to think it over. When he pulled Mom closer to him and nodded, I knew there was no point in arguing. "I'm going to head out then. I have a few errands to run, but don't be surprised if you don't see me until the morning. Cookie may need my help in the bakery tonight."

She wouldn't need my help, but she was going to get it because I wanted to give them some time alone. I stood and straightened Mom's cushion in her wheelchair before I kissed her cheek and told her I loved her. When I stepped back, I took in the image before me that emanated such deep, devoted love. My friends used to joke that my parents were like teenagers. They always had to be touching each other when they were in a room together. I didn't appreciate it back then. I do now.

"I want you to know that you're the best parents I could have ever asked for. You set an example I can never live up to, but you still make me want to try."

"You can have a love like this too, son," my dad said with a wink. "You just have to find the right woman. She's out there. Maybe even closer than you think."

Mom patted his chest and rolled her eyes. "Subtle, honey."

I laughed and shook my head at the two people who would always be there for me through thick and thin. "Subtlety has never been Dad's strong suit," I said with a wink back at her. "On that note, I'm going to take my leave. If you guys need anything, call me. I'll make it happen."

"Thanks, Ares," Mom whispered.

I squeezed her hand before leaving them huddled together like I had seen many times. It broke my heart when I remembered all the times over my life that this condition stole my mom's joy, but buoyed it to remember she had my dad's love to see her through. If I ever found a love like theirs, I was never letting it go.

You've already found it, Ares, that voice said. *Follow your heart, and it will lead you right to her.*

As I jogged down the stairs to collect my things, I couldn't help but pray that voice was right this time.

Eighteen

"Fancy meeting you here," a voice said from behind me.

"Something tells me you weren't just happening by," I replied, happy to hear her laughter as she sat beside me.

"I may have gotten a text that said you might need to talk."

"May and might, eh?"

"Or not," she added. "I'm happy just to sit here and stare at the lake with you."

"Who sent you the may and might text? My mom?"

"Nope," she said, popping the P. "I promised not to tell, but his name starts with B and ends with P."

"Not surprised, I guess. I'm fine, though."

"Would you be finer if you had a hug from a friend?"

"That would probably make me feel much finer," I agreed.

Cookie scooted closer and wrapped her arms around my shoulders, resting her head next to mine. "You can never go wrong with a hug from a friend," she said as we focused our gazes on the water.

"How did you find me?"

"I took an educated guess," she answered. "The text was enough clue to tell me that something happened with your mom. Whenever we were kids, and something happened with Aunt Amber, it was a surefire bet that I'd find you here staring at the lake and avoiding the house."

"I'm not avoiding the house," I assured her. "I'm just giving them space to be alone. I hope you don't mind a bakery helper tonight because I'm not returning to that house until tomorrow morning."

Cookie

"I'm always happy to have your help in the bakery, Ares. Tomorrow is the cookie competition, so tonight is mostly preparation and packing."

"You can count on me, Cookie," I promised. "We'll get you prepared, and then you can catch some sleep while I help the girls with the rest of the work. You need to be rested for tomorrow."

"I like that plan," I agreed. "Is Aunt Amber okay?" she asked, rubbing my back like she used to when we were teenagers.

"She will be now that my dad is there to care for her."

"Did you finally get to the bottom of her situation?"

"You mean her PTSD-induced anxiety, right?"

"I suspected it was that, but I'm not judging, Ares, just asking. You don't have to tell me."

After a heavy sigh, I shook my head and turned my gaze to the sky to keep from crying. "I went into the kitchen to get some lunch, and Mom was there. I asked her how she was doing, and for a moment, I thought she was better, but she fell apart as soon as we started talking about Florida. Dad showed up unexpectedly, and it all poured out. She was afraid to face the storms in Florida, not to mention losing her parents there, but she didn't want to say anything to Dad. She didn't want to ruin something he looked forward to after retirement. She was also worried about your mom and dad since their plans hinged on my parents too."

"Oh, man, I never even thought of that. Florida is a hotspot for storms, and I find it odd that she would even consider it."

"I don't know for sure, but I suspect it was one of those situations where she agreed to do it before she thought about the implications of that part of the country. My dad, on the other hand, had already figured out this might be the problem and was looking into some other warmer climate areas where storms wouldn't be a factor. They'll talk to your mom and dad once they figure things out, so please don't say anything."

She zipped her lip and threw away the key. "Mum's the word, but I know my family, and they will follow Amber and Bishop wherever they decide to go. It's not about where they are. It's about who they're with."

"Ironic," I said, a smile lifting my lips. "That's exactly what my dad said. Mom was so upset we had to give her the anti-anxiety meds because she could not physically do it herself. I noticed when I grabbed the bottle that it was almost empty."

"Which means she's been using a lot of it?"

I rubbed my hands over my face and locked them behind my neck. "A bottle usually lasts for months, but I picked that bottle up for her when I came home. So yeah, she's used a lot of it. I wish she would have told us sooner so she didn't have to suffer. Lord knows she's suffered enough."

"I'm glad they figured it out and are working toward a solution for her. That's the reason you're not going home, right? To give them time to sort through all this?"

"That, and I needed distance. Mom needs quiet time with Dad to feel better after a bad attack. I've been gone for a long time, but nothing has changed in that respect."

"I know it was hard growing up that way."

"It wasn't all bad, don't get me wrong. Knowing there's nothing I can do for her when these things happen is terrible. Summer was always stressful, but I learned to be flexible. That's a skill not everyone learns, so there's that."

"I feel like that's not the only reason you don't want to go back to the house," she finally said as she continued to rub my back.

"Maybe not. Watching them today, it hit home how empty my life is. I'm thirty and have nothing to show for it. I watch my mom and dad together and wonder if I'll ever find a love like theirs. That all-consuming, unquestioning love may look suffocating to others, but to those of us on the inside, we understand it's about needing the other person just to breathe." I rubbed my hands over my face again and sighed. "I must sound ridiculous. Ignore me."

"You don't sound ridiculous, Ares. I understand what you're saying. Maybe because my parents are much the same way. Some get lucky and find the other person who completes them, some find the person but can never be with them, and some never find their soulmate. I think it's safe to say in our parents' case, they fall into the first group. I never had to deal with the situations you did with Aunt Amber, but I understand what you mean about that all-consuming love. I also understand what you mean by being thirty and alone. Dating is nearly impossible these days, as I proved earlier this week, but we can't give up on finding love. Without love, life is a hard slog."

When she fell silent, I finally turned to her. "Do you want to get out of here?"

"Sure," she said, standing and brushing off her pants before offering me a hand up. I took it and stood, but I didn't let go of her hand. I enjoyed holding it too much and it grounded me to this place with her so my mind didn't spin off to the house where I grew up and the people inside it.

"What did you have in mind?" she asked as we walked up the hill from the lake.

I turned around to walk backward so I could see her face. "An early dinner and a surprise?"

"I'm down for dinner," she said as we stepped onto the sidewalk. "But you know I'm not a fan of surprises."

"You will be of this one," I assured her with a wink.

"I can't believe we drove to Farmington for a hot dog," I said, wiping the ketchup and mustard off my fingers.

"I was betting things hadn't changed since high school when you used to devour them every chance you got."

I patted my hips. "These hips are brought to you by The Fluffy Cupcake and Queenie Weenie Dogs."

"Don't tempt me, Cookie," he hissed, his body blocking mine. Toe to toe, he covered my hands with his.

"Tempt you to what?" I asked, inhaling the musky scent of his aftershave mixed with the spicy hotdog he'd just finished.

"Tempt me to put my hands on those hips the way I've wanted to for years."

"Uh, Ares, your hands are on my hips."

146

"Not the way I want them to be," he growled, curling his fingers around mine. "The way I want them to be is not suitable for work. When I put my hands on these hips and explore them the way I want to, we'll need to be alone."

I couldn't be sure, but that sounded like he had plans he hadn't cleared with me yet. Was I down with those plans? Yes and no. I was down with having his hands all over me, but I wasn't down with getting my heart broken or making life at the bakery difficult.

I pulled his hands away from my hips and held them at my side. "Maybe we better move on, Mr. Halla, before one of us makes a decision we can't take back."

He stared me down for what felt like an eternity before he hit me with that ten thousand watt grin he had down to an art. Women all over Minnesota fell for that grin and I used to be one of them. Now, being older and more mature, I knew that was his wolf in sheep's clothing grin that he used whenever evil plans were in the making.

I ran my finger in a circle around his face. "Don't give me that grin, and don't make plans that have to do with me without consulting me."

The grin fell away and he tipped his head. "I would never do that, Cookie. I hope you don't think I'd ever do anything to hurt you."

"No, not what I meant," I said, pressing both hands to his chest. "I just meant that grin was the one you'd give me when we were kids and you were hatching an evil plan."

"Well, I am," he said, grasping my hands in his but leaving them on his chest. "More like hatched. Do you want to be my partner in evil?"

"I thought it was partner in crime," I said, taking a step closer until we were plastered against each other.

"No crimes are being committed, but I do have a few things up my sleeve I should let you in on, if you're interested, that is."

Still tight against his chest, with my hands captured between us, I could barely breathe, much less put a sensical thought together, so I just nodded instead.

"Good," he said with a smile. "I want you to know how much I needed your company today. I'm sure there are one hundred other things you could be doing instead of hanging out with my lug head, which is why it means so much to me that you're here."

"Nothing is more important than helping a friend, Ares. That hasn't changed about me since we were kids. I was always there for you when Aunt Amber was going through surgeries and I'm still here for you."

"You just trust me less now than you did then."

I shrugged since he wasn't allowing me to leave his atmosphere. "Can you blame me? Once trust is broken, gaining it back takes a long time, and you've only been here for three weeks."

He ran his fingertip down my cheek and shook his head. "I wish I knew what happened all those years ago to make you think you can't trust me. Please, tell me what it was." I remained silent, my gaze dropping to our joined hands. I tried to take a step back, but he held me tightly to him and tipped my chin up. "Hey, it's okay," he said, calming my fight or flight response to the question. "I'll wait until you're ready to talk about it. In the meantime, I'll keep showing up so you know that I'm not the same boy I was when I drove out of town at seventeen. Is that fair?"

I nodded, swallowing around the lump in my throat from his tender honesty. "That's fair. I'm not ready to ruin the fun we're having with anything too heavy."

His thumb caressed my temple and he smiled. "I'm glad you're having fun. I am too, for the record, and you've taken my mind off what's going on at home just like you used to when we were kids. In fact," he said, dropping his hand and picking up mine as we started to walk back to the car. "I've made a decision to find an apartment this summer and move out of my parents place."

"What?" I asked with total confusion. "I thought the plan was for you to stay there while they were gone and take care of the house."

"That was the plan," he agreed, swinging our hands between us, "but Dad mentioned that maybe the best plan was to leave in January and return at the beginning of June. That leaves a lot of months that I'm living with them and to be honest, the house is kind of cramped with three people when I need space for an office. I feel claustrophobic in my old bedroom in the loft now."

"I'm sure you feel that way because you lived alone for so many years. You did live alone, right?"

"Right," he said, opening the car door for me. "That's probably it. I need my own space and I feel like I'm taking over theirs."

He shut the door and walked to the driver's side, sliding one long, muscular leg into the car. That offered me a view of his tight ass hugged by his Wranglers at an angle that left me more than a little hot and bothered. I wanted to rip those jeans off and put my hands all over him. I wanted to explore, taste, and touch every inch of this man and as repulsed as I was by the truth, it was the truth. Was I repulsed, though? Not by him, but I was repulsed by my weakness for him. I wanted to believe I had level five bitchitude, but the reality is, when it comes to Ares, I have zero bitchitude and one hundred percent hornitude. Maybe that was the answer, I thought as I looked him up and down while he started the SUV. Give in to the horniness but keep him at arm's length with the emotions. Now that was something I was excellent at when it came to Ares Halla—the arm's length part, not the horniness part.

"Ready?" he asked, putting it in drive and heading further into Farmington, which dragged me out of my thoughts of horny versus emotional and popped my gaze back to the road.

"Ready as I'll ever be, though I don't know for what." I ran my hand over the dashboard of the new SUV. "How long will you have this loaner? It's nice."

"Well, that's just the thing," he said, biting his lip. "This isn't a loaner. I sold the BMW and bought this SUV instead."

"You sold the BMW and replaced it with a Chevy? Are you okay, or should we find a doctor?"

"Har-har," he said, chucking me under the chin. "I'm fine, but the BMW had to go. My old life is behind me now, and that includes the car. I never wanted it in the first place, but…" He paused and then waved his hand in the air. "It doesn't matter. My point is, this is a much more sensible car for Lake Pendle."

"I think it does matter, though," I said, my head cocked. "Whatever that car represented matters a lot from what I can see."

"Remember when you said you didn't want to talk about anything heavy and ruin the day?" I nodded. "Same."

I held up my hands. "Noted, but one day you'll tell me?"

"One day," he said, biting his lip for a moment. He was so handsome with the sunshine streaming in through the window to highlight his golden blond hair. He looked so much like the boy next door that he used to be. That boy ran to me and told me everything without holding back or being afraid to look weak. We always had each other's backs. I wanted that boy back, but it was possible the man who had replaced him was nothing like him anymore.

"I do like the Chevy better than the BMW," I admitted as he slowed for a stop sign. "It feels more Ares Halla. I especially like the silver."

"I was looking for a lighter color," he explained, taking a left at the stop sign. "I plan to have the bakery logo detailed on the doors and hatch."

"You're going to have pink cupcakes and the word fluffy on your car by choice?"

"I am," he said with a satisfied grin. "It's my business now, too, and I'm not embarrassed by said pink cupcakes or the word fluffy. In fact," he said, sending a heated glance my way, "I love fluffy."

Was it hot in here? I needed air, so I cracked the window a hair and noticed his immediate smirk.

"Well," I said, clearing my throat, "if you do that, this car becomes a write off."

"Exactly," he said with a wink. He slowed and eventually parked the SUV at the curb. To my right was a small white bungalow with a lovely floral pathway that led to a white wraparound porch and a red door. "We're here."

"We're where?"

"To get your surprise." He unclicked his seatbelt and mine before climbing out and opening my door. He gave me a hand out, and I grabbed his sleeve once I was standing.

"You mean the hotdogs weren't my surprise?"

"Not even close to the surprise you're about to get," he said with a smile. "Just don't be mad, okay?"

"Oh, brother," I sighed. "Whenever you said that when we were kids, it always meant you'd already done something you knew I wouldn't like."

150

"Not this time," he said, grabbing my hand to help me up the curb. "I don't think so anyway, but if you don't like it, that's okay, I can always resell it."

"You bought something for me?"

"Yes, now stop asking questions and follow me!"

I laughed while I tried to keep pace with his long strides up the sidewalk. I couldn't figure out what he was talking about, but knowing Ares, whatever was about to happen would take me and my heart by surprise.

Nineteen

Maybe eating a hot dog before taking her to see the surprise was a bad idea. I could feel it roiling around in my stomach with each step we took toward the backyard. Would she like it? Would she hate it? Would she hate me and accuse me of overstepping? I hoped she liked it but I was worried I had overstepped, even if it was with good intentions.

"Ares," she hissed from behind me as I tugged her along with me. "Why are we walking around the backyard of someone we don't know?"

"I know them, and we have permission. They're at work, so we're not bothering anyone. Come on. Your surprise is back here."

"My surprise is in the backyard of someone's home in Farmington? Should I be afraid?"

We stopped in front of a small garage, and I turned to take her shoulder. "You don't need to be afraid, but I hope you are excited when you see this. Ready?" I asked, taking a deep breath while I waited for her to respond. When she nodded, I dropped my hands and shook out my shoulders.

It's now or never, Ares.

I hoisted the overhead door up, held my breath, and waited for her to say something.

"It's a trailer."

I let the breath out and took her hand, walking into the garage so she could see it better. "Not just any trailer. It's a fully operational concessions trailer."

"It's a what now?" she asked, her jaw hanging open.

"A concessions trailer," I hurriedly explained.

"I heard that part. Why would you buy a concessions trailer?"

"For you, Cookie," I said, grasping her shoulders to make eye contact. "I bought it for you."

"You mean..."

"The Cuckoo for Cookies Wagon."

She opened and closed her mouth several times, but no words came out.

When I noticed tears gathering in her eyes, I tenderly rubbed her cheek to calm her. "Hey, it's okay if you don't like it. Don't get upset. I knew there was a chance it wasn't what you wanted when I bought it, so I'm totally flexible with it."

"It's just. What?" she asked, her lips trembling. "You bought this? For me?"

It took everything I had not to laugh, not at her, but just out of pure happiness. The look in her eyes told me she wasn't upset that I had bought the trailer. She was happy.

"Yes, I bought it for you, Cookie Pie." I paused with a grimace. "Sorry, I meant Cookie."

"You bought me a cookie wagon. You can call me Cookie Pie," she said, laughter escaping her lips. "You bought me a cookie wagon."

The words were said with such disbelief that I pulled her against my chest and wrapped my arms around her. "I did, and if you don't like it, I can resell it, but when it came up for sale, it felt a bit like kismet. I was also worried someone else would snatch it out from under us if I didn't move on it. The season for fairs and events is starting now and I didn't want to lose it by waiting."

"How did you pay for it?" she asked, glancing up at me from her position on my chest. "I know the bakery doesn't have the money available yet since I haven't won the competition."

"When I traded in the BMW, it was worth far more than the Chevy. I invested the money that was left from the BMW into the concessions trailer. Worst case scenario, you don't like it and I resell it. If that's the case, I'll easily get my money back."

"Wow," she whispered, her voice breathy. "I seriously don't know what to say, Ares. What if I don't win the competition and I can't pay you back? I don't have the money to buy a concessions trailer."

"I know, Cookie. I'm not asking you to pay me back. I look at this as an investment in what is now partly my business too. If you don't like this trailer, we can always clean it up and resell it for a profit. Then we can find one more to your liking."

Her laughter filled the garage, and she swiped at a tear as she took a step back. "As though I'm not going to like it, Ares. I've dreamed about this day for years. I should have known it would be you who would make it happen. I suppose we should actually look inside?"

I chuckled and grabbed her hand, bringing it to my lips to kiss. "I was thinking you would never ask," I said with the wink. "Watch your step. It's a bit of a tight fit here."

I should have known it would be you who would make it happen.

Her words echoed through my head as I led her to the side door of the trailer, lowered the metal stairs, and turned the knob. Did she want it to be me? It almost sounded like she expected me to be the one to make her dreams come true. Hope swirled in my belly. If she honestly believed that, then I was further ahead in my pursuit to regain her trust than I thought.

I helped her up into the surprisingly roomy interior where she did a full three-sixty with her mouth hanging open. "This is fantastic, Ares. It's like you took my vision and materialized it here."

"Well, we did talk about it the other night in detail. I started searching forums and was surprised by this trailer only a few minutes from Lake Pendle. It can be fully operational with very little work. I know that you don't want to think about doing large events for at least a year, but I see no reason why we can't start small with the farmers' market this summer. As a bonus, my new SUV can pull the trailer if the bakery van is unavailable."

"This is too much to take in," she whispered as she stopped and stared at the back wall. "It's got an oven!" She ran to it and pulled it open. "A convection oven!" She ran her hand along the stainless-steel countertop. "Wait, are these coolers under here?" She squatted to open one of them and squealed with delight. "This is perfect, Ares!"

She ran to me and jumped into my arms, nearly knocking me back into the sink, but I caught her and myself and held on tightly.

Holding her filled me with pure joy and happiness, something that had been missing from my life in the city.

"I'm beyond thrilled that you like it, Cookie Pie. I took a chance on it because it was so close to what we'd discussed. We can put together some ideas and add or subtract anything that doesn't work. It's easy to customize these, but we were lucky that the people selling this one hardly used it."

"It's more than I could hope for, Ares. We could use it just as it is without making any changes. At least for the first year while we learn what works and what doesn't work. I can't believe this."

Her voice held so much surprise, awe, and thankfulness that my heart squeezed hard inside my chest. It had been years since I'd felt anything but pain from that organ and Cookie Pearson was the one to make it beat again. I shouldn't be surprised. For me, it had always been her. Nothing made that more evident than when I missed her every second of every day for the last thirteen years.

"You deserve this, Cookie Pie," I whispered. "You have worked so damn hard to make The Fluffy Cupcake what it is today. Our moms gave you a strong and steady foundation, but you're the one who brought us up through the digital era and put us on the map. The same will be true with the cookie wagon. You'll break barriers and open new horizons for the bakery with it."

"It wasn't all me," she argued. "Without Athena and Rye, we wouldn't be where we are today."

That was an expected statement. She never took credit for her accomplishments, instead wanting to downplay her role in things.

"Athena and Rye contribute with their wonderful baked goods, there's no doubt, but they've told me themselves that you're the one who keeps challenging them to up their game. That's what a good leader does, and there's no doubt you are the leader at The Fluffy Cupcake." I finished the statement with a kiss to her soft temple.

I lowered her to the ground and she took a step back, smoothing her shirt down over her sweet hips. "That's because The Fluffy Cupcake is my life. I know you don't understand how I could invest so much of my time and energy into a family bakery in a small town, but I truly believe I'm building something for future generations." She dropped her gaze to the floor rather than hold mine, which I didn't like.

"Cookie," I said, taking her hand in mine. "I don't know why you think I don't understand your devotion to the bakery. That's just not true."

"I got the idea from you, Ares Halla," she spat. Her eyes flared bright for a moment before the light was extinguished and they went flat.

"How? When?" I asked, stepping closer to her so she couldn't turn and ignore my question.

"Wait, where are we going to keep this trailer when we aren't using it?" she asked, turning to face the door. "It's too new to leave it out in the snow all winter."

So that was the game we were going to play? Okay, I'd play it, for now, but soon she was going to tell me about my implied transgressions so I could fix them. I didn't want this animosity to continue to flare and cause problems at the bakery or in our new relationship, whatever that may look like. My mind took me right back to that kiss on her couch when she was soft under my lips. Her satisfied mewling said more than any words she had uttered since. She wanted me and I was going to have her, regardless of how long it took.

"I have a plan for that," I said, stepping around her to block her from exiting the trailer. "We'll keep it at my dad's when we aren't using it in the summer. The pontoon pad will be empty since his boat will be in the water, so that's free parking when we aren't using it. I think we can safely keep it going through October, but then we'll rent a storage unit for the winter months. Since it will be inside, we can use that time to do any repairs or improvements on it. I also have an appointment at Hot Rod Joe's Detailing to have the logo put on and any other decals we need. We're going to take it right to Joe's today, so you can talk to him yourself about what you want done. I don't want to reveal her to the public until she's dressed and ready."

"Wow, you really have thought of everything," she said, a smile firmly in place. "I'm impressed, Ares. Impressed and still slightly dumbfounded. I can't believe you spent your money on this to help the bakery."

"No, I bought the trailer for you. The bakery had nothing to do with it. Does it benefit the bakery in the long run? Absolutely. If you weren't there, would it even be a consideration? Absolutely not. This is your dream, Cookie Pie, and I just wanted to be a little part of it."

She stepped up to me and planted the palm of her hand on my chest. "If I haven't said thank you, consider this a thank you. I promise to make Cuckoo for Cookies profitable and pay you back every penny you spent on this beauty. If I win the competition, I'll pay you immediately."

I put my finger to her lips to quiet her. "No, Cookie, you don't understand. I don't want you to pay me back for the cookie wagon. This is a gift from me to you. If you win the competition, that money will go toward operating costs for the wagon. I don't have the kind of talent in my hands for baked goods that you do, so I'll never be able to contribute to the bakery in that sense. This here," I said, motioning around the space, "is an investment in you and my business. My new life. Do you understand?" My voice was a whisper now as I balanced my forehead on hers. She nodded her head rather than speak and I dropped my hand to her face, cupping her warm cheek. "You are so beautiful, Cookie."

"No, I—"

I silenced her with my thumb and then ran it across her soft lips. "I'm going to repeat that because I want you to hear me. You're beautiful, Cookie. All of you. Heart, mind, body, and soul. I missed you every moment of the last thirteen years, but when I drove into town almost three weeks ago and saw you standing there, all the turmoil inside me disappeared. You've always done that for me, and I knew right then I was home to stay."

"I just—I don't..."

"Shh, I know," I promised. "The same words run through my mind when we're together. There is so much history between us, Cookie. Just for today, as we stand here ready to embark on a new adventure together, can we focus on that and nothing else?"

"Just for today?" I nodded and she sighed. "Okay. Just for today."

"I'm going to kiss you, Cookie. Just for today, hoping maybe someday it will be every day."

She gazed up at me and what I saw in those giant blue eyes told me she wanted the same thing. I cradled my hand behind her head

Cookie

as I lowered my lips to hers. She was soft, warm, and smelled of fresh bread, summer air, and redemption. When she slipped her arms around my waist, and up my back, my heart thumped hard inside my chest. I was kissing my best friend, and she was kissing me back. If someone had told me coming back to Lake Pendle would bring Cookie back to me, I would have done it ten years ago. Hell, I probably would never have left. I had, though, and while that canyon of our lives still loomed between us, I hoped that today added strength to my bridge. The way she kissed me said I had done at least part of my job.

I pulled her closer to me and plastered her the length of me, not even ashamed of my body's reaction. I dropped one hand to her hip and ran my palm down and across her waist, tugging her even closer. Unable to resist, I slid my hand down her ass to squeeze her cheek, drawing a moan from her lips. I returned the moan, and I wasn't ashamed of that either. She was fire without knowing she held the flame. My body was burning for her, and while I had to settle for a kiss today, her soft moans told me *just today* could turn into tomorrow if I fanned the flames with trust and honesty.

"Ares," she moaned when my lips left hers to kiss their way to her ear. "What's happening to us?"

"I don't know," I whispered into her ear before I kissed it. "But I don't want today to end."

"Me either," she whispered right before I captured her lips again and worked to show her that if she could learn to trust me, tomorrow would be even better than today.

Twenty

"I'm here, Cookie," Rye called from the front of the bakery. Rather than have her join me in the back, I jogged to her.

"Hey," I said, flipping on just one light over a table near the bakery case.

She stopped short when she saw me. "You're not crying."

"Am I supposed to be?" I asked, motioning her over to the table.

"You sent an S.O.S. text. That usually means tears will be involved."

"Not this time," I said with a shrug. There were two pieces of carrot cake and two coffees at the table, and we sat to enjoy them. "That was a 'you aren't going to believe this' kind of S.O.S. but I needed to talk to you when a certain someone wasn't here."

"I see," she said, sipping the coffee. "It does seem like he's always here."

When I shrugged, it carried a heavy load of uncertainty where Ares was concerned. "Ares told me he likes to be here because it makes him feel alive. He feels like his life matters again."

"All because of some baked goods?"

"It might have something to do with the person behind the mixer, but he was sincere when he said it."

"How do you know for sure? You don't trust him, remember."

"I know for sure because he'd had his lips on mine just minutes before he said that."

"What?" she exclaimed, her voice far too loud.

"Shhhh," I ordered, putting my finger to my lips. "He's asleep in my apartment right now."

Her eyes widened and I waved my hands in denial before I could even get a word out from between my paralyzed lips. "Not like that," I promised, crossing my heart. "Aunt Amber had an episode today and afterward we hung out for the afternoon. Ares was tired but didn't want to return to his parent's house since he was trying to give them some time alone together. I told him he could sleep at my place. He swears he's coming down to bake tonight, but I hope he stays asleep. He's exhausted and the emotional stress of today really got to him."

"Mom told me they finally got to the bottom of her problem and they're working with Bishop to find a place where she'll feel safe. I feel terrible for Amber. I can't imagine living in that kind of fear all the time. I'm sure it's hard for Ares to see his mom like that."

"It is," I agreed, sipping my coffee. "I'm still glad that he was able to get to the bottom of it before something worse happened. Anyway, since I don't know if he will stay asleep, I wanted to talk to you before we started working, just in case."

"Can we circle back around to the part where he kissed you?" she asked, leaning in to whisper the question. "What the hell, Cookie? I thought you were mad at him!"

"I'm a weak woman," I said with a frown. "When he offered me comfort after the Blake incident, I took it."

"Why didn't you tell me sooner?"

"I thought it was a one-off type situation," I explained and when she lowered a brow at me, I sighed. "Okay, that's partly true but the main reason I didn't tell you was because I wondered if I'd dreamed it."

"Had you?"

"Nope. Ares kissed me again today."

Her mouth made an O and she opened and closed it a few times before she could force words out. "Twice?" she squeaked.

I nodded, biting back a grin. "It's a little hard for me to believe too, but there's more."

Her hand went to her chest, and she inhaled deeply. "I don't know if I can handle more."

"Then you better buckle up, buttercup," I said, not holding my smile back any longer. "But you can't tell anyone this just yet." I pointed sternly at her and she nodded. "He bought me a Cuckoo for Cookies wagon!"

Rye sat back in her seat as if she'd been slapped. For a moment, she fiddled with the processor on her right implant. "I'm sorry. I don't think this is working. I swear you said he bought a cookie wagon."

"He did," I said, opening my phone and showing her a picture of the trailer that I'd snapped as he was loading it. "It's perfect, Rye."

"I thought you were trying to buy a truck." Her question wasn't judgmental, just confused. "Don't get me wrong, that's a beautiful trailer, but I'm out of the loop about my own business."

I bit my lip. Part of me had already been worried that she and Athena would feel that way when we told them the news. Ares assured me his sister wouldn't care since she had nothing to do with the sweets side of the bakery, but I told him he needed to tell her immediately. He promised he'd do it tonight when she came in to bake, but I didn't want to drop this on Rye without warning while she was trying to work. She struggled to hear everything when the bakery was busy, so there was no way she would follow an important conversation and not burn the donuts.

"If it makes you feel any better, I had no idea he was doing it either. He sprung it on me this afternoon."

"I didn't think we had the money to buy anything yet."

"We don't," I agreed, "but the bakery didn't buy it, he did. He sold the BMW and got a Chevy SUV and the trailer. We had talked early last week about how a concessions trailer would get the job done without another motor to care for all winter long. I was still in the thinking phase on it, but when he came across this one, he snatched it up."

"What if you didn't like it?"

"When he showed me, the first thing he said was, if I didn't like it, he could resell it and he wouldn't feel bad. He didn't want to risk someone else buying the trailer, so he bought it immediately."

"More likely it was an ask forgiveness rather than ask permission type situation," she muttered.

"Could be," I agreed, "but he was so eager and sincere that I couldn't be mad at him. Besides, the trailer is beautiful and I could lift the awning and start selling without changing anything."

Cookie

"If you win the cookie competition you can pay him back then, I suppose."

"He won't let me," I said, taking a bite of the carrot cake.

"He won't let you?" she asked, as though she had to double check what I said.

I sipped my coffee and nodded. "Ares said if I win the competition, we'll put the money toward the wagon's operating expenses, but the initial price of the wagon is his seed money, so to say."

"In lieu of sweat equity." I couldn't tell if the sentence was meant to be factual or disdainful, so I forced myself not to get defensive.

"Essentially, yes, at least according to him. He understands that he doesn't have magic hands like the three of us do, but when he sees a good idea that will benefit the bakery, he wants to use the math to make it happen. The math added up this time, so he went for it."

"Do we get to vote on it?" she asked, poking at the carrot cake.

"I guess we can have an impromptu meeting to talk about it once Athena gets here," I said, but I was sure she could hear the confusion in my voice. "Are you going to vote no?"

"I'm going to vote that he doesn't do this again," she said, tapping the table. "We're the ones here making this business happen and I think he should come to us before he makes decisions that affect all of us. Doing it this way makes it feel underhanded."

I nodded with my lower lip between my teeth. To say I was surprised that Rye had any pushback was an understatement. "I'm sorry this upset you. I was worried you and Athena would feel left out. That said, the reason I accepted the wagon had nothing to do with the business."

"What other reason is there for a cookie wagon, Cookie?"

"A peace offering."

"Come again."

"It was a peace offering, Rye. That shifted how I felt about it when he said he bought the trailer for me, not the bakery."

"I don't follow," she admitted, but her shoulders had relaxed as we spoke.

"It was a gift from him to me of something I'd wanted for years. All the way back to when we were kids and building a cookie wagon out of Legos. He didn't present the trailer to me as, 'Look at this great investment I made in our business.' He presented it as, 'I had the opportunity to make your dream come true and I wanted to do that for you.' My voice cracked at the end and I ducked my head, fighting back the tears to keep them from falling.

"Hey," she said, standing and pulling me up into a hug. "I'm sorry if I made you sad. That wasn't what I wanted and now I feel like I ruined this for you."

"No," I said, sitting back down. "You didn't ruin it for me. I was just explaining it to you and the truth kind of hit me full force. Ares was thinking about me when he bought the trailer, not the bakery. That's…" I made the mind blown motion and swiped at a tear with my shoulder. "I haven't had time to process it fully, I guess."

"From what I can see, that says a lot about his mindset as well," Rye said, squeezing my hand. "He's here to stay and wants to make things right between you."

"He kissed me again today after I accepted his gift," I said with a nod. "It was like he was desperate for my forgiveness."

"Have you forgiven him?" she asked, letting go of my hand to grab her fork.

"I don't know the answer to that, Rye. I wish I did, but I really don't. Do I want to forgive him? Yes, but I don't know if I can."

"Because?"

I tossed my hand up and let it fall to my lap. "I still don't know why he did what he did?"

"That was a question and not a statement. I assume you didn't talk about it before the kiss?"

"He kissed me," I said, sitting up and pointing at her. "I didn't stop it because, if nothing else, I'd always have that moment to remember. "I'm so confused."

She knelt in front of me and put her hands on my knees. "I know you are, and I think it's good." I lifted a brow, and she smiled. "He's bringing you back to life and making you question the things you were so certain were true just a month ago. Right?"

Cookie

I nodded, swallowing around the lump in my throat that had lodged there when I realized how true her words were. "It's like the last two decades just washed away and we're best friends again. We want to spend all of our time together doing what we love. I can't define it better than that right now."

"That's okay," she promised. "You have all the time in the world to work out your feelings for him and sort out the past. Take it one day at a time. He's here to stay. You don't have to rush it."

I nodded, my chest lightening a bit at the idea. "You're right. I need time to let go of my preconceived notions of what working with Ares would be like and open myself to my current reality. Maybe that will make it easier, in the long run, to talk to him about what happened in high school."

She patted my knees. "I think you're on the right track. We don't need to vote on the wagon, either. You know I would never do anything to keep that dream from coming true."

"That's because you're the best friend a girl could ask for—"

A knock on the bakery door startled us both. Rye turned and jumped up at the same time I did. Standing outside the door waving at us was Ben Lanstrom.

"What does he want?" Rye asked as she checked her watch. "It's nearly nine."

I walked to the door and unlocked it, pulling it open. "Ben, is something wrong?"

"No," he said, jamming his hands in his pockets. "I just wanted to talk to you about something, so when I saw the lights were on, I thought I'd knock. If now isn't a good time, I totally get it. I can come back when you're open."

I stepped back and motioned him in. Ben ran the bank, so I wasn't too worried about letting him into my business after hours. Besides, he knew better than anyone that my left hook wasn't to be messed with in any manner.

Ben walked inside and nervously waved at my best friend. "Hey, Rye. I hope you're doing good now. I heard you weren't feeling well."

"Who'd you hear that from?" I asked, pushing off the door and walking over to the table. "Cake?" I asked him, but he waved the suggestion away.

"Ares stopped in the bank the other day and mentioned that he'd worked overnight as the world's worst donut fryer."

I couldn't help but laugh. "He's not the world's worst, but he's no Rye Pearson."

"Wait, Pearson?" Ben asked, glancing between us.

"My sister may be slightly ahead of the game in changing my name, but Brady and Haylee are adopting me."

"Rye, that's wonderful!" Ben exclaimed. "I mean, they've always been your parents, and we all knew that, but now it will be official."

Rye nodded, but looked away as her cheeks heated. "I'm very lucky to have them."

"I heard you also own part of the bakery now. I think that's great. You deserve it. You've worked hard since high school."

"Thanks," Rye said, still not making eye contact. That was surprising since she often needed to read lips to make sure what she heard was correct.

"Ben," I jumped in to save her. "You had a question?"

"Yes, right," he said, addressing me without taking his eyes off Rye. "It was about donuts for the bank."

"Well, sure, I can take a special order for you, when do you need them by?"

He waved his hand and finally turned his attention to me. "Not a special order. An always order." That sentence lifted Rye's head immediately.

"An always order?"

"When you dropped the donuts off at the bank a few weeks ago, our customers were thrilled. We thought maybe it would be good to have some pastries, donuts, or cookies there with coffee for customers. I was hoping if we had a regular order schedule that we'd get a little break and it would help us both out. Our customers would be happy and people who haven't tried your baked goods before, will be over here immediately upon first taste."

"Not a bad idea," Rye said with a nod. "But maybe you should pick a few days rather than every day. That way, the customers will look forward to it."

"That's a great idea," Ben agreed.

Cookie

"You know what," I said, grabbing a piece of cake from the case and switching it out with mine at the table. "Rye is our donut and pastry expert, so she's the girl you want to talk to about this. I'm confident the two of you can come up with a plan. I have to get to work."

I started backing toward the back of the bakery and Rye motioned me forward "Cookie, I'll need your input on this," she said between clenched teeth.

"You actually don't, Rye. You're an owner now," I reminded her. "You make the call."

"Did you know you would own part of the bakery?" I heard Ben ask as I ducked into the back of the bakery with a sly smile on my face.

Twenty-One

The knock on the door startled me until I heard the voice on the other side. "It's Ares, Cookie Pie."

I jogged to my door and pulled it open to the man that I had spent way too much time thinking about lately. He was usually my last thought at night and my first thought in the morning. Today was different, though. Today, I only had one thing on my mind. Cookie Pies.

"Hi," he said while his eyes ate me up from top to bottom. "How are you?" He stepped inside and closed the door.

"Nervous," I answered with terrified laughter. "I shouldn't be this nervous, right?"

"Nerves are good. Nerves mean you care about what you're about to do. You don't need to be nervous, though. You're a baking queen. No one can come close to what you can do with cookie dough."

"You are good for my ego, Ares Halla."

He grinned and walked me backward until my back hit the wall. "But wait, there's more," he said with desire in his eyes. "You look sexy as hell in this outfit."

I glanced down at myself. "Ares, it's just my chef's coat and pants. I wear it every night at the bakery."

"I know," he agreed, licking his lips. "It turns me on every single night."

I lifted a brow and it drew a dirty laugh from his lips. "You don't get out much, do you?"

"Cookie Pie, I lived in the city and went to events every week with beautiful women in beautiful gowns on my arm. I wasn't interested in any of them."

Cookie

I slipped my hand up his face to cup his cheek. "What happened to you in the city, Ares?"

He lowered his lips toward mine and whispered *nothing* right before they landed on mine. His were warm and tasted sweet, as though he'd been downstairs sampling my wares. His hands slid down across my waist to settle on my hips, which ripped a moan from his throat. I parted my lips and he dug in deeper, his tongue like silk as he slid it in to tangle with mine. Another moan filled my head as he rested his tongue alongside mine to cuddle for a moment.

My experience with this man was limited when it came to kissing him, but today, I knew he was kissing me because he wanted to. He yearned to. The things he said weren't to flatter me or inflate my ego. He said them because he believed them. That was Ares Halla in a nutshell. He'd been that way since he was a tiny boy. He was empathetic, warm, engaging, gregarious, and honest to a fault. That was the part that surprised me about his constant dodging when I've asked about his time in the city. Something happened there that stole some of that empathy, warmth, and honesty. That truth had settled deep inside my soul to fester. The past had tainted my view of him for years, but having him back, engaging with him, working with him and teaching him, had slowly pushed those memories to the back as we made new ones together. That spot deep inside me that festered was also the place where my pain was buried. That told me we both had to be honest with each other if we truly wanted to be more than frenemies turned friends. He hadn't come right out and said he wanted to be more than friends, but the way he kissed me said it without words.

I slipped my hands up his chest to hold his shirt just as his hands slid down over my ass. He cupped my cheeks and the moan that left his lips filled the entire room in a way that sent white hot fire to my center, turning it to liquid. When he pressed himself to me, I was sure he wanted to be more than friends. He was long, hard, and apparently not ashamed of his reaction to my body.

"Cookie," he moaned, his lips kissing their way to my ear. "You don't know how I've longed to have my hands on you." Said hands split apart and one cupped my ass while the other encircled my back and pulled me into a hug.

168

We were both breathing heavily against the other's shoulder when I turned my lips against his ear. "Is that a baguette in your pants or are you just happy to see me."

"Oh, Cookie Pie, I'm ecstatic to see you."

"You mean that's the real you?"

"Every inch," he whispered into my ear, stealing a nip against my earlobe before he kissed away the sting. "That's what this chef's coat does to me, Cookie Pie. Or rather, that's what the woman wearing it does to me. I've had a few fantasies of you wearing nothing but that coat when I walk into work."

"I'm not sure I'm capable of handling every inch of you, Ares Halla."

His naughty laughter filled my heart and made it pound hard against my chest. Just thinking about being in bed with him usually did that to me, but today, there was more behind it. There was an emotion filling me that had been missing for too long when it came to him. "I'm positive you have everything you need to handle me, Cookie. Unfortunately, we don't have time for me to prove it."

I blew out a breath and waited for my heart to stop pounding before I spoke. "You didn't answer my question, though, Ares."

The way his brows pulled down into a V told me he thought he'd gotten away with distracting me only to learn he hadn't. "I don't want to talk about it, Cookie. Especially not today." He lifted my hand to his lips and brushed a kiss across my knuckles. "Please understand."

I slid my other hand into his hair and left it there, enjoying the feel of his silky locks against my skin. "I understand that whatever happened must have hurt you deeply, right?" It took him a full fifteen seconds of gazing into my eyes before he nodded. "I understand that makes it hard to talk about, right?" This time, his nod was immediate. "Then you must understand why we have to talk about it." He gave one nod followed by a tip of his head, as though he couldn't decide. "We have enough on our plate today, but soon, you're going to tell me the truth, right?"

He brought his lips close to mine again before he answered. "Just as soon as you tell me the truth, right?"

"Agreed," I answered, which clearly brought his thought process to a stop as he pulled back to meet my gaze.

Cookie

"Agreed?"

I nodded and tipped my head the same way he had. "It won't be easy for either of us, but until it's been said, we can't move anywhere."

"You always were the smartest of the two of us," he said, his lips kissing mine in a short peck.

"That's not true, Ares. I'm just tired of this festering wound inside my soul that I can't soothe or heal. While talking about everything will make it bleed, I can hope that it also starts a healing process. It's been too many years of turmoil to let it continue."

"Thirteen to be exact," he whispered and I nodded once, biting my lip to keep it from trembling. "That's my fault. I don't know why, but I want to fix it. As I stand here today, Cookie, if I can fix it, I will."

"For the first time in a decade, I actually believe you," I whispered, accepting the gentle kiss he placed on my lips.

"I want to stand here forever with you, but we can't, can we?"

With a heavy sigh, I stepped out of his arms and shook my head. "Nope, we can't. It's time for Cookie Pies."

"You're ready, though. You're going to wow the judges regardless of whether you win or not. No one can resist these cookies. While you slept, Rye and I loaded the bakery van and everything is ready for our trip across town."

"Our trip? You're coming with me and Rye?"

He tipped his head side to side. "More like I am Rye."

"You are Rye? Are you speaking English?"

"I'm going to be your assistant, not Rye," he clarified.

I held up my finger, lowered it and raised it again. "I need a baker's assistant, Ares, not a finance man."

He wrapped his fingers around mine and lowered our hands. "I know you do, and I'm ready to be your assistant. Not only did we create this cookie together when we were kids, but I've been with you every step of the way the last two weeks. I've got this down. You can trust me."

"What about Rye?" I asked, still unsure who was making decisions behind my back.

170

"She wants to be there, but she's nervous about being your assistant. She's afraid she'll miss a cue or not hear you ask for something."

"Then she should have come to me and talked to me about it," I said, pointing at myself and taking a step back. "This is a team and we're supposed to discuss everything together."

"I know," he said, holding his hands out to calm me. "I only found out because she asked Athena if she'd do it instead, but Athena has an order she can't miss. Athena told me about it, so I talked to Rye."

"That doesn't explain why she didn't talk to me, Ares."

"She worships you, Cookie, and she doesn't want to let you down. If I hadn't volunteered, she would have done it, but she was already a nervous wreck just loading the truck, so I don't know how much help she would have been once you were there. I don't know for sure, but I feel like something is going on with her hearing that she either doesn't want to admit or is afraid to address."

I rubbed my temple, closing my eyes for a moment to focus on Rye. "I agree with you. She can't seem to run her processors for long periods of time anymore and even when she has them on, she's reading our lips more and more. When this competition is over, I'll go over to my parent's house and we'll have a talk. Something is going on, but I know Rye, and she doesn't want to miss work or—"

"Screw up the business with her disability," he said, which snapped my gaze to his immediately. "Don't get worked up. Those were her words, not mine. When I told her that wasn't possible, she just scoffed at me."

"Okay, I need to talk to her. Is she downstairs?"

"She's double-checking the van to make sure we didn't forget anything."

I looked him up and down before I nodded. "While I'm talking to her, you'd better suit up, bakery boy," I said, grabbing my bag off the chair.

"Bakery boy?" he asked, tickling my side as we walked to the door.

"You look sexy as hell in Calvin Kleins and cashmere, but you'd be a bit out of place wearing them at a baking competition."

"Maybe we could use that to our advantage," he pondered as we walked down the stairs to the bakery. "I could throw the rest of the bakers off their game and you're guaranteed a win."

"If I win, it's going to be because my cookie is irresistible, not my baker's assistant."

"You're saying I'm irresistible," he quipped. "I like it."

"Wow, I think I'd better drive my car to the competition." I paused with my hand on the door knob to the bakery.

"Why? We're taking the van."

"True, but if you and your ego is in it, there won't be room for these hips, and this ass," I said, smacking a cheek before I turned the knob and walked into the bakery floating on his laughter.

"How are you feeling?" I asked my co-pilot as we pulled away from the bakery and headed for the high school where the competition was being held. At first, I thought it was strange that a leader in the cooking industry, with its own channel, magazine, and cookbook publications, would hold a cookie competition in Lake Pendle. My dad was able to shed light on the situation. He explained that they wanted a small-town feel to draw in viewers who loved nothing more. The district had just redone the family and consumer education room last year, so the setup was what they needed to make it work. They'd had enough interest to hold two rounds of baking for the first phase of the competition. The first round was happening now, while those of us in the second round arrived and checked in. The judges would then decide on the top three cookies, and those bakers would be brought in to do some question-and-answer interviews and a speed round. Cookie would have to create a cookie with unknown ingredients quickly. It would be a long day, but I had no doubt my girl would knock it out of the park.

My girl? That voice asked.

My gaze flicked to her for a moment and then back to the road. Yeah. If I do things right, she could be my girl. Of that I was finally sure.

"I'm trying to put everything else out of my mind and focus just on the competition. I'm glad I got to talk to Rye, though. Sometimes, I forget that I see her as Wonder Woman instead of human. I should have asked if she wanted to be my assistant. Instead, I didn't give her a choice, and that's on me. I hope I smoothed it over with her."

"I don't think it was a matter of smoothing," I said, turning left toward the school.

"It was more a matter of listening," she finished and I nodded. "Funny how she can't hear, but does a better job of listening than I do."

"It was nice of her to take your shift tonight, so you didn't have to bake all day and go in tonight, though."

"For sure," she agreed, leaning her head against the headrest. "I'm tired just thinking about what's ahead of us, but it will be worth it if I win this competition."

"Hometown school. Hometown girl. You've got it in the bag," I promised, squeezing her shoulder. "In fact, open that." I pointed at the file folder on the console.

She opened the folder and pulled out a poster, her gaze sweeping it. "Ares, what is this?"

"It's a poster for the Tenth Annual Lake Pendle Days next weekend."

"Why does it say the Cuckoo for Cookies Wagon will be there?"

"See that empty spot there?" I asked, motioning at the top of the poster while I slowed for the entry to the school. "We'll put a picture of the wagon there, but only a bit of the trailer will peek out in the image to tease the viewer."

She waved her hand in the air. "Ares, we don't have the cookie wagon ready, nor do we have it stocked. And here, it says, p.s. There will be Cookie Pies!"

Cookie

"We will and there will be," I said, biting my cheek to keep from laughing.

"Is the wagon done being detailed?"

"It will be tomorrow," I said with a grin. "I got the call from Joe this morning. That gives us the week to prep it and fill it. Easy peasy."

"Easy peasy for you to say!" she exclaimed, dropping the paper to her lap. "I mean, sure, we already have to make the cookies for our booth, but to get the whole thing ready to go might be biting off more than we can chew."

"We have help in the form of your parents."

"But they don't know about the cookie wagon. You didn't tell them, did you?"

"Nope," I promised, backing the van into a parking spot and putting it into park. "I asked them if they had time to help me with a secret project this week. They were onboard immediately."

"But your dad's party is the night before, and I have to make all the cakes and goodies for that and attend it. I just don't see how this is going to work, Ares." She was flustered and I couldn't figure out why.

"Cookie Pie, what's going on here? We already have a booth there that day and have started prepping for it. I know you're going to be busy, which is why we'll help load the wagon as you get the cookies ready. I'm not asking you to do this alone." She leaned back against the seat and let out a breath, her chin falling to her chest until I tipped it up with my finger. It only took one look into her eyes to know what the problem was. "Hey, what are you scared of?"

"It being a flop? That people will think it's dumb? That it's not successful and you'll have wasted a whole lot of money on a dumb idea."

I put my finger to her lips to stop her. "Cookie, I don't waste money on dumb ideas. I'm kind of known for making wise investments and that's what I did here. It will not be a flop, people will not think it's dumb, and it will be incredibly successful."

"How do you know?" she asked, desperation in her voice.

"Because it will be filled with your cookies, which everyone already loves, and you, which again, everyone already loves." I wanted to tell her at that moment how I felt about her, too, but I couldn't do it when we had the whole day of competition ahead of us. I couldn't blow her concentration that way.

Cookie glanced down at the poster again and finally gave a nod. "Okay, but I want to be there when my parents find out about the wagon. My mom was always my biggest cheerleader when it came to making it happen."

I leaned forward and kissed her on the nose. "I know, which is why we're going to pick it up tomorrow at two and drive it over to their house, parking smack dab in the front of Athena's. Since your mom is on one corner and mine is on the other, it's the perfect reveal to everyone."

"Plus, your mom can come out and see it without too much work," she said with a soft smile. I gave her a wink and she tucked the poster back in the folder. "I'll do it, on one condition."

"Name it."

"I get final say on the posters that go up and whether there will be Cookie Pies or not."

"But, Cookie—"

She hushed me with her finger the same way I'd hushed her. "Ares, listen to me. What's about to happen is a lot for any pastry chef to undertake. It's hours of standing around filled with nerves, and having to flip your customer service mode on and off. If the cookie doesn't do well, I may need some distance from it before I start serving it to the public."

"I'll agree only because I know they're going to rock the judges' socks, and anyone else who tries them. Are you ready to prove me correct?"

When her laughter filled the van, I couldn't help but smile. "There you are with that ego again, Mr. Halla."

"No ego. Only confidence in the beautiful woman in front of me. You underestimate yourself all the time and I'm determined to be the one to teach you how to accept the accolades you so well deserve. Now, Baker Pearson, are you ready to bake?"

"I am," she said with a head nod, "I just need one thing first."

"Anything you need, I'll get you. That's what a good assistant does."

"Well then assistant, I need a good luck kiss."

Cookie

"Now that I can do with my eyes closed," I promised, lowering my lips to hers and offering a good luck kiss that would stick with her until late into the night.

"You got this," Ares said as I gazed at the pile of ingredients before me.

We'd been baking for hours, and I had no idea where he got his unwavering confidence in me, but I was never more grateful. When my Raspberry Chocolate Truffle Cookie Pie made it into the top three, he grinned like the Cheshire Cat and blew me a kiss. His happiness brought a smile to my lips more than landing in the top three did. I was still grateful to be in the running, but having his respect was all I needed. And I had his respect. I could feel it in every move he'd made during the competition. He was calculated, calm, and precise, which I wasn't expecting when he said he'd be my assistant. I expected the competition to be cumbersome from constantly explaining what I needed from him.

Instead, we worked together the same way we did at the bakery. He often anticipated what I'd need before I asked for it, and kept me smiling with a running commentary of stories from the good old days. I missed those days, but I was also enjoying this new Ares Halla. You often hear the expression that someone is 'all in.' That defined this new Ares to a T. He was all in on the bakery, and if I was reading him correctly, he was all in on me too.

"Premade cookie dough," I sighed. "First of all, that shouldn't exist, but now I actually have to make a cookie with it?"

"If anyone can do it, it's you, Cookie Pie. Head in the game," he said, pushing the rest of the ingredients toward me. "You've also got a jar of cherries, a stick of butter, mixed white and chocolate chips, and oatmeal."

"I have to use all the ingredients," I said, worrying my lip between my teeth for a moment. "I've got it!" I exclaimed, much to the delight of the cameraman whom I had forgotten existed. I was surprised, and thankful, at how easy it was to lose myself in the baking even with all the hoopla going on around me. It made the day much easier to deal with when I could focus on my work and not the cameras.

I pulled the mixer over toward me. "I need you to drain the cherries, but reserve the juice. Dry the cherries and chop them asap."

"Yes, Chef," Ares said, swiping the jar from the table and moving over to the prep station. I dumped the cookie dough and oatmeal into the mixer and started it, patiently waiting for the oatmeal to disappear into the dough. It was slightly dry, so I added a bit of warm water. Ares slid me the measuring cup with the cherry juice and I poured some in, eyeballing the dough until it was the consistency and color I wanted. In went the chips to mix while I waited for my Halla sexy assistant to finish with the cherries. I snorted at my own joke, a grin breaking out on my face as I prepared a pan with parchment paper. It was hard not to notice that the other two teams were still looking at their ingredients when I dumped the chopped cherries in and let them spin. I let it mix just enough to work them in before I shut the mixer off.

"What about the butter?" he asked as I started to scoop the cookies onto the parchment paper.

"Oh, right," I said, almost forgetting the final touch. "I need it melted."

He swiped it and stuck it in the microwave, waiting impatiently with his hand on the door until it was ready. I finished making perfect balls of dough, grateful that there were only twelve, and grabbed a pastry brush from my toolkit. After a quick brush with butter, I slid the cookies into the oven and closed the door.

"How long on the timer, Chef?"

"I have no idea," I muttered out the side of my lip. "You start the clean-up, and I'll watch the cookies."

"Yes, Chef," he said, throwing me a wink as he turned to clean up the workspace, more than likely preening for the camera as he did so.

Cookie

Was I bothered that my giant hips and ass were facing the camera the entire time I stood at the oven watching the cookies melt into delicious globs of chocolate and cherry? Yes, but not bothered enough to take my attention off the cookies. I would have to pull them out at just the right moment. They needed to retain their pink coloring and still have a cake-like texture inside. The butter was a long shot, and I could have worked it into the batter, but I was banking on the melted butter on the outside being one of the first flavors the judge tasted rather than the preservative flavor of a premade cookie dough. A lot was riding on this, and not just the prize money. Mine and my bakery's reputation were also on the line here. Hell, my town's reputation was on the line as I watched the edges of the cookies start to firm up under the oven's heat.

My mouth watered as I anticipated what the cookie would taste like. Would it be the best it could be using premade cookie dough? Absolutely not, but I wanted it to have potential because a double cherry chocolate chip cookie would be a great addition to the bakery case when fresh cherries were in season. I grabbed a hot pad, swung the doors open, pulled the pan out, and slid it onto a cooling rack.

"Ares," I called and he was by my side in a second.

"Yes, Chef?"

"I need these off the pan, so they stop baking. I'm going to grab the paper while you slide the pan out of the way of the rack. It's hot, so use a pad."

He grabbed a towel and gripped the edges of the pan, then nodded. I lifted the paper, glad I had placed the cookies evenly across the sheet, so moving them this way didn't crack them. Ares moved the pan to cool on the other workbench while I grabbed a plate to prepare. I'd saved a few cherries and chips to use as garnish on the plate, and once it was ready, I motioned Ares over.

"Everyone else has barely started their cookies and ours are done. What's wrong with us?"

His laughter was low and sexy as hell, which made my belly do a weird flop. "Just the opposite, dear girl, what's wrong with them?" he asked with a wink.

"We have to try a cookie and make sure they don't taste like hell."

"What exactly does hell taste like?" he asked, as the camera moved around the back to get our faces. Great, now even if the cookies were terrible, we'd have to pretend they were great.

"It tastes like premade cookie dough." A shudder went through me and he bit back laughter when he noticed the camera.

"No time like the present." He picked up a cookie and took a bite, his eyes popping open as he chewed before he motioned for me to try one.

I lifted the still-warm cookie off the sheet and broke it in half slowly, watching the melted chocolate pull away from the chunks of cherry in a delicious scene of gooey goodness. "Make a note that chocolate chunks would be a better chocolate to use than chips," I said, and with a final prayer to the heavens, I took a bite, letting it sit on my tongue for a moment before I chewed. Blessed be the bakers! The butter trick had worked. The cookie was soft, rich, and perfectly sweet.

After I swallowed, I turned to Ares and gave him a wink. "That'll do. Let's plate it."

Ares carried the plate over and I arranged five cookies around the garnish then took the plate from him. I had every intention of getting these to the judges before they cooled too much since I had no idea if they'd lose their cakelike texture and turn into hard bricks when completely cooled.

"You've got this, baby," he whispered as I walked toward the judges.

He was right, I did and it was because of him that I calmly set the plate down on the table in front of some of the most talented pastry chefs in the nation and took a step back. The camera was on me now and I swallowed, nerves kicking in as we hit the last few moments of the competition. "The Fluffy Cupcake Heavenly Cherry Bites for your enjoyment, Chefs."

"Your presentation is lovely, Chef Pearson."

"Thank you, Chef, but I'm just a baker. I'm not a chef."

"Your qualifications say otherwise. You are a master baker and certified pastry chef."

"I suppose that is true," I agreed, uncomfortable with the conversation. "But those certifications came along as I learned the

179

Cookie

bakery business from the ground up so I could run my family's one day, no other reason. I'm proud to wear the title of Baker Pearson."

"Are you?" Chef Hodges asked from the end of the table. "Running the bakery, that is."

I rocked up on my toes once. "As of three weeks ago," I answered.

"If those cookies taste as good as they look, I suspect I know why. You've done the assignment in record time, so kudos to you and your team."

"Well, cookies are my specialty."

Chef Mac lifted a cookie off the plate and inspected it before taking a bite. He may have tried to maintain a neutral facial expression, but I noticed his eyes dilated slightly, and he tightened his grip on the cookie. "I see why," he said after he swallowed. "Thank you, Baker Pearson. You may return to your workspace to await the verdict."

"Thank you, Chefs, for a well-run and respectful competition," I said before I turned back to Ares at our station.

"I think I messed that up," I muttered out the side of my lip once I was next to him.

"Impossible. You had them eating out of the palm of your hand, and look," he whispered in my ear, motioning toward the table. "Your cookies are already gone. Relax now. You've done your best and that's all you can do."

He gently massaged my shoulders in solidarity as team two carried their cookies to the judges' table. This would be over in less than an hour, and the winning cookie would be announced. In the meantime, all we could do was wait.

Twenty-Two

"Alright, teams, the judges have reached a decision," the producer said from the front of the room. "As you know the show is airing tomorrow night, so no one outside of this room can know who won the competition, nor can you advertise your cookie, until tomorrow night after the program airs. For this take, we'll announce the winner and wrap up the show. Directly after we finish shooting, we'll give you all the information you'll need for advertising as a Cookie Heaven participant. We ask that the winner remain here for a short time after we wrap to record an after the show interview. You can, of course, keep your Cookie Heaven coats. Any questions?"

We all shook our heads no, but I noticed Cookie grimace at the mention of a recorded interview. She claims to be awkward and not good on camera, but I watched one she did earlier today and she's dead wrong. She's honest and graceful in the way she talks about her skills as a baker, so much so that she puts the interviewer at ease too. She's confident, but not cocky, and consistently engages with the interviewer in a way others never seem to. She's well-spoken, articulate, and knowledgeable about the topics when asked. Maybe it's her lack of ego that allows that to happen. All of that said, when it comes to life in general, I've seen that her self-confidence hasn't improved since I left Lake Pendle. If anything, it's gotten worse to the point she doesn't even date.

She can claim whatever she wants, but I know her recent spell of dating was nothing more than a ploy to make me jealous and show me I have no control over her life. I already knew that, and I don't want control over her life. I want to be part of it. When I left the city, it was to find something in life that I could depend on. I thought it would be The Fluffy Cupcake, and it was, but only because this beautiful, intelligent, funny, sassy, sexy woman

Cookie

standing next to me *is* The Fluffy Cupcake. To say I was surprised and grateful that she'd given me a second chance was an understatement, and I had no plans to blow it.

"Everyone please, take your mark. We're ready in three, two..." He backed away and motioned at the host to open the show again.

I slipped my hand into Cookie's and squeezed it gently. Silent encouragement as we waited for Nadia, the show's host, to finish with her explanation of the final cookies for the audience at home. When they got to the Cookie Pies, the camera zoomed in on the cookies for a moment before it panned back to us. I tried to take a step to the side, but Cookie held me in place with my hand gripped tightly in hers.

"The judges are extremely impressed with the talent here tonight," Nadia said, motioning at the three teams. "But everyone knows only one baker can claim the title of Cookie Heaven Champion, so let's get to it!" Nadia lifted an envelope in the air. "Inside this envelope is the name of the baker who has brought their best cookie to the table tonight." She tore open the envelope with dramatic anticipation and glanced at the name before raising her head again. "With a well-rounded display of cookie brilliance, the winner of this Cookie Heaven competition is a hometown girl who stunned the judges with her gluten-free entry. Congratulations, Baker Cookie Pearson of The Fluffy Cupcake!"

"You did it!" I exclaimed as Cookie turned toward me, her expression holding utter confusion. "You did it! You won!"

"We did it!" she whispered right before she threw her arms around me. "We did it!"

The room erupted in applause and I hugged her to me, the sweet scent of cherries still on her skin. "I knew you could do it, Cookie Pie. I'm so proud of you. Go get your kudos."

When Cookie leaned back, she had the brightest smile on her face. I hadn't seen that smile in thirteen years, but tonight, it was all I could see. It sucked me in and held me there as she patted my face once and then walked to the front of the room to stand next to Nadia.

"It is with great pleasure that I present you with the Cookie Heaven white knot champion chef coat," Nadia said, holding out the

182

coat in one hand. "There are only a handful of these jackets in existence, and your entry was such a modern day take on an old classic that you deserve to wear this for life."

Cookie unbuttoned her red competition jacket and stripped it from her shoulders so Nadia could help her on with the new coat. Once it was buttoned, Nadia bent down and picked up a giant cardboard check.

"While the coat is a trophy to wear proudly, we can't forget the grand prize! Your Raspberry Chocolate Truffle Cookie Pies have earned you twenty thousand dollars!" She handed Cookie the giant check and her hands shook as she held it in front of her for the cameras to span. "Do you have plans for the prize money? A trip to the Bahamas maybe?"

Cookie chuckled and shook her head. "I'll be using the money for a new project I'm launching at our bakery," she said into the microphone Nadia held for her.

"I hope it involves those Cookie Pies, because they are delicious!" Nadia said with a grin.

"It does," Cookie agreed, her smile shy but bright. "I plan to start a program to employ foster kids and teach them job skills for their future."

"Wow," Nadia said, taking a step back. "I'd love to hear more about that, but we're almost out of time." She turned to face the camera. "Stay tuned after this episode for an after the show interview with Baker Pearson to learn more about her plans! But, for now, The Lake Pendle Cookie Heaven Bake-Off is coming to a close, so remember," she inhaled deeply, a cue for all of us to join in with her.

"A cookie a day keeps the doctor away!" We said in unison and then broke into applause until the producer yelled that we were out.

Cookie hugged Nadia one last time and then collected her things, before running back to me and launching herself into my arms. She said nothing, she just hugged me while I swung her back and forth.

"I'm so damn proud of you, Cookie Pearson," I whispered into her ear as the teams around us started to pack up. "Thank you for letting me be here today to share it with you."

"It had to be you," she whispered. "Because it's always been you."

"Cookie? We're ready for the interview," the producer called before I could respond.

I let her go and watched her walk away from me, but all I could hear were her parting words. *It's always been you.*

Good or bad, Cookie Pearson, it's always been you too.

"I knew you'd win," he said, still wearing the same silly grin he'd had on his face for hours.

"Maybe, but I still feel awkward about it."

"Because?"

"I own a bakery!" I exclaimed, nearly sloshing my wine out the side of my glass.

"So? Some of the other contestants you were up against were pastry chefs at five-star restaurants. What you own or what your education is, doesn't matter. What matters is talent, knowledge, the ability to think on your feet, roll with the punches and get back up every time. That's what you did today."

"I'll admit that I enjoyed the speed round at the end. I love coming up with things on the fly and discovering a new recipe that everyone loves. I will be recreating the cherry chip cookies for the cookie wagon."

"Cookie Pies and Heavenly Cherry Bites are on the menu!" he exclaimed before he took a bite of pizza.

"Great name, right?" I asked, as I tucked my leg under my ass and grabbed another piece of pizza.

"It's the perfect name. You came up with the recipe on Cookie Heaven, they're cherry, and everyone wants to take a bite."

I snorted as I chewed, but tipped my head in agreement. "We'll promo them as the cookie that sealed the deal on Cookie Heaven. We can't go wrong with that kind of free advertising."

He beamed as he took another bite of pizza. It was as though being accepted into the business and having input came as a surprise to him every time. Part of me felt a bit bad about that, considering I was the one who didn't welcome him home with open arms. In my defense, I had no idea how much he'd changed and how much he cared about The Fluffy Cupcake.

"The Modern Goat's caramelized pineapple and bacon pizza should be illegal in all fifty states," I said, biting into the slice. The flavors melded on my tongue and mixed with the wine, which went right to my head. "This is the reason my hips are the size they are. The cookies explain my ass," I said as I chewed. "Don't care tonight, though."

"You shouldn't care any night," Ares said from where he sat in the chair across from me. "You worked all day baking and doing interviews with nothing to eat but premade cookie dough. Premade cookie dough!" he exclaimed, his hands to his cheeks. "Please stop putting yourself down, Cookie. You are a beautiful woman and your hips and ass only add to the beauty that makes you, you."

"I come by it naturally," I said as a lame cop out.

"Your mother, I know." His eye roll told me that he remembered how much I used those five words as a defense all through school. "You're a grown woman now and clearly, despite all your wishing, you didn't outgrow those hips and ass. Not surprising, considering it's called genetics, but I know in high school you wished you could."

I shrugged and dropped the last of the pizza slice back on the plate. "We all have things we'd like to change about ourselves."

"That's true," he agreed, "things like patience, honesty, and kindness. Not something you have no control over."

"But I have control. I just have to eat less pizza and cookies."

"I know for a fact you don't eat that many cookies and you work out every day, so the question remains, have you accepted that this is how you're built and you're not going to change that by dieting or exercising."

185

Cookie

"I know," I said, sloshing back some more wine. My gaze drifted to the white and red coats slung over the hangers by the door. "I still can't believe I won a coveted Cookie Heaven Chef's coat. It's mindboggling."

"I can," he said, relaxing in the chair with his wine. "You nailed every aspect of that competition from the planning stage to the final interview. Speaking of that final interview, you took me by surprise."

He was referring to the one where I spoke about using the prize money to start an initiative that hires foster kids to train at the bakery.

"It's been a dream of mine for a long time." My shrug was supposed to say I didn't want to talk about it, but he didn't appear to get that memo.

"I didn't see mention of it anywhere in the plans for the bakery."

"Probably because I didn't include it. It was one of those dreams I figured would happen fifteen or twenty years from now when I was old and looking for young recruits to keep the bakery going after I retired."

"You don't think your kids will want the business?"

My laughter was loud and sarcastic, which surprised both of us. "Ares, you're assuming I'm going to have children. Look at my dating record thus far."

"I can't say I'm familiar with it," he answered.

"Then let me tell you this titillating story! Don't worry, it won't take long." I noticed my words slurred a bit, but I didn't care. More wine, please! I refilled my glass and then leaned back again. "After we graduated, I went to St. Paul for some baking classes. I dated a couple of guys off and on there until I met Chance. He was a great guy, and we were together for about nine months, but I knew it would never work out."

"Why is that?" he asked, moving over to sit next to me and rest his hand on my knee.

"Well, one, he wasn't you. And two, he loved the city and his family owned a business there. When he finished college, he had a job waiting for him."

"So did you, here."

186

"Exactly," I said, giving him a finger gun. "It was bad enough I had to be in the city three days a week for school, I was never moving there for good."

"What happened when that ended?"

"We broke up in May and I didn't date much after that as I concentrated on the business. I'll admit to a few one night stands here and there when I was in the city for certifications but nothing more serious than a few dates and a good time in the sack. Once I hit twenty-four and had all my certs, I left the dating scene. It was a lost cause in Lake Pendle anyway."

"Until recently," he added, but not as a dig, more as a matter-of-fact statement.

"Which, ironically, continues to prove my point about dating in Lake Pendle."

"Then let me ask you a question. What did Chance and your one-night stands think about your hips and ass."

"They never had a problem with them to my knowledge."

He pointed at me. "Then why do you?"

"Probably because I didn't care about Chance or my one-night-stands." I pondered the question for a moment. "Since I didn't plan to commit to them, their opinion didn't matter."

"That," he said, leaning forward and setting his glass on the table. "Their opinion didn't matter. The only person's opinion that matters is yours. When you carry yourself as a sexy, independent, smart woman like you did today, everyone else sees you that way too."

"The only person's opinion I ever cared about was yours, Ares." I slapped my hand over my mouth. "Oh, crap, did I just say that?" I muttered through my fingers. "Too much wine, Cookie. Too much wine," I moaned.

Ares took my hand in his and brought it to his lips to kiss. "Why did my opinion matter, Cookie Pie?"

"It just did," I answered lamely. "What about you?" I asked to save my soul from dying of embarrassment. "You must have had a few lady friends in the city."

He dropped my hand as his relaxed and fun-loving nature became tense and dark. He stared over my shoulder at the kitchen door and shook his head. "None worth talking about."

Cookie

"I don't believe you," I pushed back. "Something happened in the city, Ares. I'm not obtuse."

"You want to know what happened? I'll tell you what happened." He inhaled a deep breath and then shook his head. "No, I won't. I never want you to know what happened in the city, Cookie. That's my burden to bear alone."

"It doesn't have to be, though. What are you afraid of? That I'm going to laugh? Because I'm not going to laugh."

"Laughing would be the best possible reaction," he answered, leaning away from me. He'd put a wall up and the fighter in me wanted to claw it down brick by brick. "Losing all faith in me is likely what would happen along with thinking I'm a fool."

"We all make mistakes, Ares. That doesn't mean it's a life sentence."

"It feels like it is," he whispered, grabbing his wine glass and slugging it back. "My parents and Athena know what happened, but I don't want everybody to know."

"I'm not everybody." I leaned forward and stuck my finger in his chest. "I'm your friend and I don't judge."

He tipped his head to the side and sighed. I was hoping he could see I wasn't going to let this go, so he may as well tell me. When he started to speak, I knew he had. "To begin with, I knew leaving Lake Pendle was a mistake the first year I was in the city, but I needed an education, so I planned to stick it out and then move back when college was over."

"But you didn't."

"I didn't get the chance. In my senior year we all did internships at finance companies. I was working for a company that showed promising potential for someone looking to make a career in finance. I decided I would work a few years in the city, get the experience I needed, and then move back and open my own firm."

"You didn't do that either."

"Nope." He shook his head. "I really don't want to talk about this." He lifted his head and met my gaze to show me just how much he was struggling to tell me about that time.

"It's okay," I promised, taking his hand in mine and rubbing my thumb over his knuckles. "I can tell whatever happened was difficult. You don't have to talk about it for us to be friends."

188

"What if I want us to be more than friends?" he asked, pulling me closer to him.

"You still don't have to tell me until you're confident that you can trust me with the information."

He was silent then, gazing into my eyes for the longest time until his breathing evened out and the color returned to his cheeks. "I was young, a small-town boy, and not wise about the corporate world," he started and I put my finger to his lips.

"You don't have to tell me."

"Your words reminded me that I have to start trusting people again and if there's one person I've always trusted without thought or reason, it's you, Cookie Pie. You've always been my safe place."

"Still am," I promised, smoothing a lock of hair back from his forehead. "Whether you tell me or not."

"I'm not proud of what happened, at least not the beginning and middle parts. The ending redeemed me some, but I have a long way to go in coming to terms with what happened."

"Because you think you're a bad person?"

"Kind of," he said with a nod. "Everyone tells me I'm not, but everyone's opinion doesn't matter. Only one person's opinion matters to me."

"Mine?" I asked with a raised brow and he nodded.

"That's why I never tried too hard to find you on the rare occasion I came home. Facing you was out of the question with what was going on in the city. Long story short, I got a job with that finance company when I graduated. The boss was ten years older than me, and pursued me until I finally gave in and started dating her. The age gap didn't bother her, but it bothered me. It just felt wrong, but I was in too deep by then. Once she convinced me to take our relationship to a physical level, not long after, she started sending me fake investment forms."

"Did you know they were fake?"

"No, I had zero idea that they weren't real. There was no way I could have known that unless she told me, which she didn't. For years I made money hand over fist, lived in a beautiful apartment paid for by the company, and I had a beautiful woman on my arm and in my bed. Every minute of those years felt wrong. I felt wrong. That man wasn't me, and finally, two years ago, I woke up. I

189

Cookie

realized my soul felt hollow because Julianna was using me. I didn't know why, but I could see that our relationship was physical and nothing more. At that point, I decided to return to Lake Pendle for a clean break from her and the business."

"That didn't happen?"

"Ha," he said, but the sound was overflowing with sarcasm. "No, that didn't happen. As soon as I tried to break it off and give my notice, Julianna clued me in on how many illegal money marketing accounts were opened by my hand and the embezzling that was keeping a roof over my head. Unsure what to do, I came back to Lake Pendle and talked to my dad."

"Who immediately told you that you did know the right thing to do."

He pointed at me with a nod. "I did. I had to report it, even if I got tangled up in it, and I did."

"You must have gotten untangled."

"I did, after spending a year working there as a whistleblower. Once I got the evidence the state needed, they shut the company down and arrested Julianna. I was cleared of any wrongdoing. I got another job working for a grocery chain in their finance department, but I was persona non grata. My reputation preceded me and there was little I could do to change that. By then I was beyond ashamed, depressed, and hopeless. Ending it all sounded like a great idea, so I tried."

My gasp was much louder than I expected when I grabbed his wrist. "Ares, oh, my God. Why didn't Aunt Amber tell me about this? I would have been there for you, angry or not."

"I made them swear to tell no one, not even your parents. Athena knew, but she's good at keeping secrets. Anyway, my dad didn't like the way I behaved on the phone with him and he was convinced I needed help. They drove into the city and found me in my bed with a belly full of pills and Jack Daniels. I woke up two days later in the hospital with a raging headache and a new psychiatrist."

"How are you now?" I asked, grasping his hands in mine with desperation. "Are you taking your medication? Am I working you too hard?"

Katie Mettner

He put his finger to my lips. "I didn't need medication. I needed to talk to someone who was neutral so I could work through the issues surrounding Julianna and the legal case. I needed someone who wasn't going to be disappointed or proud of me. My therapist helped me see that I could make a new life back here in Lake Pendle because ultimately, that's what I'd wanted all along. I drove home with the intent to tell my parents that I had quit my job and was going to move back and open a firm, when they told me they wanted to retire."

"Do you want to open your own firm?"

"I thought I did, until I started working at The Fluffy Cupcake. The last few weeks have given me clarity in a way I never expected. I'm good at numbers, but I want my work to mean something and for it to build something bigger than me in an honest and pure way. That's what The Fluffy Cupcake does. That's what you do, but I always knew that would be the case. The other thing my therapist told me was that I needed to be honest with myself and you, regardless of the outcome, before I could truly build a new life."

"Be honest with me? About what happened in the city?"

"No, honest about how I feel," he said, and I noticed his Adams apple bob in a show of nerves.

"I'm confused."

He sighed, but finally met my gaze. "She told me it was time to be honest with myself about how I feel about you and then to be equally as honest with you. I took the first step the other night when I talked to Uncle Brady and I told him how much I care about you."

"You told my father that you care about me?"

"Are you going to repeat everything I say?" His laughter was nervous and it wiped away some of the fuzziness from the wine.

"I'm sorry, but I'm confused why you would talk to my dad before you talked to me."

"Then let me clear it up for you. I told your dad that I've loved you probably since before we were born and certainly for as long as I can remember."

"Loved," I said, nodding to keep from crying. "So that's past tense. But you still care about me a lot?"

"I thought I was over you, Cookie Pearson. Then I saw you standing there by the cookie wagon and all of those years of longing

191

that I'd buried rose to the surface instantly. Time and distance didn't make the love go away, it just let me pretend I could live without you for the rest of my life. Today, when I was standing there watching you put on that white coat, I thought my chest would explode with pride for the woman I have loved all my life. I've spent every minute you'll allow with you these last few weeks for the simple reason that I'm in love with you, Cookie. I know there's a lot between us, but I don't want my feelings for you to be one of them."

My hands shook and my lip trembled as I gazed at the man I had loved all my life. Even if we love each other, after everything that's happened, how can we ever be together? I opened my mouth to speak but all that came out was a sob. Embarrassed, I stood and ran for the bathroom, slamming the door and leaning my full weight against it. He loves me but we can never be together. On a sob, I hung my head over the toilet and relieved myself of all the pain, guilt, and heartache dealt to me by the man who now claims to love me.

Where do I go from here?

Twenty-Three

It was dark and cool in the room when I awoke with distorted memories of the last few hours. How did I end up in bed? Better question, who was in it with me?

I turned my head and came face-to-face with Ares.

"Hi," he said, smoothing a piece of hair off my forehead. "How are you feeling?"

"How did I get here?"

"I carried you in when I found you passed out on the bathroom floor."

"You carried me? Did you hurt yourself?"

"Cookie," he said and his voice held a warning tone.

"I don't remember passing out."

"I'm pretty sure the combination of sobbing and vomiting made it happen. I wasn't expecting that reaction the first time I said I love you to a woman."

"First time?"

"Of course," he said, trailing his finger down my cheek. "I've only ever loved one woman in this life. I'm looking at her."

"You never told Julianna you loved her?"

"Nope," he said, his P popping hard. "There was only one woman who would hear those words from my lips or no woman would."

"It was overwhelming to hear you say those words when I had dreamed about it for so many years. I've always loved you, Ares Halla. Despite not wanting to, I've loved you for the last thirteen years. Even when I was mad. Even when I was sad, but the tears tonight were also bittersweet. They were all the *what could have beens* and *what can't be now*."

"What can't be now, Cookie Pie?"

"Us," I replied. "How do we be us when so much has happened?"

"We just start," he said, his thumb caressing my cheek as he gazed into my eyes. "We just start, Cookie. We start trusting each other. We start believing in each other. We start believing in us. We start believing in what we can be. We start and we see where it takes us."

"I feel like we started the day you walked up to me at the farmers' market in your sexy Halla jeans."

A smile lifted his lips. "You think my jeans are sexy?"

"Well, don't be getting a big head about it," I said on an eye roll. "All I'm saying is, you can still pull it off. Maybe better than high school even. You've...matured."

He propped his elbow on the bed and winked at me. "In more ways than you know."

"Oh, I know," I said, my mouth suddenly dry. "I felt your maturity when we kissed this morning. The size of your baguette makes it impossible for it to be incognito."

His laughter was low and dirty and made my stomach tip sideways. "I can assure you with absolute certainty that my baguette has never been that hard from just a kiss before. The only time my baguette is that hard is when I'm in bed thinking about you, Cookie."

"You think about me like...that?" The idea that he fantasized about me the same way I did him was powerful if true.

"Yes." His wink was sexy in the darkness as he took my hand. He brushed a kiss across my knuckles and held it to his chest. "My therapist said I had to tell you everything, so this is me telling you everything. I've never finished inside a woman before. I physically and mentally can't. The only way I can come is to think about you with my hand wrapped around my," he paused to smirk for a moment. "My baguette, the way I wanted yours to be."

"Never?" I asked in shock and he shook his head. "That probably should have been a waving red flag for you, Ares," I whispered.

"I got good at pretending," he said with a shrug. "This last year, all I had to do was remember you in your bathing suit at the lake the summer we were sixteen, and this happened." He lowered my hand to the front of his jeans so I could cup his fullness. "Then I imagine you under the water with your lips around me. I pull you up and lower you down over my dick so you can take the pain away. I come every time."

I ran my hand up the length of him until he hissed and thrust against my hand. "Whenever I use Mr. Twisty, I remember you the summer we were sixteen, shirtless in the lake with your arms stretched wide waiting for me to jump into them."

"Mr. Twisty?"

"An apt name," I said, giving him a nonchalant shrug to mirror his.

"Show me," he demanded with a growl.

I cocked a brow. "Why?"

"I want to see what has taken my place all these years. Show me."

As though I had no control over my motions, I opened the drawer next to the bed and pulled out the braided vibrator. He rolled it on his palm before he turned it on, the buzz of the motor quiet but powerful.

"I bet this feels good," he said before turning it off.

"So good," I agreed. "Best one I've ever had."

"If I have my way, it will be relegated to that drawer and only come out when we want to play."

Was this actually happening or was this a dream? I felt awake and aware, but maybe I was still asleep on the bathroom floor, passed out cold from the wine. I pinched my leg. It hurt, which meant I was awake and this man was in my bed, holding my vibrator, and telling me about his masturbation fantasies. If I didn't get out of here, I was going to jump his bones like the sex-starved woman I am.

Would that be a bad thing? That's all you've ever wanted, a little voice said.

It would be a bad thing to let him into my heart and my bed before we clear the air about what happened when he left town after high school.

Does it matter anymore? You can see how much he's changed and he told you earlier that he knew he made a mistake when he left. Will having the answer to that question change how you feel

about today's Ares? Are you going to hold the actions of a kid
against the man he is now?

Gazing into his eyes, I didn't know what the correct answer was. He loved me, but was that enough? Did anything else matter?

"I'm not the boy I used to be, Cookie Pie."

"I know," I whispered, wondering if he could read my mind. "I'm just scared of doing something I can't take back."

"Like what?" he asked, stroking my cheek with his thumb. "I love you, and don't want you to feel scared about anything."

"Don't you see?" I asked, lifting my gaze to his. "If this doesn't work out, I will lose you as my best friend again."

His lips were on mine before I finished the last word. He drew me toward him, plastering my body the length of his and holding the back of my head possessively. When he broke the kiss for a breath, he held my gaze. "I'm never going anywhere again, Cookie. Lake Pendle is my home. The Fluffy Cupcake is my home. You are my home. The only way this doesn't work out is because you decide you no longer want me. I've been yours for thirty years. I wish it hadn't taken me so long to realize it, but I will do anything within my power to make sure you understand that I want you. I want you, Cookie Pearson, and no one else. To be clear, I'm not pressuring you into doing anything tonight. I'm just trying to be completely clear about my intentions."

"Your baguette says otherwise," I tried to joke, but my voice was a little too squeaky for him to believe.

"Maybe, but that's my problem, not yours. I can head to the bathroom and take care of things the same way I have for years."

"I just pictured that," I moaned, my voice husky with need. "Is it weird that I would love to watch?"

"Weird? No. My dream come true? Absofuckinglutely, baby," he hissed. "I don't think I've ever been this hard before. Normally, it takes a long time for me to get even a little bit hard."

"Because you're so big?"

His laughter was lazy, relaxed, and dirty before he spoke. "I'm not that big, Cookie."

"Listen, I don't have a lot of experience with dicks, but the ones I've seen were nothing like yours."

"You haven't even seen mine."

Katie Mettner

"It's my business to judge the size of things when swollen, Ares. I don't need to see it to know."

His snort was amused when he lowered his lips to my forehead. "I love you, Cookie. Do you know how amazing it feels to say that after all these years? Knowing that you love me makes it sweeter each time I say it. I can wait for our relationship to be in a place of trust before we make love, but to be clear. We will make love."

"I want to," I admitted, lifting my gaze to meet his. "I want to, but I don't want to lose you again, Ares. The last time almost killed me, and we hadn't even shared a physical relationship. I won't survive another round."

"I know you're afraid, and that's my fault. I'll spend the rest of my life making up for it, Cookie, because I can't live the way I lived the last thirteen years either. The first time I saw you, my chest unlocked and I could finally breathe. I can't go back to being locked up with every breath I take. I can't go back to a life without you by my side."

"You love me."

"So much, baby. So much I will wait until eternity for you."

"I don't want to wait," I whispered. "Waiting opens a chance that we'll never find ourselves here again."

"Waiting also gives you time to trust that we'll be here again, baby."

He was right. Waiting gave me time to know for sure that he had changed. Then again, he told my father he loved me.

"What did my dad say when you told him you loved me?"

His thumb stroked my lips as he smiled. "I asked him if I had his permission to date you. He said I did for one reason. He remembered being a thirty-year-old man in love with a woman and desperate to be with her. He also said they've known all along that we belong together, but I better not hurt you again or he will find me and kill me."

One side of my lips tipped up. "That sounds like him. I'm surprised he didn't kick you out of the house, much less give his permission."

"He knows, baby," Ares whispered, scooting closer and tangling his legs in mine. "He knows we deserve a chance."

Cookie

You have two choices here, Cookie, that voice said. *You can let fear and anger control you and maybe lose out on something extraordinary or you can let the past go and take a chance on the one thing you've always wanted. Ares.*

The voice was right. People change and that changes the situation by default. I've changed. I'm no longer the person I was in high school, for the better, I hope. Doesn't Ares deserve that same grace to grow and change for the better?

The answer was clear as I gazed into his eyes. We had both changed, which was why we found our way back to each other. The things he went through in the city challenged his morals. Was he the kind of guy that let money and prestige keep him from doing the right thing? No. He did the right thing, even when it blew up in his face and nearly took his life. He did the right thing and came home to find a new life in a place that always protected him with love. I could do the same.

"Make love to me, Ares. We deserve a chance at happiness and I'm not throwing it away tonight. Tonight, I'm yours."

His lips attacked mine in a fury of passion, love, and need that told me I had made the right decision. He pulled me close and gently slid his leg up to rest against me. With his tongue in my mouth, I thrust against his leg, which earned me a moan to fill my heart to overflowing.

"You have too many clothes on, Cookie," he whispered. "I need to see you."

With his words, I froze. If I took my clothes off, Ares Halla would see all of me in the flesh. There was no hiding behind my baggy bakery pants and coat or a hoodie two sizes too big. If I took my clothes off, he was going to see it all, and then what—

"Stop," he commanded. "I know what you're thinking."

"Now you're a mind reader too?" It was hard to miss the tension in my voice despite trying to cover it with smartaleckness.

"I don't need to read your mind, Cookie. I know you that well. You realized I would see you all when I stripped your clothes off. Then there'd be no hiding those hips or ass." He got off the bed and straightened me out on it before I could say anything. "Let me assure you right now." He slipped his hands under my sweatshirt and pulled it over my head, my tank top following in the next

Katie Mettner

breath. A heavy puff of air escaped his lips when my breasts fell free to his gaze. "You are a fucking goddess, and by the time I'm done here, you'll understand that to the depths of your soul. You take my fucking breath away, Cookie. Lay back."

I did what he said without even second-guessing it. The look in his eye told me he meant every word he said. I was a goddess to him and had no right to tell him otherwise. Especially when I could see the truth straining against his pants. "I don't know if that zipper will hold you in much longer. Maybe you should let it free."

"Don't worry about my zipper. I'll let it down when the time is right. Now, you still have too many clothes on."

He slipped his fingers under my waistband and I grasped one of his hands. "Fair warning, I'm not wearing any panties."

His growl was accompanied by the ripping of my pants as he tore them off me in one motion, the material flying over his head while his eyes were nowhere but on me. He fisted his hands at his side, opening and closing them a few times as he licked his lips, raking my body with his gaze. "I want your hips in my hands and my lips on your breasts."

"Why aren't they?" I asked, scooting up closer to the pillows. "I don't see any other man in the room ready to devour me."

"There will never be any other man," he hissed. "I am the only man who will ever touch you like this again. Do you understand me?"

I could tell he wanted an answer, so I nodded. "That's going to be up to you, Ares. I'm not going anywhere."

"Neither am I," he assured me as his other knee compressed the mattress. "Except to heaven with you. I want to memorize every inch of you, but I have no willpower when it comes to you, Cookie."

"Why wait?" I asked, confusion clear in my tone. "Aren't we here for that very reason?"

"We are, but there is only one first time. The first time I touch you, the first time I suckle you, the first time I make you crumb. There is only one first time."

"Make me crumb?" I asked, grasping my lip between my teeth for a moment. "Did you just make a bakery joke, Ares?"

Cookie

"No," he assured me, his hands coming to rest at my knees as his eyes closed. "You, my dear Cookie, are going to crumb frequently and loudly. Understand me?"

"I'll do my best," I promised, a brow raised.

"As will I." He ran his hands up my thighs to sit in the place of honor at my hips. He moaned louder this time as he massaged my skin before he ran his hands under me to grasp my ass and lift it into the air a few inches. "My fantasies never came close to the real Cookie."

His words ended when he grasped a nipple in his mouth, his hand massaging the other with tenderness. He knelt on the right side of me and his hand slid down my belly to rub in a circle while he worshipped both breasts with the utmost care. I arched upward, pushing my nipple deeper, moaning when he suckled it hard and then dropped it, letting the cool night air peak it once again.

"This belly," he moaned, his lips kissing their way from my breasts to my navel. "I knew it would be soft, but I wasn't expecting the sweet way it would lead me right to your cookie center."

"It's kind of big, I know," I whispered, suddenly self-conscious enough to cover my breasts.

"Absolutely not," he said, removing my arm from my chest and resting his cheek on my stomach. "It's perfect because you're a..."

He waited and I realized he wanted me to finish the sentence. "Fucking goddess?"

"That's right. Don't forget it."

"I don't think you'll let me," I whispered as he flipped around to kneel in front of me.

"Not for the rest of my life." He slid his hands up the inside of my legs to my thighs where he slowly pushed them apart. "Oh yes, open those legs for me, baby. You have no idea how long I've dreamed about seeing you open and ready for me."

"How do you know I'm ready for you? That's a little cocky, don't you think?"

He lowered himself to his butt and slipped his finger down my opening, his moan loud as it bounced around the room. "Fuck, Cookie, that's how I know," he said, before he brought his finger to his lips and tasted me. "Now that's a cookie I could eat for the rest of my life."

He kissed his way up my thigh from my knee, feathering puffs of air along the trail until he reached my center. With a final puff of air, he buried his nose between my lips and swiped his tongue the length of me. It was my turn to fill the room with a moan as he didn't let up. He kissed, suckled, and teased until my hips were in the air and my cookie was pressed tight to his face.

"Ares," I cried with desperation. "Please, I want you inside me."

"No," he said without lifting his head. "You're going to crumb many times tonight, and this is the first. Relax and give yourself to me," he cooed, lulling me into an orgasm with little effort.

With his tongue still on me, he inserted Mr. Twisty and turned it on low. "Oh my God," I cried, my legs starting to shake as the orgasm built. "Ares, oh, God, Ares," I whimpered.

"I love you, Cookie," he mumbled from between my legs right before he shifted Mr. Twisty and sucked my bud into his mouth.

"I'm coming," I cried, my body spasming from the power of his touch.

"That's it, baby," he encouraged as he moaned against my center. "I've longed to hear you come apart under me, sweetheart."

As I floated back down to earth, that sentence hit me in the heart. He really did love me. This was real. I just had my first orgasm á la Ares Halla. He shifted back to my side and gathered me in his arms, wiping away a tear.

"Why are you crying? Did I hurt you?"

"No," I whispered, resting my head on his chest. "You healed me, Ares."

Twenty-Four

I healed her. What she saw as a sacrifice by me was actually just the opposite and I had to make her understand that. "You healed me, sweet Cookie. You trusted me with your body and that," I said, kissing her knuckles, "tells me this is real and we've finally found the right path."

"I sure hope so," she said, her fingers going to the buttons on my shirt. "Because I want to see you in the real. Fair is fair."

I leaned down and kissed her, letting her taste herself on my lips. "Taste that," I hissed. "That should tell you how damn much I enjoyed eating your cookie until it crumbed on my tongue. That will happen again tonight."

"Not until I get these clothes off you," she said, struggling with the bottom button.

"Lay back," I ordered, waiting until she was spread eagle on the bed, then I shucked my shirt and unhooked my belt. "Just so you know, I'm clean. I was tested before I left the city."

"Me too," she said, her gaze enraptured by my bare chest. "You have chest hair now. I love it."

I chuckled and leaned in, allowing her to bury her hands in it for a moment. "It never grew in high school, but the day I hit eighteen, there it was. I love how my chest feels with your hands against it. It just feels so light."

"Mine too," she whispered, offering me a genuine Cookie smile that I didn't see often. "I haven't felt this free since you left me here alone. If I had known that being with you was all I needed, I would have stopped at nothing to find you."

"I wish you had, but wishes and would haves get us nowhere. Connecting with each other like this, admitting our feelings, and trusting our hearts will move us forward."

"Let's move forward then," she said, a tilt to her lips. "I'm ready for those pants to come off."

"Now that's a wish I can grant," I promised, standing and shucking my jeans, then lowering my boxers until I stood before her naked and proud. I grasped my dick and rubbed it, anything to offer a little pleasure with the pain.

"Ares," she said, scooting backward. "I knew you were big, but that's not a baguette you're holding. That's more like a Vienna loaf."

After biting back laughter, I shook my head. "I'm not that big," I assured her, crawling onto the bed. "Maybe a few inches longer than average, but I promise we'll go slow and you are in control at all times. I won't hurt you."

Her nod was tentative, but her grasp of my Vienna loaf was not. I sucked in a breath the moment her warm hand wrapped around me. The moan that tore from my lips released more than just pent-up sexual frustration. It released all the years that felt wrong because we were apart.

"Does that feel good?" she asked, doing it again until a spot of moisture sat at my tip. "I want you to feel good."

"Good doesn't begin to explain it," I said, thrusting against her hand. "I'm unsure if I'm in your bedroom or in heaven, but I want to stay here forever."

She lowered her head and ran her tongue down the length of me and back to my tip, where she stole the moisture with her tongue. "This is why I had to come first, right?"

"Smart girl," I hissed as she sucked me in between her lips and gently ran her teeth around the edge of my head. "I had to be sure I wouldn't hurt you." She sucked hard and I nearly came right there in her mouth. "Cookie," I cried, grabbing her chin. "Stop or I'll come."

She lifted her head to make eye contact. "You said you've never come in a woman before, so I want to give you the same pleasure you gave me."

"Sweetheart, I have wanted to be inside you for as long as I've known what that meant. That is pleasure I've yearned for and you're not taking it away from me. Hang on. I have to grab a condom from my jeans."

Cookie

Cookie held my arm. "I don't want anything between us, Ares. There's been enough of that in our lives. I want to feel every inch of you knowing it's only you."

"But…"

"I'm on the pill and we're protected. Trust me?"

I growled nonsense as I laid her down under me and kissed her until we both were desperate for air. "I do trust you, Cookie. We were written in the stars and nothing will change that. I love you."

"I love you, too," she whispered, brushing hair off my forehead. "I'll never get tired of hearing you say that, Ares."

"I'll never get tired of saying it," I promised, putting my lips back on hers to tease her into a kiss. She dropped her jaw and my tongue strolled in, distracting her while I lined myself up with her heat and waited at her entrance. Her eyes came open when she felt my tip against her and I kissed each eyelid before I spoke. "I'm going to go slow. You're so wet we don't need to worry about lube."

"That's what you do to me, Ares. Every time," she moaned, her gaze flicking to Mr. Twisty discarded on the bed, which is where he would stay.

"Tell me to stop if you need me to," I said and she nodded as I pushed forward, giving her just the first few inches.

Her eyes widened and she grabbed my face, instigating a kiss that was so hot I was afraid I would burn up under her lips. "More," she said, wiggling her ass to take more of me.

I pushed forward a bit, afraid to go too far and bring her pain. Having a large dick was not what it was cracked up to be. Most women weren't built for something this size.

Then I felt it, her legs wrapped around my waist and she used her heels to push me forward, taking all the control. I loved nothing more than an independent woman who knows what she wants, so I wasn't going to argue with her, but damn, how did I get so lucky? When she stopped, I stopped and waited.

"Are you okay? I don't want to hurt you."

"Lift my hips," she hissed and I did as she ordered, grasping her ass and lifting her a few inches. "Like that?"

Katie Mettner

Without answering, she shoved a pillow in the hole I'd created and then I lowered her back to the bed. "Now I'm okay," she moaned. "Fuck me, Ares. I need all of you in all of me."

She didn't have to tell me twice. I pulled out and pushed back in slowly. The sensation, no longer dulled by a condom, came to life against my skin and when I pushed forward and dropped deeper yet, it dragged a moan from her lips as well.

"Does that feel good?" I asked, drawing out and thrusting back in gently, being sure not to hit her anywhere too sensitive.

"So fucking good," she moaned, her head rolling on the bed. "I never knew it was supposed to feel like this, Ares."

"Me either," I assured her, sliding my cock back out and in again. "I never want this to end but I don't know if I can hold back at the same time."

"Stop holding back," she whispered. "We've waited a long time for this, take me to the moon, Ares."

My hips bucked at the thought and I leaned down, capturing her lips as I thrust into her, our moans of pleasure filling the room to capacity until I lost control of the rhythm and cried her name. "Cookie! I'm going to come. Oh, God, I'm going to come, baby," I cried, nothing in the universe making sense to me other than her.

Her hips shifted and her legs fell open, leaving herself at my mercy as I pumped in and out of her. "Come with me, Ares," she called, her voice already in a far-off place as that first wave rippled over my cock. Never had I ever experienced sex like this in my life. Her pleasure only drove me higher, our cries of pain and pleasure melding together as she spasmed around me and called my name.

"Ares!" It was reverent, incredulous and so filled with love that I couldn't deny it if I'd tried.

"I'm going to come, Cookie," I moaned, stilling inside her, buried as deep as I dared without hurting her. She arched, taking me that half inch deeper to rest against her soul and that acceptance swept me up into an orgasm I couldn't stop. "Oh my God," I cried, burying my head against her breast as I spasmed inside her. When I was spent and couldn't hold myself up a second longer, a shudder racked me.

"Come here," she said, wrapping her arms and legs around me to keep us joined. "I love you," she whispered, kissing my temple.

"Thank you for showing me what I've been missing all these years."

"I should be thanking you," I said when my breath returned. "I'm thirty and that was the first time I've ever come while making love. I didn't know it could be like this, Cookie."

"It couldn't be until we were together. That was the conclusion I came to when you sank inside me and we fit together like puzzle pieces. These hips that I've hated all my life exist to hold you, Ares Halla. Knowing that, I wouldn't change a thing about them now."

"Yes," I sighed, kissing her lips as I rolled off her and pulled the wedge out from under her so she was more comfortable. "You are perfect for me, Cookie Pearson. I will never be the same after tonight. The way we fit together." I paused and buried my face in her neck, kissing and suckling without leaving a mark.

"It's like we were meant to be," she finished, her hand running up and down my chest. "We fit like we are meant to be."

A shudder went through me at her words because she was right. We were meant to be. "From this day forward, I will do everything in my power to be worthy of you, Cookie Pearson."

She slid her hand up my cheek and cupped it, kissing my lips gently. "You already are, Ares, or we wouldn't be here. I just had to trust the truth I knew about you. I hesitated on the most important second chance of my life, but I'm glad I offered it without anger or expectations or we wouldn't be here right now."

"It was April third last year that I got a second chance at life, but this will be the date I remember as the true start of my new life."

She captured my lips again and as I rolled down across her, my hand massaging her soft breast, I could see our future in her eyes. I loved every second of it.

Twenty-Five

"You haven't stopped smiling all day. And it's not the kind of smile that says you won a huge kitty at a baking competition," Athena said. "It's the smile of a woman well loved."

"I have no idea what you're talking about." I emphasized the words while I tried to wipe the stupid smile off my face. It had been there all day despite the issues I'd dealt with since we got up.

Ares and I had no sooner fallen asleep after several rounds of lovemaking when my phone rang. The Hobart mixer had gone down and Athena wouldn't finish her orders if we didn't do something about it. Since no one knew Ares was at my place, he also got a phone call for help. We made a plan to arrive separately through different doors in the time it would take each of us to get to the bakery if we were alone in our beds at home. I thought we'd pulled it off, until now.

"Funny thing about that because my brother is wearing that same grin. I'm not saying you were together last night but I'm saying you were together last night. Great job on splitting your arrival times, BTW."

Did she just say BTW out loud? Lord, what do I say now?

"Ares was at my place but only because we got back from the competition so late. We're just friends, Athena."

"Uh-huh, okay. You can stick with that story, but I have eyes. That said, he is handy to have around, right? Who knew he could fix a mixer?"

"Not me," I said with a relieved shrug. "But I do remember him taking shop classes in high school."

"I'm glad he remembered how to fix wires or I would have been screwed."

"I'm still having the Hobart repair guy come out and rewire it on the up and up. I'll also have him check it over and repair anything else. The problem is, that mixer isn't made for some of the heavy bread doughs we make now."

"I agree, but you work with what you have, right?"

"For now," I said with a nod. "But I'm going to have a discussion with the finance guy about the equipment fund and what's available for use. It's time to get you a big girl mixer."

"A big girl mixer?"

"They make Hobart mixers that can handle the dough you make. A new mixer would benefit you in multiple ways, but mostly in time. It will be faster and you won't have to wait for one of us to finish a mix with the other two. The two we have will last much longer if they aren't being abused by heavy dough, too."

"Fair, but the kind of mixer you're talking about must be pricey."

"It is, but there is financing available, which is something we can talk about once I know what Ares thinks we can spare on it. For now, I'm just glad this one is working again, but we need to be kind to the old guy until I can get the repair man in." It was past time to get Athena a mixer that could hold up to her heavy dough. If I had to use my winnings from Cookie Heaven to do it, I would. I could always use the sales money from the Cookie Pies to start my new initiative.

"You got it boss," she said, turning in her chair to face me. "Now, what are you doing at my house a mere two hours before your watch party for Cookie Heaven. You know," she leaned in to whisper the following sentence. "If you tell me who won, I won't tell anyone in the next two hours."

I pretended to zip my lips and throw away the key. "You know I would love to tell you, but rules are rules. To answer your other question, I'm here because Ares is set to arrive soon with the cookie wagon for everyone to check out!"

"Seriously?" she asked, nearly jumping out of her seat. "I've been dying to see it finished! Is it beautiful? Tell me it's beautiful!"

"I haven't seen it, to be honest. At least not since he showed me the first time. He wanted to surprise me too, which is why he made me stay here while he went to get it. We decided we'd show all of you this afternoon and then I'm going to load it up and we'll take it to the watch party so everyone can enjoy cookies while they watch."

"That's such a great idea! What a perfect time for its maiden voyage. I'm happy to help cover so you can work the crowd."

"Thanks, Athena, that would be great. At least it's only a ninety-minute show. I don't think I'll last much longer than that without falling asleep on my feet."

"That will happen when you're in bed the entire night but not sleeping." She bit her lip, likely to stem laughter.

"You're hilarious. I'll have you know yesterday was an extremely stressful day between baking, interviewing, and standing around waiting for something to happen. Your brother made quite the baker's assistant, though. He followed orders well and even made sure I had food and drink during the breaks, so I could perform at my top level."

"I can't tell you the change we've seen in him since he came back here and started being in your company again. He's a completely different person than he was in the city."

"He told me about...everything," I said rather than go into details. "It's a relief to know that Lake Pendle and The Fluffy Cupcake has given him a new lease on life."

"It's not Lake Pendle or The Fluffy Cupcake doing that, Cookie. It's you. There is no question in my mind that you are the missing piece of his puzzle, and honestly, him for you. You started out angry and sharp with him, but slowly, you warmed up. I contribute that to you being the kind of person who offers people second chances, but also because you can see he's changed, grown, and matured."

Oh, how he had matured, I thought, biting back a grin.

A text beeped on my phone, saving me from having to respond. "That's him. He will be here in a few minutes. Rye is going to bring my parents down and Ares texted Bishop to bring Amber out. Where's Taylor?" I asked, searching the yard, but she was nowhere to be found.

"Inside resting," Athena said, but it was how she said it that told me something was off.

"Why don't you go get her and I'll meet you at the driveway." That was when I noticed tears in her eyes. I grabbed her hand tightly. "Athena, what's the matter? And don't say nothing because I can see there's a problem here."

"Athena?" Taylor asked from the doorway and we both snapped our attention to her. She came out of the house leaning heavily on a cane then sat and took Athena's other hand. "It's okay. We have to tell them, right?"

Athena nodded as I glanced between them. "Tell us what?"

"I was diagnosed with relapsing remitting multiple sclerosis after a recent scan," Taylor said.

That was the very last thing I expected to hear today, especially from the woman who worked harder at the bakery than all of us put together. "Taylor, I had no idea. I'm so sorry that I didn't see that something was wrong."

"Don't do that," Taylor said with a head shake. "It's not on you to read minds. I kept it a secret until I knew for certain, partly out of denial and partly so I don't lose my job because of it."

My gasp was loud in the afternoon sunshine. "We would never do that, Taylor! Your wife owns stock in the company, which means so do you!"

She held up her hand to calm me. "I know, but denial doesn't always follow logic."

"Does anyone else know?" I asked, unable to come up with the right things to say.

"Ares, Bishop, and Amber," Athena answered. "Though, Rye suspects something is wrong. She's seen her resting a lot more than usual the last few weeks between customers."

"Do you need some time off?" I asked Taylor who shook her head, but I noticed Athena's nodding behind her.

"No, we're going into the busy season and you're going to need me."

"You're forgetting one thing. Your brother-in-law is back, and while he does the books, that doesn't take him all day. He wants to help, so you should let him."

"You think he would?" Taylor asked, glancing back at Athena who nodded again. "If he could do the heavy lifting and bending, I would last much longer during the day. Or if he could come in at noon and work until close, I could get a few extra hours of rest."

"Why don't we get everyone together tonight before the watch party and make a plan? Rye will have insight on this as well, since she does the donuts. We can all pick up a little extra slack for a while until you're feeling better. I'm sure it's not good to wear yourself out or to stress about things, right?"

"Nope," Athena answered for her. "The doctor told her for the treatment to get her back to baseline, she needs extra rest."

"What are you, my mother?" Taylor asked jokingly.

"No, I'm your wife, and I've loved you for thirty years. I'm not going to let you kill yourself over buns and cookies, okay?"

"Wow, you're celebrating thirty years?" I asked, to break the tension. "I remember when you got married, but I forget that you've been together much longer."

"We've been together longer than you've been alive," Taylor said with a wink. "That's why I know we'll get through this blip on the radar, even if my wife worries too much." She reached back and Athena slipped her hand in hers.

"I understand why you didn't say anything, but I wish you had. In hindsight, I see how exhausted and on edge you've both been. I want you guys to stay home tonight, climb into bed and watch Cookie Heaven on television."

"But the cookie wagon," Athena said and I slashed my hand through the air to end her protesting.

"We'll be fine. Do you honestly think once my mom and dad see this that they'll let anyone else in it for the remainder of the evening?"

Taylor snorted and bit back a smile, but Athena outright laughed. "You make a good point. Are you sure?"

"Positive," I said. "In fact, Ares and the part-time kids can cover your shifts this weekend, Taylor. Athena, you work your schedule however you need to so you get the orders done but you also get some time at home."

"I don't think you can make carte blanche decisions like that when there are four shareholders," Athena said bossily.

"As if the other two are going to disagree with me. Since you have to recuse yourself from the vote, it's three votes yea. Sorry."

Cookie

This time Taylor did laugh and she turned to Athena. "You're exhausted from worrying about me. Let's do what she says, I think it would be best for both of us."

"Alright," Athena finally agreed but she never took her eyes off her wife. "But I will get the baking done."

"I have no doubt," I assured her just as tires crunched on gravel. "Ready to see the cookie wagon? Taylor, take it slow."

"Yes, mommy," she quipped as she stood and used Athena's arm rather than the cane to walk to the street.

I took a moment to take a deep breath and let it back out. When you aren't expecting news like that, and it hits you unexpectedly, getting everything right in your head is challenging. Taylor and Athena have been my aunts all my life, and it broke my heart to see them battling something so serious while being afraid to ask for support from their families. I would hedge a bet that my parents already know, but I'd be sure to fill Rye in tonight. We'd all rally behind them to help them through this time. Significant changes were coming to The Fluffy Cupcake. Some of those changes would be painful, but I guess that's why they called them growing pains. I was confident we could find Taylor a position that would play to her strengths rather than her weaknesses.

That decided, I stood and walked down the steps as Ares' SUV came into view. When stopped, I wasn't surprised to see the cookie wagon covered in a custom-made tarp. I suspected he'd have one made to protect it during the summer when we weren't using it. Today, though, the cover was only to torture me. Bishop came around the side of the house with Amber while Rye led my parents down the street toward us.

Ares hopped out and winked at me then made a show of unhooking the tarp. Questions were being thrown out left and right by both sets of parents, but none of us were in a hurry to answer. Their questions would be answered soon enough. Ares took a breath and then pulled the tarp, letting it fall to the ground to reveal the cookie wagon.

I felt the collective gasp in my chest more than I heard it. The wagon had a giant caricature of me in a white coat. The left side said The Fluffy Cupcake and the right side said Cookie Heaven. I was holding a tray of Cookie Pies with a smile. Ares lowered the window shelf and suddenly, it looked like the tray was on the shelf. Above the window it said, The Fluffy Cupcake's Cuckoo for Cookies Wagon. The final touch was below the window where it said, Home of the Original Cookie Pie as Featured on Cookie Heaven.

"Ares, it's—"

"Unbelievable," my dad whispered.

Unable to wait another second, I ran to Ares and jumped into his arms. "It's beautiful!"

He rubbed my back for a moment and whispered into my ear. "It's not as beautiful as you are, baby. I love you." He lowered me to the ground and took my hand, walking with me around the trailer so I could see the back. I was shocked to see all the services available at The Fluffy Cupcake listed below our logo.

"Ares, this is too much." I swiped at my shoulder to catch a tear. "I still can't believe you did this for me."

"For us," he promised, his thumb stroking my cheek to wipe away another tear. "I did this for us, Cookie Pie, because I love you and I'm all in on your dreams. Remember?" He snuck a quick kiss from my lips before he took my hand and pulled me back around the wagon.

"Son, do you want to tell us what's going on here?" Bishop asked, his hands on Amber's shoulders.

"I'm gobsmacked," my mom said, her hand to her mouth. "It's so delightful, I don't know where to look first."

Ares cleared his throat and motioned at the wagon. "It's always been Cookie's dream to have a traveling bakery wagon for events and to promote The Fluffy Cupcake. We talked about it one night and I could feel her passion for the project as she spoke about it. When I traded in my old car, I had more money than I needed for the SUV, so I started looking for a concessions trailer we could convert into a cookie wagon. I was surprised to find this one just down the road. It was barely used and the family wanted it gone quickly. With Cookie's agreement, I bought it and took it in for detailing."

"You knew about this?" Dad asked me as he ran his hand over the window shelf.

Cookie

"I knew about the trailer," I whispered, "but not this. I had no idea he was going to do this. Wait until you see the back."

Everyone trundled around the back where I heard more gasps and excited chatter. I leaned into the man I'd spent the night making love to and smiled up at him. "You do speak my love language."

He tapped me on the nose before he leaned down and kissed it. "I wouldn't have you any other way, Cookie Pearson. Are you ready for tonight?"

"I'm going to ask Mom and Dad if they want to take a turn in the wagon at the watch party. Taylor told me about her situation and I insisted they stay home and watch the show in bed."

A look crossed his face for a fraction of a second before it was gone. "Good idea. They both need some rest. They were in limbo for so long, and now that they have a firm diagnosis, they need some time to process it together."

"Agreed, which is why we're also going to have an emergency meeting to work out a way to give Taylor some breathing room."

"I'm all in, in any way I can help. You know that."

"Which is exactly what I told them. We'll worry about that later. For now, we have a watch party to get to."

"Do you think any of them realized the Cookie Heaven coat you're wearing on the wagon is white and not red?"

"Nope. Not one of them. You're sneaky, Mr. Halla, it kind of turns me on."

His wink was naughty but it was his grin that was lascivious. "Sweetheart, when it comes to turning you on, I can do much better than kind of."

"I'm counting on it."

It looked like the entire community had turned out to the school gymnasium to watch Lake Pendle's Cookie Heaven competition. The pride from the community was overflowing, both for me and for having the district chosen as the school to host the competition. I couldn't say for sure, but I had a suspicion that an influential member of the district was the reason for that decision. Amber may no longer be owner of The Fluffy Cupcake, but his son and daughter have a lot of skin in the game. I also suspected it was Bishop that pressured Ares into convincing me to do the competition. After all, it would be hard to brag that you held a cookie competition in your town if your main baker didn't participate. One day I hoped to prove it so I could thank him. Not only had it led to an extra twenty grand in the coffers for the bakery, but it opened up time and space for Ares and me to connect. If it weren't for the competition, chances were good we'd still be dancing around each other. Instead, he sat next to me, discreetly holding my hand while he frantically chopped cherries on the big screen.

"You got this Team Cookie!" someone yelled from the back, raising laughter from everyone.

"We do got this," he whispered, giving me a wink. "No matter what it is, we got this as long as we're together."

I smiled with a nod, but didn't want to get too friendly, considering we were hemmed in by our mothers. Business had been brisk at the cookie wagon, though to everyone's disappointment there were no Cookie Pies. It was easy to say I didn't have time to make them after the event yesterday, but I promised everyone I'd have a whole wagon load on Saturday for Lake Pendle Days. Once the show started, the need for cookies ceased, so we decided to close it down and head in to watch with everyone. We were curious to see how the producers would put the show together, and thus far, they hadn't disappointed.

"Hearing what the judges thought about the cookies from behind the scenes is great," I whispered to my mom. "Yesterday, we only got to hear what they said on camera. It's a wonderful insight."

She nodded and leaned her head on my shoulder. "It is, and I've been a baker for a lot of years, baby. I know you got this." Her mom intuition was correct, so I nodded and winked, and she lit up, barely able to contain herself.

"I have to go," I whispered into her ear. "They need me out there for a moment."

"But you'll miss the end," she whispered back.

"I've seen it," I said with another wink and then nodded to Ares, who followed me out of the gymnasium side door.

I had hoped sitting that close to the door would help us get out unnoticed, but the murmurs I heard go through the crowd told me otherwise. There was nothing I could do about that now. After we wrapped shooting yesterday, the producer asked me if I would consider filming an after the show program where Nadia would come to the watch party and introduce me as the new champion, tour the bakery, and film the quaint small-town vibe Lake Pendle had going. On the heels of a victory like this one, I couldn't pass up the opportunity to introduce the country to The Fluffy Cupcake. Spending the morning with the camera crew tomorrow would add to an already jam-packed week, but by Sunday we could all rest and take a breath.

"My mom knows," I said as soon as we were alone in the hallway.

"Mine too," he said with laughter. "Your dad, too. It's hard to fool a baker and they've spent too much time at the bench not to see the writing on the wall. In fact, everyone I talked to tonight has you tagged as the winner." He kissed my knuckles and then dropped our hands. "Ready to do this?"

"Nope, wish I didn't have to, but I know how important it is for the business."

"You know that whole online ordering thing you were talking about?" I nodded and he hit me with a sneaky grin. "I've got a developer putting it together now. It will be live by the time the special airs."

"Ares!" I exclaimed, then remembered to lower my voice. "We aren't ready yet! Imagine what could happen!"

"Shhh," he said, motioning for me to lower my voice. "I can imagine what could happen, which is why I jumped on this immediately. We will only take the number of orders we can manage and nothing more. We'll discuss it all at the meeting with the shareholders, but we'd be nuts not to capitalize on this opportunity."

Katie Mettner

"I know, but Taylor and—"

He put his finger to my lips. "I've got this, Cookie Pie. You have to trust that I have everyone's back with everything I do, right?" I nodded, though it was tentative. "Good girl. I'll explain more tomorrow night. For now, I just want you to bask in the glory of this win."

That reminded me of my promise to talk to him about a new mixer. If what he said was true and he was opening up the online store, it wasn't an *if* we got a new mixer. It was a *when* we got a new mixer, preferably the sooner the better. I'd have to bring it to the table at the next meeting with the understanding that we pay for it with the prize money, since we'd already ordered extra coolers with our operations budget. It would take longer to start my training initiative, but that wouldn't take a lot of capital, and we'd still have the sales from the Cookie Pies to earmark for the project.

"Cookie, Ares, so nice to see you again," Nadia said, motioning us into the girls' locker room. "Do you have your coats?"

"I'll grab them," Ares said, jogging to a locker where we'd stowed them away.

"Once the winner is announced, the show will end," Nadia explained and I held up my finger.

"Are we not doing the after the show segment?"

"We decided not to until we've toured the bakery. We'll use your interview there because it will play nicely with the reveal of your cookie wagon, which is beautiful, by the way."

"Thank you," I said, a smile on my face, but I noticed it was Ares who was brimming with pride. "It's a dream come true and I can't wait to use it to do good things."

"I have no doubt that you will," she agreed as Ares helped me on with the coat.

"Now, let's go wait by the door. When the crowd goes wild, we go in."

Ares put his hand to my back as we walked toward the door, probably because he knew I'd bolt if I had a chance. I didn't want to do this, but the town deserved a colossal celebration for supporting us all these years. I would do it for them.

We couldn't hear what was happening until the moment a roar hit our ears. Nadia grinned and the stagehand pulled the door open

217

for the three of us to walk through, followed by a cameraman. When the crowd saw us on the stage, the cheering intensified until everyone was simply chanting, 'Cookie.'

The screen had gone dark and Nadia started motioning with her hands for everyone to settle down so she could speak. Once everyone was back in their seats, she brought her microphone to her lips. "I'm so pleased to be here tonight with all of you," she said as another cheer went through the crowd. "Cookie Pearson impressed me so much yesterday that I wanted to share in the celebration of having a Cookie Heaven Champion Baker in your town!"

More roaring from the crowd until she got them to quiet down again. The entire time I was dying inside and focusing on the warmth of Ares' hand on my back. If he hadn't agreed to be with me, I probably would have faked an illness and hid under my blankets. My job was to create something that stole the show, not be the show.

"I have to say, of all the contestants I've seen come through Cookie Heaven competitions, there have been few like your Cookie Pearson. She is focused, intelligent, quick on her feet, eloquent, and brilliant in all things baking. More than that, she has a kind heart. She works day in and day out to make sure all of you have the products you need to celebrate the good days and for comfort on the bad, and she does it without need for recognition. As part of the filming, we do several interviews with the contestants throughout the day, but it was her last one that told me what a gem Cookie Pearson is. I'll let you watch that interview yourself in a few weeks, but for now, suffice it to say that this woman doesn't just create baked goods. She infuses love into every single bite knowing that's what's important in life. To that end, I'd like to ask Superintendent Bishop Halla to the stage."

More cheering ensued as Bishop kissed Amber's cheek and then jogged to the stage. At sixty-five, he may be sporting grey hair, but he was as fit as he was the day I was born.

"Superintendent Bishop's wife was notified that Cookie Heaven was looking for a small-town to host a new event, and he pulled out all the stops to shine the best light on Lake Pendle and this beautiful school. Not only were we welcomed warmly, but he was integral in assuring the taping went smoothly. However, Bishop didn't write his letter of nomination as the district's superintendent. He wrote the letter as a man who had been loved, mentored, and welcomed into this town with open arms at a time when he was desperate for a connection. He wrote it as a father who brought his homesick daughter here where she too was loved, mentored, and welcomed with open arms, even as a member of the LGBTQ community, or, as he put it, maybe because she needed a community, no one cared who she loved. His son was born and raised here, graduated from Lake Pendle and has now taken part ownership in the bakery with his sister when their mother retired. To say it has come full circle for Bishop is an understatement, especially as he is set to retire in just a few short days."

More clapping ensued, occasionally broken by boos for his retirement until he took the microphone from Nadia and used his teacher's voice to settle the crowd. Bishop handed the microphone back to her with a grin. "Good to know I've still got it."

Ares and I snorted as Nadia addressed the crowd again. "I'm telling you here tonight about all of this because Bishop's letter, and Cookie's performance, along with her teammate, Ares—we can't forget about him," she said, opening up the crowd to more cheering. Thankfully, it didn't last long. "Brought the producers and directors to the table last night with one request. More Lake Pendle!"

As expected, the crowd went wild and I couldn't help but turn to Ares and shake my head with a silly grin on my face. "Is this even happening?"

"Appears so. Wouldn't mind if she'd wrap this up so I can take you home and enjoy my cookie with a glass of milk."

My face heated immediately and I leaned into his chest to hide my laughter. "Don't make promises you can't keep, Mr. Halla," I said before I turned back to face Nadia and...his father. The smirk he wore told me we hadn't pulled anything past them about how our relationship had evolved.

"So," Nadia said to quiet the last few revelers. "Instead of an after the show segment that you're used to seeing with Cookie Heaven, we'll be doing an entire special on Lake Pendle. Over the next few days, we'll be in town shooting footage including a tour of the bakery, school, and the town hot spots. We'll be interviewing some of you as well as visiting the lake so we can show our viewership what else Lake Pendle has to offer besides great cookies!"

"Cookie, would you like to say a few words?"

I took the microphone and nervously cleared my throat. "I'd like to thank Superintendent Halla for pushing to have the competition in our town. I've known Uncle Bish my entire life, and he's always been about showing off Lake Pendle in the best possible light, which I think he did quite handedly this time. I also want to thank my esteemed baking assistant, who not only convinced me to sign up for the competition, but jumped in at the last second, quite literally, to assist me on taping day. A huge thank you to my mom and dad, for instilling in me the importance of hard work, and passing down the baking gene so that I, and my sister Rye, could continue providing all of you with the goodies you've come to love over the years. Finally, a life size thank-you to all of you for supporting the bakery year after year. Okay, I'm sorry, I didn't mean to make this sound like an Oscar speech!" Everyone laughed, and my face burned hot with embarrassment until I remembered that I'd worked hard to be here tonight. "Then again, being crowned a Cookie Heaven Champion is a bit like the baking Oscars. Thank you to Cookie Heaven for being here tonight, for hosting a wonderful and safe event, and for recognizing the beauty, talent, and community that is Lake Pendle. Now I hope you all understand why there were no Cookie Pies at the cookie wagon tonight." Another round of laughter ensued as heads nodded. "But I assure you, Cookie Pies and Heavenly Cherry Bites will be available Saturday at Lake Pendle Days! Thanks again, everyone."

I handed the microphone back to Nadia while everyone stood and clapped. Ares slid his arm around my waist and gave it a squeeze. "I'm so proud of you, baby," he whispered.

Nadia brought the microphone to her mouth. "Again, on behalf of Cookie Heaven, I want to thank all of you for being here tonight. Remember, if you see us around town, don't be afraid to say hello. You never know who will end up on the big screen when the special airs." With a final wave, Nadia walked offstage, and we all followed her into the hallway. She handed the microphone to a stagehand and clapped her hands together once. "Thanks so much for being here tonight, guys. I know the special is going to be fantastic. We will see you tomorrow morning?"

"We'll be ready for you," I promised, even though, on the inside, I was grimacing. We had so much work to do tonight, but with any luck, we'd have the baking done and everything cleaned up by the time they arrived tomorrow. It would be cutting it close to get everything baked and ready for Lake Pendle Days and Bishop's retirement party, and I didn't see a lot of sleep in the foreseeable future. All of that said, the work and lack of sleep would be worth it if we put The Fluffy Cupcake on the map.

Twenty-Six

Exhaustion had set in a few hours ago already, but I refused to let it show. As long as Cookie kept going, so would I. The minute this tour was done, I had every intention of dragging her up to her apartment for some sleep. I'd rather spend the time making love to her sweet body, but we both needed to catch up on a few winks before we had to do this all over again tonight.

We managed to hold a quick meeting before we started baking last night, by calling Athena and Taylor by video. I assured my sister that I would be here to help Taylor prepare every morning that we didn't have a part-timer working. Thankfully, school was almost done and once our summer help arrived, we would have no problem covering Taylor's shifts. Then we'd have the summer to find someone to take over her full-time position when school resumed. The answer was simple in my eyes. Taylor would take over all special orders including online ordering, packaging and shipping. That would allow her to stay off her feet for the most part, and give her new treatment time to work. Growing the business meant growing pains, but those pains were not going to be felt by my sister-in-law.

That was barely settled when Cookie surprised me about needing a new floor mixer. She wasn't wrong. Our mixers are as old as we are, and we're on borrowed time with them. Since a new one can run close to ten grand, Cookie insisted that we use the prize money from Cookie Heaven to purchase the new mixer. At first, I fought her on it, but her reasoning did make sense. If we invested the prize money back into equipment, we'd get a tax break on the winnings. Then we earmark the money from the sale of the Cookie Pies and online order money for her foster care initiative. When we all agreed, Athena especially so, we ended the call to start baking.

We had cookies stacked everywhere, cupcakes and donuts filling the case, and a clean bakery primed for a nighttime special for Cookie Heaven. I checked the clock, and we had ten minutes until the crew arrived.

That gave me ten minutes alone with the girl I loved. "I'll be in the back with Cookie for a few minutes, Corey," I said. "Holler if you need anything."

"Thanks, Ares, but I'll be fine. I know you're going to be busy with the production company today. I'll keep the front running smoothly."

"I know you will, thanks again for jumping into the bakery at a crazy time."

Corey was one of our summer front end workers who happened to be done with classes already. When I called her to see if she could start sooner than Monday, she was happy to come in and cover Taylor's shifts. I was grateful and would be giving her as many hours as she wanted this summer for her loyalty.

When I got to the back of the bakery, Cookie stood at the bench, both hands planted on it and her eyes glued to the oven, though I suspected she was off somewhere in space. "Hey, baby, are you okay?"

Her gaze flicked to mine for a moment and she nodded. "Yeah, sorry, I was going over the list of everything I needed to do in my head. Everything has to be perfect when the camera crew arrives."

After a quick glance around the room, I offered her a smile. "I can assure you the place hasn't been this clean since I got here. It's going to be fine." I walked over to her and slipped my arms around her for a hug. "Hey, let's run upstairs for a minute."

"Why?" she asked as I led her from the bakery and jogged up the stairs, giving her no choice but to follow me. Once I unlocked the door, I pushed her through it and closed it behind us.

"Ares, what's going on? We don't have much time."

"We have nine and a half minutes until the crew arrives. I plan to spend eight and a half of them kissing you."

I leaned in, putting my hand behind her head as I pressed her up against the wall then lowered my lips to hers. It had been way too long since I'd put my lips and hands on her, so I took a full tour of her beautiful curves while I dipped my tongue in to taste her. She tasted so damn sweet that I moaned with abandon. Mid-kiss, I wrapped my other hand around her ass so I could press myself against her. I trailed my lips along her cheek to her ear and whispered softly, "Do you feel what you do to me?"

"It would be hard to miss," she said, but her words were breathy. "Too bad we only have seven minutes left before the camera crew arrives."

"Darling, I only need two."

Her naughty laughter made my dick pulse against her. I wanted to be inside her, and I knew she wanted the same. I took her hand and led her to the couch, placing her hands on the back and pulling her hips backward until that ass of hers aligned perfectly with my dick. I lowered her pants and trailed a finger down her slit, both of us inhaling sharply at how wet she was already.

I leaned over her back and nipped at her ear. "Did any of your other lovers bend you over the couch and fuck you in the middle of the day, Cookie?" While I awaited her answer, I lowered my pants, my dick primed for a bit of action.

"No," she answered, but it was more desperate than matter of fact, considering my finger was on her clit, rocking it back and forth.

"Why not?" I lined my dick up at her opening and waited for her answer.

"I wouldn't let them."

With a thrust, I was inside her. I grasped her hips, leaning over to whisper in her ear. "But you'll let me fuck you in the middle of the day because?" I asked, pulling out and pushing back in until the only sound that left her lips was a moan. After a few more thrusts, and with my patience waning, I slapped her ass playfully. "I'm still waiting for an answer, Cookie."

"I let you fuck me in the middle of the day because I love you, Ares Halla. I love the way your dick stretches me wide open until I can't help but come all over you."

"Hold on then, baby. Here I come," I whispered before I wrapped an arm around her breasts and the other around her belly so I could hold her up as she started to come. "That's it," I hissed. "That's it, come hard for me, Cookie," I ground out, pushing through her orgasm to bring us both up to a higher plane until I couldn't hold out any longer. "Fuck," I moaned, my dick pulsing as I came inside her, both of us muttering nonsense as the sensations overtook us. I leaned over her back again as our orgasms faded and kissed her ear. "I love you, Cookie Pie," I whispered as she finished shuddering in my arms. "I'll never get tired of knowing when I need to feel complete, all I have to do is come to you."

She sighed and dropped her forehead to the couch as her final spasms faded away. "I love you too," she said as she pushed herself up. "But that took more than two minutes and we're going to be late!"

I pulled out and grabbed her shoulders as she started to turn without pulling up her pants. "Hold on. We have time. Give me thirty seconds in the bathroom, and then I'll wait downstairs. Join me when you're ready. I'll tell Nadia you're freshening up."

She smiled and kissed my lips. "Are you going to tell her it's your fault I needed to?"

"Only if you want me to," I quipped, a smile on my face that wasn't going anywhere anytime soon.

She swatted at me and laughed. "You better not! Or there won't be any more quickies in your future."

I gasped and threw my hand to my heart. "We don't want that! Be right back."

After a quick wash down in the bathroom, so I didn't smell like sex the moment the camera crew arrived, I opened the door to her smiling face.

"I'll see you in two?" I asked and with a kiss to my lips, and a wink of her left eye, she walked into the bathroom and closed the door.

That was the moment I knew Cookie Pearson had always had me, and always would.

"Cookie?" Nadia asked from behind me as the camera crew were packing up their gear. "Do you think your parents would do an interview with us for the special?"

"Absolutely," I said as I turned. "Without my parents and my Aunt Amber and Uncle Bishop, this place wouldn't be what it is today. I'm sure they would all love to sit down and talk with you about how they started, and the ways the bakery has changed over the years."

"What would be the best way to contact them?"

"I'll shoot them a text and let them know you're going to reach out? Does that work for you?"

"It sure does," she agreed with a smile. "If you want to put in a good word for us that would help too."

I laughed and shook my head as I leaned against the floor mixer. "Trust me, they'll be more than happy to talk to you about their years of owning The Fluffy Cupcake. Ask them about the time Bart broke down and was out of commission for several weeks but they still managed to get all the baking done."

"Bart?" she curiously asked.

I patted the giant machine I leaned against. "This is Bart. He's been around longer than I have and he's starting to show his age. He broke down on us just the other night, and we managed to fix him, but we're going to have to buy a new one. Come to think of it, maybe you should leave that part out of the interview where I talked about using the prize money for my new foster care initiative. Unfortunately, that money is going to go toward a new Bart."

"Are you tabling your initiative all together, then?"

"Oh, absolutely not," I emphasized. "We're just going to take the funds from the sale of Cookie Pies and the online orders that were starting, thanks to Cookie Heaven. The funds for the initiative are there, and since I don't need a large sum immediately, we can take time to build the fund over the summer from sales. We have no choice but to buy the mixer if we're going to keep up with the orders coming in now that I'm a Cookie Heaven Champion."

"That's understandable," she said with a nod. "I see no reason why the interview can't remain as it is then. You're not pulling your foster care idea. You're just funding it differently. Besides, I can't imagine you need a large sum upfront?"

"Not since Ares bought the cookie wagon as a personal investment in the bakery. That would have been the biggest expense. Now all I'll need for funding is money to buy uniforms and tools for the kids we hire. Since we'll only be having one or two at a time, summer sales from the cookie wagon will cover most of it."

"My years as a producer, and as a woman, tell me that Ares bought the cookie wagon as a personal investment in you, not the bakery."

I tried to fight the smile, but it tipped my lips anyway. "Ares and I have been best friends since we came out of the womb. It's fair to say if he has a way to make one of my dreams happen, he will. That's why I know he's currently looking at the books, trying to figure out any other way to pick up another mixer so the prize money can go into my planned initiatives. I'm confident, one way or the other, that by this time next year, we will have several foster care kids working here under our guidance."

"Make me a promise?" she asked.

"I'll try my best," I promised.

"Email me after you've had your first kids working for a few months. I would love to come back and see how you're all doing. Maybe do a story about how baking can change lives."

"Now that's a promise I can make," I assured her, accepting the hug she offered.

"I think we have everything we need, but if we need more shots, I'll give you a ring and we can stop back later this week? We'll be here through Lake Pendle Days, so there's plenty of time to get the interviews that we need."

"You bet. We will be here baking away. Well, actually, right now I'm going to go upstairs and collapse into bed because I've been up for twenty-four hours."

"I think that's more than fair," Nadia said with a chuckle. "We'll get out of your hair, and you get some rest. I know Cookie Pies wait for no one, but it's hard to bake in your sleep."

"If I could bake in my sleep, I would take The Fluffy Cupcake nationwide!"

Cookie

We both busted into laughter until we had to wipe tears from our eyes.

"Hey," Ares said as he walked into the bakery from the side door. "What's so funny?"

"Cookie," Nadia answered. "We're about ready to get out of your hair, so I suggest you take this woman upstairs and put her to bed."

"That's exactly why I'm here," Ares said with a wink. "Thanks for filming this special and introducing your viewers to the wonderful Lake Pendle and The Fluffy Cupcake. I can't wait to watch it, but until then, I wish you a good night."

He hooked my arm in his and led me to the door. I waved at Nadia as the door closed, and I dragged my feet up the thirteen stairs to my apartment.

"They want to interview our parents," I said as he pushed the door open for me.

"I'm not surprised. I figured they would cover all their bases before they left town. But, enough about the television show. It's time for Cookie heaven in real life. Let's start with a shower," he said with a naughty wink.

Twenty-Seven

Our hands swung between us as we walked toward the shore, the stars shining above us to light our way. The night had been long, and we had less than two hours until we had to start baking, but I wanted to spend those two hours with him. I wanted to spend all my hours with him, which made my stomach squishy. How had I fallen so hard so quickly for the man I'd been angry at for so many years?

The truth was I had never fallen out of love with him, which made forgiving him easy once I put the anger aside. When I looked back at my reaction to his proclamations, I realized that my own anger was the reason I suffered so long. Had I stepped up and asked him why he was saying those things or even told him how it made me feel, maybe we could have avoided all the pain. Was I ever leaving The Fluffy Cupcake? No, but for Ares, I would have made a long-distance relationship work. It certainly would have been a hell of a lot easier than carrying so much pain and anger for the last thirteen years.

"You're deep in thought," he said when we reached our favorite spot by the lake. Since it was private property and no one was around, he spread the blanket on the sand so we could lay back and watch the stars.

"I was just thinking about us. Your dad cornered me at the party and asked me why we were trying to keep our love a secret."

His laughter was soft as it filtered into the night. "They must have an evil plan because Aunt Haylee cornered me tonight, too. She asked me the same question."

"What was your answer?"

He pulled me in closer to him and wrapped his arms around me. "I told her that we've been so busy we haven't even had time to talk about us, where we're going, or what we want this to look like. Some of that was true, some of it wasn't."

"That's what I told your dad, too. What do you mean some of it was true and some of it wasn't?" Nerves skittered through my belly. Was he already thinking about leaving Lake Pendle?

"It's true that we haven't had time to talk about us, but that doesn't mean I don't know where we're going or what I want us to look like. Anywhere we go I want it to be together, and I want us to look like my parents or your parents in thirty years."

I smiled up at him, his eyes telling me his words were trustworthy and honest. "I feel the same way. I know it's fast considering you've only been back in town for a few weeks, but it felt like the time we were apart just fell away."

"Like the moment we came back together, we were best friends again," he finished.

"Best friends who were finally old enough to realize their love for the other person was more than friends. In my defense, I knew that a long time ago, but there was nothing I could do about it." He was quiet as he stared out over the lake, and I cupped his cheek, forcing his gaze toward mine. "Something's bothering you. It has been since we left your dad's retirement party."

"We were joking around right before you brought the cake out," he said, dropping his gaze to his lap. "Mom raced off in her wheelchair laughing and Dad just got this look on his face that was such pure emotion. He told me was so glad we were both happy again because for a while, he thought he was going to lose us both. It made me feel like total rubbish for what I did to them. I should have thought about them when I tried to end everything, but I didn't. I'll live with what I did to them forever."

"No," I said, my finger to his lips. "You weren't thinking about anything other than ending the constant pain you were living in. No one holds that against you. I'm sure it was hard for them, and they feel guilty too, but love will heal those wounds if you keep going and keep telling them how much you love them."

"It sounds like you have experience with this and that scares me."

I shrugged and dropped eye contact with him. "There was a time I considered ending the pain too."

"But you didn't?"

"Only because Rye realized there was a problem and told my parents. They got me help and were a support system for me, which is something you didn't have."

"Your dad intimated as much that night we were at their house, but I didn't want to believe it. He said it took a year for you to return to them, and when you did, you were a completely different person."

"He's not wrong, but I'm no longer the person I was then either. We all change, grow, and learn, Ares. If that wasn't intentional, we'd be born with all the necessary knowledge."

He flipped around so he could hold my hands. "I'm going to ask you a question, and I want you to answer me honestly. Agreed?" I nodded once, and he took a breath as his gaze floated out toward the water. "Back when you contemplated ending the pain for good, was I the reason?"

I paused, prepared to lie, till he locked his gaze with mine again and I no longer wanted to. Honesty was the only way for us going forward. "You were the catalyst, but not the reason."

"Cookie, that's basically the same thing."

"No, it's not. You leaving Lake Pendle was the catalyst, but my emotions were the reason for my pain. There was so much anger tied up with all of it that it kept me from finding you so we could talk. It seemed easier not to have any feelings than to talk to you about the ones that hurt me."

He hung his head and inhaled deeply. "I'm sorry for all the things that I did to hurt you, Cookie. Nothing, and I mean nothing, will make up for the pain I caused you, but I promise you tonight that I will spend the rest of my life being the man you thought I was."

"No, you'll spend the rest of your life being the man you are. That is the man I love."

He took my hand and feathered a kiss across my palm. "I'm a lucky man to have fallen for a woman with such a forgiving heart. All of that said, and all of that accepted as part of our history, does this feel fast to you?"

Cookie

"No, it feels like the longest wait of my life is finally over, and the one certainty I've carried forever has finally arrived." I tossed my legs over his thighs so I could see him better.

"That we're supposed to be together?"

"That we were created for each other. It was always going to come back to this, the universe would make sure of it."

"You believe in the idea of soulmates?"

"You've met our parents, right?" I asked, my head cocked. "Everything that happened in their lives led them to each other. Look at your mom and dad. There was no reason for your dad to take a job in this little town other than to meet Amber. There was no reason my dad should have stayed at The Fluffy Cupcake for seven years when he had the talent to go work in any five-star restaurant. He stayed because that's where his soulmate was, even if Mom was hesitant to that idea."

"That's the part that gets me, though," he said, taking my hands in his. "Both our moms were resistant to getting together with our dads. If that's the case, can it really be soulmates?"

"I didn't say they were resistant," I reminded him. "I said hesitant, and for good reason. My mom was my dad's boss, but he was also the only other baker she had. He was moving The Fluffy Cupcake forward in the industry, which added another layer to her consideration. She was hesitant to admit how she felt because she loved him enough not to trap him in Lake Pendle forever when he had the potential to go out and advance his career. Amber was hesitant because of her disability. She didn't want your dad to have to deal with what she dealt with every day. That was a legitimate reason to be hesitant since she was the only person to know what that looked like. It wasn't that she didn't love him. She loved him enough not to want to put him through that kind of hell."

His face took on a faraway look even as he held my gaze. "Yeah, and sometimes, it was hell. When you look at it that way, though, I see what you mean. Finding the one for you isn't always a straight road without horrific car crashes."

I chuckled but slid my hand up his face to rub his temple. "Exactly. Our hearts were connected and we were written in the stars, but there was no timestamp on that process. How long it takes to get there and what we go through in the meantime is what makes the bond concrete. If we don't bring life experience to the table, then we can't appreciate how far we've come and how wonderful it is to have each other."

"I know I'm the luckiest man alive," he whispered, his fingers holding my chin gently. "Not only have you allowed me back into your life, but you've welcomed me as though I never left. As though I never hurt you when I know I have."

"I'll be honest, the first day I saw you standing by the cookie wagon, I was angry, I never made that a secret. You had hurt me and I didn't want to forgive you, but also, seeing you again made my head spin in the sense that the magnet in my compass was finally lined up with the earth again. A piece of me that had been missing for so long was filled in again, even if I wanted to ignore it. That was the moment I knew holding onto the anger would only delay the inevitable, and if I wanted to find happiness again, I had to let it go. I'm so glad I did, Ares," I promised, scooting forward until I could kiss his lips. "So glad," I murmured around his tongue as it slipped inside to coil with mine.

The kiss heated and he lowered himself to the sand, bringing me down on top of him without breaking the kiss. It was easy to straddle him, his dick hard and throbbing under me as I leaned in to kiss him. With a thrust of my hips, I dragged moan after moan from his lips until he finally broke the kiss to catch a breath.

"You're going to be the death of me, woman," he hissed, his hands sliding under my shirt to caress my breasts through my bra. "I want these in my mouth." I sat up and stripped my shirt off and then my bra, throwing them behind me as his eyes widened. "Cookie," he hissed and I leaned down, stealing his lips.

"Yes?"

"You can't be out here naked!"

"Why not? It's my property, so no one else should be out here. If they are, well, they'll get a free show." To punctuate that statement, I leaned over him so my right breast was lined up with his lips and then lowered myself toward him until he couldn't help but grasp my nipple and suck it in, drawing a long moan from my lips.

"You're so beautiful," he murmured around my nipple before he moved to the other one, offering it the same kind of love until I was grinding against his hard dick right through my pants.

"You're so fucking hard, I want you inside me."

I stood long enough to do a short striptease to whet his appetite. His gaze was pinned to my hands as I slowly lowered the zipper of my pants. I lowered the pants even slower until a whimper left his lips when he saw the red lace thong I wore under them.

"You're killing me, Cookie," he moaned as I dropped the pants and stood in only the thong.

"It's not often you see a fat girl wearing a see-through thong."

"No," he said, sitting up instantly. His expression turned hard and his fingers gripped my thighs as though he was trying not to rip off said thong. "That is not a word you are allowed to use about yourself." I opened my mouth to object, but he squeezed my thighs. "No. You are a beautiful woman wearing a thong. The last time I checked," he looked down at his belly, "my dick agrees with that assessment. Never use that word in my presence again or I'll have to punish you."

I lifted a brow and planted a hand on my hip. "Oh, you're going to punish me? I'd like to know how. I'm as big as you are."

"I have my ways," he promised, licking his lips as his gaze took hold of the thong again. "Take it off."

The strings tied at my hips, so I pulled the loop until the thong fell to the ground. The wind blew cool across my breasts, peaking my nipples into hard mounds and pebbling my sex before his gaze.

"I have to taste you. Now. Sit on my face. I want to have my cookie and eat her too." His grin was devilish but I shook my head slightly as I lowered myself to the blanket.

"I'll suffocate you. Better go from the side."

"Wrong." Rather than explain, he grabbed my hips and lifted me over his head until I knelt by his neck. "Mmm, you smell amazing." In a breath he had his lips on me, his tongue lapping until I fell forward. I braced my hands in the sand as he moaned beneath me, his fingers kneading my ass while he took his fill of me. "You're so wet," he moaned as his tongue dipped inside me to suckle steadily. The sensations heightened and I ground myself against his lips out of desperation. His moan against my skin raced a shiver up my spine. That was the sound that told me we were made for each other. A tendril of smoke worked its way through my belly until I was nearly breathless for release.

"Ares," I moaned, his tongue taking me to new heights in a position I was unaccustomed to.

"Tell me what you need, baby," he cooed around my lips.

"I need to come, please," I begged, unsure where this forward, unabashed woman had come from, if I were honest. The old Cookie would never beg a man for an orgasm, but the new Cookie would beg this man without question.

"Are you going to call my name when you come?" he asked, blowing against my sensitive skin, pushing me to the top of the mountain where I stood on my tiptoes, arms wide open and my gaze focused on the clouds below.

"Ares," I called into the blue sky from the mountain.

"You're ready, sweetheart," he hissed, his lips going back to work as he took a long, slow, wet stroke with his tongue.

I pushed forward with my toes off the mountain and soared into the sky, his lips and tongue driving me higher and higher as I called out his name. When my orgasm slowed, his motions did too until he was barely stroking me, allowing me to relax at my own pace rather than his.

"I'd ask if it was good, but the fact that my face is dripping wet means I don't have to," he whispered against my soft belly where he'd moved his lips. "I love making you come."

I scooted backwards, dragging myself along his t-shirt until I was over his hard cock. Rocking, I stroked it up and down until he was panting, his hands fighting against me to get to his zipper, but I didn't allow it.

"Cookie, please." His demand was weak as the sensations filled him. "I need you more than air right now."

His desperation evident, I worked myself backward until I could get to his pants where I unhooked his belt, button and zipper in fast fashion. I couldn't wait to get to the good stuff. Once I'd stripped him of his jeans and tossed them aside, I lowered his boxers until he was naked from the waist down. "I love your dick," I whispered right before I took the tip in my mouth and suckled. He thrust upward, nearly choking me before he remembered and backed off.

"I love having my dick in your mouth," he hissed, his hips working in a rhythm all their own. "It makes me want to come over and over just to spend time there."

With a pump of my hand, his moan filled the night sky. "You can come," I whispered, swirling my tongue around his tip. "I'm not going to stop you."

"The only place I'm coming is inside you," he hissed, grasping my hair as he thrust against the roof of my mouth carefully. "This feels good, but your sweet, wet, hot sex takes me to new planets, Cookie."

"Oh, you mean this sweet, wet, hotness?" I finished stripping him of his boxers and moved over him again, rubbing my clit against his dick. We both moaned, but he spoke. "Fuck me, Cookie," he begged, his hands grasping my tits as I held myself over him. "Remind me why I live."

Before he could say more, I lowered myself over his tip and held myself there, my thighs shaking and my sex clenching at the size of him. "No one else has ever filled me this way, Ares," I sighed as I slid down to nestle him against my center.

"No one else ever will, Cookie," he moaned, his eyes rolled back in his head as he thrust upward gently, searching for something he'd only find in me. "You are mine now, forever."

I dropped down, my hands next to his head and my lips on his as I set the rhythm to our lovemaking. His hips met mine thrust for thrust until our cries meshed at the same time our bodies did. He curled his hands in mine so we could soar into the night sky together to read our story written in the stars.

Twenty-Eight

Had it only been twenty-four hours since we'd laid under these same stars and made love by the lake? It felt like a distant memory after the busyness of this day. The debut of the Cuckoo for Cookie Wagon at Lake Pendle Days had been cuckoo for sure. We had a line a mile long before we opened the window and it had been a steady stream all day long of people coming to try the now famous Cookie Pies. Rye had made multiple trips over with new batches of cookies she was making like an assembly line at the bakery. My sister had even jumped in and helped bake off the cookies so Rye could put them together and deliver them.

Was it a flash in the pan? We couldn't answer that yet. We hoped not, but anything was possible. We hoped if we kept them as a special event product rather than a regular case item, that people would continue to beg for them. Their availability online and for special orders would also hopefully spur people to order them for parties and events that they otherwise might order cupcakes or cake.

"I think we're officially out of cookies," Cookie said from behind me. "Quick, close the window!"

Laughing, I pulled the locks and lowered the canopy before I locked the window down. "We did it, sweetheart," I said, pulling her into my arms. "What a day!"

"We both smell like frosting and chocolate," she said, giggling as she buried her nose in my neck. "Thank you, Ares. I couldn't have done it without you."

"Yeah, you could have, but I'm glad I got to be here to see the community fall in love with your dream of a cookie wagon the same way you did. The same way I fell in love with you. Instantly and without question knowing that anything you handed me was going to be sweet and worth every bite."

Cookie

She giggled against my neck and it made all the hair on my body stand at attention. "You are amazing for my ego, Ares Halla."

"You are amazing for my heart, baby. What do you say we load up this wagon and get the heck out of here? I'm ready to take a shower and have some milk and a cookie."

She groaned with laughter when she leaned back to make eye contact. "I'm so tired, I don't know if I'll get through the shower without nodding off."

"Oh, you will, I assure you," I promised with a wink. "We're not even going to unload the wagon until tomorrow. We'll park it behind the bakery and deal with it then."

"Thank goodness," she sighed as her shoulders drooped. "I need food, I know, shocker, but also some sleep."

"No, you deserve food," I reminded her with raised brows and she finally tipped her head in agreement.

"Okay, I deserve food and rest, but first, I have to go to the bathroom. Can you start breaking this down while I run to the restrooms? I'll be back in five."

"I'll go with you," I said, glancing out the window on the door. "It's pitch black out and I don't want you out there alone."

"I'll be fine," she said, patting my chest. "There are a ton of people in the park still and the bathrooms are well-lit. The faster you get this place tied up, the faster we get to that shower," she said, waggling her eyebrows at me.

She turned and headed for the door but not before I got a pat to her ass. "Okay, be careful."

"You don't need to worry," she promised, hand on the doorknob. "These hips are a weapon and this ass is lethal."

"Oh, baby, you're not kidding," I said, biting my lip with one brow up. Her laughter trailed her as she disappeared into the night.

The trailer was a disaster but it was the kind of disaster I didn't mind cleaning. I'd have to run the numbers, but I had little doubt that we broke every record we'd set at Lake Pendle Days over the years. There was no way we hadn't and I couldn't wait to get the tally on the number of cookies sold. It would be another way to prove to Cookie that she was changing the face of The Fluffy Cupcake and Lake Pendle.

There was a knock on the door and I jogged to it. "I didn't think that locked automatically—" I paused when I pushed the door open and it wasn't Cookie standing there. "Oh, hey, Nadia," I said, hopping down from the trailer. "I didn't know you guys were still in town."

"We head out tomorrow," she answered. "I sent everyone else back to the resort but I was dying to find out how the Cookie Pies did."

"There isn't one to be found in Lake Pendle," I said, my chest puffing with pride for the beautiful woman behind it all.

"Wonderful!" she exclaimed, clapping once. "Can I talk to Cookie? I won't take much of her time."

I pulled my phone from my pocket. "Sure, I'll text her. She just ran to the bathroom, but should be right back." I typed out a quick text and then motioned at the trailer. "Want a tour while you wait?"

"You know I do!" she exclaimed as I held the door open for her. "Knowing Cookie, it's brilliant. She told us you bought it for her."

"I did, but she has certainly added her signature touch to it."

For the next ten minutes we talked through the set up and what Cookie hoped to do with it once our trial phase was over. I pulled my phone out and noticed she hadn't even read the text. She'd easily been gone twenty minutes which gave me a bad feeling in the pit of my stomach.

"Cookie hasn't responded?" Nadia asked, and I glanced up, realizing I had tuned out what she'd been saying.

"No, and it's been twenty minutes to the five she said it would take."

"Maybe she ran into someone and got to talking," Nadia suggested.

"I'll call her." I hit the button and listened to it ring until it went to voicemail.

"Something is wrong," I said as I hung up.

"Maybe she's sick and can't answer the phone?"

"I don't know, but I have to go look for her."

She followed me out of the trailer and jogged along next to me. "I'll come too. I can go into the women's bathroom, at least."

Cookie

Nadia had a point, so I motioned her along as we ran for the bathrooms. My gut said Cookie was in trouble and needed me. When we arrived at the bathrooms, Nadia ran into the women's but came out seconds later.

"She's not in there."

She barely finished the sentence and a cop car, sirens blaring, came roaring to a stop in the parking lot. The officer climbed out and I recognized him immediately since we'd gone to school together.

"We got a 911 call from Cookie's phone at this location," Officer Gordon Booth said as he ran toward us.

"She left the trailer almost twenty-five minutes ago for the bathroom and never returned."

"The call came through but no one answered when we called back. Since I was close, I decided to check it out."

An idea struck me. "Let me call her phone." I hit the number, and it rang once in my ear before her ringtone floated in the air. Gordon followed the sound and quickly snatched her phone from some tall grass at the edge of the restrooms.

After I hung up, we all stared at each other momentarily. "We need to search the park," Nadia said, her voice wavering slightly. She sounded like I felt, so I nodded.

Gordon compressed the button on his walkie and spoke into it. "I need back up at the east end of the park near the restrooms. We have a 10-57."

"Let's wait for more officers before we fan out," Gordon said, but I shook my head.

"It's already been twenty minutes. She could be anywhere and without her phone, we can't even track her!"

Gordon held his hands out to calm me. "I'm sure she's fine, Ares."

"Fine? Fine? What kind of person calls 911 and then ditches her phone? Something is wrong!" I paced back and forth a few times as my words echoed in my ears. I snapped my fingers and turned back to him. "I need her phone!"

"Why?" Gordon asked, still holding it in his hand. "The phone is passcode protected."

"It is, but I know the code. I also know she has an Air Tag on her keys for the bakery so if she ever loses them, she can find them quickly. If her tag recently paired to her phone, we should be able to see where she is!"

Gordon held the phone out immediately and I punched in her code, then pulled up the Find My Phone app. After inputting the information, I clicked the air tag and waited, my breath held tightly in my chest. "If the air tag hasn't connected to her phone recently, it will be useless, but if it did, we might at least get a starting point," I explained as I waited for the system to find it. When it did, I let out a breath and held up the phone. "It pinned her by the lake ten minutes ago."

"No other pins since?" Gordon asked.

"No, which means she's either still there or that's where the tag lost the connection."

"Let's go," he said, taking off in the direction the pin on the screen told us to go. Nadia and I followed him after he flicked his flashlight on and aimed it ahead of us.

"Cookie!" I called, desperate for her to answer me. I'd never been more desperate for anything in my life than I was for her at this moment. "Cookie!" I cursed myself for being so stupid. "I should have gone with her!"

"You had no way of knowing," Nadia said, her breath coming in pants. "There was no reason to think she couldn't go alone."

We came to a stop in the area where the air tag had pinned her, but she wasn't there. Gordon pointed his flashlight to the right. "Ares, you go left while I go right. Whoever you are," he said, pointing to Nadia, "head back to the restrooms and inform the rest of the officers of our location."

"I'm Nadia," she said as she took off again toward the restrooms.

I flicked on the flashlight on Cookie's phone and started walking along the shore of the lake. It was heavy with reeds in a swampy marsh, so there would be no reason for her to be here. "Cookie!" I called, hoping to hear her sweet voice, but the night was silent other than our footsteps in the grass. Ahead there was an extended jutting of heavy swamp grass and weeds. I'd have to work around it carefully so I didn't fall into the muck.

Cookie

Where could she be? My gut was knotted and I wanted to puke at the idea that she was hurt or worse because I didn't walk her to the bathroom. I should have insisted! "Cookie!" I screamed and when the sound died away, I swear I heard a moan.

I stopped and called her name again. "Cookie?" Another groan followed and I turned the flashlight to the grassy outcropping. That's when I caught a flash of white. I parted the weeds, and there was the woman I loved, on her back in the swampy mud.

"Cookie!" I cried with equal amounts fear and joy. "Oh, God, what happened?" I asked, as she moaned again. I had to get her out of the cold water before she froze to death. "Gordon!" I screamed. "I found her!"

I knelt and felt her neck for injuries, but it all felt normal to me, so I gently lifted her under her armpits and slid her out of the water and onto the grass. "Talk to me, baby," I said, dropping to my knees next to her and aiming the flashlight at her face. "Oh my God," I whispered when the left side of her face was one giant purple bruise and swollen to twice its normal size.

She moaned again and her right eye fluttered open just a hair as she brought her hand up to her face.

Before she could touch it, I grabbed her hand and held it to my chest. "You're okay, baby. We're going to get an ambulance here in just a minute," I promised.

Gordon rounded the side of the lake and stopped short when his flashlight caught the extent of the damage to her face. He pressed his radio button again. "I need 10-78 at my location. We have a 10-45b." He released the button and knelt next to Cookie. "Can you tell me what happened?" he asked her, while she blinked over and over as though it would help clear her head.

"Blah," she said, her tongue coming out to try and wet her lips, which were also swollen. She lifted her right hand and slowly formed letters in the air in sign language. B L A K E

"Blake?" I asked, realizing she was trying to tell us who did this.

She signed yes into the air, but she was getting weaker with every attempt.

"Blake Edington?" Gordon asked and she signed yes again.

"Grabbed me," she signed and I translated. "Called 911."

Katie Mettner

"He grabbed you and you tried to call 911?" I asked and she nodded. "That's why Officer Booth is here. He got the call. Rest now. We have an ambulance on the way to get you to the hospital." She closed her eyes again and I glanced up at Gordon. "That piece of shit needs to be behind bars now."

"I couldn't agree more," he said, stepping back to speak into his walkie, sending dispatch the information about the suspect.

"I love you, Cookie," I whispered, kissing her knuckles as a commotion above us reached my ears. "I'm so sorry I wasn't there to help you."

Her eyes came open again and she shook her head a bit. "Not your fault. My fault," she signed.

I gently caressed the right side of her face to calm her. "Just rest, baby."

"EMS!" someone called and then a bright spotlight lit up the lake.

I squinted, but locked gazes with her for a moment. "Don't leave me," she signed, grabbing my hand when she finished.

"I'm here, baby. I'm not leaving you."

Before I could say more, the EMS guys were pushing me out of the way as they prepped her to leave the lakeshore. I worried the trip on the stretcher back to the parking lot was going to cause her excruciating pain, until I noticed one of the EMS guys inject something into her new I.V.

"That's just a little something to help the pain until we get to the hospital," he told her as they lifted her onto the stretcher, which was actually a sled. They'd pull her through the grass to the stretcher that waited on the concrete path above.

The feeling of helplessness was overwhelming as I followed behind the stretcher, making sure it didn't get caught on the long grass or run over anything to cause her pain. The whole way I wondered if this was how my dad felt all those times my mom got hurt or needed surgery. Like your heart had been stomped on by a heavy boot and you wonder if it will ever beat again. I remembered feeling something akin to this every time my mom had surgery, but this was different. This was worse. This was a reminder that love hurts.

243

Cookie

The bakery was quiet for the first time all day and I leaned against the baker's bench with relief. It had been a week since Blake had taken me by surprise when I came out of the restroom. While we danced around each other, I'd used my emergency call button to connect to 911. Unfortunately, he managed to punch me in the face and knock me out before I knew if the call ever connected. Thank God it had.

I don't remember what happened after that, but Blake told the cops he dragged me down to the lake with every intention of killing me. After taking several shots at my face, he didn't have the stomach for it, so he tossed me into the lake unconscious, thinking I would drown. He didn't realize the spot he tossed me was all reeds that held me up out of the water. He was currently in jail being held on attempted murder, since he outright admitted that was his plan all along. A shiver ran through me at the thought. To think what started out as innocent dating would turn so violent. All because he was tired of chicks dishing him. Those were his exact words to the cops in his statement. I couldn't help but think that maybe if he didn't threaten and abuse women, they may not dish him. Just sayin'.

My face pounded once as a reminder that it still wasn't healed. I had two facial fractures that the doctors said would heal on their own, but I had to be careful while they did, which meant no heavy lifting. I was managing to do my work at the bakery by having Rye and Athena get my sweets baked off, while I decorated them. I had another week before I could even think about doing the baking myself, so I was happy they'd stepped up to help.

That made me think of the person who hadn't stepped up. Ares. At least not since the night I left the hospital. Once I was cleared by the doctors to go home it was early in the morning, but Ares was nowhere to be found. My parents brought me to their place, since I couldn't be alone, and I'd spent three nights there, but never once saw Ares. Rye told me he would come into work like a robot, but never hung around longer than he had to. Since I'd returned to the bakery, he hadn't been in once. He told Athena he was working on the online sales site, but none of us bought it. Thankfully, our summer help was here and in full swing, so we didn't miss his help as much as we would have two weeks ago. That didn't mean I understood it.

He'd told me on the shore that night that he was never leaving me but as soon as the going got tough, the not-so-tough got going. I had no idea why he was angry or even if he was angry. All I knew was, he hadn't returned a text or a call of mine in days. I half expected to hear from Athena that he was leaving town. I wouldn't even be surprised considering the cold shoulder I'd gotten this last week. Was I angry? No. I was hurt and sad that he wasn't here for me, but I sensed there was more to this story. I was going to have to get to the bottom of it, but I needed a few more days to feel better before I tackled Ares emotions too.

There was a knock on the back door and I walked to it, wishing it was Ares, but knowing he would use the front door during business hours. It was probably a delivery I'd forgotten about. I pulled the door open and indeed, a delivery man stood there. It was the logo on his shirt that threw me for a loop.

"Hobart?" I asked and the guy nodded. "You already came and fixed my mixer."

"I know," he said, pointing at his clipboard. "This is a delivery, not a repair. Sign here."

I took the clipboard in hopes it would tell me what was going on, but all it told me was the sender. Cookie Heaven. I handed the clipboard back and tipped my head. "Why is Cookie Heaven sending you guys here?"

"Prop the door open and head back into the bakery, we'll need the space," he said, jogging to the truck where another man waited.

They opened the back doors just as Rye walked up behind me. "What's going on?" she asked, her voice throaty after working all night.

Cookie

I propped the door open and motioned her back toward the baker's bench. "Cookie Heaven sent Hobart out. I have no idea why since we already got Bart fixed."

It wasn't long before the answer arrived. "Where do you want this one?" The guy who asked stood there with a commercial mixer on a wheeled cart.

"This one?" I asked completely confused. "What?"

Rye snickered and pointed at the mixer. "I think Cookie Heaven sent you a new Bart."

"I'm glad someone understands," one of the guys said. "This thing is heavy."

Rye motioned for them to put it next to the one already sitting there. They lowered it to the ground and then stood back up and headed for the door again. Rye walked over to the mixer with her mouth hanging open much like mine was. "Cookie, this is a spiral mixer for—"

"Bread dough," I said, stunned. "The top of the line one."

"Cookie Heaven never said a word to you about this?" she asked, turning to watch my lips.

"No, not an email or a text," I assured her, pulling my phone from my pocket to be sure.

Before I could put it back in my pocket, the men returned with another mixer!

"Where can we put this one?" he asked, motioning at the new Legacy mixer. "Nadia said it was time to give Old Bart a rest," the guy said. "Whatever that means."

I couldn't help it, I started to laugh. I stood there in my bakery laughing hysterically while Rye told the guys to put the mixer next to Bart. By the time I got myself under control and wiped my eyes, the delivery guy returned with a box and set it on the baker's bench. "I'll let you take a look at this while we install the mixers and get them up and running." He took a folder from the other guy who was holding it out. "This is all of your warranty and service information. Before we get started, are you sure this is where you want them placed?"

To say I was dumbfounded was a bit of an understatement. Rye walked over and took my arm gently. "You'll have to forgive her. She had a recent head injury and has trouble processing things

246

quickly right now." She turned to me. "I think it's smart to put the spiral mixer on the left side of the bench, so Athena can work on that side of the bakery. We should put the other new mixer on the right side for you to use, which will keep the flow moving without running into each other. Old Bart can go next to the mixer for the donut station. I can split my batches between them and make them last longer. Does that make sense?"

All I could do was nod, so Rye directed the men while I turned to the box on the table. I pulled open the flaps and took a step back when I saw what was inside. It was a custom tabletop mixer that was pink and white with the Cookie Heaven logo on one side and my Cuckoo for Cookies logo on the other side. An envelope was stuck in the mixing bowl with my name on it, and once I got it open, I read it aloud. "Cookie, all of us at Cookie Heaven hope you are doing better since the incident. We're working diligently on the special, but in the meantime, we wanted to lighten your load by hooking you up with three new Barts for your team. The old guy has served you well, but it's time for you to play with the big boys now. We hope the mixers are just what you need to send your business shooting off into the stratosphere. Nadia insisted that we couldn't forget about the Cuckoo for Cookies wagon and thought this would be the perfect finishing touch for the counter. We'll be in touch soon when the special is complete. In the meantime, rest, heal, and enjoy the new mixers! Your friends at Cookie Heaven."

I lowered the note to the bench and wiped my eyes carefully. Just when I thought I was at my lowest, along came a reminder that people cared. I turned and watched Rye give directions and nod as the men spoke to her, her gaze locked to their lips so she didn't miss a word. For once, I didn't interrupt or insist on being the boss. For once, I was accepting the love and care of the people around me. My face would heal with time and rest, but my broken heart would remain that way forever if my god of war decides I'm not worth defending.

Twenty-Nine

"This was…unexpected," Rye said after the men were gone and she'd read the note. "I don't even know what to say beyond that."

"Same," I agreed, holding an ice pack to my cheek as we stared at the new additions to the bakery. "I want to throw a batch of cookies in that bad boy just to see it in action, but I won't."

Rye laughed and the sound was joyful and happy, two things I didn't feel at the depths of my heart. I was beyond grateful to Cookie Heaven, but I couldn't work up that same kind of joy. Probably because a broken heart doesn't know how to laugh.

"As for me, I can't believe I get Old Bart to myself! I don't have to work around anyone else. Can you imagine how efficient life is going to be now?"

"I can," I said with a nod. "We are incredibly lucky. I texted Nadia and she said they just wanted to encourage me to keep going and not let the Blake situation get me down or keep me from pursuing my next initiative."

"The foster care initiative?" she asked and I offered a nod. "It's a great idea, Cookie. It really is, but there aren't many foster kids in Lake Pendle. I doubt kids from the city would be able to get a ride out here to work."

"I know," I agreed, as I leaned on the bench. "Which is why I'm looking toward newly graduated foster kids who have left the system but aren't able to go to college."

"That's a good idea, but then you run into the housing situation."

"Also a consideration, but I was thinking I could find a new place and that would leave the apartment open. There are two bedrooms, so I could house two kids while they worked here."

"Not a bad idea," she agreed with a nod.

"I have a lot more thinking to do on it, but my head hurts too much right now."

"Cookie?" voices called from the front of the bakery

"Did you call Dad and Athena?"

Rye smirked. "They have to see this!"

Before I could answer, Dad, Athena, Taylor, and Mom arrived in the back of the bakery. They nearly bumped into each other in a comical case of dominos when they laid eyes on the mixers.

"What on earth?" Athena asked, her voice shaking. "Why is there a spiral mixer sitting next to my station?"

"Uh, so you can use it to create fucking kick-ass out of this world bread." I held up my hand. "Nadia's words, not mine."

"Nadia?" my mom asked. "From Cookie Heaven?"

"Yep," Rye answered. "We got a surprise delivery this morning."

"They sent two new mixers?" Dad asked, his mouth hanging open as he walked to the Legacy and ran his hand over it.

"Three," I corrected him, pointing at the tabletop mixer on the bench. "This one's for the cookie wagon."

"Holy shit," my mom said without apology. "Do you know how much these mixers cost?"

I chuckled and moved the ice pack away from my face. "Since I own the place, I'm well aware. I was planning to buy a new one with my winnings from Cookie Heaven, but Nadia wants me to put the money toward things that will do good," I said making air quotes, "so they sent us the mixers to keep us moving forward."

"This is incredible," Athena said, stroking the spiral mixer as she checked it out. "Like, I might cry."

"Been there."

"Done that," Rye finished.

"This is going to simplify our lives to the point we may not know what to do with ourselves," Athena said, leaning her elbow on the mixer.

"I know my wife," Taylor said, inspecting the mixer with Athena. "She always knows what to do with herself, and it always involves a new bread recipe."

Cookie

Athena laughed and gently shoulder bumped her wife. "Did you text Ares?" She pointed at my phone as though I didn't know what texting meant.

"Nope, and I have no plans to."

"You need to tell him about the mixers. Suddenly, the bakery has twenty grand in its coffers," Athena said.

"He will see them when he comes in next time—if he comes in next time. Otherwise, feel free to tell him."

Athena frowned, but didn't say anything more as she walked around the mixer, mumbling about starting a line of pizza crusts.

"My head hurts," I moaned, bringing the ice pack back to my cheek. "What time is it?"

"Time to rest," Dad said, putting an arm around me as Mom held the side door open.

"You might be pushing the work thing a little too soon," Mom scolded once we were inside the apartment and I'd lowered myself to the couch. She sat next to me and removed the ice pack to inspect my cheek. "At least most of the swelling has gone down," she said, her critical mom eye taking it all in. "The massive bruising makes it hard to tell if it's healing or not."

"Oh, it's healing," I promised as Dad returned to the room with a bottle of water. I hadn't even noticed him leave. Sleep was next on the docket for sure. "It pounds every minute or so to remind me."

"We could have covered the bakery for a few days," Dad said. "In fact, we're covering the bakery the next two nights."

"No," I said, setting the bottle down and regretting it immediately when my face pounded in pain. "I refuse to let you do that, though the offer is sweet. I told everyone the first day we took over that we wouldn't fall back on you guys as subs or extra help. That's not a smart way to do business when you'll be gone half the year."

Dad glanced at Mom. "Should we tell her?"

"Tell me what?"

"We aren't going to be gone for half the year," Mom said, stroking the hair off my face.

"But," I sputtered and she smiled and shushed me.

"The four of us talked, and it turns out that some of Amber's anxiety is stemming from the idea of how hard it is for her to travel

250

for extended periods of time. She just can't do it, but feels like she's dragging us all down with her."

"That much is easy to see," I said with a nod. "Short trips, sure. But I can't see her living in an RV somewhere for months. How would she even get in and out."

"Exactly," Dad agreed. "So, collectively, the four of us have decided to embark on a different adventure."

I tipped my head and blinked. "You just said you didn't want to travel."

"We don't," Mom said. "Our new adventure is going to be foster care. We're each going to take a foster teen who is close to graduating into our home. We're hoping we can partner with The Fluffy Cupcake for employment and job skills while they finish school."

My heart was pounding hard in my chest by the time she finished explaining. "Oh my God. Are you guys serious?" The words were barely audible in the room as I tried to speak through the tears.

"Never been more serious," Dad agreed. "We love what you're doing here, Cooks, and we want to be part of it. We're retired but we can still make a difference in a child's life."

"I love you guys so much!" I said, throwing my arms around them in a hug.

"We'll talk more about it when you're healed," Mom promised, ending the hug and patting my hand.

"I talked to Gordon today," Dad said, taking my other hand. "Three more women have come forward to report abuse they suffered under Blake's hands. From what Gordon tells me, the DA is currently working a plea deal with Blake and there will be no trial if he takes it. He'll plead guilty to attempted first degree murder, since it was premeditated, and the other charges will be dropped. He'll still spend his life in prison, but he won't go to a federal one."

"No trial means I don't have to testify, right?" I asked and they both nodded.

"I hope he takes the deal then. I want him out of my life."

"That's understandable," Dad said. "I'm sure the detective on the case will update you soon, but I thought I'd give you a heads up so you weren't taken by surprise."

"Honey, have you talked to Ares since the accident?" Mom asked and I shook my head. "You can't work anything out if you don't communicate, sweetheart."

"I don't even know what's wrong!" I exclaimed, throwing one hand up in the air, but regretting it immediately when my head pounded. "He left the hospital and I haven't seen him since. I don't know what I did or what I didn't do, but I would bet my new mixer he's getting ready to run."

"Can I ask you a question?" Dad's words were measured and careful when he asked.

"Sure," I said on a shrug. "But I might not answer it."

"Fair," he agreed with a chuckle. "Did you ever find out why Ares said all those horrible things to you in high school?"

"No," I answered honestly. "He'd changed so much, a change that I could see and a change I thought I could believe in, so I let it go. I decided holding him responsible for the person he was thirteen years ago was unfair to who he is now. Apparently, I was wrong on all accounts and should have realized he was the same person under the guise of maturity."

"I don't think that's true," Mom said. "He has changed and so have you."

"This isn't my fault." My words were as adamant as the tears in my eyes.

"No, we know, honey," Dad said, kissing my temple. "But I think it's time the two of you talk it out. Reach out to him, Cookie. He needs to know you want him to be part of your life or he just might run. For whatever reason, he's scared and doesn't know how to react to what happened. He needs reassurance and not the cold shoulder."

"You don't know that, Dad." My words were lame and weak, but I was running out of arguments.

"You're right, I don't know that for sure, but I still remember the moment I found your mother on the ground stabbed and the sheer terror that went through me at the thought of losing her. If he feels half that amount of terror, then I know he needs reassurance, not radio silence."

"I've texted and called him multiple times. I'm right here. He's the one who has gone radio silent. If he was so scared of losing me, he'd have done the same thing you did, and that was never let her out of your sight for months. Ares didn't do that, Dad." With a moan, I lowered my chin to my chest. "I'm so tired." My words were slurred, which prompted Dad to lift me into his arms and carry me to my room.

"Time to sleep," he whispered, kissing my forehead. "No baking tonight. Mom and I will help Athena and Rye. You can try out your new mixer in the morning with a batch of Cookie Pies if you feel up to it. Okay?"

I had no energy to argue, so I nodded as he lowered me to the bed.

"We'll check on you later, Cooks," he said, pulling the blanket over me and flicking off the light. "Love you."

"Love you more," I managed to say before my eyes closed, and the darkness stole the pain in my face and my heart.

I slid my leg over a barstool and waited for the bartender to walk by. When he did, I was grateful I didn't know him. I wasn't in the mood to talk to anyone, especially a bartender. "Whiskey sour," I ordered. When the glass was set in front of me, I downed it in one swallow. "Another," I said, laying some bills on the bar so he knew I was good for it.

I drank the next one slower, pondering my options as they stood. There weren't many that didn't involve leaving town. "You're such a coward, man," I muttered, bringing the glass to my lips to sip.

"No, you're not," a voice said and I grimaced when the man that owned the voice slid across the bar stool next to me. "It's even early for day drinking, though," Uncle Brady said, ordering a Coke.

Cookie

"It's late for me," I assured him since I hadn't slept in three days. I tried, but I just laid there seeing the image of his daughter battered and bruised.

"Want to talk about it?"

"Not even a little bit."

"I just left the bakery. You'll need to stop over and see what's going on as a partner in the business. Don't worry. Cookie is upstairs in her bed, asleep. She's worn out from working and worrying."

That got my attention. "She's working?" I asked in shock. "She shouldn't be working."

He gave me the palms up before sipping his pop. "No one is there to stop her, I guess. Though, I did tell her I was taking over tonight with Athena and Rye. She needs sleep and time to heal. That's the least I can do as her father who knows how to bake."

"What did the doctor say about healing time?" I regretted it the second I asked because the question meant I cared, and that was a bad spot to be in when talking to her father.

"He said two weeks before she could do any heavy lifting, but you know Cookie. She does what she wants, even to the detriment of her health. You'd know all this if you had stuck around the hospital or shown up at the bakery this week."

"I've been working on the online sales site at home." That was a lie. I was staring at a blank screen and wishing words would appear.

"Twenty-four-seven? As the kids say, sounds a little suss to me, Ares."

I snorted, but didn't smile, just shook my head and took another swig.

"Listen, Ares, I hunted you down for one reason and it wasn't to bust your chops about walking out on my daughter, okay?"

"Seems like you are, though." My words held laughter but no mirth.

"I know, but that's not my intention. My intention was to tell you that we've got Cookie and we're taking care of her. It's okay to be scared and not know how to react to what happened, but it's not okay to shut her out."

"Mmm," was all I said as I sipped my drink.

He grasped my shoulder and squeezed it. "When I found Cupcake bleeding from a stab wound on the ground, do you know the only thing I remember?" I shook my head, so he continued. "The terror. Soul-paralyzing terror. It still makes me want to vomit when I think about how close I came to losing her, especially when I see everything we've built together since that time."

"It's my fault," I said, sticking my finger in my chest. "I should have walked Cookie to the restroom."

"Cookie said you offered, but she told you to stay put."

"She did, but that means nothing, Uncle Brady. I should have walked her there."

He shrugged. "I should have been at the bakery when Haylee was that night, but I was a few minutes late because we'd had an argument and I wanted to make sure she was already working so she couldn't walk out on me. If I'd just gotten ready a few minutes earlier. If I hadn't checked my phone that one last time before I got in the car. In the end, it wasn't my fault, and this wasn't your fault."

"You're forgetting one thing," I said, finishing the drink and motioning for another. "It is my fault. Cookie started this serial dating nonsense to get back at me. If she hadn't done that, she never would have met Blake."

He tipped his head back and forth while I accepted the drink from the bartender and stirred it with the little red stick. "True, but then it's also Rye's fault. She's the one who set her up with Blake."

"Doesn't matter. Cookie is what matters." There had to be a way out of this. The alcohol was already going to my head, and I didn't want to get into a pissing match with Brady.

"You're right. Cookie does matter, but so do you, Ares. Your feelings and emotions about what happened are just as legitimate as hers are, but you're running the wrong way. My daughter needs the man she knows you are."

"That man doesn't exist." He said nothing, and I groaned, dropping my chin to my chest. "He doesn't exist, Uncle Brady. I thought I could be like you and my dad, but I'm not. My name means God of War. What a joke."

"You thought you were like me and your dad? I don't understand what that means."

"Just forget it," I mumbled, drinking half the glass in a swallow.

"I'm going to ask you something, Ares. Do you remember telling Cookie in high school that you had bigger dreams to chase that didn't include working at The Fluffy Cupcake or her? Do you remember telling her you were only friends because you grew up together, but there was no place in the adult world for it?"

"Do I remember saying that?" I reiterated, fear lancing through me. There was no way I could forget those words and several others I'd said to Cookie before I left town. "Yeah, I remember every single letter, syllable, and word. They were why I didn't turn around and run back to Lake Pendle within two months of heading to the city."

"You thought it was a lost cause or?"

"No, they reminded me I had to make something of myself. I couldn't do that in Lake Pendle." I lifted my head to take in his surprised expression. "No offense." I held up my hand. "I meant I wanted to make it in the financial world. I couldn't do that in a small town."

"So, your reason for saying them was simply that you wanted to make something of yourself? I don't think you had to shatter Cookie in order to do that."

I shook my head and stared into my glass. "It's water under the bridge now, Uncle Brady."

"But it's not," he insisted, taking the glass away from me and sliding it to the bartender to dump. "When you came back to town, you showed her that you were a different person and she took that at face value and forgave you without demanding an answer about the words that plagued her life for a decade. Cookie has always had a forgiving heart, but if you blow this second chance, there won't be another."

"What do you want me to say or do?" I asked, frustrated and angry.

"Be a man," he said, patting me on the back. "Be a man and talk to her. Show her you still love her. Tell her how you feel about what happened to her, but above all, come clean about why you said those things in high school."

I opened my mouth to speak, but he held up a finger. "Not to me. To her. Six days ago, you loved her enough to share her bed." I raised a brow, and he chuckled. "I'm not an idiot, Ares. Was I happy when I saw that grin on both of your faces? Yes and no. I wanted to pound your punk ass into the ground for touching my daughter, but I was also happy you were finally on the right path together. Get back on the path, Ares. It will be a difficult uphill climb, but it will be worth it once you're walking next to her again."

"Do you think she'll give me the time of day?" I asked as my spine stiffened with determination.

"She already gave you her heart, buddy. The time of day will be easy for her."

I nodded, swallowing back the tears that wanted to fall as I thought about how lucky I was to have the entire Pearson family in my life. "Can I ask you a question, Uncle Brady? It's an important one and I'll understand if you say no."

"I'm listening."

"Do I have your permission to marry your daughter? If she still loves me after all of this, I'm never letting her go."

His lips turned up and he got that twinkle in his eye that only happened when the discussion turned to Cookie. "I thought you'd never ask. Ares, we'd only be so lucky to call you our son. You've always been part of the family, but we'd love for you to make it official when you're ready."

He patted my back and walked away with a whistle on his lips and his hands tucked in his pockets. I stood, pushed the bills to the edge of the bar, and walked out of The Modern Goat. I'd check in at the bakery to see what was happening, then try to find the courage Uncle Brady believed I had to talk to the woman I loved with my entire soul. If I didn't start that uphill climb soon, I was going to wallow in this muck forever. A reel of memories played through my mind as I walked, and I realized all the important ones, the ones that truly mattered, had Cookie standing right next to me.

Uncle Brady was right. That was worth fighting for, even if the terror made me throw up and the shame made me cry. I had to be honest with Cookie and let her decide if she can be with the man I am now instead of the boy I was then. First, I had to let her rest, so I'd use the time to my advantage.

Thirty

When I woke up at seven p.m., I couldn't get back to sleep, so I decided to take a walk. I'd been banned from the bakery until morning, but a little fresh air might help clear my head and let me fall back asleep sooner rather than later. At least the evening air was cool with a light breeze to carry the scent of lilacs. The birds called to each other as the sun lowered in the sky preparing to end its reign for the day. I was grateful that my face felt better after a good long nap, and that gave me hope that in another week, I could get back to work full-time and rely less on everyone else.

I took a sip of pop from my straw and leaned back on the soft grass to gaze out over the lake. Funny how the lake had been where I nearly died, but it was still my first destination when I needed to clear my head and heart. Try as I might, I couldn't clear my heart of Ares, though, and I didn't know what to do. On the one hand, I was mad as hell that he would go on and live his life somewhere else without a second thought about me, but on the other hand, I didn't believe that would be the case. He might go live his life somewhere else, but the man I'd gotten to know in the last month would be as miserable as I would be if we were apart.

My parents were right. I needed to reach out and talk to him, but I didn't know how to approach it without looking needy or demanding. Bossy or bitchy. Hurt and confused. All of those emotions were jumbled inside me and sorting them out was going to be a job for an older, more mature Cookie. I picked up my phone and took a deep breath while I worked out what kind of simple statement would get the job done without any of the above emotions entering the equation.

"Fancy meeting you here," Ares said from behind me and I jumped, my phone landing in the grass as I threw my hand over my heart.

"You scared me," I said, my body shaking from the adrenaline. "I didn't hear you walk down here."

"I'm sorry," he said, sitting next to me and giving me a gentle hug. "I didn't mean to do that. I'm an idiot, forgive me."

"It's fine," I said, pulling out of his embrace before I wanted to stay there forever. "I'm not a wilting flower."

He chuckled and shook his head. "No, you certainly have never been that. How are you feeling?"

"Better." The answer was lame, so I took a breath and kept going. "I was hurting pretty bad earlier, but my mom and dad showed up and made me go to bed. When I woke up, my face didn't hurt as much, so I decided to go for a walk."

He tipped my chin toward him and grimaced when he saw the bruising and mottled skin. "God, baby," he hissed. "I should have been here for you. I'm so sorry."

"Where have you been?" The question was asked without judgment, and for that, I was proud.

"Living in my coward cage," he answered, and I heard the truth in the words. "Uncle Brady helped me see I wasn't being a coward as much as I was letting my fear control me."

"Your fear?"

"Yeah. Your dad called it soul-paralyzing terror, which sums it up better," he said, turning to face me. "I didn't know how to react when the doctor told us that your face was broken and that you were lucky to be alive. I felt like I was in a tunnel. On one side of me was my mom and all her experiences; on the other was Taylor being diagnosed with something life-changing at a young age. It was like the carpet had been yanked out from under me, and it all piled on me at once. I let my fear take over and did what I've always done best. I ran."

"You didn't run far. Though," I said, motioning at him, "you do look like hell."

"I know," he said, running his hand through his hair. "Uncle Brady found me drinking in the bar at noon. Not my proudest moment."

Cookie

"You talked to Dad?"

"I did, and let me just say, holy hell those are some beautiful new mixers!"

I reminded myself not to smile and cause pain, so I nodded as tears gathered at my lids again. "Incredible, Ares. I wanted to text you, but I was afraid."

"I know, that was my fault too," he said, wiping away a tear from my right eye. "I should have been there for you. Honestly, I'm still in shock about what Cookie Heaven did for us."

"Same," I said with a head nod. "I'm going to pay it forward, too. I promise you that right here."

"There is no doubt," he said, leaning in and kissing away another tear from my right eye. "I'm so sorry, baby. I want to be part of everything you do. I know you're angry, but can you ever forgive me?"

"I don't give third chances, Ares," I said, gazing into his eyes. They were filled with undeniable depths of pain and anguish. "That said, I also understand that fear makes us do things our otherwise rational minds wouldn't do. Are you telling me that's what happened here? That you were too afraid to love me after Blake attacked me?"

"No!" he exclaimed, grabbing my shoulders and squeezing. "God, no," he said, a tear falling from his eye and down his cheek. "I was afraid I wasn't good enough to love you, Cookie. I should have walked you to the bathroom. I should have insisted that you let me, but I didn't. If I had, you wouldn't be sitting here with a broken face."

"Maybe, or maybe he would have just waited until the next time I was alone. This wasn't your fault any more than it was my fault, Ares. It was Blake Edington's fault. Full stop."

"Uncle Brady helped me see that," he agreed with a nod as he wiped his face on his shoulder. "You're not mad at me?"

"Mad? No. Confused and hurt? Yes."

"I wish like hell I hadn't made you feel that way," he whispered, his finger stroking my cheek. "Your dad told me it's time I'm completely honest with you, so you have all the information you need to decide if you want to give me a second chance squared."

"Second chance squared." I straight up laughed. "I should have known a money guy would figure out how to avoid using third chance." He winked but took my hand and held it to his chest. "What haven't you been completely honest with me about?"

His swallow was hard, and his gaze darted to the lake momentarily before he looked down at our hands joined together. "What happened when we were in high school."

"Water under the bridge, Ares," I jumped in, but he shook his head.

"No, it's not. It applies to this situation in ways you don't even know."

Whatever he had to say, it was a closely guarded secret. I could see the war he waged in his eyes, and the way his lip trembled every so often told me it was deeply rooted in something highly emotional. Maybe I needed to help him along.

"Our senior year of high school, you changed your plans and told me you had bigger dreams to chase than The Fluffy Cupcake. You also said our friendship was nothing more than a forced proximity childhood thing that couldn't be carried into adulthood. Is that what you're talking about here?"

"Yeah," he said, clearing his throat. "It broke my heart, but I thought I was doing what was best for you."

"Why would you think breaking my heart and telling me our friendship meant nothing to you would be best for me?"

"I don't even know how to explain this, if I'm honest," he said, his lips trembling still. "When I do, I'm going to sound like a total asshat. Try to remember I was just a kid?"

"I'm not judging you, Ares. You don't even have to tell me. It was easier to love you than to hold onto the anger any longer, so I let it all go."

"Maybe that's true, but it applies to what happened last weekend. Do you remember what happened right before Christmas our senior year?"

"I'm drawing a blank, but it's probably the head injury. The doctor told me I might struggle with that for a while."

"It was when Mom got the bad infection in her knee."

261

"Then she had the major amputation," I finished. "I know you struggled every time Aunt Amber was in the hospital, but you never let on that it was more than that."

He shrugged and stared off over my shoulder rather than meet my gaze. "Real men don't cry, you know."

"You weren't a man, Ares. You were a teenager with a lot on his plate."

"Agreed," he said, running a hand behind his neck. "I didn't want to add to my dad's worries, and I took it out on you. That was wrong."

"But, Ares, by the time you changed your plans, Aunt Amber was healed."

"She was but it festered, you know?" he asked, running a hand down his chest.

"What festered? The fear? The anger?"

"Both along with guilt and sadness. There was this neon flashing light that said love hurts, and you better have the means to care for love if it goes wrong. I watched my dad move up the ranks of the district, not necessarily because he wanted to, but he needed to in order to take care of Mom. Every time something happened to her leg, I could see in his eyes how it killed him to watch her go through so much pain. He'd do anything to make sure she had whatever she needed."

"Ares, Uncle Bishop moved through the district ranks because he wanted to. I remember hearing my parents talk over the years about Bishop's drive to make a difference in the school district. He understood that he would impact the children in his class as a teacher, but he would have to be an administrator if he wanted to impact all of the children in the district and make it a better place for them to learn and grow. He wanted to grow the district by encouraging open enrollment and higher education initiatives. All these years later, he's done that."

"Maybe that's true, but those shifts always happened when Mom needed more care, better equipment, or more expensive therapy. I know that because I lived it," he said, poking himself in the chest.

"Ares, I know you lived it, and I'm sorry," I whispered, kissing his lips gently for just a moment. "I'm not denying your experience growing up. Maybe your mom's challenges did impact when he chose to move up in the ranks, but he had every intention of doing it regardless."

"But it was proof to me that I was going to need a job that gave me opportunities to move up."

"Which you couldn't do if you worked at a bakery?" I asked, wiping a tear from his face with my thumb.

"I guess?"

"Only you know the answer, Ares."

He blew out a breath and shook his head with his face tipped to the sky. "I wasn't thinking right, but I couldn't talk to anyone about it either."

"Why?" I asked, confused by that line of thinking.

"You don't get it, do you? No one could know how angry I was that my life revolved around whatever medical emergency or episode Mom was having at the time. That made me an asshole. I hated what happened to her with every fiber of my being, but by the time the amputation happened, I was emotionally exhausted from being on constant alert all my life."

"I would have listened, Ares," I whispered, holding his chin so he couldn't look away. "I never would have thought you were an asshole for having emotions. I know your parents wouldn't have either."

"Hindsight and all that," he replied. "I told myself I needed a four-year degree so I had options even if I never planned to marry anyone and put myself in the same position as my dad."

"Is that why you told me we couldn't be friends anymore? You wanted me to forget about you?"

"In a nutshell." He grasped his bottom lip for a moment. "I'm not as strong as my dad is, Cookie. The idea of something happening to you as it did to my mom paralyzed me. You needed to forget about me and find someone better to love. I don't have the same constitution as my dad. I cry when Mom is in pain, throw up when she's in the hospital from the massive fear in my gut, and run when the going gets tough. I proved that this week without even trying."

"Wait. If you think your dad doesn't cry or worry or throw up from fear when your mom is in trouble, you're dead wrong. I've seen it with my own eyes, Ares. When your mom was in the operating room for the amputation, I vividly remember my dad kneeling on the floor before Bishop, hands on his shoulders, and talking him through breathing. He was hyperventilating that she wouldn't survive, and if she did, he wouldn't know how to care for her. He hated that you were caught up in the middle of it and wanted to protect you from it even though he knew he couldn't."

"I don't remember that."

"You'd left for the bathroom, probably to throw up. After thirty minutes they asked me to find you."

"When you did, I was staring out the windows overlooking Lake Pendle and trying to hide my tears."

"Yep," I said, wiping more from his face. "Listen, Ares, this idea of men not having emotions is the most ridiculous thing someone ever started. You can be sensitive and caring and still be a man. Your manhood shouldn't be defined or comprised of the number of emotions you shove deep inside you to avoid looking weak. When you're faced with a situation that you don't know how to deal with, it's okay to reach out to people who do and ask for help. It such a basic idea that I hate the fact that I even have to point it out, but I understand why in this day and age. Personally, I like the Ares that cares. I like the Ares who feels all the feels and who isn't afraid to tell people how he feels about them. The Ares you became during our senior year was someone I didn't like even if I still loved him. Did you like that Ares?"

He shook his head and dropped his gaze to his lap. "I think the answer is evident by the disgraced way I returned to Lake Pendle."

"No," I said, tipping his chin up to face me again. "You returned to Lake Pendle as a warrior after what you went through. Do I regret you going away to get that degree? No. You're an excellent finance person who is going to drive The Fluffy Cupcake into the next decade with record sales. Do I regret that I didn't love you harder during that time? Yes. Maybe I could have saved you from what you went through after graduation. If I had put my anger aside and told you that I still wanted you in my life, it might have been the lifeline you needed. That's my biggest regret, Ares, but we can't go back. We can only move forward. I want to move forward with you in my life. Do you want the same?"

"Yes, so much, but I've never deserved you, Cookie, and I sure as hell don't deserve you now."

"That's where you're wrong, Ares. Love isn't about who's deserving and who isn't. Love is about knowing that the other person will make you a better person just by being with them. I know that's the case for me, Ares. My entire childhood I tried to emulate your empathy and kindness until it was weaved into my soul. If you let that boy lead you again, we're going to be just fine. Do you think you can do that?"

He was silent for the longest time as he gazed into my eyes while the sun set and the sky darkened enough that the stars could come out to play. I didn't break eye contact or rush him. He needed to come to the conclusions on his own, or there would always be a ribbon of uncertainty between us.

"The more I think about it," he finally said, "the more I realize that boy has been leading me for the last year. When I woke up in that hospital last year, it was like I had someone tugging on my hand until I followed. Maybe it's time to stop fighting that tug and just be who I am."

"In my opinion, that makes life much easier and more enjoyable. When you lead with your heart, it's never wrong, Ares."

"My heart has led me to you over and over, Cookie Pearson. It's time I listen to it again without doubting what it says."

"What does it say, Ares Halla?" I whisper-asked.

"That Ares Halla loves Cookie Pearson. I'm tired of denying the way I feel, Cookie. The last month I've been free to love you has been the best month of my life, but the last five days have been utter hell again. I want to be the man I was Saturday as we laughed together selling Cookie Pies and sneaking kisses."

"Then be him, Ares, because that's the man I love."

He slid his hand up the right side of my face and caressed my temple with his thumb. "I promise you here tonight that this will never happen again," he whispered, touching the left side of my face gently. "No one is going to hurt you again."

"But one of us could get hurt or sick, and if we do, we face it together, right?" I asked, lifting one brow.

"Together," he agreed as he leaned in and kissed my lips gently while carefully examining my face. "Speaking of together, I made another stop today after talking to your dad."

"For what?"

"I hope it's for our future."

"Tell me you didn't buy a second cookie wagon," I teased. "I don't think there's enough of us to go around."

"There isn't," he agreed with a wink. "It would, however, affect how we do things at the bakery. There would be ground rules, like no making out in the cooler and other boring and unlikeable things."

"I'm so confused," I admitted. "Might be the head injury, though."

"What I'm trying to say is where I stopped today could change everything if you agree."

He rose on his knees and reached into his pocket, pulling out a ring. The image before me stole my breath. "I saw this today in the window of The Jolly Carrot, and I walked right in and bought it. I'm sure it's the wrong size, but I couldn't risk someone else buying it while I figured out what size you wore."

"It's a sunflower," I said, gazing at the beautiful ring. The center of the sunflower was a diamond and the petals were done in a yellow jewel. The leaves hugged the band to finish the look of a flower on a stalk.

"It reminded me of your—"

"Sunshine on a Rainy Day cookie," we said in unison.

I lifted my gaze to his with uncertainty. "Is this what I think it is, Ares?"

"I hope so," he answered, a nervous smile on his face. "After I asked Uncle Brady for permission, and got it, I promised myself if you forgave me and accepted me, faults and all, that I wouldn't waste another minute of our time together. So," he said, getting on one knee and holding the ring out between his fingers. "I love you, Cookie Pearson, with my whole soul. These last few days of being without you have made it clear that we belong together. I don't know where the future will lead us, but I do know that as long as we're together, we can face anything. Will you be my best friend, lover, and business partner, but most of all, will you be my wife, Cookie? Will you marry me?"

With my hands at my lips to stem the trembling, I could only nod for a few moments while I reminded myself to breathe. My childhood dream was coming true, and while the path to get here may have been winding and bumpy, we'd made it. Ares was asking me to be his wife. That meant he was ready to commit to me and the bakery until death do us part. I had no doubt that was true. There wasn't a shred of doubt in my heart that he wasn't the man I was meant to marry. I was in love with the Ares who drove back into town with the scars of war and the humility of defeat. This was the Ares who invested himself in the bakery and Lake Pendle again because he needed something to believe in. This was the Ares who believed in me, worshiped my body every night, and nurtured my heart and talent all day.

"Yes," I whispered, lowering my trembling hand to my lap. "I'll marry you, Ares. I've loved you my entire life and will until I take my last breath. I want to wear your ring, be your wife, and find happiness in this life together."

His shoulders relaxed, and he hit me with a good old-fashioned Ares smile. "Thank you for being you, Cookie," he whispered as he slipped the ring on my finger. We were both stunned when it fit like a glove. He glanced up and smiled. "I guess it was meant to be."

"Just like us," I promised as his lips captured mine.

About the Author

Katie Mettner wears the title of 'the only person to lose her leg after falling down the bunny hill' and loves decorating her prosthetic leg to fit the season. She lives in Northern Wisconsin with her own happily-ever-after and spends the day writing romantic stories with her sweet puppy by her side. Katie has an addiction to coffee and dachshunds and a lessening aversion to Pinterest — now that she's quit trying to make the things she pins.

Katie Mettner

A Note to My Readers

People with disabilities are just that—people. We are not 'differently abled' because of our disability. We all have different abilities and interests, and the fact that we may or may not have a physical or intellectual disability doesn't change that. The disabled community may have different needs, but we are productive members of society who also happen to be husbands, wives, moms, dads, sons, daughters, sisters, brothers, friends, and co-workers. People with disabilities are often disrespected and portrayed two different ways; as helpless or as heroically inspirational for doing simple, basic activities.

As a disabled author who writes disabled characters, my focus is to help people without disabilities understand the real-life disability issues we face like discrimination, limited accessibility, housing, employment opportunities, and lack of people first language. I want to change the way others see our community by writing strong characters who go after their dreams, and find their true love, without shying away from what it is like to be a person with a disability. Another way I can educate people without disabilities is to help them understand our terminology. We, as the disabled community, have worked to establish what we call People First Language. This isn't a case of being politically correct. Rather, it is a way to acknowledge and communicate with a person with a disability in a respectful way by eliminating generalizations, assumptions, and stereotypes.

As a person with disabilities, I appreciate when readers take the time to ask me what my preferred language is. Since so many have asked, I thought I would include a small sample of the people-first language we use in the disabled community. This language also applies when leaving reviews and talking about books that feature characters with disabilities. The most important thing to remember when you're talking to people with disabilities is that we are people first! If you ask us what our preferred terminology is regarding our disability, we will not only tell you, but be glad you asked! If you would like more information about people first language, you will find a disability resource guide on my website.

Instead of: He is handicapped.
Use: He is a person with a disability.

Instead of: She is differently abled.
Use: She is a person with a disability.

Instead of: He is mentally retarded.
Use: He has a developmental or intellectual disability.

Instead of: She is wheelchair-bound.
Use: She uses a wheelchair.

Instead of: He is a cripple.
Use: He has a physical disability.

Instead of: She is a midget or dwarf.
Use: She is a person of short stature or a little person.

Instead of: He is deaf and mute.
Use: He is deaf or he has a hearing disability.

Instead of: She is a normal or healthy person.
Use: She is a person without a disability.

Katie Mettner

Find All of Katie's Books on her website at www.KatieMettner.com

Torched
Finding Susan
After Summer Ends
Someone in the Water
The Secrets Between Us
White Sheets & Rosy Cheeks
A Christmas at Gingerbread Falls
Love on the Lake (Three first in series collection)

Sugar's Dance
Sugar's Song
Sugar's Night
Sugar's Faith
Trusting Trey

Granted Redemption
Autumn Reflections
Winter's Rain
Forever Phoenix

Snow Daze
December Kiss
Noel's Hart
April Melody
Liberty Belle
Wicked Winifred
Nick S. Klaus

Calling Kupid
Me and Mr. IT
The Forgotten Lei
Hiding Rose

Magnificent Love
Magnificent Destiny

Cookie
The Magnificent Box Set

Inherited Love
Inherited Light
Inherited Life

October Winds
Ruby Sky

Meatloaf & Mistletoe
Hotcakes & Holly
Jam & Jingle Bells
Apples & Angel Wings
Eggnog & Evergreens
Gumdrops & Garland
Candy Canes & Caroling (November 2023)
Bells Pass Box Set 1
Bells Pass Box Set 2

The German's Guilty Pleasure
The German's Desperate Vow

Cupcake
Tart
Cookie

Butterflies and Hazel Eyes
Honeybees and Sexy Tees

Blazing Hot Nights
Long Past Dawn
Due North
His Christmas Star
The Cowboys of Bison Ridge Box Set

Going Rogue in Red Rye County
The Perfect Witness ~ Available for preorder

Printed in Great Britain
by Amazon

31161773R00155